BRIGHT SOUL

This novel is entirely a work of fiction. The names, characters and incidents portrayed in it are the work of the author's imagination. Any resemblance to actual persons, living or dead, events or localities is entirely coincidental.

Flutterbye Trail Press
797 Sam Bass Road #2541
Round Rock, TX 78681

First edition

Chapter Art by Etheric Tales
Cover Design by Covers by Kellie Arts
Discreet Cover Design by Gombar Cover Design
Editing by Red Loop Editing
Hardback Case Design by Olga Sauchenia
Printed Interior Design by Enchanting Covers
Published by Flutterbye Trail Press

ISBN: 978-1-954582-19-4 (E-book)
ISBN: 978-1-954582-54-5 (Discreet Paperback)
ISBN: 978-1-954582-24-8 (Paperback)
ISBN: 978-1-954582-30-9 (Hardback)

Feedback: Encounter a problem with this book? Let us know at ellahendricksauthor@gmail.com

BOOKS BY ELLA HENDRICKS

THE MOONGROVE UNIVERSE

Wicked Spells
Academy Paranormal Romance (RH)

Librarian Witch
Shadow Slayer
Bright Soul
Wicked Spells: The Complete Series

Cursed Ashes
Paranormal Romance (RH)

Elemental Alchemy

THE UNSEELIEVERSE

The Omega Masquerade
Sweet Romantasy Omegaverse (RH)

Fated or Knot

The Arcane Alliances Universe

House of the Sanguine
with Nicole LaBrocca
Dark Vampire Romantasy (RH)

Thirst

BRIGHT SOUL

MOONGROVE ACADEMY: WICKED SPELLS
BOOK 3

ELLA HENDRICKS

CONTENT OVERVIEW

This is a paranormal RH romance, meaning that the main female character does not need to choose between love interests. There are graphic sex scenes (some including more than one partner) between consenting adults. *Bright Soul* is book three of a trilogy that ends with a guaranteed HEA!

Please be aware that this book continues to show depictions of grief because of the death of a friend. Also contained within are fight sequences that include death, gore, and magical violence. This trilogy is classified as dark academia because the main antagonists have magic that affects the souls of others.

This trilogy does not include a pregnancy for the FMC or MM content.

If you find anything in the contents of this book that should be added to this page, please let me know at ellahen dricksauthor@gmail.com.

1

CRESS

My heart was still a thrumming pulse in my ears when we emerged onto a dirty backstreet. Flies buzzed around what smelled like days-old garbage left to fester in a weak winter sun. The chill, stale air nipped my cheeks.

There was a silent neighborhood beyond where we paused to regroup as the last of the pack of survivors emerged into the light. Those who'd lived through the fight we'd fled from were in various states of injury. We'd walked for what had felt like hours through an underground tunnel lit only with red bulbs, giving us the bare minimum to see by. Worse, there'd been no cell service while we made the trek to safety, so I had no idea if Mom and my sister, Carly, were okay.

Healers like my friend Áine wove between the ranks of guardian witches, Crystal Court fae, and my coven, mending the worst of our wounds. They'd been too busy stabilizing those most hurt throughout our trip through the tunnel to fix the minor scrapes and bruises we all had, and by the time Áine's bouncy hoofed stride came my way, she had mere sparks and curls of green magic left on her earthen-toned fingertips.

"I'll be okay," I told her, though I wasn't sure that was entirely true. I barely saw her concerned frown, too busy watching my phone's screen as I restarted it, hoping it would find a connection.

Physically, I was fine. I should count myself lucky, because the vampire Garroway had interrupted my coven's petition to the Crown Coven with a small army of assassins and enslaved witches, and yet here I was, alive. Terrified, but alive.

My phone buzzed in my hand. Several messages and missed calls flashed across the screen, all from Mom.

"My mom's safe. She found a hospital and is pitching in there," I told Áine with a trickle of relief, cut short when I saw Mom was also asking if I'd seen Carly. My thumbs moved as I spoke, asking Mom for a name or location of this hospital.

A few of us needed more medical attention than could be applied on the fly, like Ben's brother, Lucas, whose unconscious body Geo carried in his gargoyle form. Both of my boyfriends were distracted from me, speaking in low tones and inspecting Lucas. I understood the worry Ben wore openly. Our healers had revived almost everyone who'd passed out, but Lucas remained limp and wan in Geo's arms.

Áine shifted on her cloven hooves. "I, uh, have to tell you some bad news," she said quietly.

My belly soured. I didn't think I could handle anything else going wrong after watching so many people die to summon a truly evil being, the soul-hungry goddess Myuna.

It's too late for me, bright soul.

God, I was going to be sick. I'd done my best to put it out of mind, but a world-ending creature had just arrived on Earth behind us. And she had Phaeron.

"I'm pretty sure someone closed the pocket dimension," Áine continued. The faun paused to wait for my inevitable questions.

"What do you mean, closed?" I asked.

"There's pressure in the air above us. Maybe you feel it a little bit? Well…it's really oppressive for me. It's my fae magic." Her deerlike ears pinned back, and she winced, as if she noticed it so much more by talking about it.

Pocket dimensions were rooted in fae magic and a complicated concept I still didn't fully understand. An individual fae could create a space that existed just for them, like an extension of the natural world. Together, a large enough group of fae could declare a leader and invest their powers into a Mother Tree, which would anchor the space and make it into a pocket dimension that could further be augmented by the magic of other supernaturals. These places existed completely out of a normal human's awareness.

We were in Cerris City, a supernatural metropolis parallel to Washington, D.C., and I had felt a change in air pressure sometime after Myuna's arrival but thought little of it. Now that Áine mentioned it, I closed my eyes and lifted my chin, letting the crush of voices around me fade to background noise.

There was an oppressive force in the air, like humidity. I wouldn't want to go for a run right now, as my whole body felt extra heavy. "I do feel it," I concluded. "What does this mean for us, though?"

"The Protector of the Mother Tree has sealed off any

entrances and exits to the pocket dimension. We're trapped," she said grimly.

"Shit," I muttered.

My heart doubled its beating. With trembling fingers, I checked my phone again and tapped the address Mom had sent me. One of my supernatural-exclusive apps popped up with a map and a blue line connecting my phone's current location with the hospital as a destination. It was several blocks away.

I looked around and spotted Madigan Ashbough, my friend Roe's mother, huddled up with a small group, undoubtedly discussing what to do next. Madigan was also known professionally as Mad Ash, a storied guardian witch who headed up a company that protected important artifacts and people. She'd led the survivors to safety and was the best choice for the leader of our mixed group while Phaeron was gone.

Áine moved on to offer what was left of her magic elsewhere when I went to approach Madigan, phone in hand. With her Crystal fae husband, Orthus, next to her, I assumed she already knew we were trapped. They turned to look at me, along with the rest of their group.

Madigan's suit of armor, made of red crystals from Orthus's court, gleamed and sang a soft note of harmony in the sunlight from portions of facets that weren't blemished by drying blood. She'd removed the helmet that made her look like an old-fashioned knight, having balanced it on the handle of her geode-formed warhammer that she had resting head down. Waves of orange hair stuck to her neck from where they'd escaped her low ponytail.

I felt a crackle of fire within me for the muscle-bound woman and Hana Graygazer, who stood unmarred by combat on Madigan's other side. She was an augur, capable of seeing the future. And judging by how she and her husband, also in this meeting of the minds, hadn't fled with us but still met us here...

"You knew this would happen," I accused.

"I did," Hana replied. She laced her fingers before her, the image of poise. She'd tied her pin-straight black hair back from her face in a practical style and wore worn traveling clothes, having changed out of the formal wear I'd last seen her in. She and her husband were some of the few around us with duffle bags at their feet.

That short, blunt answer didn't satisfy me. "All those people died because we showed up to petition the Crown Coven today!" I jabbed a finger back toward the tunnel we'd just used to flee, my voice rising with every word. "Why didn't you warn us? Why didn't you stop this?"

"Watch your tone with her," Madigan said flatly.

My whole body tensed. I had yet to give her a piece of my mind for tearing me away from Phaeron earlier. Which was foolish, I told myself, trying to get my emotions back under control. If she had left me, I might be a soulless husk right now. But I had no idea of what'd happened to the princely dimensional after we fled. Was he alive? Was he between Myuna's teeth or worse right now?

Hana shifted to put herself between Madigan and me. "It's all right. Let her be angry. Cress, I apologize for withholding information from you."

My lips quirked to the side. I had a distinct feeling there was a "but" following on the heels of this apology and about to ruin its sincerity.

"But I gazed hard into the gray for any other way and didn't find one. Look around. What do you see?" Hana asked and barely gave me a chance to do as she instructed before she continued. "I'll tell you what I see: standing around us is the team that will defeat Myuna the White. She was destined to be summoned to our planet. If not today, in Cerris City, where she can be contained...on Earth itself, where nothing would stop her from glutting herself on billions of souls."

The moisture left my mouth at the thought. "But—"

"It had to happen," Hana stated, steel behind every word. "At this time, in this place, with these people. I give you my word. Do you know what happens when a Graygazer denies their fate?" She gestured between herself, her husband, and the older gentleman sitting on a curb nearby, Kwan Graygazer. He was one of two members of the Crown Coven to survive.

I cringed, moisture stinging the corners of my eyes. "Don't say that," I croaked. "The last time you said that to me..."

It was burned in my memory like a brand, along with the follow-up. *Someone else dies instead. Often horrifically.* Lanie, her daughter and my friend, had just sacrificed herself to prevent the Hungering Darkness from killing and eating the soul of a different witch. It was the curse of a talented augur—knowing when, where, and how they would die.

Hana's dark gaze softened. "I know. And if it makes a difference, it hurt to lead us all on this path, knowing what you would have to witness and endure. Now, you came over here to suggest where we go next, right?"

I'd nearly forgotten I had my unlocked phone in hand, the map route waiting to be shared. "Yeah," I said, clearing my throat and blinking rapidly. I offered the device to Hana, who passed it to Madigan. Orthus leaned over to look at the screen too. "My mom found the nearest hospital, and it's not all that far from where we are."

"The streets will be safe for now," Hana shared.

That seemed to make Madigan's decision easier. She exchanged a glance with Orthus before declaring, "A sound position for us to rest properly and plan our next steps. Let's move."

I stayed by Hana's side as Madigan picked up her helmet and hammer and began circulating to share the news that we were heading out. The group moved slowly toward a main street, our leader up front, consulting my phone and its map. I was so used to having my device disappear to be used by others that it didn't bother me.

Madigan's guardian witches and Crystal fae spread out to surround the perimeter of our group with fighters. Ben and Geo, still carrying Lucas, were pushed toward the center along with most of the members of my coven and all our assorted familiars. Roe supported Willow, who wasn't the steadiest on her feet.

Bella, my brown tabby cat familiar, jumped into my arms with a chirp for attention. Milo and Jin remained with the rest of our animal companions, pressed close to the bigger, stronger ones of the group. I snuggled Bella to my chest, finding some reassurance in her soft fur and faint purr. "You're safe with us," I murmured to her.

"It's going to be okay," she echoed in her squeak of a voice. As one of my bonded familiars, I alone could hear her meows as words.

I could hear Roe also trying to encourage and comfort Wren. The blonde had just watched her father and boyfriend die senselessly. She muffled sobs into a handkerchief and wobbled uncharacteristically in her heels as she shuffled along with the group.

I itched to go be with them rather than toward the back of the group with Hana. But I had a burning question for the augur who'd pushed us toward this situation that'd put the tears in Wren's eyes and the grief in all of us for what we'd already lost.

"What about Phaeron?" I asked. Hana glanced up at me, her expression unreadable. "Did Myuna eat his soul? Did she corrupt him? Is...is he alive?"

"He's alive, just suppressed by her presence," she answered, measuring each word carefully. "His fate branches in several directions, and the most likely outcome is yet unclear to me. I am thankful, though."

"Oh?" I asked faintly.

"You will have an opportunity to affect which fate he meets. Because of your influence, I have hope we will avoid the future where Myuna twists him into one of her monsters," she stated. The thought made my insides feel like they were trying to wrap into a knot, drawing out a pain in my gut.

Hana was as serious as ever and I felt the weight of her words keenly. "But if she succeeds and he becomes corrupted, we're doomed. Each and every one of us."

2

PHAERON

The goddess Myuna the White did not chew her food. It'd always unsettled me deep down that she didn't have teeth. But once, I'd been naïve enough to think that, as a higher being, she had no need to eat.

She slurped down all that was placed before her in offering now, her face a thin veneer over a bottomless hole. Her mouth stretched grotesquely around the whole bodies of human beings, and she uttered the occasional rumble of dissatisfaction.

I was forced to watch. While she was aware I was tethered to her, all she wanted to do was eat and eat. Endaeron fed her, dragging over the soulless corpses left behind in the Crown Coven's audience chamber. The metallic smell of blood was heavy in the still air, and only the grunting and cursing of Endaeron's newest vessel, a vampire named Garroway, broke the silence between Myuna's gulps and quaffs.

When I refused to help bring her the bodies littered around the chamber, she'd pointed a clawed finger, and I stood where she indicated, waiting with dread in my heart for her feasting to cease. My body was turned toward hers, standing with rigid obedience to await her next order. Purple-tinged blood still dripped down my leather armor, courtesy of the burning wounds left behind in my fight with Endaeron in his last vessel, the boy Lucas. I let the pain ground me, its sting reminding me of who I was.

There was a small hole in my soul and a pinprick of corruption left behind within it. It formed the strand of control by which she could command me. My logical mind was shut under a layer of her magical influence, and even now, I pushed and probed at the barrier between Myuna's control and my free will.

Once she realized there were no souls left here for her to eat except for mine and Garroway's tainted one, my life was forfeit, or worse. I had to find a way to defy the control her mere presence gave her.

"Useless fuck," muttered Garroway as he dragged another corpse past me. Though most of my body was locked in place, I could still move my head to see that he struggled with the bulk of a fallen Crystal fae, whose body was encased in a suit of armor with solid stone plates. Myuna would still consume it in one giant swallow.

I knew he was trying to insult me, but I ignored him. There was little intensity left in Garroway's voice, and I had to preserve what fight I could muster for Myuna. He carried what was left of my brother, the Hungering Darkness, within him and thus was more hopelessly enslaved to her will than I was.

Myuna sat upon the lip of the raised dais where the Crown Coven once reigned, their throne-like seats pushed around haphazardly to make way for her bulk. She was over twice my height, with bone-white skin that glowed dimly even now. Her visage still appeared to be that of one of my people, with forward-facing horns, leathery wings, slitted eyes, and a tapered tail that swung midair like a pendulum. We had once revered her as a goddess of light, not realizing the dark hunger lingering inside her until it was too late.

She'd appeared on my home planet of Soiluire within an egg-like comet, emerging a savior and a beacon for my people, who, at that time, lived in near-complete darkness. For centuries, she built her base of worshipers, biding her time until the moment was right, or her cravings for souls grew too great.

Our society had collapsed when she turned on us. Those that'd served her most faithfully as her torchbearers were killed and enslaved first, forced to bring her millions to consume. Her glutting was the beginning of our Age of Decay and eventual exodus from Soiluire.

I'd slain her monsters and endured a trip through the Void to lead the dregs of my people here, to Earth. We'd tolerated the prejudices of humans, who'd thought our features resembled the hellish demons of their worst imaginings, all to get away from Myuna. My people became known as dimensional travelers by escaping to a new world. We'd sealed the way behind us, intending to close the door back to Soiluire permanently.

I simmered with a low boil of fury. There was no end to my rage with Endaeron for undoing all our sacrifices and leading her here, but I kept my emotions contained and my breathing slow and deep. I knew I could not act in anger if I wanted to escape this room and return to Cress. I also knew I could not kill Myuna alone.

"That is everything, my lady," Garroway said in the

two-toned voice that meant the Hungering Darkness was currently in control of their shared body. White shadow flickered around the vampire's form like flames, slowly enveloping his body and hiding his human features.

Myuna worked the stretched-out material that should have been her jaw. It'd come unhinged and spread wide enough to allow her to feast unimpeded. What should've been flesh and bone quickly flowed back into place. Then she…melted. I watched in horror as her entire body ran like candle wax, puddling down the carved stones of the dais.

The mass of white substance quivered before drawing into a ball. It was like witnessing a master sculptor manipulate Myuna's body as it formed four tubes and an oval for a head before etching in details. Wrists, knees, fingers, and nails formed, and the oval sprouted a nose, hair, and two almond-shaped eyes that glowed a little brighter than the rest of her.

Myuna had transformed into a human. Worse, I recognized her new face. She had assumed an all-white visage of the fallen leader of the Crown Coven, Tempest Wildsong. Instead of having flowing raven-dark locks and a dress of soft green, though, Myuna was a pale imitation in pure white, save for the toothless black hole behind her lips as she spoke.

"Is this what mortal females look like on this world?"

Her voice held power; it shook me to my very center. She spoke every possible language layered on top of one another. For her to utter anything wrapped her first exhalation and last in a blanket of incomprehensible nonsense. To listen too closely would inspire madness in most.

"Yes, my lady," Garroway responded with Endaeron's breathless awe of her.

She dipped her chin. The dots of her pupils pointed my way, even under a filmy sheen of white magic. "What small, soft people. I yet hunger for more of them. But first there's you, Phaeron et Sudair. We have unfinished business."

The language I heard my name in was my native tongue, separating my title rather than treating it like a surname as humans did. "Because of you…" she began before trailing off. Her attention snagged on a book that flew past her head.

A whole flock of books flapped above us. The audience chamber had representations of magic from all seven affinities available to witches, and these books of law were enchanted to fly with librarian witch magic and a tiny creature from Soiluire called a wispfly. For a moment, Myuna was like a fascinated cat, watching them circle the room unaware of the fight and subsequent summoning of an otherworldly goddess.

She snatched one out of the air when it flew too close. It was not malfunctioning like Cress's handbook, so it settled and reported its title with one last flick of its front and back cover. It was *The Rule of Supernatural Law* and was halfway through listing its copyright information before she sucked it into her mouth and swallowed.

"Hmm, dry," she commented. A glowing tongue emerged from her mouth to lick a slimy trail over her lips. "But that wispfly… I need more like it."

"The books will come to you if you state their title, my lady," simpered Garroway. The lack of the two-toned quality to his voice and his brief smirk told me the suggestion was all the vampire.

Myuna was tall enough to glimpse a few titles. Those books came to her hand and quickly disappeared into her maw. As she did this, I noticed a metal device mounted out of reach that seemed to be pointing our way. A red light flashed beside a dome of black glass. I gazed at the unfamiliar technology with hope for a moment. Was it a weapon? Perhaps something that nullified magic?

The sounds of rattling paper ceased, and Myuna cleared her throat. I turned away from that blinking light with a sigh. If it were something useful, then it would've been utilized in the fight that'd killed most of the Crown Coven and their protectors earlier.

"As I was saying." The goddess wove light into threads between her fingers. Watching her brought back hazy memories of seeing her do the same thing when she was bored at functions or needed to keep her hands busy. "I spent too much time sitting in place on Soiluire, feeling the advancements and indulgences of the mortals on planets innumerable. Their peoples growing plump for harvesting... but I could not reach them."

She crushed the braid of light when her fingers fisted on the dais, cracking the stone underneath. "Because of *you*, Phaeron. You and the other souls that fled the death you were due."

I drew breath to reply and felt the force of her will. She didn't want to hear my voice.

"You meddled in forces outside your control. I am entropy, the death of civilizations, the reaper of worlds." She leaned forward, her finger pointed accusingly. The hairs on the back of my neck lifted from a shift in air pressure. Here it was...the moment she consumed me for saving what I could of my people.

"I came short on power when you disappeared alongside thousands of souls. I have been stranded, sitting alone on a rotting world. I ate my half-formed interstellar vessel waiting. I endured the pain of eating my own power, pleading with my fellow gods to take me away in my darkest season. Their silence was damning. And yet, I am saved."

She turned her head toward Garroway and whispered, "You shall be rewarded beyond measure."

I slanted a glare his way, my lip curling in disgust. He would enjoy that reward for half a second before I made his death as painful as possible.

Myuna made a come-hither gesture, and my legs jerked forward at her unspoken command. Light sputtered against her palms before she managed to make them both glow. She had an old trick that she used on me, where she lifted and suspended me in a bubble of light she formed between her hands, making it seem like I floated before her looming, all-powerful presence. Pain twinged in my chest as the muscles shifted from the lack of gravity.

My forehead was level with her mouth, which leaked the carrion smell of her last meal. "Any last words, Phaeron?" Her words boomed, her presence all-consuming.

She returned my voice to me, and I wasted little of my limited time left. "You are a foul, narcissistic shade. To tell me of *your* suffering, as if you have no concept of the damage you have wrought... I wish you had agonized further, for you deserve so much worse. You would be doing innumerable worlds a favor by feasting upon the last of yourself and leaving the rest of us in peace—"

Myuna made a pinching motion, suffocating the last of my words before I could utter them. She seemed to roll her eyes while I coughed off the choking sensation. "I should have known better," she remarked.

She unsheathed one of my swords between three of her fingers, drawing it out to inspect it. They'd been sheathed in a hurry, so the weapon was dirty. Of course, she had to lick her way up the side, cleaning off the dimensional language etched into it. I began to sweat as the moments passed. If she was going to consume me, she would've gone ahead and done it. Her intentions had to be far more sinister.

"Hmm, half of Soiluire, half of this planet. You must value this weapon very much," she stated. "It is fortunate you have two. One for each of my most loyal servants."

She slid my weapon out of sight, toward Garroway. I stared at her in defiance, unable to do more when caught in the trap of her light and will. So it would be death by a thousand cuts, starting with losing one of my last physical links to my home planet.

Myuna wove magic between her fingers just like she'd made threads formed of light. She wrapped me in a potent spell that sank into my mind. This, I could still fight with a jerk of my head. I closed my eyes tight against her intrusion and pushed her presence away.

A slimy, warm sensation coated my wounds. While I struggled against her mentally, she'd licked the blood from my chest. A shrill tone of panic and disgust rose in my ears before she delved further into my thoughts and memories, ripping through them with little care.

"So bitter," she whispered, no more than another voice in my head. I saw what she did as it played over the back of my eyelids in vivid detail.

She watched me wake in Moongrove Library, disoriented and slow.

I tried to push her away again, but her talons had hooked in deep. She combed through the faces of the humans I'd grown fond of and the knowledge of who they were. We pushed and pulled our way closer to my memories of Cress, and I heard her utter an "ahh" when she finally won this contest of wills and beheld my bright soul in all her glory.

Cress was unique amongst librarian witches, with a soul that haloed her in a glow. She dazzled me constantly with the power of her presence. I twisted to jerk the memories of her out of Myuna's sight, yet she quickly learned she was looking at my True Light. It was my duty to protect and cherish Cress, to make her my mate.

The goddess viewed her from all the angles she could wring from me. She saw the surprised and uncertain Cress who first freed me from Moongrove Library. The heartbroken Cress who'd caught me standing over her friend's body. Tired Cress, angry Cress, silly Cress...coy Cress, her lips around my cock as I rode the feverish lust induced by a manipulative cupid.

I shoved Myuna back again, feeling further violated by the way she lingered on that memory. She obliged by switching to rest on a moment before a mirror, my fangs pressed to Cress's neck. So close to claiming her as my mate...yet the awful hunger born of the goddess had been there, urging me to consume some of her radiant soul instead and taste its sweetness.

Myuna laughed, releasing her hold on my mind. "You have grown weak, Phaeron. Leaving your mate without your protection or even your mark."

My eyes opened. Little had changed around us, except that I was drenched in sweat under my armor. I was sure to develop an infection in all the wounds she'd licked, as my chest smelled of her foulness.

Myuna set me down from the bubble of light. The only reason I didn't collapse was her control, which steered me to stand back in my original spot.

"Endaeron," she breathed, a toothless grin spanning the

empty void of her mouth. "Go forth from this place and bring me a purple-haired human named Cressida Rollins Darkmore. Her life and soul are mine to take."

Garroway bowed, but under his breath, he muttered, "Her *again*?"

3

BEN

We weren't the only group that'd come to this hospital upon being stranded in Cerris City. The waiting room for emergencies was overflowing when we arrived, alive with energy in a city that'd seemed dead on the outside. Luckily —if you could count anything that'd happened to us lately as "lucky"—Lucas had jumped to the top of the list of priorities for the medical staff.

I sat in a quiet room with him on the third floor. My brother was hooked to several machines, so pale and still in the heaps of white sheets he'd been buried in. They'd just allowed me in the room after a doctor had cast a hurried set of spells and then rushed off to the next patient.

An equally harried nurse had told me not to touch anything, then left me with Lucas. I'd withstood the silence afterward for only a few minutes before jittering in place, all my excess energy and worries spilling over. I could barely look at the state the Hungering Darkness had left my brother's body in, but I had to. The sight had to be permanent in my mind. This was the evil we faced...the evil I hadn't protected him from.

I sat alone for a while, until there was a tentative knock on the door, followed by Cress peeking inside. I gestured for her to come in, sweeping her into a hug and a quick, delicate kiss. It was a relief to have her here, to touch anam cara marks with her and feel the spark of wholeness between us. She wore a couple butterfly bandages over the cuts on her face and had the bulk of wrapped wounds peeking through her torn sleeves.

"My mom told me where they put Lucas. Is he...?" She bit her lip, looking over at the bed.

"The doctor called it a magic-induced coma," I answered quietly, weighed down by worry. "There's not enough healing magic to go around for everyone right now, so they... He's on life support."

"Oh, Ben, I'm sorry." She gave me a squeeze around my middle, still standing in the circle of my arms.

I tried to give one of my usual carefree shrugs. "Hey, it could be worse, right? The Hunger could've gobbled him up...or..." I wracked my brain for how this moment could be worse. Having my brother alive but unresponsive and sickly was somehow more severe than if he'd simply died.

There was no guarantee he'd wake up or if he'd be the same person after carrying the Hungering Darkness within him for months. The brother I knew may be long gone.

I choked on the burning sensation of tears. Out of long habit, they lingered at the corners of my vision, half formed. Cress gathered me closer all the same, holding the back of my neck. She smelled of antiseptic and the musky staleness of the tunnel we'd come through. But she was okay and had scrubbed the blood from her clothes and skin...something I still needed to do. We stayed that way for a few long minutes. I was glad to have her with me, warm and whole.

"He'll be safe here, for now," she eventually said.

"Is there such a thing as 'safe' anymore?" I asked with a sigh. "Did you hear that we're stuck in this city?"

"Yeah." She shared what Áine and Hana Graygazer had told her, drawing a muttered string of curses from me.

"But there's some good news," Cress added with a hesitant lift of her lips. "Hana says we're not going to be kept in the dark anymore. We're invited to meet with the leadership of Ashbough Protective Services, plus the Graygazers and the surviving members of the Crown Coven, tomorrow to decide what to do next. The rest of the day is for us to rest and recover."

My gaze veered back toward Lucas. I didn't know how much of either task I would be doing. As a blood witch, I'd already healed all the cuts and bruises I'd sustained in the earlier fight. My body was ready for another round, even if my heart and soul remained wounded and in denial.

"And your aunt is waiting to talk to you, too," she shared.

She released me so I could open the door out into the hall, and standing there patiently were two people. I should've expected as much. Aunt Jordan had yet to see my little brother, and Geo was never too far from Cress if he could help it.

Jordan had escaped any serious harm. She still wore a beautiful formal robe stitched with falling stars, but dust clung stubbornly to it and the limp brown hair around her head. She had a soft face made for kindly smiles and sympathy, which I could barely stand to see on her expression when our eyes met briefly.

"You want to see Lucas," I said, stepping to the side so she could enter the room.

She pushed off the wall and went straight to me for a

big hug. I froze, surprised. "Tell me you're all right first," she said.

My aunt released me just to look me over critically, and I wondered if this was what it felt like to have a mom... someone who would fuss because they liked you whole and healthy, even if it was a little embarrassing.

"As good as can be expected." I felt stiff and awkward. Before we'd met about a month ago, I'd never been fussed over. There had been no mother figures amongst Garroway's coven of assassins, only blood and pain.

She nodded and gestured over her shoulder. "I made sure to take your staff with us. Unfortunately, the case was left behind...but such a thing can be replaced."

Propped against the wall were two celestial witch staves. The first was made of golden wood and embellishments, with a single piece of paper hanging from a bar that crossed under a small, molded sun resting at the top of it. That paper was a prepared spell, waiting in reserve. Since high-level celestial magic was a long and grueling process, it was typical for spells to be ritually created and then stored on paper slips on a staff.

"My" staff was the impressive creation next to it. Its name was Evening Guidance, and it'd been my father's before his untimely death. The wood was coated with black varnish and painted with silver trails of stars to match the centerpiece of a silver-plated crescent moon wrapped in the tails of several falling stars. Dozens of prepared spells were still attached to it.

The last time it'd been used was in Cress's hands, firing a ray of pure power at Lucas to separate him from the Hungering Darkness. Neither of us was a celestial witch, but somehow, she'd called upon the power to use it anyway. I saw Evening Guidance as her weapon now, even if it were sized and balanced for a man's use.

Her magical book's spine was perched on it, front and back cover flickering like a strange butterfly. As I ushered my aunt into my brother's room, I heard it utter, "Hey Cressie-poo, were you worried about me too?" It sounded a lot like a squeaky toy, and Cress loved it to death even though it was a flying, talking, know-it-all nuisance.

"Of course I was, *The Librarian Witch's Handbook*," she cooed.

Oh, and she had to address it by its full name, else it pouted. "Annoying" was part of its charm.

Their voices were muffled as I closed the door behind us, letting my aunt meet Lucas for the first time. She took his hand and prayed to the witch goddess while I stood back to give her some privacy. Something told me his condition was not for the divine to heal.

His soul needed Phaeron's help, the one thing we didn't have.

EVENING CAME SWIFTLY, and I'd been dragged from Lucas's bedside to join my coven and friends in one of the only rooms left unused on the fourth and final floor of the hospital. It had two curtained beds, and we drew straws for who would pile into them versus sleep on the cold floor tonight.

It was like a strange slumber party, all of us huddled under blankets, watching the evening news from a tiny television mounted in the wall, and eating our rationed share of hospital food. Geo, who'd returned to his human form finally, helped me bracket Cress between us in the back of the group. I played halfheartedly with my familiar, Flit, who was full of ferret energy despite everything.

The supernatural news stations were dominated by grainy footage taken of a glowing white figure sitting on the Crown Coven's dais as if it were a throne. News anchors warned viewers multiple times before playing a few carefully curated shots of Myuna interacting with the two men still alive with her.

Though the news jumped around to avoid showing the reality of the situation, Myuna's mouth and chin were streaked with blood, standing out in shades of gray and black from the grayscale recording.

"She's eating the bodies left behind," Cress murmured, the first to acknowledge the gruesome truth.

"And Garroway's feeding her," commented Bianca.

The olive-skinned woman was the only other person in this room that didn't bear any injuries. She and I were perhaps the only two blood witches to escape Garroway's coven and live to tell the tale. We would always bear the runes he'd carved into our skin and the scars from his relentless training. That made us trauma siblings, even if she was about as friendly as a lit fuse most days.

As much as I wanted Garroway to suffer for everything he'd done to us, I hoped Myuna didn't kill him. I'd vowed to finish him myself and intended to keep that promise.

Cress's voice drew me out of my dark thoughts. "But not Phaeron." She sounded like she was clinging to hope.

The news only showed the dark gray figure of the dimensional prince standing there, watching. He appeared to be standing in the same place in every shot.

The talking heads on every station reported that it was Myuna, quoting a red-skinned dimensional woman who'd come forward earlier to set the record straight for the greater supernatural community. She'd shared who Myuna was and why she was there. And once that footage was exhausted, talk turned to that of survivors and missing family members who hadn't had the means to escape the pocket dimension in time.

It looked bleak for them...for us. Cerris City would not come off lockdown for anyone when a world-eating goddess could escape behind them.

"I bet you someone is streaming the uncut footage." The husky-voiced suggestion came from Wren, who sat on one of the beds. Though she'd stopped crying, she looked and sounded exhausted, wearing her grief with her spine curled in.

Several of us spoke up at once. Wren ignored it all, typing away on her phone screen.

"We need to have some eyes on the inside. Why not a camera?" suggested our resident changeling in disguise. We only knew him as Grant Norwood, the verdant witch he appeared to be at the moment. Since Áine was also in this room, he kept his true form hidden. As they were from enemy courts, she was bound to be the last to know we had a changeling in our midst, and I didn't want to be around for her wrath if she ever learned the truth.

I glanced over at him, wondering if we could send him to spy on Myuna. It would be more accurate than the news or a recording presumably being streamed online.

An awful buzzing noise came from Wren's phone, startling most of us. She grimaced and turned it down with a few rapid clicks on the side of her device. "This hacker is saying that when Myuna spoke for the first time, all the audio got messed up. But this is what's happening right now," she said.

Her phone was passed from hand to hand, quickly

ending up with Cress. "They're just...doing nothing?" she asked. Myuna hadn't moved from the dais, and Phaeron was a motionless statue below her.

The device stopped in Roe's hands last. She angled its screen away from Willow, who had recently received magical healing for a concussion. Our coven's leader was the only one here willing to scroll as far back in time as the stream would go, making a sound of disgust as the black and white shadows played over her face. "Okay, gross," Roe muttered. "So she eats everyone...then she starts talking to Phaeron... Oh, this might be something."

We gathered into a tight knot behind Roe as she played the video at three times its normal speed. Myuna made a come-hither gesture, and Phaeron responded. She worked magic over him and blinded the camera with beams of light...

"Fuck," Cress spat in frustration. "What'd she do to him?"

When the light cleared, Phaeron was assuming the same spot where he'd apparently been standing since this moment. Myuna turned to Garroway and said something, then Roe paused the video. "He's taking one of Phaeron's swords and leaving," she said.

"We have to go get Phaeron," Cress said.

"Not yet," Geo rumbled. "He has to leave the goddess's side first. And something tells me she won't allow him to do that unless he is fully under her control."

"We'll figure out how to nab him, promise," Roe put in.

Everyone voiced their agreement in their own ways. Willow, Áine, and Wren gave weary nods. Grant, Bianca, and I cracked our knuckles, signaling a readiness to fight. I raised a brow at Grant since he'd said more than once that his pretty changeling ass was no good in combat. He offered a brilliant smile and a shrug in reply.

Roe, Geo, and Cress exchanged glances, determination in their faces.

"In the meantime, I'm declaring Yule to be on pause. I bought a gift for each and every one of you, and you'll get them when we escape this pocket dimension," Roe continued.

"If you haven't noticed, they're not unsealing the pocket dimension for anyone to 'escape,'" Grant said with air quotes.

"Not until Myuna is dead," Cress spoke up. "And Hana Graygazer believes the right group has been trapped in here with her to make that happen."

"Who...*us*?" Wren asked, glancing around. A bit of that rich girl judgment returned to her gaze and tone. "Most of us can barely cast five spells."

"Two of us are trained assassins with many kills to their names," Bianca retorted. A claim she could make about herself, especially in hunting unnaturals, but less about me. I had the "trained" part down, but Garroway had barely sent me on any missions.

Wren turned a glare her way. "You're not even in this coven."

I knew that look on Bianca's face, ready and excited for a fight. I murmured her name, practically begging for her to glance my way and not start this conflict. Not now.

She said without pause, "I will be tomorrow."

Several emotions passed over Wren's face before she settled on betrayal. She tilted that look toward Roe. "Heath's body isn't even cold yet," she said, going breathy with emotion. "I mean, before some monster everyone calls a goddess ate what's left of him. He can't be replaced like that." She snapped her fingers.

"Wren, you have to understand—" Roe began to say.

"I'm not having this conversation around everyone," the other woman said abruptly. She stood and snatched up her phone, putting it in her pocket and sailing out the door. If she was trying to outrun the first sob before we all heard it...I could pretend it hadn't happened before she was out of earshot.

Roe heaved a tired sigh before following after her. After a few moments of hesitation, Cress followed, motioning for Geo and me to stay behind.

4

CRESS

THE NEXT MORNING, Bianca was sworn in as the seventh member of A Little Wicked Coven with the rest of us bearing witness over a cold breakfast. Wren hadn't had it in her to argue when Roe and I had presented Biana's strengths as a talented assassin who knew one of our main enemies, the vampire Garroway, with more familiarity than even Ben.

That didn't mean she liked it. Not that I ever got the feeling she ever particularly *liked* any of us, anyway. She stared off into the middle distance in the hospital's cramped cafeteria and ate her ration of food without relish. If someone had told me I'd feel this much sympathy for Wren even a week ago, I'd have cackled like it was a bad joke. Yet here we were.

The meeting Hana had invited me to started right after breakfast, in a conference room on the hospital's first floor. I attended with Ben, Geo, Roe, and Bianca and wondered why we were invited at all when I saw the faces that ringed the other half of the long table. Madigan and Orthus represented Ashbough Protective Services. Hana sat with the remnants of the Crown Coven, Kwan Graygazer and Daire Grimsbane. A few fae and verdant witch doctors, all carrying a tired, fearful gleam in their eyes, were here too as hospital leadership.

And sitting in one of the only unoccupied seats was a ghost only I could see, of my deceased birth mother, Eris Darkmore. Ever since Phaeron had called her spirit back on Samhain to talk to me, she'd remained on the mortal plane to haunt me on and off under the guise of helping.

She could be helpful, but it was awkward at the same time. We barely knew each other. She was endlessly judgmental about my decision to become a librarian witch, and I was sure there was an unpleasant day ahead when she popped in while I was having private time with my boyfriends. Just the thought gave me a full-body cringe.

"We're gathered today to discuss what to do next," Madigan said. She'd claimed the head of the table, fingers steepled as the room quieted down and faces turned her way. "The goddess that destroyed Soiluire is now here, locked inside the Cerris City pocket dimension with us. The majority of the city's population received the emergency alert about the lockdown and fled, including many medical professionals. Thank you for staying to support and heal the sick and injured." She nodded toward the doctors present.

I smiled their way briefly. I hadn't realized the crew keeping the hospital running had had to make the conscious decision to stay. No wonder they'd thrown scrubs at my mom so readily when she'd volunteered to help.

"Unfortunately, there are civilians still stranded here, and many of them are kids or young families. We have to act fast to bring them to safety and gather supplies," Madigan continued.

Hana interjected, "Myuna will not sit idle for long. She has one loyal servant right now, but that will change as time passes. As a goddess, she is used to being served by a legion."

Bianca raised her fingers as Hana spoke. Madigan gestured for her to speak. "The 'loyal servant' you mentioned is the vampire Garroway, who won't be able to take anyone to her while it's daylight outside," she said, punching into her palm. "We should hunt him when the sun sets, to cripple her further."

"She will then turn her attention to Phaeron to break his will early. This is a future we do not want," Hana replied.

"Early?" I echoed in a pained whisper.

"Right now, she wants him aware and in pain. Last night, she sent Garroway out to hunt you," Hana said, her gaze flashing to me. My ghostly mother gasped in surprise. "We might have one more night where he tries again. One thing is for certain...Myuna will remain in place and expect her every desire to come to her. That makes her predictable and thus something we can outwit and kill."

"So, she can be killed?" asked Crown Grimsbane. He was a tough-looking Black man and the only blood witch in the Crown Coven. He still wore a bandolier lined with daggers but had replaced whatever expensive clothing he had been wearing for a plain t-shirt and jeans. It was probably the miraculous healing powers of his affinity that'd ensured his survival of yesterday's attack.

"She can be," Hana confirmed.

"Hell, why don't we go do that now? We've been

patched up. We know where she is and who her allies are. All of us versus the three of them," he commented.

Hana drew breath to reply, but it was Crown Graygazer who spoke up next. "We would lose and feed ourselves to Myuna. And afterward, there would be no one to stop her from taking over the pocket dimension until it has to be collapsed."

I wasn't the only one paling at the implication of collapsing Cerris City. I'd only heard of it being done once, when the Fall Court's Mother Tree was burned, but a collapsed pocket dimension simply ceased to exist, as did any living things within it at the time.

If that meant Myuna died, great. Except I wanted to live...as did the hundreds, perhaps thousands, of other supernaturals still trapped here with us.

The elder Graygazer continued talking while we reeled from this revelation, "There are a few paths to victory we can take...but they must be selected with care. Hana and I will guide us in the right direction."

I nodded to myself. Hana had gotten us into this mess with the idea that we were the right ones to fix it.

Geo cleared his throat, drawing attention even though it wasn't the sound of clashing rocks like it would be in his gargoyle form. "I have a suggestion," he stated, voice still flat with how recently he'd been in his stone form.

"Let's hear it," Madigan said with some of her usual enthusiasm.

"As you've said, once she gets her bearings, one of Myuna's first goals will be to recruit allies. Is there a library here?" He looked around, asking the room at large.

"Cerris City Library, yes," one of the doctors confirmed.

"We need to secure it before she realizes it exists. Most of the unnatural creatures and artifacts stored by librarian witches can trace their corrupted origins back to Myuna," Geo said.

"That's true. She could gain a lot of dangerous servants, depending on what's in the library," I pitched in.

"Civilians can shelter in the lower levels," Geo rumbled. "And I will activate the library's gargoyle units to defend them."

Madigan dropped her voice to whisper with Orthus for a brief conversation. "We can split our people into three groups. One to rescue survivors; one to secure food, water, and other supplies; and one to head to Cerris City Library," she said finally.

"Let's talk locations," Orthus added. Like the crystals that originated from his home court, his voice was resonant with power, soft but deep. His crystal armor blended in seamlessly with his granite-colored skin and the sharp emerald crystals that grew from his shoulders and formed points at his elbows and fingertips. "It would become an extra challenge to hold both the hospital and the library should they be too far from each other."

A few of us dug out our phones to look at the digital map of the city. The hospital was at the corner of a block, occupying a lot of space considering its conjoined parking garage. Unfortunately, the library was two miles away and a close landmark to the Crown Coven's complex and Myuna's new seat of power.

We noted a supermarket between the library and the hospital, and the planning began from there. Several vehicles had been abandoned in the hospital's garage, and it was Bianca who suggested some grand theft auto to speed up the process of gathering supplies and people. Roe, who'd been quietly absorbing the information around her, made a disapproving hum.

"A Little Wicked Coven will go to Cerris City Library. Cress and Geo can help us convince anyone remaining there to work with us," Roe said.

A flash of protectiveness passed over Madigan's expression. "I will send a few friends to help you," she said.

Roe shook her head. "We can do this, Mom. More of our people should be securing food and survivors before things get really dangerous."

Though hesitant, Madigan agreed and began divvying up those healthy enough to undertake these tasks. While she was occupied, Eris turned her ghostly head toward me. "Just don't go out after dark. If that vampire is hunting you, he had better not realize you're in the library," she said.

"Right," I whispered.

If Myuna wanted me, she must know I meant something to Phaeron. Maybe that's what she'd done to him when her light magic had blinded the camera. Read his mind...or made him admit things against his will. If she aimed to break him, consuming friends and family in front of him would be an evil first step.

As I tuned out of the meeting, my worries for him flooded back in. He'd been wounded when we were separated. We'd checked the hacker's stream this morning to see that he and Myuna had still not moved overnight. I doubted she'd let him care for his wounds properly.

His absence was a loss for this meeting. I had no doubt he would know what to do to take Myuna down quicker than our plan to gather survivors and entrench ourselves. Maybe we'd even put him at the head of the table, as the only ally who'd fought Myuna and her creatures before.

I knew we had to protect ourselves first before helping others, but I wanted to do more for him than this. And, on that note, for Carly. I swiped over to my texts and tapped her name, worried when I saw she still hadn't read any of the messages I'd sent her. Hopefully she'd just lost her phone fleeing with the crowd and had either been pulled out of the pocket dimension by another supernatural or was hunkered down somewhere safe.

A message from Mom popped up on my screen—her telling me to come find her after the meeting was over. It wasn't much longer before we were done, and Roe set off with Geo to get our group together. Mom told me she was working on the second floor.

I waited for her at the nurses' station and texted her back, waiting a good few minutes before she emerged from one of the occupied rooms red-faced and fuming. Mom, angry? She was a nurse with nerves of steel, but her usual kindly air was frazzled.

"Did something happen?" I blurted.

Her blue eyes flashed before she took a deep breath and put on a smile for me. "I'm just finding Crystal fae to be more difficult patients than I'm used to," she told me in a low voice.

I glanced over my shoulder to make sure we were alone. Even ghostly Eris was faded out for the time being, and the other nurses were hustling to keep the hospital functioning.

"I'm sure they can be as stubborn as rocks. Fae take on some of the qualities of their court, after all," I answered.

"As amazing as it is to live in a world where fae exist, you're probably wondering why I wanted to see you. I want you to sit down with one of the doctors for a few minutes."

I agreed warily since she said the doctor was already waiting to see me next in a room being cleaned and prepped for the next patient. Mom made herself scarce, then the steel-haired verdant witch doctor started asking the general questions I would answer for an annual physical.

Then she inquired if I was sexually active, and it all clicked into place. My ultra-perceptive Mom had made sure I was leaving with my friends for Cerris City Library with a new prescription of birth control pills in my pocket. Sure, it was a little embarrassing, but I couldn't wait to tell Geo and Ben.

5
GEO

The trip to the library was short, aided by two cars borrowed from the hospital's parking garage. Getting them started was Bianca's job, something she did with practiced ease. Cress and her coven packed themselves into the small vehicles, while the larger ones and especially the trucks went to the guardians and Crystal fae for the task of gathering supplies and people.

If I wasn't escorting the two cars making the brief trip to the Cerris City Library, I would've flown right past it. It was a building made of chrome and glass, modernized with a flat roof and sharp angles. I'd gotten my hopes up for nothing. There were no gargoyles here, waiting in stasis for when they would be needed most.

It seemed the building was made very recently, without the spacious eaves where a gargoyle could perch. I flew overtop it, frowning to myself and recognizing why modernization had moved away from my kind.

The creation of gargoyles was outlawed some time ago due to a moral argument, something I had experienced personally. Ritually placing a witch's soul inside of a stone heart to animate a gargoyle made the resulting construct a new person with its own life to live, if they came to realize it.

Once most of us took our human forms of flesh and blood, we were loath to return, inevitably abandoning the duty we'd been created to perform. It was unfortunate I was seeing the downsides of this, with a lack of protectors to call upon when this library needed it most.

What a hypocrite my disappointment made me. I felt muffled and numb in my stone form now. I'd been out of it long enough that it felt like I was suffocating the complexity of my emotions. If I stayed this way too long, it would all fade until only cold reasoning was left, and what a shame that would be.

I was no longer comforted by unfeeling duty. My heart belonged to the purple-haired witch exiting one of the cars two stories below where I flew. When I'd awoken from self-imposed stasis, my duty had simply been *her*.

Her wants, needs, goals, dreams. My stone heart resonated for Cress, and she was mine. My purpose, my future. The reason I craved the warmth and illogicality of emotion within me once more.

I completed one last, wider pass overhead to check for threats before coming in for a landing on the sidewalk nearby. At the last second, I checked my momentum to set down my obsidian body without cratering the cement underfoot. I only remained a gargoyle for the authority it gave me...if the librarians within this space would give me jurisdiction as its new protector.

"Door's open," Roe said, holding back what looked to be a solid pane of glass for everyone else to pass through.

"The defenses here are insufficient," I ground out. "How are we to hold control of a house of glass?"

Cress was the one who answered. "Easy. Everything of value is down below."

"I don't like the idea of enemies three layers above our heads," I replied.

She went ahead of me into the library's inside foyer, head bent over her handbook. It replied in a squeaky, "You got it, toots! Look for hostiles quietly!"

"*Quietly*," she hissed back.

"Yup!" It flapped off to fly around the first floor. I stood next to Cress and watched it go with a low, rumbling chuckle.

In my stone form, I towered over her, taller in stature than any human man and much broader even with my wings folded as tight as they would go to my back. I carried a new addition, too, a shield made of tempered crystal. It was a gift from Prince Orthus and as large as my torso. It'd already come in handy in our last fight, and Cress liked it, finding how it rang from the touch of sunlight and glittered like an opal delightful. If I appreciated its function and she enjoyed its form, then it was perfect in my eyes.

I likened it to myself, as I had been sculpted and given new life for her. She enjoyed my form and functions quite a bit in private. My longing was a meager ember compared to normal, yet I yearned to touch her, to take her hand. I flexed my digits as much as they would bend, frustrated with how it felt I was working with an oven mitt rather than graceful fingers to twine with hers.

Later, I thought. In my own head, I was as taciturn as ever.

Would I have Cress to myself soon? *Yes.*

Would Ben join us? *Probably yes.*

Did I care? *Hmm.*

No. He could assist in clearing away her troubles for an

evening. And if the dimensional returned... When he returned, Phaeron could join us. His absence was grinding through her thoughts, creating the shadows that danced in her eyes. If he was that important to her, then it was time for my pride to take a step back so I could fulfill my duty as her man.

"...Geo? Are you even listening?" Cress's voice cut through my thoughts. I refocused my quartz-formed eyes, realizing I'd stalled in place, gazing down at her absent-mindedly. And apparently, she'd been trying to talk to me all the while, as her lip was quirked with annoyance and she'd crossed her arms.

"My apologies," I said. *I was merely daydreaming of you.*

"I was saying we should head down a level and see if there are any librarian witches still at work here."

"A sound plan," I answered. The library's inside was familiar, though the stacks were sparser than I was used to.

"Wait," whispered Áine. She'd declared herself the eighth member of the coven and tagged along with us, along with Jordan Evenstar, as Ben had not been able to dissuade her. A good thing, too, with their abilities.

Áine pointed to the left, where the handbook had stopped and bobbed in place ten feet above the ground. It was analyzing something.

A vine as thick as one of my stone fingers sprang from Áine's wrist, unspooling at her will as curls of green mist rose from her palms. Someone yelped behind one of the stacks when Áine made a circular motion with her hand and tugged backward. The plant returned to her, towing along a young teen by a loop of vine curled around his ankle. He clawed at the ground in futility. When I checked his aura, sure enough, he bore a weak but fluid halo of shifter magic.

He also hissed when Áine released him from the vine. "You are not a librarian," I stated.

"Obviously," the kid muttered, standing and dusting himself off. His gaze flickered between us, and he ran a hand through unruly russet-brown hair a shade darker than his skin. "If you guys are looking for a place to stay, keep going. The library's closed."

"We are looking for the librarian witches," I stated.

He shrugged sharply. "And they don't want to see anybody."

"We're here to help," Cress put in hastily. She patted the sword fastened to her hip. "I'm a librarian too."

His eyes widened. "That might be different. Wait here," he said. Without waiting for a reply, he moved behind the nearest stack and shifted. His clothes hit the ground with a rustle before he dashed away on the four padded feet of a brown tabby cat.

Cress watched him go, smiling broadly. "Aww, look how cute he is." She stooped to pick up one of her familiars, Milo, who purred in her hold. The other two had listened to her instruct her handbook and disappeared into the first floor to search for dangers.

"Not that I know many shifters, babe," said Ben. "But I think they'd object to being called cute."

Her expression barely dimmed. "I thought shifters were only able to turn into bigger animals?" she asked.

Roe was the one to pitch in while everyone else waited in various states of nervous idleness. "There are shifters of pretty much every animal you can imagine. They just keep to their own clans for the most part."

There was a loud snap. Several of us glanced over at Wren, who was chewing gum with a few aggressive pops in her mouth. "Two bucks says the kid ditched us," she said.

"Let's give him a little benefit of the doubt. The librarians will trust him more than us," Cress said.

Wren released a little "hmph."

A few minutes later, the cat shifter returned, leading a woman toward us who didn't look much older than Cress and her friends. "Oh, wow. A real gargoyle," she said, stopping short when she spotted me. "No wonder Steven was in such a fuss!"

The cat's ears pinned back, and he growled before going back around the stack to shift back. I heard the rustling of clothes before he emerged wearing what he'd shifted out of. "There's a gargoyle and a librarian, and they wanted to talk to you," he said.

"Hi, I'm Aurora," she said, waving to me shyly.

"Greetings. I am Geo."

"Nice to meet you, Geo. Is that short for anything?"

"No."

Ben muffled a snicker behind his hand. The librarian shifted on her feet, still looking uncertain as she took in our group. "Well, okay then. If you're trying to find shelter, I'm afraid we've closed the library. There are dangerous, unstable creatures down below that are trying to escape their containment rooms. It's not safe."

"We are here to offer assistance and partnership," I said.

"And Ashbough Protective Services is only a couple miles away to shelter and protect any civilians you might have," Roe added, gesturing toward the shifter boy.

She glanced at him. "Oh, Steven? He's practically our mascot. We, err..." She leaned in, lowering her voice. "Most of the staff abandoned Cerris City right before the lockdown. If you're really here to help, jump in and do it. Those of us who stayed can barely keep up with what's going on down below."

"We definitely want to help," Cress said.

"We'll do so as a group, though. As a fair warning, you should know that many of us are new to our magic," Roe added.

The other librarian nodded, waving the concern away hastily. "Let's be on our way. The powercore is going to need contact with you first"—she nodded to Cress—"and then it will communicate where you're most needed."

Cress nodded, determination creasing her face. "Let's go."

6

CRESS

THE POWERCORE WAS on level sixteen of thirty. I eyed the buttons on the elevator's wall as I descended in relative silence alongside Aurora and Geo, my handbook now fluttering just off my shoulder. Since Geo refused to leave his gargoyle form, we would exceed the weight limit with all of us in here, so the others would follow along shortly.

Moongrove Library had had fifty floors, with many levels specialized for the containment of specific kinds of creatures, unnaturals, and artifacts. I'd met dozens of librarians who'd worked there, often seeing more than one person working every day on the more labor-intensive floors. To think Cerris City Library only had three librarians left. Even with its smaller size, it would become unmanageable quickly.

Geo's suggestion that we come here immediately was rock solid...pun not intended. He was my protective shadow as we followed Aurora through a foyer that looked like it could be any modern office's reception area and passed a waiting area with a cluster of plush chairs.

"What's your home library?" Aurora asked.

"Moongrove," I answered.

"Ah, I went to college at NSU too. The powercore here is different, and so is the process of drawing from it," she said.

I quirked a curious brow. "How so?"

"Moongrove's powercore felt a lot like talking to a person, especially when I touched it. It felt ancient and mysterious. There's no mystery here. The powercore in this library is a computer," she said, gesturing us into the next room.

"Can a computer be a powercore?" I asked mostly to myself.

My handbook rustled its pages. "Yeah, almost every powercore across North America is powered by artificial intelligence. You've been spoiled by one that thinks like you do," it said.

"It was weird at first, but I've gotten used to it. It monitors the library just as well as Moongrove's powercore," Aurora said.

I bit my lip. She was so close to the truth. Moongrove Library's powercore *was* a person, once, named Braza. After her death, her soul had become the beating heart of the library. She'd formed into a large, immobile sphere that rested on a ley line, siphoning raw magic from the earth to create a reservoir her librarians could tap. Through her awareness of the fifty underground floors of her domain, Braza guided her librarians to maintain order.

I'd only learned this much about her because of Phaeron, who'd known her in life. She'd healed me of some devastating injuries and sheltered me within her dome. I was disappointed I was about to let go of the magic she'd given me so I could attune with a computer-controlled powercore instead. It just wouldn't be the same.

The powercore chamber came to light slowly as I

approached the sphere at its center. It reminded me of an LED with its faint but growing light, marked a pure and crisp white. Like with Braza, the massive powercore rested in the cradle of a stone loop.

"The other change is that you can climb inside of it. There's a seat and a terminal within to enter your information," Aurora explained.

"That does seem weird," I said. I took a couple steps up to the powercore before I touched its jellylike surface. It wasn't as dense as Braza, and I pushed my hand through to the pocket of air within it.

"Just step forward!" Aurora encouraged. She and Geo waited a few paces away. He'd crossed his arms, gazing up at me with a vague frown. With his stone form, even a small downturn of his lips was as intense as if he were about to rush over and snatch me away from danger.

I braced myself and took the suggested step. The powercore blinded me for a moment, but the sole of my foot found a solid surface on the other side. Blinking away dazzled streaks from my eyes, I inspected the computer terminal and seat that took up much of the space inside. I sat and put my fingertips on the keyboard extending out from under the monitor.

There was a jolt of static over my skin. "Beginning startup procedure," a robotic voice said from the terminal.

The hair rose along my arms. There was some kind of magic analyzing me, and it felt reminiscent of the same magic Braza wielded. My handbook giggled. "That tickles!" it squeaked.

After a minute of this, the sensation faded and the machine said, "Scan complete. Welcome, librarian witch. What would you like to do?"

The monitor flashed with a menu list of options. I used the arrow keys on the keyboard to highlight option three, which was to attune to this powercore, and hit enter.

"My sensors detect lingering magic from the powercore in Moongrove Library. Enter identifying information to begin the transfer process."

The screen went dark before loading in what looked like a job application. I started typing in my name and date of birth with a sigh, hoping I wouldn't leave my friends waiting for too long. There was a spinning wheel in the corner of the screen that kept distracting me as text flashed next to it. "Connecting to Moongrove Library..."

I was halfway through the application when the connection went through and the screen froze. I muttered a curse and tapped the keys with more force than necessary, past annoyed with this cumbersome system.

A voice entered my head, sudden and loud. *"Brightest of souls! Why are you trying to switch libraries?"*

"Braza?" I whispered.

"What has happened? Did I not grant you sufficient power for your audience with the Crown Coven?" she demanded.

I had questions for her, too. Like how she'd managed to bring her presence across so many miles to shout in my head. I could feel her lingering in the air with me, a presence of power and static.

"It comes with the job of needing others to do what I physically cannot," she answered. She could also skim the thoughts off the top of my head, which meant there were no secrets I could keep from her.

Instead of using my words, now that I knew she was in my thoughts, I projected my most recent memories to her. The interrupted audience, the fight and deaths, Myuna's summoning. All the while, her magic thickened further in the air.

"Uhhh, Cressie-poo, maybe we should get out of this thing," my handbook said nervously, flapping circles around my head.

The small space filled with the humidity of a mounting storm, and I teared up as it reminded me of Phaeron. I could close my eyes, and it would be him next to me, his magic on a short leash. But I knew that was a lie. Braza had a zip of electricity to her that he did not. It felt like potential I could reach out and take to wield as well as I could.

"Step out of the powercore," she instructed.

I scrambled from the seat and took a leap out of the white powercore. The room shuddered as my feet landed. "W-what's happening?" Aurora asked. She clutched the front of her chest and gasped as the tremors under our feet grew.

Geo grabbed me with one arm and her with the other, shading us with his heavy wings. I was pressed between his shield and the outside world, my eyes twice their size as the computerized powercore went dim. Aurora screamed and reached out for it as its jellylike surface shrank and fell into the hole underneath its stone dais.

"The powercore!" she shrieked.

"Wait!" I shouted. Something else was flowing up from the hole, its soft form expanding once it'd cleared the stone and emitting a piercing purple-black glow.

I had no idea how, but it was Braza, and her presence expanded out rapidly through the room and likely the library as a whole. *"Emergency protocol initiated: temporary placement of an ancient powercore. Reinforcing all existing spells..."* Braza projected this outward, and Aurora's mouth fell open.

Geo released us both as the shaking beneath our feet stopped. A door slammed, and in ran Ben, followed closely by Roe and the rest of our friends and coven. "Hey," Aurora tried to shout, but she was breathless. "Only librarians and gargoyles this close to the powercore."

I whispered Braza's name, awe keeping my face slackened. Her magic flowed from her in waves, like a beating heart.

"It is quite all right. I have welcomed this young coven in my halls before. As I used to see you daily, small shimmer. Fret not, I have secured the creatures attempting to escape. Come attune with me so we can hold this library against..." Braza faltered for a moment. *"Hold this library for as long as we can with the few resources that remain here."*

"I didn't know you could switch places with another powercore like this," I said. And my thoughts added, *"Aren't you afraid Myuna will come for you?"*

"In my prince's absence, you need me more than ever. We shall fight. Together," she answered. No one else seemed to hear her reassurance or feel the way her power curled around me like an embrace.

"Together," I murmured aloud in agreement.

"You will see how literal that is soon. For now, I must meet with the three librarians who remain here, and you need to claim a place to rest. Might I suggest the rooms on floor negative two?" She hummed, adding as an afterthought, *"The living spaces set aside on floor negative one bear signs of occupation. I don't think they have grounds to complain if you borrow their things. Clothes, especially."*

I looked down at myself and the wrinkled and torn formal robe and pants combination I was still wearing. She was definitely telling me to change into something else.

As I turned to go, motioning to my friends to come

along, a woman who looked like she could be Steven's grandmother stalked into the chamber. She had a similar brown skin tone and the first touches of gray through her dark hair. The cat shifter peered around her ankles as if he were a familiar taking shelter behind his witch.

She wore a sweater and jeans but carried an ornate silver sword in one hand and had a book flapping just over her shoulder obediently. Her brows drew in a surprised scowl. "Is it true? An ancient powercore just arrived?"

"That is correct," Braza answered for us.

The older librarian's voice broke as she said, "Thank the goddess. We were bound to be overrun without some kind of help."

"Do I smell a round of firings once this is all over, boss?" asked the last librarian as he sauntered in. He could've been Lars Eriksson's American twin, with sideswept blond hair and a leanly muscled build. His sword was sheathed at his side and his stance cocky. A low whistle escaped him as he eyed Braza's glow.

The boss in question smacked her lips. "You're not coming any closer to my job, Jonah, if that's what you're really asking."

Roe cleared her throat, stepping forward with her hand extended. "Sorry to interrupt, ma'am. Since you're in charge, I wanted to let you know who we are and why we're here."

"Yes, I was wondering what you all were doing this close to the powercore," she commented, shaking Roe's hand. "Leona Whiteside, head librarian."

We gathered for a group introduction, and even Braza presented herself formally. Leona seemed like a strict woman who didn't take much shit yet had seen too much of it lately. She still was visibly relieved that our group included another librarian and a gargoyle. She offered us rooms, same as Braza had, and accepted a partnership with Ashbough Protective Services through Roe.

"If the monster eating corpses on the nightly news is the reason our dimensional aberrations are suddenly gaining the power to wake from stasis, we will need any defenders you can spare. Preferably people who won't hesitate to slay anything that tries to escape," she said.

I only hesitated for a few moments before telling her that monster was Myuna, the goddess of said aberrations. Jonah paled beside her, while Leona's eyes flashed with defiance. They exchanged a glance before Leona said, "Then we must initiate a new protocol. Please, put me in contact with your leader. I believe we must do something quite desperate."

She told us not to worry about it for now and practically chased us out of the room so we could claim places to rest for the evening. I, at least, would not be leaving the library once it was after dark, knowing a vampire was hunting me in Myuna's name.

Braza reached out to me, whispering the idea that'd come to Leona. *"She was not willing to tell you that the only way to keep Myuna from summoning the servants and magic waiting for her in this library is to destroy it all first."*

I swallowed thickly, thinking that we locked the monsters away because they were dangerous, unknowable, or both. And the books and tools of occult use were kept here for careful study, considering they could never be replaced. To set all of that alight represented a huge loss of knowledge.

"I know, brightest of souls. But we must mitigate the threats we can."

I trembled as I thought of how unprepared my friends

were to fight the creatures that even a fully staffed library had preferred to keep in containment rooms. I couldn't lose any of them, especially not after having to leave Phaeron with Myuna and an uncertain fate.

7

PHAERON

THE ACHE of my injuries prevented me from focusing on counting the heartbeats thrumming within me. Time passed with the madness of the Void. Hours felt like minutes; moments felt like days. The goddess must have taken the chill of it with her for time to dilate in such a confounding way.

There was a Void between dimensions, an endless blackness. The closest thing humans had come to understanding the Void as a concept was through their study of the celestial bodies. It was similar to space, but *things* still existed out in space, hanging there suspended with vast distances between them. As much as the Void held the illusion of nothingness, it also retained an echo of all that touched it. It was a chamber where voices and experiences remained, slowly twisting into nightmarish form.

I'd had a few brushes with the Void before, even though I was not of the Vrassorm tribe, the Void-touched. I'd had a friend once who was, and he was excellent at making the darkness answer to his whims. The same friend had helped me guide our people through the Void to Earth. It'd felt like walking through an endless tunnel, the atmosphere cold, cold, *cold*.

My skin prickled, and I shuddered. I'd lost enough blood to miss it, some of it dried in the creases of my shredded armor. Myuna had not licked me again, but her carrion smell lingered to sting my nostrils. I hadn't left this spot in...days?

No, that's not right. I blinked away the fog starting to creep over my eyes. Garroway had yet to return, so it had not even been a day yet. He was bound to the day-night cycle as a vampire, so I could judge time passing by his arrivals and departures.

I knew for a fact that Myuna would eventually rest as well. Until then, she occupied herself with consuming the rest of the enchanted books in the chamber. It would've been easier for her if she stood and snatched them, but she was as lazy as I remembered. Either she read their titles aloud and they came to her hand obediently to meet their end, or she lassoed them out of the air with the strands of pure light she'd woven into rope.

This was fun for her. Her occasional laugh threatened to split my head in half, the *ha ha* layered with so many other voices. It felt like the souls she'd consumed screaming out while she had her gaping maw open to laugh.

Or a small amount of Void doing what it did best, echoing. Its chill lingered in the atmosphere, its many lurid eyes watching Myuna with me. She was too busy trying to call down the final two books from the rafters to notice.

I couldn't close my eyes for longer than a blink, not when Myuna had forbidden me to sleep or rest. Time's passing increasingly felt like torture, with me trapped in a silent, alert body with no reprieve.

So, I embraced the Void, just a little. Letting it giggle for me when she grew frustrated. Her lassos broke several human fixtures, casting us into full darkness, even knocking off the object I'd hoped was a weapon secretly pointed at her. It fell to the bloodied ground and shattered with the crunch of smashed glass and fragile metal.

With no artificial light in the chamber, it was obvious when the sun rose. Garroway returned, dragging two unconscious people behind him. "My lady," he said in the Hungering Darkness's two-toned voice. "I was not able to find the purple-haired witch. But I brought you a meal..."

Myuna's lasso flashed out and closed around the torsos of the two victims Garroway placed before her. Her magic faded, allowing her to hold up the man and woman in either hand as if they were dolls.

"...for us to share," Garroway finished in a whisper since it was already too late. Myuna consumed their souls with all the fanfare of taking a deep breath, then swallowed the bodies together in one ravenous gulp.

"You have forgotten my appetite if you believe that was a meal for me," she tutted, dabbing at the corners of her mouth with her sleeve.

"Yes, my lady."

"Forget the girl for now. Bring me *more souls*."

Garroway bared his teeth. I doubt the blood baron had made an expression of chagrin like this in decades. "I will remind you that this vessel cannot go out in the daylight, my lady."

She gazed down at him as if he were a bug to crush. "Worthless. I will make more servants since none of the ones I sense want to answer my call." Then she turned that look on me, instructing me to walk myself out of the audience chamber to wait five paces from the door for her summons.

My feet moved for me, pivoting me away before she could read the realization on my face. There was a library in the city...and Myuna could sense the denizens within it. It was only a matter of time before she corrupted a small force and tried to raid the building for access to her captured unnatural creatures. It'd be ruinous for this world if she went there personally to slurp down the powercore's accumulated energy. If she grew powerful enough, she might be able to muscle through the closed doors to leave Cerris City.

I'd figured out at some point overnight that the pocket dimension had been sealed shut. The change in air pressure was noticeable once Myuna was no longer bearing down on me. That meant the supply of unwilling servants was the small pool of people who didn't, or couldn't, escape from Cerris City in time.

A group of people that might not include Cress and her friends. Perhaps they had escaped not just the audience chamber, but Myuna's grasp completely. I hoped that was the case. The last thing I wanted was for Cress to see me become one of the goddess's servants, but it was only a matter of time. Myuna could already command my body. She'd make it as slow and torturous as possible, but she would inevitably seize control of my soul as well. A fate that loomed over me with great, ever-present dread.

Thankfully, five paces from the audience chamber took me to a battered bench I turned upright. My legs became one constant ache once I sat and finally took the pressure off my feet. I wanted to stray farther and find a restroom to clean my wounds and scrub away Myuna's stench, but I couldn't defy her order to wait five paces from the door.

I massaged feeling back into my muscles and reminded myself that I was still nearly whole. *Cress will still recognize you. She will still want you.*

I clenched my hand around one knee. *I will return to her,* I vowed. No matter what tortures Myuna inflicted upon me, I had a mate to claim and protect. It was up to me to find a way out of this situation before it was too late.

The Void's madness struck again while I was lost in my own thoughts. It felt like a blink's worth of time before Garroway stood before me, arms crossed. "I was sent to retrieve you," he said without the two-toned voice that indicated Endaeron was in charge.

I stood, wincing and reaching for the wounds that crossed my chest. They were weeping a hint of fresh blood. I spoke with effort, "Before we go back in there, I need to clean my—"

"Quiet," Garroway practically purred. My teeth clacked together so quickly I tasted the cut on my lower lip before I felt it. "Ah, it seems she's given me the end of your leash."

If I could correct him, I would. It was my brother, the one who'd swallowed a piece of my soul, who had originally had a finger's hold on my consciousness. With the Hungering Darkness inside of him, Garroway had it too, and I was too weakened to fight back.

He took a more confident stance; this was familiar territory for him, having his orders obeyed unquestioningly. I tamped my anger down with a deep breath. *He's a blood baron. He's used to mute glares and the futile struggles of those he controls,* I reminded myself. When I met his gaze, I wore my calmest expression.

He eyed me for a few moments, his face also a practiced mask. There was no telling if my reaction was also expected or if he was even a little unsettled. "I'll take you to a public bathroom in exchange for an honest conversation," he said.

I waited with patient blankness.

With a soft huff of breath, he added, "You may speak."

"I find these terms acceptable," I said.

He motioned for me to follow. There was a men's restroom just down the hall. Unlike the waiting room, which looked as if a hurricane had ripped through it, the restroom was mostly untouched. I could've used a shower, but this public space was better than nothing. I bent over one of the sinks and got to work with soap and lukewarm water, soon ringing the drain with my fuchsia blood.

My skin was purpled and puckered around the wounds as I scraped them clean with cheap paper towels. The paper ripped when I scrubbed the remains of my leather chest piece too, desperate to be rid of Myuna's dried saliva.

Endaeron had made the furrows across my armor and chest with his claws, ruining the new chest piece I'd painstakingly etched with runes next to the seams. Once it smelled of soap rather than carrion, I inspected the damage with a tisk.

"What did you wish to discuss?" I asked while I continued to clean myself. Not because I wanted to hear Garroway's voice, but if I kept him talking, it was less likely the Hungering Darkness would rouse.

Garroway had changed into a new set of clothes since the last time I'd seen him. He undid his belt to tug the line of his pants down on one side and removed his shirt, revealing a gigantic blood rune. Its magic was dormant and black, forming three spiky rings of runes that encompassed most of his right side from hip to armpit. Four healed and scarred slashes crossed the rings in jagged lines.

"I was wondering if there was any salvaging this, to regain control of myself," he said.

I pictured the moment of his possession by the Hungering Darkness. Endaeron had made those scars to prevent this blood rune from... I leaned in, reading the intent of the many runes Garroway had tattooed onto his skin.

He'd wanted to make his body a cage. The intricate spell bore marks of suppression and containment. If Endaeron had not destroyed it immediately, Garroway would have gained all the power of the Hungering Darkness with no foreseeable downsides.

It was unthinkable. And now he sought my help, as if I'd allow him such unchecked power.

"It is not possible," I stated.

Such a flat answer displeased Garroway. He bared his fangs and said, "The truth, dimensional. Tell me what you know about how to fix these runes."

Pain hooked behind my eyes the moment I thought to defy his order. I knew a great deal of things I wasn't willing to share, but I told him enough to soothe the pounding headache setting in. "There is a pinprick of hope for you. Your kind has always used dimensional magic to make these blood runes," I commented. "From a single weapon shattered into several pieces."

"Yes. And your fool brother destroyed the part I possessed," he stated through gritted teeth.

I tipped my head. "If you were to get a second piece..."

"There is nothing else that will fix the magic of these runes?" he demanded.

Again, the pain dug into my skull. I hissed with all the banked hostility within me. He was poking a predator through the bars of its cage, and I was just about ready to snap off his finger for it.

I answered in a low voice. "The weapon you were using to make the runes was unique. Endaeron was the one who forged and shaped the original great sword. It was made less for carving intricate displays of runes like this"—I gestured to his body—"and more for branding the flesh of any he faced in battle. It marked body and soul alike for his control."

"Ingenious," Garroway breathed.

I was about to call it *cruel* and share that I'd convinced Endaeron to shatter it, but the remains of my goodwill shriveled up. The few pieces of the sword that'd come to Earth with us had ended up filtered into the hands of the blood barons. They used them to mark the skin of their victims, witches like Ben, who bore the Agonia rune embedded into him permanently.

I knew his type. I'd slain a couple vampires like him in my time searching for the pieces of the sword, trying to destroy Endaeron's legacy before it endangered too many lives.

Unfortunately, I'd learned the hard way that destroying those shards also killed those who were being directly controlled by the man or woman who'd branded them with it. The mass casualties that'd followed when Endaeron had crushed Garroway's piece a mere day ago were additional stains on Garroway's already black soul.

"This is Myuna's work, marking souls, permanently branding others for control." He traced one of the runes marked in his own flesh.

Hatred flared within me at the reverence in his tone. "Myuna had little to do with it," I said, but he wasn't listening anymore.

"She is the most powerful being I've met in my long life," he continued. "A true *goddess*, not like the imaginary figurehead witches pray to. And she has chosen me as her right hand. Since it's not feasible to repair this rune, as you've said, I think I will accept what she's given me." A slow, cruel smile shaped his lips.

The Void's chill seeped into my voice. "That only means she will eat you last. You are a servant now, truly disposable to Myuna. She will slurp you up without a second thought, just like those two poor witches you brought before her," I sneered. I finished scrubbing my wounds clean and threw away a bloodied wad of paper towels.

He jabbed at my inflamed skin with a finger. "Don't take that tone with me, dimensional."

I snarled as his control dug in yet again, this time swiping my claws at him. He reared back with vampiric reflexes. "You wanted honesty. Here it is: you are a fool to think you're anything but a pawn," I snapped, switching to full venom since he forbade cold judgment.

"Wait. Pause." He held his hand palm up, and I froze.

I probed at his control, finding it as solid as Myuna's.

His voice became a velvet drawl. "We don't have to be enemies. Don't you want to see your purple-haired girl again?"

My whole body tensed further, recognizing the threat.

"Now, I'm going to let you go, and we can discuss what we can do for one another."

The moment he released his hold on my body, I grabbed him by the throat and shoved him through the bathroom mirror. Glass shards fell to the ground in a clanging rain around him. His eyes bulged, and skin reddened, face going slack with fear as shadows erupted from my body, closing around my head to form a wolflike visage protected by curled horns.

Yes, much better. I hated Garroway's presence less when he wasn't wearing that look of smug superiority. I caught his wrists with tendrils of shadow, pinning his arms down to his sides and his legs together with them.

"Let's get one thing straight, *blood baron*," I growled,

baring ebon fangs at him. My voice deepened with shadow-born power. "I do not tolerate petty tyrants. You will not dare speak of my mate if you want to leave this bathroom intact."

"*Is that so?*" asked the Hungering Darkness, disembodied from the choking grip I had Garroway in.

"Fuck," I said under my breath. There went the opportunity I had to make good on my promise and be rid of Garroway forever.

"*Release my vessel, Phaeron. That's a good brother. Now, let's return. You obviously can't be trusted away from Lady Myuna's gaze.*"

I jerked away from him and didn't move to the door until he ordered me to walk. We marched our way back to the audience chamber and the waiting goddess. Garroway spoke behind me in a two-toned voice, "Our lady will be quite interested in the interaction we just had. How do you think she'll react to such an assault on her favored servant?"

"Her only servant," I muttered.

"We'll fix that. You'll join us very soon."

I stopped in my spot before Myuna, who had her chin propped on her fist. Her white-filmed eyes were dull with boredom. She would rest soon, which would delay Endaeron from sharing anything with her.

"*...I can't wait to have you back, brother,*" Endaeron whispered. I glanced over my shoulder, but it was just a trick. Only madness from the Void lingering around us.

A fine shiver worked its way up my spine.

My breath came shorter. I was trapped...an animal in a cage of wills, stuck between a goddess and my brother, a victim she had corrupted beyond saving.

No help was coming. How could it? No one could stand against Myuna, even as weakened as she was.

Everyone left in this pocket dimension would end up dead or worse. And I stared into the maw of *worse* as the white figure on the dais yawned impossibly wide and closed her eyes.

She rested for a minute, or perhaps an hour, or it could have been an eternity. But her eyelids popped open again suddenly at a disturbance underground. Something had shifted beneath our feet, but it emerged as a beacon to my magical senses, glowing with pure power.

Braza.

My hopeful smile came and went quickly. *Braza, here?* The powercore's energy was a buffet in front of Myuna's single-minded hunger. "That soul's power...it is familiar," she commented, turning her gaze my way.

She beckoned me forth, lifting me in an orb of her energy so I floated before her. "Tell me what you know," she ordered.

Talons of pain sank into my skull when I tried to keep my silence.

"Don't make this so difficult on yourself. I know the feel of souls...but it has been so long..." She tapped a finger to her lips. "Hmm. She feels like the girl you were going to adopt. But I ordered her dead. Endaeron, why is she alive?"

My eyes widened, but shock turned to pure wrath. Many deaths in my family could be traced back to Myuna, but here she gloated over one that was still a ragged wound within me.

"I'm not sure I know who you're talking about, my lady," he replied.

Her lips spanned a toothless grin. "Perhaps Phaeron is ready to enlighten us."

The pressure was mounting, making it feel like my horns were about to implode and crush my skull. "Her name is Braza," I muttered.

"More," she demanded.

"I *did* adopt her." I stared at her in defiance. My hatred was an unsheathed blade before her, ready to cut.

Her expression shifted. Something like worry tugged at her brows before they creased with growing wrath. "*More,*" she hissed.

"And then my brother murdered her. She was one of his first victims on Earth. We thought we were safe from you and your creatures, your madness, your endless hunger for our life force," I spat, picking up fervor as I spoke. If she would just silence me before she probed for the relevant information. "But we had no such luck. He cleaved her soul nearly in two in his frenzy before I killed his vessel. We gave them both the best funeral we could, but—"

Myuna made a silencing gesture. "Yes, yes, yammer more about how terrible I am." She rolled her eyes. "If she is dead, why is she here? And why does her soul feel so *powerful* and *juicy*?"

Slowly, she unspooled the truth from me about libraries and power sources. Her eyes glittered with interest as we discussed the possibility of there being a Cerris City Library and what "delights" might be locked within it.

8

CRESS

The first thing I did was shower and change into a clean, fluffy robe left behind in the room I'd claimed. With my damp hair still piled on my head with a towel, I took up my phone and flopped onto the bed. The room was little more than a rectangle of space with all the essentials lined up—a small kitchen area, a bed and closet, and finally a bathroom, with utilitarian decorations that were probably uniform across all the temporary living spaces on the second floor of this library.

I paid my surroundings little heed as I waited for a website to load. When it did, I muffled a curse in the off-white duvet I lay on and jabbed the refresh button like that would change the fact that the hacker's feed of the Crown Coven's audience chamber was disconnected.

I scrolled past a couple paragraphs the hacker had written, gaze snagging on a moving GIF. Myuna was swinging a startlingly bright rope that blinded the camera before the viewpoint went dark. Had she known the supernatural community was watching her? I took a breath to calm my racing heart before reading the text above the GIF.

In it, the hacker explained there were no other working camera feeds in the audience chamber. He also linked a petition, which I tapped.

Thousands of digital signatures already graced the plea to open up Cerris City again for long enough to evacuate everyone left behind. It read like the powerful men and women debating collapsing the pocket dimension were nearing a decision and that it looked bleak for us.

"It is an unnecessary cruelty that they should die with the dimensional monster we've seen on the news," I read out loud, my dread rising. "Please save these innocent people before it's too late."

Hana had mentioned the possibility that Myuna would be winked out of existence this way if we failed. A future she'd seen that didn't need to happen if we killed Myuna. But someone had to reach out to the supernatural community on this side of the pocket dimension to mention that we were going to try fighting her and needed more time to regroup. Had Madigan or Hana already done that?

Was the greater supernatural community just going to collapse Cerris City anyway?

As cynical as it was, the hundreds of lives stuck here were a small sacrifice compared to Myuna escaping and consuming the whole world instead. With a ragged sigh, I closed my eyes.

Everyone I held dear was here. If the pocket dimension was destroyed now, the mother who'd adopted me and the sister I was raised with would be gone. I saw Carly in my mind's eye and wondered where she'd fled to. She still hadn't answered her phone or any texts I'd sent. I hoped she was all right.

There was also my coven to consider. All of them were my friends...maybe even prickly Wren. She had come here to stand behind me in the audience chamber and confronted her father's misdeeds head-on. I found myself hoping that she would be all right too, after the loved ones she'd lost and all the emotions that'd rocked her rich-girl world.

My mind strayed back to my men, though. With the softness of bedsheets under me, it was inevitable I thought of the three guys I wanted here with me.

First Phaeron, the one who kept me at arm's length despite acknowledging something between us. I felt the ghost of his touch skimming goosebumps up my arms. He liked to lean down and whisper in his deep, smooth voice over the shell of my ear. Though he didn't trust himself and his instincts not to harm me, he'd still teased and tasted and given me glimpses of the animal that lurked underneath his princely veneer.

I only hoped those moments weren't all I was left with. I missed him with a fierceness that made needling pains in my chest. If he were here, I'd slip this robe off my skin ever so slowly and watch the heat light in his otherworldly yellow eyes. Maybe he'd touch, maybe he wouldn't. He'd seen it all before, even had the self-control to watch as Ben and Geo took me right in front of him without joining in.

Hell, both Ben and Geo were a shout away, and here I was fantasizing without them. But with Geo in gargoyle form for so long and Ben burdened by his brother's condition, would either of them want me right now? I moved to sit at the foot of the bed, robe gaping around my body with how the tie had come loose.

Well...I wasn't going to be much of a seductress like this. I went to the bathroom mirror to dry my hair and lamented my plain face. I hadn't packed anything, least of all makeup, and I wasn't about to go take some half-used cosmetics from one of the librarians who'd abandoned the pocket dimension.

I supposed my men were getting serious, plain-faced Cress for a while. My face didn't rest in a friendly expression, but I poked color into my cheeks and forced my lips to turn upward in my reflection.

"It's not all bad. They've seen this before," I said for my own benefit. We'd gotten past the stage where all they saw of me was the primped, polished Cress rather than the rumpled, morning-after Cress. Ben usually enjoyed tousling my purple hair further, mirth a shine in his eyes.

We should be sharing this room, not going to different parts of the library. I secured my robe firmly and peered out into the hall, looking left and right to be sure it was quiet. On bare feet, I padded to the door I thought Ben had claimed and knocked.

He answered as I was raising my knuckles to knock a second time. He'd been scowling, but his expression brightened the moment he saw me standing there. "Hey, babe. Come tell Geo to eat," he invited, stepping aside.

Puzzled, I came inside and spotted Geo in his human form. His tall body was folded awkwardly over the squat table in the kitchen area, a plate of smoked meat and crackers set out next to a steaming mug before him. His eyes gleamed with quicksilver irises, a sign that he'd just recently changed back from gargoyle form.

"You need to eat," I parroted.

On cue, Geo coughed up a puff of dust. We'd learned that eating and drinking gave his human side a kick start, drawing back the man I loved from the shell of stone he could encase himself in.

"As you insist." His voice was deep and guttural, yet his

generous lips curled into a smile before he drank from his mug.

They'd made coffee, the smell of it lingering. I searched for creamer before committing to a mug of it, knowing I couldn't stomach it black but wanting the kick of energy all the same. Ben came behind me while I poured and stirred, his hands warm pressure around my hips. I placed everything on the counter and leaned back, tilting my head toward his.

The same longing I'd been feeling reflected back at me. I knew Ben well enough to gauge the slant of his clever mouth. "We were going to come find you," he said. His fingertips skimmed up my waist, finding the soft tie of fabric holding my robe together.

"Well, I found you first. What is my reward?" I snared his fingers with mine, drawing them away from freeing me of my clothes so soon.

"Us, of course," Geo answered. Straight to the point, as always, while Ben punctuated it with a kiss on the curve of my neck.

I shivered, the chill in the air only a contrast to the heat of him. I should've told him about the online petition, one representation of the executioner's axe looming over us regardless of whether we had a chance to confront the evil in Cerris City. Maybe I should have mentioned the destroyed camera that'd once offered us a glimpse at Myuna and Phaeron.

But what would we do about any of that now? I twisted in Ben's hold, taking him in again now that we were face to face. His worries were shadows in the hollows of his face. The last thing he needed was more to shoulder.

"I'll take that reward. Let's forget what's outside this

room, at least for tonight," I said, tracing my fingers up his freshly shaven jaw.

He leaned into my touch. "That's the best idea I've heard in a long while," he said.

My hand drifted to the soft strands of his honey-brown hair, drawing him down to meet my lips. He opened up, kissing with the intent to forget. He tasted of coffee with a hint of his usual breath mints. Effortlessly, he lifted and spun me around, my lower back hitting a hard surface.

I opened my eyes, meeting Geo's gaze, which was darkening with lust. My head was next to his plate. Ben smiled against my mouth, holding up a strip of cloth...the tie to my robe, which pooled around me to reveal my naked form. I hadn't bothered with underwear.

Ben released me suddenly, skimming his touch up my curves. His calloused fingertips rubbed the chilled pucker of my nipples. "Hey, babe, lean back. I need to eat too," he said with a hint of his usual smirk.

"What if I'm hungry as well?" I asked playfully.

Geo eased his meal aside and helped guide me so my back was fully on the table. He stood and left my line of sight while Ben cupped my thighs and eased my legs around his shoulders. A little sound of pleasure left us both when he ran his tongue up the seam of my slit and kissed the bud at its apex. I moaned from the electric thrill that jumped through me.

I heard Geo return to his seat and the scrape as he repositioned it. He set something ceramic down close to my ear. "I will feed you anything you desire," he rumbled.

He pressed the pad of his fingertip to my lips, and I opened, surprised by the taste of sweet coffee. I licked his finger clean and sucked on the digit. The swirl of my tongue hinted that I expected him to "feed" me something else.

In response, Geo next placed a circle of smoked meat in my mouth, and I chewed carefully, experimenting with this while Ben coaxed his way between my lower lips with shorter licks. He'd picked up on the mood and slowed down from his usual eager feasting to prolong the moment.

I swallowed, accepting a cracker next. Though a little stale, this food packed more flavor than the last meal I remembered...my breakfast in the hospital. My belly rumbled, suddenly ravenous. I tightened my thighs around Ben, grinding against his face for more. His eyes were slanted with amusement as well as the lust that grew sharper when I closed my lips around Geo's finger again for a small taste of coffee.

I was glad they'd brewed some, even though we were taking in the caffeine later than we should. I'd come in here feeling drained and stressed, but my heart zipped with new energy as they teased out my pleasure. They just so happened to meet two needs at once, though any hunger I felt faded when Ben closed his lips around my clit.

I came and bit Geo's finger; he moaned deeply. He breathed without trouble now, no sign of stone dust or the apathy of his other form. The eager way he watched the pleasure break across my expression and how I threaded my fingers through Ben's hair told me that Geo was fully with us, completely a man.

As I lay there recovering from my pleasure high, they motioned between themselves, negotiating how they'd share me next.

"If we're doing food-themed tonight," I said, my voice husky. "Then I had better be sandwiched between you as soon as possible."

"You heard the lady." Chuckling, Ben flipped Geo a condom. We'd discussed the birth control I'd started taking in a private moment, but they still had to use protection until the pill took effect. I was just glad Ben had taken a few condoms in his wallet.

Geo caught my chin between his thumb and forefinger, stealing a kiss. "He got to taste you. I want you next," he practically growled.

I felt a brief pang of worry that he was letting his old reluctance to share me rise to the surface until his fingers skimmed down my lower belly, cupping and rubbing my slippery womanhood. His thick digits spread me, and I moaned as he curled them, shooting a bolt of pleasure through my core.

"Fine by me," Ben said.

I nodded in breathless agreement and slipped off the table, the fabric of my robe making it a fast trip to land on my jellylike legs. Ben caught me and helped pass me to Geo. Soon, I was lip-locked with the gargoyle, pressed firmly to his clothed front.

Geo had to release me to get the shirt off his body. I took that moment to help him, shortening the time between acts so I wouldn't need to think. After freeing his erection from the confines of his pants, I stole the condom from his fingers and slipped it onto his heavy shaft in one loving stroke.

I'd been shared by these two men enough to prefer having them at the same time rather than needing to choose between them for an evening. Sometimes I wondered what it would be like to add a third man, especially one with a tail and shadows solid enough to feel like stroking fingers. But I shook off thoughts of Phaeron, knowing longing would sour the night if I let it into my heart.

We didn't make it to the bed. Geo was strong enough to

lift me without trouble halfway there, and I anchored myself with my legs around his solid thighs, arms braced on his shoulders. I tugged his white locs and shivered with anticipation as Ben stepped up behind me, squeezing my waist while Geo had my ass cupped in his broad palms.

Ben's teasing touch ran up and down my back, his mouth on my neck from behind. He brushed my slit and teased his thumb between my cheeks, using my own slick to prepare my ass for a bigger insertion. My breath came in slow, eager pants against Geo's mouth. Ben leaned down, lips brushing my ear. "Is this when I make a sandwich pun?" he whispered.

"No," Geo answered shortly.

He practically pouted. "I had a clever one. Salami was involved."

I struggled not to burst out laughing. I'd missed their back-and-forth. "Actions over words, Ben," I said.

Geo grunted in agreement, lowering my hips to spear me on his manhood. He caught his lower lip between his teeth on a hiss of pleasure.

"All right, all right," Ben conceded quickly. I knew he was taking himself in hand, waiting for me to sink halfway on the gargoyle's cock before he made his move. He pressed me more firmly between the heat of their chests and helped angle himself into my ass.

Mouth hanging half open, I moaned loudly at how full I felt between them. I tried to shift in Geo's hold, but he dug his fingers into my skin to hold me still, as immovable as stone. By unspoken agreement, they moved like two pistons; where Ben pressed, Geo withdrew, and back again.

I held on to Geo's back. His skin was slick, already sheened with sweat. I would marvel later at how quickly he bounced back from his stone form. Maybe it was just the food, as his kisses still tasted faintly of his scrounged meal, but I wanted to think it was me. Us. That this act was the true switch to flip for him.

I was glad to have him back...to have both of them still here with me. I cried their names out until I came and jumbled them up together. Once we cleaned up and lay out together, with me still blissfully between them, they had a good-natured debate over who I called out to when I'd said something akin to "Beneo."

$$9$$

CRESS

Leona Whiteside met with Madigan, Jordan, and Hana early the next morning, before most of us woke up. I learned about it when they emerged from a room on floor negative one and the door slammed behind them, startling me into looking up. I was rummaging through the break room with Ben for anything edible, my laughter from a story he was telling fading as I spotted the group of women walking by.

The four of them exchanged a meaningful glance. Each time a secretive look was shared with Hana, the tension along my spine notched a little tighter. I wondered what future she was guiding us toward now.

"Good morning," I said.

"Before you ask…yes, we know about the online petition. The other governing covens and councils around the world are debating our fate as we speak," Hana said.

I bared my teeth in a cringe. That was the opposite of comforting to hear from her.

"Well, damn, not such a good morning after all," Ben muttered.

Madigan brushed a hand through her hair. Unbound orange curls tangled around her head, mussed like she'd been tugging on them in frustration. "I'm going to trust Hana, as I always have, and say it will be handled. I have new instructions for you and the rest of your coven in the meantime." She gestured broadly toward Leona. "I am entrusting you all and your training to the head librarian."

Leona's mouth was set grimly. "I don't know much about other affinities...but there's little you can't learn by doing. We start purging the containment rooms today."

I swallowed down a surge of nerves and looked over at Madigan. "That sounds dangerous. Are you sending any more of Ashbough Protective Services to help?" I asked.

Madigan nodded. "Of course. We're supporting the library with an equal share of people and supplies."

"Aunt Jordan, you're going to be here with us?" Ben asked, earning a warm smile and a confirmation from her. She twirled her staff with its single stored spell, brandishing it with a flourish.

"And we'll all be helping...even Willow?" I added.

The last time Willow had used her magic had been in the Crown Coven's audience chamber. Her control had gone haywire, and many of the people who'd been around her had clutched their necks and gasped for air like they were drowning on land. It'd only been Madigan's timely intervention in knocking Willow unconscious that'd saved those people.

"I've seen a lot of spells in my day," Madigan answered slowly. "I believe what I saw was her performing mer magic."

"Yes, for the first time," Hana confirmed.

Madigan nodded, unsurprised. "It looked like an explosion of magic that'd been under pressure for a long time.

It's difficult to be half witch and half a different kind of supernatural, but it's not something to be feared. If we gather any mer survivors, we will seek a mentor for her amongst them. But until then...keep her with you. It'll be better for her if she's with her coven, doing what she can without pushing her magic that far again."

The seer nodded in echo to her. If Hana wasn't offering a warning of impending danger, I would gladly have my friend here helping us.

"Additionally, I offer you a suggestion," Hana said. "Grant and Wren will need more space in the coming days. Do with that as you will."

"And don't let any interpersonal drama come between you and your duties to this library," Leona added with the air of a final word.

When Ben and I murmured in agreement, they moved on, speaking quietly amongst themselves. I turned to my man, whispering, "Grant should go spy on what Myuna is doing."

ON OUR WAY TO Grant's door, we gathered up Roe, who had donned workout gear from somewhere and was about to try to find a place to exercise.

Her familiar, a stout Belgian Malinois named Tank, panted eagerly by her side. He seemed disappointed when we distracted his witch. All of our familiars had to be getting bored. We'd set aside a room for them to take over, ensuring they were safely tucked away from danger for now.

Roe had paled at the thought of sending Grant out as

our spy but didn't air any protests, only coming along and standing behind Ben and me as we knocked on his door.

Grant answered after a few minutes, looking disheveled. "It's too early for such long faces," he said, standing aside so we could come in. The moment he closed and locked the door, his real form spilled out.

The true Grant, if that was even his name, had light brown skin reminiscent of pinewood, with wood grain striations up his arms that continued at the bare vee of flesh at his collarbones before disappearing under his shirt. What marked him as a changeling were the four pretty, faceted dragonfly wings folded down on his back.

And part of what proved that he was a fae of the dangerous Autumn Court was his hair, evergreen at the roots and tarnishing to orange halfway down, and the amber-brown eyes he turned our way, alight with intrigue. He had a handsome, angular face and pointed ears that poked a bit out of his bedhead.

"I'm guessing you all want something," he said, sounding curious. He tried to call Tank over, but the dog gave him a look of distrust and refused to budge from Roe's side.

"Myuna destroyed the camera we were using to watch what she was doing," I said. "I know it would be dangerous, but I was wondering if you would be able to spy on her."

His green eyebrows rose to his hairline. "Yeah, I suppose I could..." He drew out the moment, and I waited, expecting the "but" that came after that statement. Maybe he wanted something in return, even after striking a deal with Roe to use his talents to help us in exchange for information and our discretion.

"I just have to wait until she has a few minions. Then I can slip in no problem. Think I'd make a good monster?" He swiped his hand through the air as if it were tipped with claws. Instead of growling, he rolled his tongue to purr and grinned over at Roe.

She was looking a little pink around the edges. "Not *that* kind of monster," she protested. "Are you sure? This seems really unsafe."

Grant's expression morphed into an easygoing smile. "It's my job, Roe. I'd much rather use my talents to try instead of standing behind you and hiding from whatever violence is on the horizon. Don't you worry about me. I'm going to gather up the finest tea that's ever been brewed and share it all with you."

Roe sighed. "Fine, but be careful."

"You know I will," he answered. "It's my ass on the line too."

The tension between them seemed to break when she rolled her eyes.

"Right, so, Wren next?" Ben asked, sharing a quick look with me. He was moments away from a smug, knowing smirk, and I tamped down the urge to return that look back to him.

"What about her?" Roe asked.

"She probably isn't back yet," Grant put in.

"What do you mean?" she demanded. "Don't tell me she left the library...without us?"

That spark of interest was back in his gaze as he covered his lips with a finger. "Shh, it's a secret."

"It's probably fine," I put in when Roe placed her hands on her head, her eyes bugging wide as she started to freak out.

"The Hunger is out there unchecked, but sure, leave the library at night," she said, breathy with panic. Tank whined and nudged her. My heart beat faster in my chest, imagining Wren being wrenched away into darkness. Hana would warn us, right, rather than let us worry over discovering her body out in the streets?

"I think she was trying to prevent this." Grant circled a hand her way.

"I'm going up to look for her. You guys coming with?" Roe asked. She gave herself a shake and strode for the door without waiting. Ben and I scrambled after her while Grant locked the door behind us.

The stairs were closer, so Roe charged up them. She cleared the door to the ground-level floor first, and I found her standing a few feet away from it and motioning for us to be quiet. I heard the faint sound of a woman trying to cry and talk at the same time, making distinctive sobs of distress.

I didn't realize it was Wren at first. We crept closer when there was quiet for a few moments, before the sounds of crying intensified. "You don't understand, Mom!" she burst out. "Listen to yourself."

Another pause. "He murdered an *entire family* for that job! What do you mean? You *knew* about it?" She gasped. I felt a twist of dread and fury, realizing they were discussing my family. The death of my birth parents so her father could be voted into his spot on the Crown Coven with my mother out of the way.

Roe made a sound low in her throat and strode forward with purpose. I wished we could've eavesdropped a little more, as the raw expression on Wren's tearstained face morphed into wide-eyed surprise at seeing us before she schooled her expression as best she could. She had a pair of earbuds in and held the edge of her phone close to her face.

Wren and I met gazes, and something passed over hers with the welling of new tears. "I don't want to talk about it anymore," she said, sounding defeated. "Just…please tell the emergency council that we're going to make a stand against Myuna. They might still listen to you. We just need more—"

She winced, her tears spilling to make new tracks over her face. She wiped them away, then pulled out her earbuds and put them into their case. "She hung up," she muttered.

My heart tugged, seeing her curled in on herself like this. "Do you want a hug?" I asked. The offer felt wholly inadequate when she was hurting deep enough to show it.

She nodded wordlessly, and Roe intercepted her to pull her into a tight embrace first. "I'm glad you're okay. We heard you went out after dark without us," she sighed.

Wren pointed, and for the first time, I noticed she'd been sitting on a crate that looked like it didn't belong in a library. There were a few more piled nearby, and her staff was propped up against them, its sunny centerpiece glowing faintly. There was a swirl of magic in a matching yellow underneath the crates, buoying them up by several inches.

Once Roe released her, Wren and I hugged briefly. It was a little awkward, but it was a start. "Yeah, I couldn't sleep, so I decided to be helpful," she said, sniffing and lifting her shoulders back, speaking more confidently. "I did some adjusting on my magic and got us everything silver I could lift from a weapons emporium."

"That's a lot of silver," Ben commented.

Wren shrugged. "Whatever the coven doesn't need, I'm sure Ashbough Protective Services can take. I left a credit card for the owner to charge if they get a chance to return, though I'm not sure it will matter…"

She drifted off with a sigh before turning abruptly

toward Roe and Ben and asking, "Could I speak with Cress alone for a few minutes?"

Roe's lashes fluttered. "Yeah, sure. Let's go get the coven to look at what you brought. C'mon, Ben."

Wren deflated again once they were gone and walked over to retrieve her staff. The crates landed on the ground with a jarring clatter. "You used celestial witch magic a few days ago," she said, inspecting the length of fine wood in her hands.

"I did. It was a stored spell on Evening Guidance. I'm not sure how..." I began to explain, drifting off when she held up a hand.

When she turned to look my way, her eyes were red rimmed with grief and a new wave of tears. "I want you to know that I don't regret defending you. My family wronged yours... My parents did the unthinkable. I...I'm not part of it anymore."

"Wren, it's okay, I promise. I don't blame you for anything," I murmured.

"Good, because I..." She breathed out raggedly. "I'm not a Starsurge anymore."

All the air left my lungs, a reply drying up on my tongue. Did that mean what I thought it did? "The rest of your family..." I couldn't even complete the vile thought.

"D-Disowned me," she said in a miserable whisper. "The only thing I can keep are the clothes I came here wearing and my staff. And I don't know if I even want the staff."

What vile people, I thought. I channeled my inner Roe for what to say next, knowing her family would take Wren in if the other woman so much as suggested it.

"Wren, I'm sorry your birth givers were..." I searched for a respectful enough way to say this without hurting her further. "That they made the decisions that led us here. Family is also what you make of it. You still have the coven. We'll support you through this if, uh, if you will let us."

She gave me a hesitant lift of her lips. "I'll try to be a better friend." After a scuff of her foot, she changed the subject quickly. "And to start, I want to experiment with your magic."

I tilted my head, my gaze searching the air above us for my handbook. It held my excess magic, the whole celestial might of my family line. "Experiment how?" I asked.

"I've never met anyone with access to two affinities. Do you have anyone to teach you how to use celestial witch magic?"

Well, there was my birth mother's ghost, but she wasn't here for this discussion. Her comings and goings were pretty unreliable, but she'd wanted to be around to help mentor me. And Jordan, though I didn't know her well enough to ask for magical training.

"If you're offering, count me in," I said.

We agreed to meet up after dinner time this evening, or whenever we called it quits for the day on purging the library. Then, we waited in companionable silence. She schooled her face to hide the worst of her grief, and I decided not to mention anything to our friends about what we'd discussed. When they arrived, they were occupied with awe as crates were pried open and weapons were laid out on the floor, all made with silver.

There were a few guns and cases of silver bullets. We set those aside for now, going for the weapons associated with our affinities. Our leaders would know who could make the best use of the limited supply of guns and ammunition.

I eagerly traded out my old training sword for a newly made one with a longer cross guard. My decision was fairly easy, so I stood back to watch what everyone else took. Ben secreted away a couple daggers, while Roe tested the weight behind a length of metal with sharp bits extending from the ball at the end—a flanged mace, she called it. Each test swing she took disturbed the air audibly.

Willow lifted a delicate silver trident like she'd break it, twisting it in the light to admire the patterns of fish scales etched into the long, thin pole and up to the three wicked points at the end. It appeared ceremonial, like a celestial witch staff, not meant to actually skewer something.

"Can I really take this?" she asked in her whisper of a voice.

"Absolutely," Wren answered. She didn't even glance around as she set down her sun-topped staff and picked up a smaller, less ornate one about the length of her forearm. It was crowned with a silvery-blue glass globe framed by a pair of crescent moons. Her shoulders loosened like she'd dropped a weight from them as she gave the new tool an approving nod.

Bianca was the one to share that these were made standard for teams of unnatural hunters. Creatures determined to be aberrations or unnatural were almost always twisted from dimensional magic or simply weren't from our world at all. Silver was the one weakness most of those creatures shared.

"The perfect weapons to kill them easily while they're trapped in the boxes here," she said.

Ben elbowed her, scowling. "Don't jinx us."

10

CRESS

Before the purge was underway, I joined the other librarian witches in the powercore chamber to commune with Braza. She spoke with all of us mentally as we went one by one to place our hands within her jellylike sphere to take in her magic.

"I've already begun the extermination protocol on containment rooms with inanimate objects and the weakest creatures. Approximately a third of the occupied rooms will not need your attention."

"Where should we start, then?" Leona asked. She'd gone first to take Braza's magic and had stood there a long time, teeth gritted as she absorbed more and more while purple mist swirled around her.

"There is a mated pair of doskalo that are imprisoned in separate rooms on floor negative twenty-nine. They are attacking the runic seals with everything in them as we speak. Though they are not the strongest creatures in the library, they are the closest to escaping."

Next to me, Jonah muttered, "Fuck. I remember bringing those two in."

"My best estimate is that one will breach by midday. It will help its mate escape too, and then we have a serious problem," Braza said, projecting a feeling in my head. It was like I took in her urgency and concern as if it were my own.

Leona finally had enough and stepped back from the powercore, panting. Jonah motioned for Aurora to go up next. "What is a doskalo?" I asked him.

"Imagine a dog with the worst mange you've ever seen. Then picture it standing on two legs and being eight feet tall, with acidic saliva and a taste for human flesh."

"No thanks," I said under my breath.

Leona picked up where he left off. "They hunt in packs made up of a mated pair and their juvenile kids. They reproduce like crazy if left unchecked and go berserk if separated from their partner. I should've guessed the doskalos would be our first big challenge."

I went up to Braza last, still picking up on Leona whispering to Jonah and Aurora, "We'll see if the coven of kids Mad Ash left us can keep up."

Braza fed me a surge of power. *"I wish to witness the experimenting Wren tries with your magic. You two may use my chamber this evening,"* she said to me privately.

"Thank you," I thought back to her.

A feeling like the caress of cool fingers drifted across my hand. I wondered if Braza would take her full humanoid form with others in the room, but she soon traced the circular pattern that marked my left wrist. It was Phaeron's mark of protection, a bit of magic that connected us. Hope thundered through my heart as she channeled her power into it rather than me.

The last time she'd utilized this trick, I'd been too new to my magic to realize what she was doing. But now I felt the electric current and the way it flowed from me into him, a single bright line of energy extending out to him that resonated with a feeling of shock when it connected.

Phaeron's voice filled my head like Braza's did, in the alien syllables and hisses of their native language. I had an overwhelmed smile, tears pricking the corner of my eyes. His deep, smooth voice was unchanged. Even if he spoke with clipped urgency, it was still him.

"I have not yet given Cress a boon to understand the language of Soiluire. She is with us as well," Braza said to him. Her power waned, like the dimming of a light, until our connection was a filament of spider silk.

"Cress?" he breathed, as faint as a whisper from one room over. *"I had hoped you would escape."*

"Not without you," I answered in my head.

He laughed, and goosebumps erupted over my body in discomfort. It was off-tune, a scrape of sandpaper rather than the velvet I would expect. *"What manner of the Void is this? A reflection of my mate to haunt me?"*

Braza's presence nudged aside my own. *"No tricks, my prince. Ask us anything for proof."*

She pushed me from the powercore physically, through a bank of purple smoke that swirled around me and eddied around Leona's concerned figure as she approached. The connection persisted, a tense strand at the back of my thoughts.

"You must've been quite depleted," the head librarian said.

At the same time, Phaeron transitioned back to Soiluirian, and Braza replied. I couldn't focus on them and the woman in front of me at the same time, so I gave my head a stern shake. "Yeah, something like that," I said vaguely.

We went to retrieve my coven and a handful of Crystal

fae who'd recently arrived alongside a nervous-looking verdant witch nurse. They were our support from Madigan and the only staff member the hospital could spare if something went wrong. The fae had armed themselves from the silver weapons we had left, and any that remained were packed up and in transit back to our allies.

We started the process of descending to the second-lowest level of the library while Leona outlined our strategy. Considering the weight of the fae's crystal armor and Geo's stone form, we would use the elevator in shifts to floor negative twenty-eight. From there, we would take the stairs to our destination.

My three cat familiars would scout things out first, along with Ben's ferret, Flit. Dimensional creatures of all kinds tended to overlook small furry companions, making them the perfect little spies.

Somewhere in the planning, Phaeron whispered my name, and I tuned out all the noise around me. He was still there, a desperate little voice over the many miles separating us. I echoed his name back, yearning for his presence and the night-air scent of his magic.

"Tell me of my name for you so I might know you from the Void," he urged.

"It's bright soul. I don't know if you picked it up from Braza or just decided to start calling me that because it's literal," I said.

"Cress... How I've desired to hear your voice again rather than the echoes of my own desires. Are you well? Wait. Do not tell me too much, for Myuna may compel it from my tongue."

"I'm fine," I said, a little puzzled. When we'd first met, he spoke like this...a touch old-fashioned. Maybe I hadn't questioned it enough when he'd picked up on modern lingo with ease.

Besides...why did it matter? He was in serious danger if

Myuna was able to "compel" him to do anything. *"Has she hurt you? How do we rescue you?"*

"We are in a battle of endurance," he said. I had the impression of his weary sigh. *"I have slept not a wink since I last beheld your face. How long has it been?"*

My brow furrowed with concern. *"Three days."*

"Three days," he echoed back. *"Yet it feels like the trickle of minutes through time or a pair of eternities intertwined."*

"Are you okay?" I burst out. *"Tell me what you need. Should I sneak into the audience chamber and grab you?"*

"No!" he shouted.

I flinched, drawing Ben's attention. I affected a carefree shrug and rubbed my arms like I'd caught a sudden chill.

"Stay as far away from Myuna as the pocket dimension permits. Give me your word that you will evade her, bright soul," Phaeron continued with feverish intensity.

"I can't do that...not while she has you."

He chuffed with frustration, and I recognized the cadence of cursing in his first language before he switched back to English. *"She is a hundred times more powerful than you, even in her much-diminished state."*

Someone took a hold of my arm, and I jumped again. It was Ben, who squinted down at me. "We're going," he said, indicating where our coven was heading toward the elevator. "You good?"

"Talking to Phaeron," I whispered, tapping my forehead.

"Uh huh," he replied skeptically.

I followed with an annoyed scoff. "I think Myuna is torturing him. He doesn't sound like himself."

What he didn't know was that, without an immediate reply from me, Phaeron was repeating my name a few times in a panic. *"We're going to save you. I don't know how, but we will,"* I promised him.

"Cress," he said, but this time, he caressed my name. *"Don't. Your time should be occupied with finding an escape, not me. Do you not yet see the danger I pose to you? Myuna snatched control of me without effort. I crave to consume your soul every time I see it. I fear the desire will only grow worse with my exposure to her fell presence. You've bonded to two strong, stable men... Allow my act of love for you to be of sacrifice so you may live without fear of me losing control in the darkest corners of night."*

"Okay, Phaeron," I replied pointedly as I got into the elevator with my coven and we started to descend into the pits of the library.

"Your agreement comes too readily," he replied in a suspicious tone.

"Isn't that what you want?" Tears pricked my eyes, and anger churned in my gut. *"You should have come with us, you know. Instead, you gave up, and now you expect me to do the same. Well, I'm not! And I won't promise you something that goes against my very being. No matter how much you shout at me in my head, you're coming home with me. Hana saw that I would have a chance to save you in the future, and I will."*

For a long, terrible moment, he was silent. I worried our silk-strand connection had snapped somewhere in the middle from my raised voice.

"I did not give up." He was far angrier than me, and I immediately wanted to duck away from the sharpness of his response. *"I felt Myuna's presence create a controlling tether between her and me. If I had gone with you, she may have been able to compel me from afar. Instead of languishing here with her, I could have delivered her the souls of everyone who*

escaped while I stayed behind. I ask in turn, is that what you want?"

"*Of course not,*" I murmured. I was amongst the last to exit the elevator when it arrived on floor negative twenty-eight. Bella brushed against my ankles before disappearing into the library with Milo and Jin while we waited for the elevator to retrieve Geo and the other librarian witches.

"*Sometimes I forget you are a shortsighted mortal,*" Phaeron scoffed. "*The passion of youth with no bracing of sense.*"

I gaped, then gritted my teeth. "*Excuse me?*" I demanded.

"*There is no saving me!*" he roared. "*Do not court a fate worse than death trying!*"

A headache throbbed between my ears immediately. "*You know what? I really don't need this right now,*" I replied. "*We're about to face some mangy giant dog things, and I can't have you distracting me.*"

"*Mangy...dog...*" he repeated slowly.

"*Doskalos,*" I supplied.

"*Fuck. Who is we?*"

"*I thought you didn't want to know what I was doing,*" I snarked. This was about the time I'd hang up on an argument or leave a text on read, but we were connected by magic Braza controlled, as I had no idea how to get his stirred-up presence out of my head. Not that I truly wanted to, even with our disagreement.

He scoffed. "*Fine. How many doskalos?*"

As he started probing for the strategy we were using, I realized I'd missed almost all of the plan in favor of talking to him. We were creeping down the stairs to floor negative twenty-nine, and it was a little late to ask, *wait, what are we doing?* I hated being that person at school, let alone on the edge of a seriously dangerous situation.

So, I told Phaeron everything I knew while we waited for the familiars to return. "The hallway is clear," Jin reported. The small black cat was the first to come back and accepted a single pet down her back before she stepped out of my reach. She projected a feeling of fear to match the way she hunkered down. "You can hear them on the other side of the doors. The one at the end of the hall is much louder."

I repeated her report aloud. The other librarians conferred briefly.

Meanwhile, Phaeron was giving me instructions on how to handle the doskalo pair. I wished again that he was here. *"You must fight each of them separately. If one of them sees its mate bloodied or dead, it will go berserk. The good news is they're not intelligent enough to realize you've already killed one if it does not see the body."*

Leona led the group into the hallway. The floor beneath my feet vibrated in time with a hard *thud* from the closest door to our right. A complicated array of librarian witch magic flickered with purple light over the threshold when the creature on the other side struck it again.

"Leave it. This one," Leona announced, pointing her sword toward the containment room Jin had indicated was closer to breach status. The metal of the door was dented outward and creaked ominously when hit from within by something large and desperate.

Leona signaled to us, and the Crystal fae stepped forward with Geo, who raised his shield and flared his wings to make himself a solid wall of defense.

With a complicated sweep of her sword's tip, Leona deactivated the array holding the metal together, and out tumbled a massive creature with patches of dirty brown hair and pinkish skin.

Its stench stung my nose and made my eyes water instantly. *"It stinks,"* I complained to Phaeron.

"All that matters is that you avoid being bitten," he replied, level and calm compared to the panic-fueled adrenaline pumping through my veins.

The group bristled with spells and silver weapons as the doskalo lurched to its feet. It seemed like some middle evolution of a massive dog becoming a werewolf, with arms that dragged the ground and scraped along with unevenly sharpened claws. Opening its mouth wider than any living thing should, it roared and lunged at the closest target, Geo. He clipped its jaw with his shield. Without sunlight, the crystal didn't ring, only making a dull thud as Geo leveraged it to knock the doskalo's head aside.

Behind us came an answering roar, muffled. I glanced over my shoulder. Shit, we were going to be fighting both of them very soon.

I also noted with relief that the creature might be dead before I got close enough to slash it with my sword. Geo and the fae created an effective semicircle that protected us from it, but there were only small windows for Bianca's crossbow bolts, Ben's throwing daggers, and the shards of glittering light Jordan hurled from the tip of her staff. Each brush of silver drew a whine from the creature, who started to retreat into its containment room from such a fierce onslaught.

Still, I cast Lux and inched closer. I wasn't expecting the freed doskalo to yip in pain and raise its clawed hand. It was shielding its face from the light...*my* light. The blade of my sword glowed like an incandescent shard, far brighter than any Lux I'd cast before. I nearly blinded myself looking down at it in shock.

Leona was shouting, "Make way! Chase it the rest of the way into the containment room!"

She gestured at me, my friends parting to the sides. The doskalo, bleeding from several wounds smoking from silver exposure, backed away from the blade I waved at it, snapping its jaws wildly and tripping over itself to be as far away as possible. Its acidic saliva sizzled on the ground from it frothing at the mouth, pupils contracting to invisible points. Geo moved with me, shield raised, ready to leap ahead of me if I needed support.

When the doskalo was back in its room, cowering down in a nest of sticks and rotting…I didn't want to think about what the scraps of gray skin and fur might've been, Jonah stepped around me and cast the Inemos spell perfectly. A wave of nearly invisible magic arced off his sword tip and hit the monster, freezing it into a new temporary stasis. With its muscles locked, Leona strode forward without fear and lopped its head off with a few brutal swings of her sword.

"Now the other one," she said grimly, steering me by the shoulder out of the room before I could retch at the smell and sight of the dead unnatural in its messy nest.

"Cress?" Phaeron asked tentatively.

"It's dead. I don't think it was supposed to be that easy?" I asked. Like he'd know, several miles away.

He seemed bemused. *"I shall wait for your business with both doskalos to conclude before pestering you further, however long or short a time it may be."*

The second doskalo died much like the first, leaving Ben and Bianca a little frustrated. "Put the spotlight away. I want a challenge," Bianca muttered.

I would've apologized, but when I squeezed the hilt of my sword to dispel the Lux spell, I stumbled and held my forehead through a dizzy spell. It sank in just how much of my stored librarian witch magic it'd taken to power that much light. The hallway seemed much darker without the blinding magic.

I looked down at the blade, wondering if it was special in some way. Maybe it tripled the power of any spell cast through it. Lux was a basic spell, power level one. It should've never been strong enough to strike such fear in monsters like those two doskalos.

"There are more creatures to put down," Braza reminded us when Leona started my way, a question obviously poised on her tongue.

"Let's talk about the magic later?" I suggested.

"Later," the head librarian agreed.

WHEN LATER CAME, it was after six hours of us facing down a handful of the unnaturals Braza deemed the most likely to break out of containment first. One would think those were the biggest, baddest creatures in the library, but they were just behind the oldest or weakest seals. Leona and Braza warned us of about a dozen more monsters still locked away that were deadly and unique. The kind of creatures strong enough to have titles and urban legends.

We'd handle them in the coming days. Tonight, I was the one under the microscope, and the ones doing the inspecting were Braza, Leona, Wren, and Phaeron still in my head. The head librarian had insisted on helping when I'd told her that we were experimenting with my magic.

"I've never seen a librarian with command of light like yours," she said when we were in the private sanctum of the powercore.

"I have a theory," Wren said. She'd come in carrying two staves—one was her old one, with the gold-plated sun at its top, and the other the scepter-sized one with silver crescent moons that she'd been casting with today. Without much preamble, she handed me the larger of the two.

The wood was warm and hummed beneath my fingertips. Unlike with Evening Guidance, which was sized and weighted for a man's use, this one was clearly designed for someone shorter.

"Try one thing for me. Cast Lux with my staff," she said, gesturing to it.

"Isn't it super dangerous to use one affinity's magic with another's tool?" I asked.

"Just humor me," she urged.

I looked up at the tip of the staff and shrugged to myself. The rays of the golden sun came to a point, which I used to form the midair X of the Lux spell by manipulating the staff with both hands.

The weapon erupted with light. I turned my face away, shutting my eyes tight. It felt like I'd cast a level-three spell, Luminare, which set off an explosion of light like a ground-level firework. Slowly, I peeled one eyelid up to peek at it in my periphery, seeing that the staff still pulsed with light. I'd lit the centerpiece brightest of all, and its golden halo formed a circle on the ceiling.

The remaining librarian magic stored within me rapidly depleted. I'd never felt it suction out of me quite this fast before, but the fatigue that came with being completely emptied of a powercore's magic had me squeezing the staff, fumbling with it to get it to stop glowing. The painful lurch of running dry happened first, the light fading as I struggled for my next breath past a spasm in my chest.

Wren steadied me with a hand on my shoulder, taking back the weight of the weapon while I recovered. "I think that proves it. You're not just a librarian witch… You're somehow two affinities in one. The light of a celestial affinity pushing out the shadows of your librarian affinity."

"That's not possible," Leona said.

I pointed at my handbook, which flapped down into my waiting palm from where it was circling the ceiling. "All of my Darkmore hereditary power was stored in this," I said, shaking the spine of the handbook. Its pages rattled with the motion.

"Hey!" it protested. "Careful. I'm sensitive."

"We made the handbook into an artifact, separating the celestial magic of her family line from the librarian magic stored within her. Although, Cress has always had a soul unusually suffused with light," Braza supplied.

"Bright soul, beacon in the night." Though I felt that Phaeron was still connected by a silken thread, his responses were distracted whispers once night fell.

The handbook took flight from my palm once I released my hold on it. "It's possible I'm leaking," it said slowly.

It seemed all of us asked at the same time, "Leaking?"

It flew loop-de-loops over our heads, seemingly carefree. "Hehe! You didn't think little ol' me could hold the might of an entire storied witch line, plus all the secrets of the great Morgana Voidbinder herself?"

"Uh, yeah?" I said, incredulous.

"You have entirely too much faith in me, Cressie-poo! I'm flattered!"

My cheeks tinted when Leona raised an unimpressed

brow. She had a normal, obedient copy of *The Librarian Witch's Handbook* flapping behind her, unlike my malfunctioning one.

Braza hurried to pitch in, *"Perhaps it is not the worst thing that her affinities are mixing. Cress was able to cast a spell stored on Evening Guidance, if the memories she shared were correct."*

"Not just any spell," Wren muttered. "She cast Sun Surge without any preparation. Just picked up the staff, aimed, and fired."

"I had help. My... An ancestor, showing me what to do and say." I wished my ghostly mother would make a reappearance for this conversation. She'd been the one to lay her hands over mine and tell me how to unleash the power waiting to be used on the staff. That beam of concentrated light had been the miracle we'd needed at the time to turn the tide of battle.

Wren offered the sun staff back to me. "Imagine if you could do it on command, with your own knowledge and prep work. How much do you even know about celestial magic?" she asked.

"You all can make portals?" I ventured.

Her nostrils flared with a delicate snort. "That's fair. It's the most complicated and ritual-driven affinity. We have what are considered sub-affinities that we call alignments. At the beginning of each moon cycle, a trio of celestial witches link hands and align to the moon, the stars, or the sun. For the next month, they complete their rituals under the light of the celestial body they're aligned to to draw its energies. Most celestial witches inherit an alignment to one of the three options, and sometimes, like in your case, it's really obvious which one it is. Make sense so far?"

I nodded slowly, wondering where she was going with this.

"Sun Surge is the biggest, showiest spell someone with a sun alignment can cast. It's a variable power level spell, depending on stored power. The freaking laser you cast a few days ago was probably power level five or six. Judging by how your magic seems to work...you're clearly meant to be sun alignment. Maybe your mother was, too?"

Eris whispered out, "I was sun-aligned, yes." Her translucent form appeared from the shadows of the room, as perfect as ever in the dark evening gown she'd been wearing when she'd died, her brown hair styled in a fancy updo. When her gaze caught on me holding Wren's sun staff, a wide, approving grin stretched her face.

"She was," I confirmed. No one else in this room except Braza could see or hear Eris's ghost, which could be awkward if I got into a seemingly one-sided conversation.

"And Ben's mother?" Wren prompted.

I barely needed Eris to tell me she was star-aligned. Her job had been reading star charts for infants before Eris's murder, after all. I shared this information and then asked, "What's your alignment?"

Wren rubbed her thumb over a curl in the design of the scepter-sized staff she held. "Up until now, stars. But the other night, I let go of it in the dark of night, like my..." She cleared her throat and took a moment to right her train of thought. "I was never fully comfortable with the star align-ment, but I was expected to excel at it with a family name like *Starsurge*. I would like a change, to experiment with the moon and her four faces. Let's try the alignment ritual with you and Ben. You're clearly the sun, and he can try the stars with his fancy staff."

"It would be highly dangerous," Leona interjected.

"Ben hasn't had an ancestor give him magic," I added, wishing the head librarian wasn't here to dissuade us. It sounded like something worth a try during this desperate time. "I only have so much access to celestial magic because I'm the sole inheritor of an entire family line."

Wren flashed a hint of a wicked smile. "There's a trick he can use to ask." Her blue eyes darted toward Leona for a moment, and she seemed to bite back on further comment. But I shared that glimmer of excitement Wren had—we would try the alignment ritual later, when we weren't under the watchful eye of an older, disapproving witch.

Maybe this would lead to the kind of power boost I could leverage to save Phaeron.

11

BEN

CRESS SHOOK me awake in the dead of night. I'd waited until my eyelids grew too heavy but eventually slipped into rest without her. She explained where she'd been and handed me a tightly knotted bag that smelled of an old-fashioned apothecary.

"Since when were you and the queen bee in cahoots?" I asked groggily once she finished talking.

Turned out, the bag *was* from an old-fashioned apothecary. Wren had slipped out of the library again without anyone's permission and left another probably worthless credit card behind to pay for the several bundles of herbs she'd lifted, along with a stockpile of verdant witch potions and tonics.

"Since the audience chamber fight, I think," she answered. "Well? Will you give it a try?"

Her suggestion was something I'd wanted to do eventually, to get in contact with my Evenstar ancestors and ask for access to my magical inheritance. I got tired of her standing over me and wringing her hands waiting for my reaction. I dragged her, giggling, overtop me, and we ended up entangled with the covers and each other.

"As long as you're in this bed with me," I said, kissing the end of her nose.

She melted into me with a tired sigh. "There's nowhere else I'd rather be."

I recognized the look she wore and bundled her close until she fell asleep, fully clothed and all. With a dismissive glance at the bag of herbs, I stuffed it under my pillow before pulling away from Cress to untie her shoes and drape the sheets over her properly. Once I turned the bedside lamp off and got comfortable, I closed my eyes and tried not to notice how strongly the herbs smelled.

It was supposed to be a soothing blend, I guess. Lavender and valerian couldn't completely cover up something foreign and spicy mixed in with them. The scent was meant to influence my dreams and open my mind to a visit from a deceased family member. My chest ached when I imagined my one memory of Marie Evenstar when I'd met her on Samhain night. My kind, doomed mother.

Cress would've liked her. In another life, they'd be close, and Cress and I would've chosen to become celestial witches. While she seemed a solid enough librarian witch, I wore the blood affinity I'd been forced to take like an ill-fitting shirt. If it were truly possible to draw forward some of the magic I was *supposed* to have, well, I'd do it even if it meant I had to accept Wren's help. I'd drag my aunt Jordan into the mix too for some more solid advice.

Despite me drifting off with my mother on my mind, I slept through what remained of the night without as much as a hint of a supernatural visit. Cress and Wren hid their disappointment quickly over breakfast, stealing glances over at Leona when she took too much of an interest in what we were discussing from her place at the head of the table.

"Today, we continue purging the lesser creatures," the head librarian announced.

Jonah, the male librarian never too far from her side, remarked, "When presented with the conundrum of one horse-sized duck or a hundred duck-sized horses, the boss chooses the big one for last."

Leona frowned over at him. "We will clear the whole library."

He nodded slowly. "If there's time."

I ate the last of my cereal without relish. We were having it dry with sides of protein bars. *Mm-mm*. The library's share of the rations didn't include anything perishable.

My appetite left me swiftly when I was reminded of what was at stake. When Myuna turned her attention to the library, anything we didn't kill would return to her side. With that in mind, we split into two groups, considering the "lesser" creatures posed less of a threat overall but there were a lot of them.

Once powered back up from a visit to the powercore, Cress shone like a prism. She was an asset in cutting down unnaturals for the rest of the time we spent in the bowels of the library. Leona pushed us harder and harder still to get our grim task completed. I felt like I barely slept a wink during this time...not the most ideal situation for a poten-tial visit from an ancestor to fish for magic I *might* be able to combine with my existing affinity, if I was anything like Cress.

I would be the first person to say I wasn't anything like Cress, though. In the evenings, she disappeared with Leona,

Wren, and soon Jordan as well to continue practicing what they were starting to call her hybrid magic, testing the bounds of what within her was librarian, celestial, or *both*. She returned late each night with an exhausted smile and the occasional superficial burn on her arms or face.

In the meantime, I put off thoughts of reclaiming my family's celestial magic for a one-sided rivalry with Bianca, who gleefully slayed monsters with the zeal of someone searching out a true challenge.

Eight days later, once all the lesser creatures were killed, we prepared for the kind of epic encounter that had Bianca salivating. We all gathered around a table where Leona had laid out articles and small artifacts depicting artist renditions of a strange aquatic creature. "When I was a young woman, this unnatural animal washed ashore just north of Myrtle Beach. It took out two SPDI combat teams before Cerris City Library was contacted to contain it. We called it the Jellywalker."

I couldn't help a poorly muffled snort.

She shot me an unimpressed look. "Laugh if you like, but I watched it tear apart two senior librarians and maim a third in the time it took to cast a stasis spell. And keep in mind, it's the lowest power level of the eleven greater creatures that remain in the library. Best case scenario…it is already dead within the dry containment room we stuffed it in.

"In the much more likely case that it is awake and biding its time like the good little ambush predator it is, you have to be aware of what it can do and how it moves." She picked up a wooden carving. "It is mostly legs. Eight feet of looming legs studded with jellyfish stingers that shred skin. It moves in quick bursts to overwhelm its prey, and its sting causes paralysis."

The carving was passed around so we all could get a good look at how bizarre the Jellywalker was. Its head was helmeted like a jellyfish, with solid plates on top that might resemble rocks if it buried itself in sand or dirt. Under the rim of its cranium, it had dozens of eyes for full sight in every direction. It supported itself on five tentacle legs and had a hidden tooth-filled seam of a mouth on the underside of its head.

"Imagine the ocean having more of these things," I said.

Willow glanced around before saying in her wisp of a voice, "The merfolk hunt unnatural creatures in the water like some of us do on land."

"So there *are* more." A few of my friends paled at my suggestion.

"Ben," Cress warned.

I cocked my usual half smile her way. "Just confirming for my nightmares, thanks."

"Anyway," Leona said pointedly. "We are running out of time. Myuna's new creatures howl outside our walls every night."

I wasn't the only one shuffling in discomfort. By some unspoken agreement, none of us had acknowledged that it seemed like unnaturals were calling to each other every evening above our heads. Their trills and screeches were muffled by several layers of dirt and metal, but they were still present. It was easier to pretend the sounds were from the monsters still trapped in the library...but there were only eleven of those left, and they were all far below us.

Geo had taken to standing guard over us at night, posting up in gargoyle form in the shadows of the library's ground floor. Cress visited him before bed. They'd have told me if they killed any monsters...I think.

"The Jellywalker and the rest of our targets are unlikely

to be as cowed by Cress's sunshine as the lesser creatures we've faced. So, not everyone at this table will be fighting the Jellywalker. Sorry, kids, but Mad Ash would have my head if you got seriously hurt," Leona said.

She more specifically had Willow, Áine, and Wren agreeing in various states of reluctance to sit this fight out. Áine would be helping the twitchy verdant witch nurse care for any wounds, while Willow was still too unpredictable in her magic and Wren was *out* of magic except for the level-one and two celestial witch spells that didn't require storing. She needed time and rituals to store stronger spells.

Cress squeezed my hand under the table, beaming. "She wants me to fight," she murmured under the planning going back and forth between Leona, Jordan, Geo, and one of the older Crystal fae that'd been assigned to the library.

I smiled back, not having the heart to tell her that she was probably coming as a spotlight to blind the demented jellyfish. She needed to work on her channeling, because most days, she used up her storage of magic just by managing her overbright Lux spell.

If only I could share my channeling ability with her. Our mothers had had the same general problem—Eris Darkmore was all power, and Marie Evenstar had channeling for days but little oomph to back it up. Because they were of the same affinity, they could share power. All the more reason I hoped to see my father's spirit every night as my nostrils were tickled by the packet of herbs still under my pillow. My mother's ghost had given me a spark of her channeling as a gift and promised to wake Liam Evenstar in the next life so he would visit too.

So, where was he when we desperately needed him to visit me?

It took a little over an hour to devise our full strategy for the Jellywalker. Geo would be the only one to engage it at first. Its expected tactic of jumping off the ceiling to wrap all five legs around its victim would be ineffective with all those stingers scraping solid obsidian. After that, we'd whittle it down while keeping a safe distance.

A small smile lifted Geo's face, a subtle sign of how pleased he was to protect us from this danger. "Let's go," he rumbled.

We headed down to floor negative thirty for the fight. I was in the second group down and took the short ride as an opportunity to apply my blood runes. I pricked the pad of my index finger with a blade and traced the familiar shapes in my own blood up my arm. Strength, speed, agility, stamina.

During my inspection of my gear, I flicked out the hidden vial of blood secreted within the ring I was wearing. It was a weird shade of purple...a gift from Phaeron, who'd taught me a couple new symbols where it'd be appropriate to use dimensional blood. I could use it to give myself shadow talons or paint a third eye on myself to see through unnatural magic. I was saving it for a dire emergency.

As we faced the Jellywalker's door together, waiting for Leona to unseal it, I swallowed my nerves. The fights were only going to get more difficult from here. We were lucky to be healthy and whole and have the advantage over this creature's natural weapons in the form of Geo. Even the five Crystal fae, with their armor of rock and mineral and natural geode-like growths, would be assets. Roe stood with them, her silver mace at the ready and the magical armor flowing from her necklace to encase her in a suit of polished orange crystal with reinforced fists.

Bianca and I stood to one side, prepared to shoot and stab the creature from afar. The librarian witches were another cluster, swords and books at the ready. Cress's handbook fluttered in graceful loops over her head, chattering away about the best places to get sushi that it'd recorded in Cerris City ten years ago with its last owner. She was blushing faintly, caught asking a rhetorical question that it made literal.

"Hush," Leona said sternly.

"Hushing!" It dropped its voice to a whisper and flapped closer to Cress's ear. "As I was saying, there's a place on Fourteenth Street that's to die for..."

Sighing through her nose, Leona went ahead and unsealed the door, opening it for Geo to step through. He lifted his shield high and rushed inside.

There was a screech of something scraping unfeeling stone. The fae and Roe pushed into the room next, with the rest of us following suit. I was so grateful I'd seen the Jelly-walker in theory first, as it helped me make sense of the hissing, pungent creature unwrapping its limbs from Geo and scuttling backward.

The monster's five legs were fully flexible, currently bowed to drop its helmeted head several feet. Its many orange eyes darted in separate directions all at once, taking in the crowd invading its containment area. We were in an extra-large room, a twenty-foot box with a ten-foot ceiling and a dirt floor it'd been burrowed in for who knows how long.

Dust flecked off its moist skin as it used those flexible limbs to start climbing the wall.

"Heads up!" one of the fae shouted.

A silver-tipped bolt flew, and one of its eyes exploded with a splash of blue blood. I threw a few daggers while it reeled from the injury, getting them stuck in its helmet and a second eye.

One of the librarians hit it with a stasis spell at that moment, but the creature shrugged it off and scuttled further up the wall, clinging to the ceiling with its many stingers sticking it in place. It inspected us from above for a more ideal target, and that's when Cress hit it with the concentrated light of her Lux spell. The Jellywalker screeched in distress, its limbs retreating under its head that it suctioned to the ceiling to seal out the blast of illumination.

Leona unleashed a level-four spell, something I'd never seen Cress do. Living shadows curled into a ball shape at her side before answering to her will and the point of her sword tip. The ball became a giant hand, which attempted to pry the Jellywalker off its perch. In the meantime, a bolt cracked one of its protective plates, and I narrowed in on the weak spot, aiming to let fly a dagger to impale it in the brain and end this conflict.

Light suddenly flared from a new source...all of the monster's intact eyes. They turned white and refocused in one direction, its next victim. It unstuck from the ceiling and lunged at one of the fae, ripping his head off his body with a brutal twist of multiple limbs, accompanied by the crunch of stone.

Shit. It'd been so fast; there was nothing we could've done for him.

The closest person to it, Aurora, screamed. It grabbed her next, its many stingers wrapping around her body. "Help!" she cried, her hand dropping her sword and freezing half extended toward us. The Jellywalker bundled her up in two tentacles before it scuttled out of the containment room in a desperate burst.

"Fuck!" I exclaimed.

Bianca and I ran after it the quickest with our speed

runes. It seemed to glance around with intelligence before sprinting straight for the stairwell and heading upward with impossible speed by skipping the stairs and using its three undulating legs to climb straight up the walls.

Bianca flashed a grin. "Race you," she said to me.

She refreshed her speed and agility runes before charging up the stairs after it with superhuman haste. I, of course, did the exact same thing, only ducking from a warning shout from Geo. He half flew up the stairwell, landing and pushing off the handrails since his stone body was too cumbersome to maneuver back and forth for a seamless flight. The metal buckled under his weight, but he outpaced Bianca and me this way.

I worried the creature was somehow scouting for Myuna when it burst onto the first floor and paused, taking in a panoramic view of the library with a sibilant hiss. It resumed its flight upon spotting Geo cocking his arm back, preparing to skewer it with one of his signature quartz spikes.

Heedless of anything, the Jellywalker scuttled straight for a glass wall helmet-first and smashed its way through it into the streets. Bianca was starting to sing-song "Fuck fuck fuuuuuck *fuck*" since it was clear the monster was racing for the audience chamber and the soul-eating goddess awaiting its arrival with one of our librarian friends in tow. She shot a silver-tipped bolt at its retreating back.

Geo circled higher to drop on it from above, but he wasn't the humanoid form that landed on its helmeted head first. It was a block away and starting to truly outpace us when this new person grabbed the ridge over its eyes and dropped their weight toward the ground, unsettling its balance. Silver flashed, and one of its scuttling limbs came free in a gush of blue liquid, flopping like a boneless eel.

The Jellywalker squealed and shook the person free. As we gained on the monster and took aim at its back, our new ally landed on her feet and spared us a fleeting glance before sweeping her sword at the leg it tried to ensnare her with. It wrapped the limb around the edges of the weapon instead, and the woman released the handle, dodging being ensnared by the loops of its leg with impressive agility.

Bianca shot it through an already wounded eye, and the creature collapsed with one last hiss of air, deflating sideways to resemble a jellyfish in death. Geo landed on its head shortly afterward, further destroying the corpse.

"The fuck was that thing?" the woman asked in a voice like a roughened purr. She eyed the Jellywalker with disgust as she pulled her sword from its limp leg and went over to sever the two limbs still encircling Aurora.

"Identify yourself," Geo rumbled. He bent to help disentangle Aurora at the same time she did.

She was murmuring, "Monster slain and a civilian saved. You got the footage, T?" Upon seeing his stone hands, she released the back of one of the legs and let him carefully peel it from Aurora's shredded clothing and skin.

It took me longer than a blink to realize she had a small microphone taped to her ear and was angling a body camera toward the scene and Geo. "I know. I wasn't expecting survivors either," she said to the person on the other end of that mic.

Bianca got impatient and pointed her crossbow at the woman. "The gargoyle said to identify yourself, bitch," she said.

Smirking, the other woman stood and said, "I just saved your friend, and this is how you treat me?"

"You could be an unnatural in disguise," Bianca replied.

"By that logic, you could as well."

I inspected the newcomer's aura, seeing nothing unusual in the moving waves of power around her. She had subtle signs of a big cat shifter with her beast close to the surface. The fingernails she pretended to inspect were lengthened to claws through small slits in her gloves, and her naturally uptilted eyes were slitted and amber. Fur seemed to pattern the back of her neck under the messy fall of a platinum blonde ponytail.

"Ladies, please. Let's put the claws away and get Aurora back to our healers," I said, stepping between them. Bianca immediately pointed her weapon toward the ground.

Geo lifted Aurora in his arms and turned to me. "Handle this," he ordered. He fanned out his stone wings and flew toward the hospital, leaving me to deal with the two women, who eyed each other carefully.

"You must be an unnatural hunter, then," Bianca said.

The cat part of the other woman was fading. She had a feral kind of grin that still lent a feline edge to her face along with her pointed nose and strong chin. Her blue eyes lidded at a lazy-seeming angle, and she had the kind of tanned skin that suggested she often worked out in the sun.

She touched a pin high on the leather armor she wore, close to the body cam. It resembled a hissing Medusa head, with several of its hair snakes baring their fangs. "Damn straight. Soon to be a part of the highest-ranked team in Chaos Inc. The name's Grace. You're survivors, huh?"

Bianca and I exchanged a glance and introduced ourselves. "You won't be ranked anything if we don't figure out a way to leave this pocket dimension," I commented.

"Ah, well, do I have good news for you! I just got here with my teammate. Do you have a safe place for us to join you?" she asked.

"You tell us how you 'just got here,'" I said with air quotes, "and we'll take you there."

I ignored Bianca's hiss of warning. We needed all the help we could get to kill the last ten unnaturals waiting in their containment rooms, and this woman was a specialist in doing just that, with a teammate hiding somewhere.

"Lead the way, then," the shifter purred.

12

PHAERON

"*No!*" Myuna roared.

I muttered a curse as pain shredded through my already aching head. The Void laughed behind my ears. It knew I was weakened by mortal needs despite my kind's functional immortality. Myuna didn't notice my wince, and it was better that way. The moments that trickled by in her presence were more pleasant when the mistress didn't notice me.

I hissed under my breath. *No,* I told myself. *You have no mistress.*

It was hard to focus for long enough to remind myself of that fact. I'd been awake five eternities now or longer, clinging to the merest trickle of power and sanity at the back of my head. Braza couldn't feed me more than a drop of energy at a time without Myuna noticing the drip-drab of relief and coherency. Still, my body should've long given up.

Myuna and Garroway ignored the occasional unhinged laugh I uttered, in chorus with the Void or off-tune, when I was just so exhausted all I could do was chuckle at my own flaws. I was going mad one excruciating minute at a time, and surely that was the purpose of my continued existence at the goddess's side. She wanted me desperate enough to bend a knee to her. She bid me every day to submit to her will for the opportunity to finally rest.

And Cress help me, there seemed no other option than to give in.

Cress. The tones of her voice haunted me, and I was convinced it was the Void playing a trick. The version of her in my head was a distorted mirage of sound, and yet I listened anyway. She lisped in my mind in pleading tones. A human dialect, strange and blunt... I did not understand the words anymore.

"They killed the first of my children that managed to escape the pit they call a library," Myuna sighed. That's right. She'd called out in distress six seconds or hours ago, upset over something.

Garroway, who'd taken to whiling away many of the daylight hours on the dais next to her, patted her arm. He simpered something her way, and I nearly mustered the energy to sneer. How quickly he'd fallen in line and served her with devotion, even when Endaeron was not the dominant personality in his body.

Considering every supernatural he brought before her was consumed, Garroway had taken to catching animals for Myuna to experiment on. She'd twisted more than a few stray dogs into creatures resembling doskalos and created new unnaturals from other animals.

The goddess delighted in corrupting the fauna of Cerris City, as they could hunt survivors for her at the times Garroway could not. Her white skin had gained a pearly sheen from regular feedings. She was a beautiful, deadly monster again, making sure to tap my awareness so I would be forced to watch as she bloated poor grackles and seabirds into bulbous harridans and other innocent creatures into her twisted slaves.

She took to playing with her food, sucking souls one piece at a time so their screams of agony joined the Void's chorus long after they were gone. "Don't you want to look away?" she'd invited. "Just submit to me. I will do the rest."

Submit. Rest.

Had she just said that? *No, just a recollection.* Yet another voice stirring in the Void.

What she was really saying was, "...consume the group murdering my children and take the powercore for myself. We grow stronger each day."

"While time may be of the essence." Garroway pitched his tone to soothe as he rubbed her shoulder. His voice had gained the two-toned hiss of the Hungering Darkness. "You have yet to claim any other supernaturals to serve you."

"I have hungered so desperately. Surely you do not fault me for eating the candidates you've already brought me?" she asked. Their foreheads leaned toward one another, and her white-filmed eyes gave his a searching look.

"Of course not, my lady," Garroway and Endaeron purred. The vampire skimmed her cheek with his fingertips, drawing her ice-white hair back behind one ear. A daring touch, so close to her mouth pit.

I recognized what I was witnessing with a sick lurch. Affection. The worst monster to grace Soiluire had found what may be the most desperate on Earth. As Myuna slowly caressed her hand down the vampire's back, I wondered if her expression was that of lust or avarice. Did the self-proclaimed reaper of worlds have what it took to feel romantically for another? Or would she consume his soul the moment he stopped giving her what she wanted?

"Come nightfall, I will bring you new candidates, my lady. We can try until you succeed in taking their souls to serve you," he promised.

"Very good," she said, sitting straight once more. She loomed over him, glowing vibrantly in anticipation.

ONCE NIGHT ARRIVED, Garroway came and went thrice, delivering victims one at a time that Myuna held in her massive palms, hesitated over, and then consumed in a few gruesome moments. She couldn't seem to help herself.

Time whirred on, and my body grew too heavy to support. Myuna did not permit me to sit, so I collapsed, splayed before her like a dying animal. The hunger and thirst had grown nearly as unbearable as the fatigue, my needs eclipsing Braza's careful drips of energy.

"Give in," she whispered. "Submit."

My tongue felt like a flap of parchment in the desert of my mouth. "No," I rasped, tasting blood. Perishing here and now would be a kinder fate than what she intended.

"Very well... Watch," she ordered. Wavering, I lifted my head and did as she bid. She consumed a wounded animal brought to her and twisted a dozen more, releasing a new pack of her monsters into the city to hunt for her.

I dipped my chin, humiliated. The great Phaeron et Sudair could not save a housecat, let alone the innocents still trapped in this pocket dimension. The blood and gore, corruption and death... They blurred together into the Void's giggling seams.

Until she arrived, days or moments or years later.

She screamed my name with a human accent. I knew

the girl struggling in Garroway's arms, and my eyes widened in recognition.

Some of the madness drained from my head, dimming the Void and muting the nonsense of time's passing. I was truly returned the moment I whispered her name, *Carly*, an ordinary human with dirty ocean-blue hair and torn clothes.

My mate's sister, here, being presented to Myuna. Panic turned my heart into a racing blur as Myuna's white-glazed eyes danced toward me and a smile curved the morass of her mouth. "You know this girl, Phaeron. I seem to recall her likeness too, from your memories."

"Leave her be." My demand was weakened by the huff of effort it took for me to stand. Shadows lengthened in the room, bending to my command.

Carly babbled, tears streaming down her face. She stared at my mouth all the while. The only thing I made out from her sobbed words was my name, repeated like a plea...

My translation spell, I realized. She had to be begging me for help and it was not being translated in a way I understood. Myuna had broken the spell I relied on so heavily, probably with the sheer force of her own mind-turning voice.

Myuna gestured for Garroway to release the girl and caught her in a weave of light. Her usual trick had Carly clawing at the boundaries of the bubble she was trapped in, still staring at me, probably wondering when I would do something to help her. The presence of Myuna's magic evaporated what few shadows I had the energy to call, rendering me useless for what was about to happen.

"What will you give me in exchange for her?" the goddess asked.

I could not give her anything.

I could not give in to her will.

But I also could not allow her to have Carly. I remembered a much more vibrant girl, who wished so desperately to be a supernatural like her adopted sister. She'd had me check and recheck her soul for any speck of magic in the hopes that proximity to the supernatural community would sprout something within her and spread flower petals toward the sun. She'd only seen the good side of magic; the Crystal Court with its friendly, honest fae folk and a tight-knit community of witches.

Her soul flickered within her now, weak and ordinary, shrinking away from the monster that had her trapped in a cage of magic. Already, Myuna eyed her like she observed every other humanoid brought to her: like a full-course meal.

"Has bringing me low not already been sufficient payment?" I growled.

In response, Myuna opened her mouth and sucked, tugging Carly's soul loose within her body. The blue-haired girl screamed and clutched her chest. "Phaeron," she begged. "*Phaeron!*"

What else did I even have to offer? My full will and body were the only things Myuna had not already taken from me. Falteringly, I offered the only other thing I could think of. "I will give you my knowledge. Several mortal lifetimes of information. Anything you would want to know about this world, here for the taking, if you would just let her go."

Carly's screams hit a feverish pitch as Myuna pulled on her soul in a nearly playful way, untethering it from her body ever so slowly.

"Please. She is still so young," I begged.

Another tug, and her soul left her body, which crumpled within the bubble of light, pristine except for the way her pupils rapidly smudged out of her unseeing eyes. Myuna cycled Carly's soul around her lips, tongue darting out to taste it.

I was seized by the inevitability of Myuna. The death of civilizations here to spread entropy, starting with Cerris City. In a couple days at most, I would be too overcome by my body's mortality, and then she'd wring control of me to help her agenda along.

Through the fog in my brain, I recognized the truth. The real reason for the methods of her torture when she so obviously wanted my subservience. She couldn't take full control of me unless I agreed or she corrupted my soul. Unlike Carly's soul, weak enough to be twisted from one lick, mine made for a challenge Myuna was obviously not willing to undertake in her current state.

I'd watched too many of the women in my life die; Carly could still be saved. And if I worded my surrender correctly...with a larger ration of luck than I deserved, so could I.

I breathed out, "Spare her, and I will slumber."

A deliberate word choice, *slumber*, the kind of blackout exhaustion she was pushing me toward. As long as I did not wake, she could reach through the tiny hole in my soul and puppet my body and powers as she willed.

It was a close second to the complete submission she desired from me.

The goddess paused with Carly's essence poised to be sucked into her pit of a mouth. "Very well," she agreed, far too readily.

She blew the soul away from her maw and manipulated it like she tied strands of light. It gained a new shape, and then it was shoved back into Carly's body, jerking her awake with a jolt. White light poured from her irises, marking her as the first human servant Myuna had successfully claimed. Back on my planet, we would call her a torchbearer, capable of wielding the goddess's white light.

I watched her sit up and breathed out with relief. If I saw Cress again, I could tell her that I'd done everything I could to protect her family.

"There. Spared," Myuna mocked. "Rest up."

Before she could change her mind, I closed my eyes, feeling how dry and aching they were. It was the biggest gamble of my life, to go into her hands willingly, if temporarily.

Her awful, multi-layered voice whispered into the last remnants of my awareness. "We have a library to claim. Perhaps your slumber shall end...with your sweet mate in my hands."

13
BEN

"You were difficult to find," my father said.

The dream I'd been waiting for was made by a surrealist. Bursts of color surrounded us, hazy and out of focus, leaving Liam Evenstar the only solid figure around. I didn't dare look down.

He was younger than I expected, wearing a navy button-down and slacks. He'd died dressed for work, as he'd been in a wreck one ordinary afternoon when I was barely more than a toddler. A tragedy in any person's life, but doubly so when it was the event that'd forced my mom to seek out Garroway for a private loan.

The rest, as they say, was history.

I felt bad. I didn't know anything about this man except that I somewhat resembled him. Yet I needed him to acknowledge me as his heir so some of the Evenstar family magic could flow into me. Sure, it was based off of a wild hunch, but one Jordan and Wren grew more certain about every time they tested the weirdness of Cress's jumbled-up magic.

"I was starting to wonder if you were even looking," I said with an awkward little laugh.

Liam grimaced in return. It appeared I wasn't the only one who was feeling off about this meeting. "Of course I was," he replied. "I was at peace in the next life until your mother found me and told me everything you'd shared with her."

"Oh, um, sorry about that."

He gripped my shoulder. In this dream, at least, he was more solid than a ghost. "I know this is uncomfortable, but I need you to know...you deserve better than what life has dealt you. When I was alive, I wanted you and your brother to have the world. Now, all I can do is give you the power to take it instead."

That was all the preamble we had before golden light haloed his form. Raw power and knowledge flowed through him into me, and it was about as pleasant as molten lava coursing through my veins and head. But the pain faded, giving way to his memories and emotions and intentions.

Liam knew how much I needed aid and at least a cursory understanding of celestial magic. I needed to properly use the staff that was my inheritance, Evening Guidance. And I was suddenly sure that I could if it were possible to suppress or supplant my blood affinity.

Once the urgency between us faded, I opened my eyes and drew my father in for a hug. "Before you go, won't you tell me more about you?" I asked, unsure if I would see him in another dream. He deserved to go back to a peaceful slumber while I used the gift he'd just given me.

"Of course," he said. The abstract colors around us solidified. He and I sat before a campfire in his favorite park, roasting sausages and marshmallows.

I woke after hours of conversation with a huge smile on my face. That was my *dad*. His power and knowledge settled in my mind like I was always supposed to have Evenstar light just under the surface of my skin.

Cress was just starting to stir from where she was snugly pressed to my side. "Guess what, babe," I whispered excitedly. "I met my dad. I wish you could've as well."

Her answering look was bittersweet. "I wish I could've met him too," she said.

I refused to let sadness into this moment. "Sure, he's gone...but it was amazing that he could visit with me for a night."

I kissed her until she stopped frowning. We got ready together in our small shared space with growing familiarity and went up to breakfast, where we saw Geo running face-first into the one usage of the Internet he didn't understand.

He was in his stone form, coming down to greet us after a night of standing guard. Wren pointed the camera of her phone at him. "Ladies and gentlemen, our resident gargoyle has arrived. This obsidian giant has kept us protected as we continue to fight back here in Cerris City," she narrated aloud.

"Hello?" Geo gritted, still confused about what she was trying to do.

Grace and her body camera had inspired Wren. Without much useful magic to fight with, she had turned to playing in the court of public opinion. Since her ex-family had not spoken a word on our behalf, she streamed everything safe to share about what we were doing in the library and beyond. Thousands of strangers could be watching right now as we ate breakfast and planned.

We'd taken out three more of the greater unnaturals

since the Jellywalker's death, but not without cost. A second one of our fae protectors had died, while a third had joined Aurora last night in the hospital for intensive care, leaving us only two fae to fight with. We'd gained one fighter in return with Grace, who'd revealed she was a mountain lion shifter, while her teammate, Tish, was her support woman.

Tish was a tiny young lady with a lavender-colored pixie cut and wide, haunted eyes. She was a hybrid of some kind, with a soul that moved like a shifter's but ears that came to small, fae-like points.

She was hard at work typing away on a laptop while taking distracted bites of dry cereal. With a click of a few keys, she had the lights flickering overhead with a dramatic buzz. According to her, this was for *ambiance* to heighten the sense of danger. The fact that she'd hacked the library's systems and could manipulate aspects of it like the cameras or electricity so easily annoyed the hell out of Leona.

An apparent tech genius, Tish had jumped in with enthusiasm and gotten Wren's stream and social media accounts set up. This not only boosted our message that there was still hope inside Cerris City, but also generated visibility for the unnatural hunting team she and Grace represented.

That was why those two were here, after all. They were chasing internal points with their organization, Chaos Inc., by killing the unnaturals here. Apparently, there were several more teams that'd chosen to enter Cerris City of their own volition through the only way still open: an ocean gate.

That the ocean gate was still operating despite the fae magic that'd shut down Cerris City was a ticking time bomb, but one we handed off to Madigan and our other senior leadership. They were the ones to decide how we would use the knowledge. If we abandoned ship now, there were still hundreds of unaccounted people out there that we'd be leaving to the monsters. But it could be used to usher out the civilians that'd already been saved.

Until a decision was made, we were all very careful not to mention the ocean gate when Wren had the stream rolling. We didn't want the mer to catch wind of it and shut it down.

I still thought the unnatural hunters were incredibly stupid to chase imaginary clout competing for a prize they might not escape the pocket dimension to see. My stay in Cerris City had made me a pessimist, sure as anything.

Tish bounced in her chair with an excited coo. "A hundred-dollar donation," she gasped, and Wren forced a big smile for the camera and thanked the generous soul.

I exchanged a glance with Cress, sure we were beyond the place where money could help, yet the stream donations were flowing in the absence of anything else from the outside world.

The only thing that might shift the landscape of the war we were in was more power...something we would experiment with tonight.

CRESS

Ben's father chose a good day to visit him, as our fights ended with Leona calling for a break in a meltdown of frustration. A corrupted dimensional had used his magic to teleport away once we'd opened his containment room, a flub Wren caught on camera. I felt for Leona, who took the embarrassment personally, as she'd overlooked this ability of his while briefing us.

It was our first true failure in a long string of successful fights, and she wasn't the only one carrying the weight of defeat. Wren shut off the stream with a quick fumble when Leona began to yell and Jonah rushed over to talk her down.

"It's been a really stressful time. We just need a rest," he said.

It gave us a chance to slip away that evening without being questioned. I met Wren, Jordan, and Ben in Braza's chamber. Jordan carried a bag to this meeting and began pulling out ritual implements while I went up to the powercore.

I reached for it, and Braza reached back, pulling me into the inner chamber of the powercore, where she stood in her dimensional form. She was made of the same purple and black material as the sphere we stood within, as the powercore was her soul and this space was where she could manifest as a shadow of herself.

I drew her into a hug and held her slightly squishy body, letting her snuggle close to my warmth. She was petite compared to Phaeron, about as tall as I was, with forward-facing horns and bat wings.

"Do you think this ritual is going to work?" I asked her.

Despite how young and soft her features were, she answered with the same air of wisdom as always. "It is a gamble and a guess, as it was to put your family's whole might into your handbook. The side effects of that decision have led to a leakage of light into your librarian affinity already. Perhaps the ritual will bolster you and Ben and somehow you will both become hybrid witches in a world that's never seen the like."

Jordan and Wren, both more experienced in this kind of ritual, thought that would happen too. "I'm just worried it will go all wrong," I admitted.

She blew out a sigh and took hold of my shoulders with a serious expression. "The worst is still possible, brightest of souls. Most who choose one path and are given an ancestral magic of another do not get to choose both because one never answers to their will. And there are books recording the celestial attunement ritual stripping potential hybrids of their non-celestial affinity. That is a trauma that can damage you down to your soul."

"I remember you mentioning that when my mother's ghost wanted to give me everything directly," I said, biting my lip on a surge of nerves.

"Unlike that situation, I believe you should still attempt the ritual. Your magic *feels* different, and your anam cara will be taking the same risk as you. If ever there was a setup for successful hybrid witches, it is this." Her hold dropped to my hands, and we both squeezed. "If you remain a librarian witch at all, I have a proposition for you."

"Oh?"

She nodded, releasing me and inclining one horn toward where I'd left my friends. "Your ritual awaits. I'll tell you later," she said.

Reassured, I stepped out of the powercore. I'd learned that Braza was lonely in her afterlife, and I meant to visit with her like that more. While we'd been talking, Jordan had drawn runes in chalk, with three large circles touching to form a triangle.

"Over here, dear," Jordan said, pointing with the nub of chalk toward the empty circle.

Wren and Ben were already sitting cross-legged in the other two. I settled in the last one and took in the markings around us. The likeness of the sun and its rays formed some of the runes around my spot, connecting to the moon phases circling Wren and the constellations around Ben. Herbs dusted an offering bowl in the center, along with an unlit candle and three of Ben's smaller throwing knives.

"You good?" Wren asked, raising a brow my way.

"Just getting some reassurance that this might work for Ben and me," I answered honestly, and she gave a little shrug of acknowledgment.

"It's going to work," Ben said without a moment of hesitation.

Jordan took a moment to confirm one more time that we wanted to do this before lighting the candle with a stray match. We let Wren speak the Latin incantation for us. We were seeking alignment outside of the new moon, when trios of celestial witches were supposed to meet and perform this ritual. To successfully align, we had to shed a few drops of blood in offering while stating the proper words.

According to Jordan, it was completely normal and even common to align when the moon wasn't new in modern times, since it was often difficult to find time for sitting in a circle under the stars with your two witchy besties with how busy our lives could get. I still had my heart in my throat when Wren went first and pricked her thumb, muttering over the bowl as the crimson drops fell. "Lunae maiestas." Majesty of the moon.

Ben was next, his confidence starting to show its cracks as he blew out an unsteady breath. He added his blood to the bowl. "Magicae stellae," he said. Magic of the stars.

They turned to me expectantly as I lifted the last clean

blade and poised my hand over the bowl. My fingers were shaking. In two simple words and a few drops of blood, we'd see how this ritual would end up working for us. I drew a steading breath and poked my thumb. "Potentia solis." Power of the sun.

Power was what I'd already harnessed with the Sun Surge I'd cast from Evening Guidance. The same light I held each time I cast Lux and Luminaire. The kind of heat I felt mounting in my chest as Wren seized my hand and I fumbled for Ben's as I started to sweat.

She closed out the ritual with one last phrase. I focused on my breathing and the runes around us. The chalk turned colors…black around Wren, silver for Ben, and gold for me. A sign of success as I rode out the sensation of the worst heartburn of my life.

Ben was grinning, flexing his hands with anticipation. "You don't feel hot?" I asked.

It was Jordan's fingers that landed on my forehead first. "You have too much magic in you. Try this." She had me hold out my hand and cast a level-one celestial spell, Lumen. My palm heated and projected a gentle flashlight-level of brightness.

I gaped at it as the heat within me calmed over the duration I held the spell, which was easily canceled by shaking out my hand. "It worked," I said with a little disbelieving laugh. "Quick, teach Ben a level-one spell!"

I felt a soft probe of my awareness. *"And even better news, you are still a librarian,"* Braza told me privately while Ben learned to produce handfuls of magic that glittered like tiny star confetti and sizzled like embers.

Ben and I laughed and hugged, and I think Wren hid a little teary moment when she successfully swirled motes of moonlight around her fingertip. She covered her mouth with one hand and took up her scepter with the other, lighting it with a glow of soft silver.

"It's so easy," she whispered.

"Will you tell me your idea now?" I asked Braza.

"Very soon, brightest of souls. The hour grows late, and you must practice with one magic before I empower the other." She projected a sensation of pride. *"You are one of the strongest witches I have had the chance to witness in my time. No wonder you are fated to my prince."*

14

GEO

While Cress and Ben engaged in their ritual, I separated myself from them for our mutual sanity. If Cress wanted to explore her magic...who was I to stop her? She was fairly certain it would be fine, and Ben was more confident still.

Rather than loom over them, I went to my evening post. I was staying in stone form longer and longer by necessity, not consuming valuable rations and not sleeping when our enemies were sniffing around the library at night.

In fact, it was irresponsible for me to take human form... but I craved it. Even as I stood sentry in the shadows of the library's first floor, I ached within to transform back and hold my love through the night once I was sure she was okay.

No. I had a duty.

And *no*, that duty wasn't waiting in the same room as her ritual. It was ensuring her safety, as I was doing. She could rest easy knowing that no unnaturals had slipped into the lower floors of the library, because I was standing guard.

Someone else would have to be tasked with this if I

abandoned my post. They could fall asleep while keeping watch. Everyone in our little group was in some stage of exhaustion and hurt at this point. Most of our various wounds resulted from careless mistakes no one made when we first started clearing the library.

I didn't shift my considerable stone weight side to side, but I realized after an hour that I was *bored*. I had never been bored in this form before. Could I still be considered a patient rock if boredom was leaking into me from my human side?

Had I truly changed so quickly to be considering this question during an ongoing crisis?

Hmm, yes. For better or worse, this was Cress's doing as well. I would never be an unfeeling stone construct again with duty as my only comfort. I loved my woman too much to revert to that state.

Glass crunched under someone's tread, drawing my focus. "Halt. Identify yourself," I stated without hesitation. I already had one quartz spike primed and ready to fire if I had just announced myself to a roaming unnatural.

"Geo?" answered Grant's uncertain voice. "It's me, your favorite changeling."

"You are the only changeling I know," I said.

"That you're aware of," he said with a lilt of playfulness. I decided he sounded unapologetically like Grant and tilted my crystal shield, letting it reflect what little light remained outside from a distant streetlight so he knew where I was standing. The upper floors of the library were completely dark to discourage unnatural scavengers.

"Is that supposed to be a joke?" I asked.

His outline approached, and he felt for the stack closest to me. "Depends. Did you find it funny?" Only now did I notice the hitch in his voice and how he stumbled and held his side. "Áine hasn't figured me out yet, right? She'll heal me?"

"She has more pressing matters than your secret identity," I confirmed. "What happened?"

I saw the impression of his bright teeth bared in a grimace. "Turns out it's nigh impossible to spy on someone who eats every supernatural placed in front of her. Still, I saw a glimpse of some real shit, my stony friend, and then the monsters discovered me."

"Were you followed?" I demanded.

"Please," he wheezed. "I'm not that much of an amateur. But...they might pick up on the smell of my blood. I had to land a couple blocks away to avoid the attention of Myuna's flying blobs."

"I will handle it," I stated. For a split second, I hesitated and warred with the desire to shake him down for all of his information, despite concern for his well-being. "Tell me the most pressing details of what you learned. Without jokes."

"Yes, sir." Grant didn't have his mocking tone anymore. "Straight to the point...Myuna is making monsters out of any animals that are brought to her and was consuming the souls and bodies of the people she gets her hands on until very recently. She's successfully turned three people into white-eyed zombies, that I've seen, and..." He spent a few moments catching his breath. "Phaeron has switched sides. He's started gathering people for Myuna to zombify."

A sick feeling gathered in my chest. "You are certain? You have seen this for yourself?" I confirmed. Cress would be heartbroken. She'd been so certain the powercore had allowed her a connection with him to send him support. But even the greatest men broke under the right kind of pressure eventually, and we knew it couldn't be easy to stand in a goddess's presence unaffected.

"Yeah, I did. Hard to mistake a big scary shadow dude hauling a screaming woman toward Myuna." He shuddered, which became a painful cough.

"Go seek healing. Don't go back out again. There is no point in endangering yourself," I said.

"Worried about me, huh? If you weren't made of stone, I'd daresay you were getting soft," he said with a hint of a fae's musical, teasing laugh as he left me, finding the elevator and disappearing into the depths of the library.

Little did he know how right he'd been, and how annoyed I was that he taunted me for it.

THREE DOGLIKE CREATURES followed the trail of Grant's blood scent. I heard them snuffling and fired a quartz spike through one of their elongated skulls, killing it and sending the other two yipping away in fear.

Come morning, I went to retrieve my weapon and got a good look at the body. Its eyes had glowed faintly with Myuna's white power, making its head a target even in low lighting. The corpse, though...it was simply sad. It appeared that the goddess had stretched an already emaciated street dog, trying to form it into a doskalo. Fur and skin were split over joints not built for the sudden weight and size of its transformation.

"Rest in peace," I rumbled. I would have to show the body to the rest of the group as an example of the unnaturals prowling the city streets.

When one of our remaining Crystal fae came up to swap

places with me, he had his phone out. "We're getting a resupply soon. Mind staying here just in case there's trouble?"

I grinded a nod, and together we stepped outside. Cold wind and a bite of freezing rain hit us, and the fae shuddered. I scanned the drab gray of the skies, which were free of flying creatures, but a few of them lined up on the buildings around us, their glowing white eyes unblinking.

The unnatural birds were hulking, inflated in the chest with...muscle? Pus? Something of the sort. Their claws were transformed into oversized and gleaming talons.

"We are being spied on," I said quietly to my fae companion, indicating the birds. If Myuna had even a smidge of tactical capability, she would have already corrupted and sent out a legion of these birds to have her eyes on every inch of Cerris City's streets.

"Shit, yeah, they're looking right at us," he muttered back, scoffing. "Think the bounty hunters will come knock 'em down for imaginary points?"

"The endeavor may not be worth the reward," I answered.

I did not have to explain further. Usually, I didn't, but as the minutes rolled past and nothing else happened, I spoke up out of my usual turn, pitching my voice low so it might be chased away on the cold wind rather than reach the birds' awareness. "I imagine they are newly installed spying units. Their job right now will be to watch us and see what we are doing. We can resupply in peace, or we can kill them and risk a hostile response in return."

"I get it. I was just trying to make a joke, man," he said through chattering teeth.

People and their jokes, I thought with a thread of annoyance. I supposed it was asking a lot for a non-gargoyle to be as direct as I was.

A large truck rumbled down the street, its bed full of crates. A second, similarly laden vehicle followed. I noted my surprise. A lot more people piled out than were needed for a supply run. I helped heft more than a person's share of the weight and fell into step with Madigan Ashbough carrying several crates too, her arms enlarged with extra muscle from a guardian witch spell.

"Hello again, Geo," she said cheerfully enough, her voice betraying a hint of strain.

I waited until we were in the library to say, "I was not expecting our leader to deliver supplies personally."

We put the crates down and her muscles relaxed to their usual size slowly. She motioned for me to stand aside with her as the rest of the men and women took care of moving the crates deeper into the library. "That's because we've had a change of strategy."

"You are aware of Phaeron switching allegiances," I surmised.

"Yes. We've always known it would happen, but not exactly when. Our seer allies are now certain the library will be the subject of an assault with him as its head," she said with a grim set of her lips.

"How long do we have?"

As we spoke, I noted the presence of her mates, the Crystal Court's Prince Orthus and the twin guardian witches, Ajax and Aaron, identical save for their different tastes in dressing style. The blood witch Daire Grimsbane was also here, fully equipped for combat; despite being a politician, he was willing to get his hands dirty fighting with us. It also seemed he was friends with the other men now, carrying on with the twins as they worked.

Orthus placed Madigan's massive geode-formed warhammer next to her, and she smiled prettily, reaching up to kiss his cheek in thanks.

"Days," she answered me. "But it will depend on Cress and the powercore to trigger Myuna's greed. We still have some agency to prepare with traps and spells."

"I will accompany you to tell her that." A frown pulled at my stone lips, made more severe when I took a moment to transform back to human form. My concern for Cress practically pulsed out of me, along with a new emotion: anger. Phaeron was the perfect agent for Myuna to hurt Cress. Despite everything, I was halfway moved toward blaming him for this situation.

Madigan nodded. "That's a good idea," she said with a look of understanding.

We descended with the next set of supplies and emerged into a bustle of movement on floor negative one as crates were opened and the items divided and put away. Cress was there helping, red-nosed and puffy-eyed, and my heart sank to see her this way. She put down a jug of water moments before I swept her off her feet and into my arms.

"Hey, Geo." She hugged me back with a soft sigh, burying her face in my shirt.

She breathed a mild protest when I carried her away to an empty conference room so she could sit with Madigan and me. I was loath to let her go, and it seemed she felt the same, as she remained in the circle of my arms when I settled. Her hand rested casually on my knee.

"How did your ritual go?" I asked.

Cress released a little watery laugh. "Fine. It was...good. I don't feel very different, but I have to do this occasionally so I don't overheat." She raised her palm, which put off the same type of glow and warmth as a lightbulb.

I found that to be of dubious usefulness but kept the thought to myself.

"You will be luminous, my love," I murmured.

Madigan cleared her throat from where she settled across from us. Cress and I jerked apart, having been about to kiss right in front of her. "I just wanted to share a few words Hana wanted me to tell you," she said.

"About Phaeron?" Cress asked. There was a hopeful hush to her voice as her fingers knotted in her lap.

Madigan nodded. "She wants you to know that Phaeron slumbers, and if you wake him, he is yours."

My mate's brow knit. "What's that supposed to mean?"

With a sigh and a shrug, Madigan leaned back in her seat. "Kid, I'd be a wealthy woman if I got a dollar for figuring out every cryptic thing an augur has said to me. I took it to mean you can shake him out of Myuna's control by making him aware of his surroundings. But he's coming for us soon with the rest of the goddess's forces."

Cress grew rigid in my lap and craned her head up toward me. "The rest of the greater unnaturals still need to be killed," she stated with realization.

"We have reinforcements to help us," I said.

"And Myuna has a corrupted dimensional who will teleport them away the moment their prisons are unsealed. But we will still try. It's better than them escaping unexpectedly," Madigan added.

Cress gulped audibly. "I need to go speak with the powercore about this and...other things."

15

CRESS

Braza had heard our conversation, sensed my distress, and filled me with urgency to leave the private meeting with Madigan and Geo on a promise to finally tell me the idea she'd been withholding.

My face felt stiff as I took the elevator alone, assuring my companions this was something I had to do on my own. I needed to have more than two moments to myself so I could shed a few more tears and process what'd happened.

I'd known Phaeron was suffering and losing his sense of self, but it hurt so much worse to know he'd given in before I'd done much more than whisper to him encouragingly over the tenuous thread Braza was able to bridge between us. That silken strand was gone now, likely severed the moment Phaeron submitted to Myuna.

I should've done more. I *would* do more. I would "wake" him somehow, and he would be mine again, just as Hana foretold. All I had to do was figure out how to go about that.

Otherwise...he would die.

Tears continued to leak from my eyes as I exited the elevator and walked to Braza's chamber. I couldn't make them stop, not when I was on the edge of accepting that there was a future for Phaeron if we didn't successfully save him, which would be worse than death.

I loved him too much to let him become an unnatural. I would swing the sword to end him myself before he had his legacy tainted and became a monster like his brother. But only if I had to.

Braza absorbed me into the powercore and took her dimensional form within the inner chamber. Her cool, jelly-like fingers brushed the tears from my face as she framed it with her hands. "Brightest of souls. I had hoped you would have a chance to practice your new celestial magic, but it seems we are out of time at last."

"Braza...he's..."

"Shh. I know," she murmured. "Come and sit with me for a moment. We have an important decision to make."

Braza had transported the stone platform and its furnishings that'd been within her at Moongrove Library. There was a bed, a couch, and an old-fashioned chest. We settled on the couch together, with her leaning against me companionably, one of her wings curled around my back and opposite shoulder.

"I would like to bestow upon you an honor that hasn't been seen since the early days of librarian witches. Before my attention was needed to contain so many rooms and monitor a busy library, I was able to elevate one librarian by merging a significant piece of myself with him or her and empower them for as long as they may live," she began.

I gaped at her. "You're picking me for this?"

"You are the only mortal I trust this deeply. But I must admit, that is partway because you are Prince Phaeron's next mate and this is a desperate measure to save him." She patted my hand to take away some of the sting of her admission. "Soul magic is heavy, Cress. If you accept the burden of Guardian of Moongrove Library, you will witness a portion of my memories. It's more intense than the after-effects of a mating bite, or so I've been told."

"Wait, Moongrove?" I asked, overwhelmed.

"If we survive this, I will transfer back, and then the title will fit."

I bit my lip, not missing the *if* in her statement. There were no guarantees we would escape Cerris City before tragedy struck in its many possible forms.

"Memories of what kind?" I asked next.

"Nothing of my time as a powercore. You would witness my short time alive." She sighed, shifting to take hold of my hand. "Cress, before you agree to this, you have to understand that I have seen a completely different side of Phaeron. Centuries before you were even born, he had a better life, a higher place in society, and a family I witnessed him love deeply. He..." She choked on emotion for a moment and bowed her head, whispering the rest. "He was my adopted father."

I squeezed her fingers, sensing she was loosening the cork on some emotions she'd bottled up and buried deep. "I didn't know that," I murmured.

"Since my death, it has been easier for us both not to acknowledge what came before. And he has not confronted me as such...but my keeping him contained alongside his brother for so long has clearly dampened any love he used to feel for me," she said, sounding miserable.

"You were trying to protect him when you thought he might turn into a monster." I could see why she thought she owed him the most desperate measure she could reach for. "He's barely had time to process what happened to him. I'm sure he will come around to forgiving you for doing what you thought was necessary. I was just thinking he'd prefer to die than become unnatural..."

"I know. And you're right, he would," she replied.

As my hand slowly warmed hers, the other thing she said sank in. About Phaeron having a family he loved centuries ago... There was someone before Morgana. Of course there was. I wasn't sure exactly how old he was, but it made sense for there to be other women in his past. Still, I knew if we did this, it would be hard to see a happier version of him with someone of his own kind and a *family*. Dimensional kids.

Braza heard my thoughts, of course. "As an immortal culture, my people avoid talking about past mates in much depth, like humans dodge discussing religion and wages. It's considered rude. He would never tell you what you will undoubtedly see in my memories."

I breathed an uncertain sigh. "I can't let that be the reason we don't do this. I'll get over myself if it helps Phaeron. How, exactly, does this process work?"

Her nod seemed approving. "When I died, my soul was split nearly in half. It's since become two pieces..." She gestured first to the dome of the powercore above us and then to her jellylike body. "This gives me the option to empower you with one piece when you need it. I will need to leave a sigil on your person like Phaeron did with his mark of protection, except this one will create a significant tether between our souls."

"So you're saying...this has connected me to Phaeron's soul all along?" I asked, pointing to the circular rune he'd left on my wrist. I'd never quite understood how it worked.

"The tiniest thread, yes. Its only function is supposed to be a tug on his awareness when you need his attention. I've been abusing it a smidge." She gave me a brief fanged smile.

"My mark will be larger and will glow when active. I suggest you put it on your back. I can try giving you something stylized, like a set of wings."

I agreed to that readily when she mimicked how large a tattoo we were talking about. It would take up the majority of my shoulder blades.

"As I create the mark on you, you will experience my memories. It will take only an hour of real time at most, but you will feel like years have passed. The truly dangerous part is that at the end, a surge of power will ring out to supernatural senses attuned to dimensional magic. We will project a buffet for Myuna to salivate over. Madigan did not tell you directly, but Hana has seen that this moment will trigger an all-out attack on the library."

"Okay, right, well..." I stammered. "We have to prepare for that fight before you and I do this. I think we should, though, when the time is right."

"I agree. I mean you no offense, but when you are forced into combat against Phaeron, you will stand no chance without me. He has had lifetimes with blades in his hands, while you have had months at most. But with us tethered, I will be able to fight him with you. I was once Phaeron's most devoted shadowborn pupil." She smiled sadly at that.

"I'm not sure your memories will turn me into a swordswoman of his caliber—"

"No, but you will be able to carry me like you have a shadowborn form of your own. I can augment your movements with dimensional speed and grace and indicate the patterns of his fighting style. My reflexes will protect you properly."

For a moment, I had a sinking suspicion that I had no idea what I was truly agreeing to. My eyes narrowed. "What can this new partnership do for you?"

"There are no sinister motives here. But I suppose you have realized...I am capable of the same kind of haunting and bodily control Endaeron is. His abilities were my inspiration to experiment with my own capabilities." She held up a clawed finger while I shifted uncomfortably. "However, I still have a home here. When half of me is not with you, it will return here. Endaeron does not have the luxury of any other vessel than the victims he possesses."

"And you said this is permanent?" I asked.

She tilted her head, undoubtedly reading all the concerns underneath that question. Things I was too polite to say aloud because she was still a friend and I didn't truly believe she was trying to trick me. "I give you my unbreakable vow as a dimensional traveler and an ancient power-core that I will not possess you against your will or do you and yours harm. I only propose a partnership for our mutual benefit."

I cleared my throat, both embarrassed and relieved that she'd cut straight through my fears. "Thank you."

WITH OUR NEW REINFORCEMENTS, we attempted to kill the rest of the greater unnatural creatures still held in the library. The blue-skinned dimensional—the teleporting, unnatural one—beat us to two of them, but we caught him by surprise the next time and killed him. The remaining monsters died before evening's fall.

There was little time to rest, though. We started setting traps on the ground floor of the library, knocking over stacks and scattering books and broken glass as part of our efforts to slow down the dozens of monsters and "zombified" supernaturals that would be coming for us the moment we triggered Myuna's greed.

According to Grant's intel, we were racing the clock more than ever. The more supernaturals Myuna turned to her side by making them white-eyed zombies, as he described them, the faster she'd be able to gather stragglers and animals to further bolster her army.

As we worked, some of my friends helped me turn over Hana's instructions.

"Perhaps he is in a deep trance. Since it's magical in nature, there has to be a trigger to snap him out of it," Áine said quietly. She and I were on book scattering duty with Wren and Willow, while Geo and Roe distributed freshly smashed glass and arranged the stacks. Roe, of course, wore her crystal armor and cracked a few smiles by getting to be the one punching the windows and walls.

Ashbough Protective Services worked around us, setting snares and other traps, hiding them under the layers of junk we set down.

All the while, there were screeches nearby as Bianca, Ben, and Grace killed the warped birds staring at us from the nearest rooftops. It made for a disconcerting background chorus, so I tried to focus on the problem at hand.

"Why can't augurs just say what they mean?" I muttered.

"Don't be such a whiner," Wren said, rolling her eyes. "At least you have a warning."

I had to agree and check myself. Hana could've just left me to my own devices with no help. It just wouldn't hurt her to be a smidge more explicit in her instructions.

"How do you think we should go about waking Phaeron from Myuna's trance?" I asked the irritable blonde.

A frown tugged at Wren's mouth. "You know, it's

almost funny. Most spells or tonics we have access to are for inducing sleep, not waking someone up. Since we'd never guess what trigger phrase or spell Myuna has used..." She pondered, biting her lip. "We could lock him in a containment room until her magic runs its course."

I was already shaking my head. "If he's not placed into stasis, he'll be able to escape without much trouble."

"Well, that's an option. Her influence should fade if we manage to kill her."

Áine spoke up. "Maybe if we teamed up and beat him soundly?"

I stifled a sigh. That sounded like a great way to get several people killed, Phaeron included. But it seemed the only options we had were the not-so-good ones.

"Well, there is something else I could try," Áine said when we didn't jump immediately at her first idea. "Remember after we fought the Hunger the first time... Phaeron swore an admission of debt to me?"

My brow furrowed. That first near-deadly fight seemed like it'd happened ages ago, not months. "Did he?"

"Yeah. More specifically, it was a debt of gratitude for healing him, which is the most benign-seeming debt you can swear to a fae." She had an impish little smile. If it weren't for her deer legs and poofy tail, I could forget Áine was one of the fair folk. But with an expression like that... she was clearly versed in the kind of trickery that had formed legends about her kind.

"Can you call in a debt while he's entranced?" Willow asked, her own face pursed in deep thought while we spoke.

"I can always try," the faun answered. "If the trance is not tied with a soul debt, he should immediately respond."

Willow seemed in, at least. "What can you ask for?"

"That's where it's tricky. I could hit him with the direct one we want. 'To show your gratitude to me, wake up and say my name.' But he could fall back under Myuna's sway immediately afterward if he needs longer than a split second to fight her control." Áine tapped her lips thoughtfully, standing aside while we finished scattering the last few books for this corner of the library.

"To show your gratitude to me, release yourself from Myuna's control?" I suggested.

"It has to be something he can reasonably do on his own on the spot," she said, shaking her head and shaking loose a few flower petals from the sad-looking blooms woven into her long curls. "Mother Tree, I don't want to do this, but...I could hit him with one of the banes of the long-lived. Before you all ask, those are experience, memory, and wisdom."

I was glad I wasn't the only one looking at her in bafflement. Willow and I exchanged a glance. "Can you explain more than that?" asked our soft-spoken friend.

"All right, fine. Most people think swearing a debt of gratitude is formally promising a fae a favor. Honorable fae would never ask for something that would actively harm another when the origin of the debt is, well, a *thank you*. But when you're immortal, like a fae, vampire, demigod, or dimensional, certain things are made more unpleasant by the passage of long stretches of time. It would not hurt Phaeron if I asked for him to recount every time and place he's ever taken a sip of water, but he would be really fucking angry with me when he was compelled to speak continuously for however long it took to do it," she explained.

"Could you actually do that?" I asked out of sheer curiosity.

She adjusted one of the flowers in her hair, causing it to bloom vibrantly again from a tiny touch of magic. "I mean, yeah. But I like him, so I think I will use the much shorter but just as baneful 'Remember yourself.' There's an old fae story about a villainous king who was defeated by those very words. He stood in place, paralyzed by years and years of things he'd forgotten all crushing his head at once. Ripe for the deposing and such. All the Crystal Court fae are going to roll their eyes, but if I have to, that's the gratitude I'd ask of Phaeron."

"Okay, that's cliché as hell, but it just might work," I said. We'd probably try some variation of all three; holding him in stasis, beating the hell out of him, and paralyzing him with memories. Though we continued to mull over possibilities as we worked, nothing else jumped out as a better solution.

Madigan wanted me to become Guardian of Moongrove Library tomorrow morning, when our enemies would be at their weakest after a full night of scavenging. More importantly, they would not have the Hungering Darkness, with Garroway's weakness to sunlight preventing him from making the trip here.

That left enough time to eat, worry a hole in the floor of the room I lived in with my men, and ignore Ben's offer to tumble into bed together until I went to retrieve Geo from his post in the shadows of the first floor. A pair of better-rested witches were already standing guard with him and helped me convince him to take the night off.

One round of sharing later, I fell into an uneasy sleep and woke blearily. Someone was going around knocking on doors.

"Sun's up! Let's go!" exclaimed a muffled voice that sounded like Orthus.

I headed down to the powercore chamber while everyone else refreshed themselves on battle stations and last-minute planning. Too nervous to eat any rations, I sipped on a bottle of water as the elevator descended. In as little as an hour, I would see Phaeron again...then we would see if he would be mine, Myuna's, or no one's.

I'd gotten fully equipped for this fight, wearing the haggard hybrid witch garb I'd since washed after wearing it new to appear before the Crown Council. I had my sword on one hip and my handbook flapping with uncharacteristic silence over my shoulder. My familiars accompanied me as well, ready to lend their small contributions to the battle ahead. When the cabin arrived on the correct floor, I picked up Wren's sun staff from where I'd leaned it against the wall. Its centerpiece and gold paint sparkled from just my touch.

It was a fairly bygone conclusion that Phaeron would appear in the powercore chamber looking for me once Myuna noticed the tether between Braza and me falling into place. Together, we would exude the kind of power the goddess wanted to devour, all light and dimensional might.

"Just like with the ritual...and putting ancestral magic in my book," I muttered to myself. "Everything that follows this is a gamble and a guess."

I marched myself into Braza's inner chamber before I could back out of our agreement. I trusted her and showed it by taking off a layer of clothing and lying down on her bed so she could start to etch magic onto the skin of my bare back.

There was a pinch of pain, then Braza saying, "If you feel drowsy, don't resist..."

Her memories came flooding in the moment I closed my eyes.

16

BRAZA

MY MOST DISTANT memories of life begin some short time after my birth. Mercifully, not with the death of my parents, but with a hazy recollection of the patterns of whimsical creatures painted on a wall. I was in a holding house, a rare unwanted orphan who took to staring at the illustrations next to the tiny bed where I regularly tucked my legs under my chin and covered myself with my wings.

I was a miserable child. All orphans of my kind are, especially those too young to realize they were cut off from the embrace of the *animaris* of their birth parents.

But I was probably the worst example of what went wrong when separated from that essence too early. I was an animal who would bite the hands of adults who wanted to treat me kindly. My claws would extend with magic, strange, overlong, and black against the blush red of my skin. The same claws that'd saved me from sharing the fate of my parents had a parade of adults leaving the holding house with disgust, calling me "unnatural."

All that changed when a different-looking person visited. She didn't immediately try to pick me up like I was one of the brightly colored toys piled up against the far wall.

Instead, she'd sat a tail-length from my bed, with me hunched on it. "Hello, little one," she'd said gently. I didn't reply, only inspecting her with a child's curiosity over the line of my knees.

She was from the Moihan tribe, the first one I'd ever seen, with feminine features exaggerated by a dusting of silver on her cheekbones and eyelids, around eyes that glowed crimson from within. Her glossy black hair was neatly pinned to stop just behind the thin curves of her spiraled horns.

She was dressed really nicely. The fall of red and silver fabric complimented her gray skin and stopped just short of her ankles and small, pointed shoes. Gems glittered on her fingers. That kind of finery didn't belong in this holding house, on the floor where so many adults had already stood and gone.

When I didn't reply or move, she smiled and pulled a book from the folds of her skirts. "I have a daughter your age and brought a book of her favorite stories. Perhaps you would like to hear one?" she offered.

I gave her the barest of nods and listened as she cracked open the first page and began to read to me. Her voice was its own magic, luring me to her. I watched the pictures seem to dance on the pages from where I sat on the soft textured fabric of her dress.

When the story was over and the title of the next stood out as she flipped the page, my eyes widened as I realized where I'd moved to. I froze, but she didn't do more than turn her red gaze my way.

"Did you like the story?" she asked. I nodded mutely. "Would you like me to read the next one?"

Shyly, I shook my head no. I didn't trust this pretty Moihan woman. She accepted my answer and told me her name, Keshora et Sudaira, and smiled wide in motherly amusement as I whispered mine back. "Bwaza."

"I'll visit you tomorrow, Braza."

I'd learn later that her title meant Keshora, mate of the second prince. My backwater town had never seen a noble Moihan before. They viewed the shadowy gray peoples of their tribe and the chilly blue Vrassorm with heavy suspicion.

In retrospect, I recognized I was caught under the same web of scorn with my barely restrained shadow powers. Those claws of mine, contrasted with my Iorsio heritage, were why none of the red-skinned townsfolk wanted anything else to do with me.

They were also part of the reason why Keshora returned the next day, this time with her daughter. Her kindly presence was overshadowed by Ravai, who, in that time, always wore her hair in a high tail with a bow of red fabric that matched her eyes. The immediacy of our friendship started at first sight. It was an anam cara bond all the way in another world, when two lonely girls became immediate best friends.

Ravai and I sat and played the day away while Keshora bargained with the bitter matron who ran the holding houses for orphans and the sick in town. The perfect day ended with Keshora seizing Ravai's arm and leaving in a whirlwind, with the matron muttering about "Moihan scum" once the door closed behind them.

THE DAYS in that holding house were made lengthy by my young age. It couldn't have been too long before Keshora and Ravai returned, but they'd brought someone else too. One moment, I was bored and alone, and the next, Ravai was in my room like a burst of color. She pulled me by the hand to come meet her father.

"You're coming home with us today!" she said gleefully, listing all the fun things *home* entailed as we headed into the front room of the house.

"Really?" I wasn't so sure I'd be released to go, not with all the bad names the matron had called her and her mother.

The matron's tune had apparently changed when face-to-face with a prince, though. My first impression of Phaeron et Sudair was of the shadows that moved with him as he spoke and gestured, deep in conversation with the matron. They eddied around his boots and added extra coils where his tail twined companionably with Keshora's. They stood together across a counter from the Iorsio woman.

He was offering her a stack of coins, but his fingers made a cage over them. The shadows suggested claws like mine.

I'd never seen the matron so nervous. "The people of this town have never seen her like before. It *is* unnatural for her to have a Moihan power," she was saying.

"All the more reason she should be raised by a family that understands her abilities," he replied.

Ravai ran up to him and tugged on his cloak. "Dad, Dad! Look, I got Braza!"

He picked her up with a coil of shadow, affectionately pressing foreheads with her before passing her to Keshora. I was next, weightless for a moment, until he sat me on the counter next to the money. I inspected him with shy wonder. Dark blue stain dusted his cheeks and marked runes and patterns over each section of his spiraled horns.

He was Moihan-strange, and were I a bold, outgoing child like Ravai, I'd have rubbed one of the patterns on his horns because I wondered if they were permanent. But it was his eyes that fascinated me. Slitted and yellow, they were familiar in a way the rest of him was not. I'd later learn he was half Iorsio himself, and while hybrids didn't truly exist in our world, he'd still inherited his mother's flame-inspired eyes.

Phaeron held out a palm full of shadows that curled and billowed like a small black fire. He didn't say anything, but his power called to mine, and I played with it like it was putty, squashing and stretching it. Everyone watched me, the Moihan family with understanding and the matron with fear.

"She is shadowborn," he said.

With a wiggle of his fingertips, the crude wing shape I'd made became a pair of them. They took flight around my head, and I giggled despite myself when they tugged my hair.

I missed warm wing hugs and the vague memories of a mother who would envelop me completely. Moihan didn't have wings, but still, the matron allowed my adoption and even waved with the money in her other hand as I became the fourth member of the second prince's family.

PHAERON RETURNED to an ongoing war once we arrived at the capital. The location would become my home, but at first, it seemed far too big as we traveled through it to the palace.

The capital had sprung up around the crater of Myuna the White's landing spot, curved like a crescent moon. Unlike the town they'd plucked me from, it was mixed with all three tribes co-existing and inter-mating with almost no judgment.

They placed me in a bedroom with Ravai, and we grew older and closer together. Those days were a blissful haze of dress-up and tasty food. Keshora became "Mom," and even though she couldn't give me wing hugs, she still treated me as if I were Ravai's pinkish-red double.

I knew of Phaeron only from their stories of him. The first prince—his twin, Endaeron—was even more vaguely a family member. My white-skinned cousins were adult age and served as torchbearers, so I only saw them at formal dinners and observed some uncomfortable family dynamics during those times. The king and queen merely tolerated one another and slavishly loved our goddess and the first prince's family, who were all blessed by Myuna down to their unnatural coloring.

Mom relied on Ravai and me to tolerate years of over-sight, calling us *Ravita* and *Brazita* affectionately. We were the shadows that balanced Myuna's light, her less favored subjects, and even as a child, I noticed the goddess looked at Keshora specifically with something less than kind in her gaze.

THE TWIN PRINCES returned when there were two red stars above Soiluire, an auspicious sign that followed their victory. I was to meet my adopted father again when it was starting to become obvious that Ravai and I were of different tribes. She'd grown tall-ish with skinny limbs and a tail just long enough to trip over, with me a head shorter and broader than her with my wings to add to the effect. I, too, tripped over my tail in graceless moments, though.

We wore silver on our faces for the occasion and dusted up Mom's cheeks and horns for her a little too zealously. The reunion happened at a banquet for our soldiers, with Myuna and the king and queen sitting at the head of the table. In those times, Myuna did not eat, and it seemed she did not need to.

The first prince arrived at the table before Phaeron, as was tradition. He was a broad Iorsio man, his skin and hair bleached white from the goddess's touch. His mate anointed his face and horns with gold as our people cheered. He was Endaeron et Myudair, the crown prince blessed by Myuna, and the love in the room for him was palpable.

Ravai practically vibrated with her excitement as the celebration for the first prince lulled and he took his seat. We both turned in our chairs as Phaeron joined the celebration. He emerged from a whirl of shadows, casually showcasing his shadowborn powers so close to the goddess.

He and Mom touched foreheads and murmured together before she brushed dark blue powder over his high cheekbones and slid a heavy signet ring back onto his finger. The crowd loved the second prince too. They cheered for him when Mom took his hair out of its tail and twisted it to pin behind his horns. The ritual showed that he was no longer at war, and now that both princes were returned to their finery and families, the feasting could begin.

I didn't have much to say to Phaeron, ever the quieter child next to Ravai. She chattered away about our palace life and schooling for me when he asked, the buffer I needed when he was akin to a myth in my life, the man who'd intimidated my old matron into allowing me to be adopted into a Moihan family.

"I have a surprise for you all," he said, smiling with all his fangs. "Endaeron and I have bought an estate far from here to retire to. It will be a school for shadowborn...as I have noticed neither of you have been educated in your extra powers."

Mom was delighted immediately, while my heart sank like I'd done something wrong. Was I supposed to be practicing with my shadows more? They were mere wisps compared to the power he seemed to have at his fingertips. She occupied his time with questions about where, exactly, the family would be escaping to and how often they'd have to return.

"As infrequently as you prefer, my heart," he'd replied in an undertone.

Mom suggested something that had me shifting shyly late into the banquet. They were both deep into their cups, and while he fed her bits of fruit from his fingers, she leaned heavily against him and drew sigils on his horns all crookedly. Between giggles, she said, "Why don't you take the girls to our new home? I've had them to myself for years. I'll follow behind with our things."

IT WAS a great idea once we figured out the awkwardness of absence in the long carriage ride to our new home. Ravai sat on her hands and clamped her jaw so I could get to know the man who would be my father better. He was smart, athletic, and so very powerful. I ended the trip giddy to finally finish the animaris ritual with him and Mom and become their child by soul and essence.

I held a twist of fragile hope in hand for the days we waited for Mom to arrive. Phaeron had gone quiet sometime in the hours before and during a family dinner, staring into the middle distance with his food untouched. He kept rubbing at his shoulder.

I picked at my meal too, sensing something was wrong but not the scope of it. A servant burst into the room and held the door open, startling all of us. Phaeron jumped to his feet, hand on the hilt of his sword, when in stepped a familiar Moihan man. The family's head of security, who was supposed to protect the caravan of our valuables.

He placed a shrouded body on the floor and dropped to his knees. "My sudair," he said in a broken voice.

Ravai and I exchanged frightened looks. I recognized the general shape of the body and its curved horns.

"I-it happened suddenly—"

"Stop. Use some sense," Phaeron hissed. "There are children."

The head of security looked up, noticed Ravai and me for the first time, and lowered himself further. Phaeron beckoned to us, and we went to him, dinner laying forgotten on the table. His broad palm and shadowy magic covered my sight. We walked out of the room, and he closed the door behind us with his tail.

Ravai was already keening, making high sounds of mourning in her throat while her eyes shimmered with the onset of grief. I was a trembling animal next to her, my leathery wings making shivery sounds. I waited for Phaeron to tell us it wasn't the sudaira...that Mom wasn't dead.

Voice heavy, Phaeron said, "Ravita, Brazita, go back to your room. I will handle this."

Still keening, Ravai took me by the hand and tugged me away. We waited together until our room's lamp flickered with the end spurts of its oil reservoir. Phaeron let himself in. The meager light reflected the pronounced facets in his eyes.

He told us as gently as he could. Mom had died unexpectedly, her body unmarked but her skin cold and her heart stopped. There was nothing anyone could've done for her. We stayed huddled on the floor together for the rest of the night, mourning her.

The head of security continued working for Phaeron at the Royal Shadowborn School. Gossip spread amongst the staff and students about Mom's unexpected death and led me to take a peek under her eyelids before she was buried to see if the rumors were true. They were. Her pupils were gone, leaving her eyes flat circles darkened to maroon. I didn't tell Phaeron I'd seen them, but the sight haunted me for years.

Soon after the funeral, he took me aside and held out a flower with gleaming blue petals. In a world of darkness, it was one of the only pieces of flora that dared to shine as bright as our eyes. I keened low in my throat when I took the bloom, knowing it was Mom's favorite.

"I know we don't know each other well yet," Phaeron said carefully. "But your mother's love for you came through clearly in every letter she wrote to me. It is my duty to care for everything she cherished."

He'd knelt before me so I wasn't craning my head. I felt a familiar glimmer of hope as I stared into his flickering Iorsio-inspired eyes, but dread threaded through me at the possibility he was going to send me away.

"Without her, I cannot 'properly' adopt you, but I would like to be your father all the same. You and Ravai deserve to grow up together." He put his hand over the one I used to hold the flower's stem.

"I would like that," I said in a small voice. I hugged him fiercely when he scooped me up, our foreheads touching briefly in affectionate acknowledgment of one another. He was my father from then on.

Dad treated Ravai and me the same as time passed. He loved us in his own way, as the one to personally tutor us with blade and shadows alike. The other instructors thought we were child prodigies, but it was really endless drills and a ruthless regime of early wakeups and long dinner conversations about values and strategy.

As we grew into our adult bodies, Ravai and I had our petty little rivalries, but we were still the definition of inseparable. We were the star pupils of the Royal Shadowborn Academy. Other students would gather to watch our rooftop duels, the same as when Dad and Endaeron would get a wild hair and show off their skills with battles of blades and black and white shadows. Those days, my sister and I always wore shadowborn black.

I HAD a quiet dislike for the garish white shade of Myuna and her followers even before the Age of Decay. But the day it started, it became the color of death and betrayal. The teachers and students had paired off in the school's court-yard for practice duels. It was a completely mundane morn-ing...until it wasn't.

Myuna's soul feast was marked by a palpable shift in the air. I'd felt it like a creep of dread across my scalp, step-ping away from Dad mid-practice duel to gaze at the sky and then across the courtyard, where the other students were edging back from a flash of bone white.

Endaeron writhed on the ground, his claws sunk into his head and his wings tangled around him. Ravai had placed her sword aside and turned him over in a misplaced effort to help him as corrupted magic started to twist and rend his skin and bone apart.

"Ravai! Get away from him!" Dad screamed.

Even then, he'd been suspicious of Myuna, but he couldn't have predicted that she'd empower and corrupt my uncle's soul the way she had. He became the Hungering Darkness as a flash of white mist, abandoning his ruined body to jump into Ravai's. And then he hopped into several more bystanders, leaving behind soulless corpses and further spreading panic.

Dad personally killed the last student Endaeron jumped into, panting with shock and horror as the kid slumped to the ground. Not knowing the true evil Endaeron had become yet, we both thought we'd lost him and Ravai in the same breath. I saw her eyes, chilled by the pupil-less maroon circles staring across the grass at nothing.

"Her eyes...like Mom," I stammered out, giving away the secret I'd held within all that time.

"*Myuna*," Dad growled, hatred turning his face into a snarling mask.

Myuna had killed Mom. We still didn't know why, and we never would; everything happened so fast after the Age of Decay kicked off.

We received word from the growing stream of survivors fleeing to the school. Myuna had consumed countless others, first reaping the capital city and moving outward from there. Her ghostly torchbearers brought her feast to her. Murdered and twisted by her magic, just like my uncle, they were immune to common weapons yet were cut down easily by shadowborn claws.

Thanks to this, we hosted a refuge for survivors, and amongst them, the Hungering Darkness lurked unseen, biding its time. No one was untouched by loss and grief. Most faces were unmarked of colored dust and paint, wiped clean a final time after the deaths of mates and loved ones. Chief amongst them was my father, who dressed for war each day and cleared paths to the school for survivors, cutting down unnaturals with ruthless fury.

I went with him every time I could, afraid he'd get himself killed with the single-minded rage that'd consumed him. The two of us made for an unstoppable team. With my help, he returned to the Royal Shadowborn Academy every day, usually with a new group of survivors in tow.

Though I was still just a teen, I was a witness to history by my father's side. When it became obvious killing monsters would never be enough to stop Myuna's single-minded consumption of our people, he sought the insight of others.

"There must be a way to defeat her," he would say at the beginning of each meeting with the most intelligent of us left. It would kick off hours of debate and ideas.

It was Auric et Vess who came up with a mad plan that just might work. He was a Vrassorm man and an old political friend of my father's. Unfortunately, for it to work, they needed the help of a vicious rival in the Iorsio woman Mencha et Syroni. Complete with Dad, they were the most powerful survivors of the three tribes.

We could escape through the Void and deny Myuna our souls by heading to a different world far from her reach. As a Vess, Auric would bend the Void to allow them through.

Dad's shadows would protect us, while Mencha's flame would light our way forward. All tribespeople with magic would follow their lead to magnify their abilities for the long journey.

"Shall we do it, my prince?" Auric asked. Everyone looked to Dad for direction now that the king, queen, first prince, and my cousins were all deceased. The second prince, who would be king if he stood still for a coronation. I stood at his right side at each meeting, trying to hide the fear from my face to look tough and capable.

Dad agreed. We gathered everyone we could and left, stepping into the nothingness between worlds. The magic of the Void marked us as we spent an unknowable amount of time walking and walking and walking without fatigue or rest. Our features and teeth smoothed out to better resemble humans', the dominant species of the world we approached. The mark of language and humanity appeared on the membrane of my wing, while the same one showed up on Dad's back and random places for everyone else.

These subtle changes were beautiful to us, but when we made first contact with humans...they were horrified by our appearances, calling us demons and fracturing the alliances within our peoples.

Most of the Iorsio tribespeople followed Mencha in becoming the monsters they decried us as. She preached that we were larger and more powerful than humans could ever dream. *Why not prove our superiority by enslaving them?* She led her followers away in disgust when Dad met and fell in love with a human woman.

Morgana was present when the Hungering Darkness started making one of my school friends act erratically. I barely remember the actual circumstances of my death, come to think of it, only bits and pieces as moments fractured into frayed strands.

The agony of having Endaeron's teeth ripping my soul into two messy pieces.

Blood spattering me when Dad killed my assailant.

His panicked face swimming in and out of my sight.

"Stay with me, Brazita," he'd begged, gathering me in his arms.

We pressed foreheads for a final time, my labored breathing and erratic heartbeat proving I was already three limbs in the grave.

I still gasped out a request and a consent to something I barely understood as my tattered soul unhooked from my body and my pupils smeared into the dull gold of my still eyes.

17

CRESS

"And that is how I became the powercore of Moongrove Library."

Braza was seated on the ground by my head as I came to and jolted upright with a twinge in my shoulders. I didn't know who I was for a minute, confused to see my teenaged dimensional face rendered in black and purple energy looking back at me.

Empathy flooded my eyes in the next moment. "My god, you weren't even my age when you died," I said.

She handed me the clothes I'd shed so she could mark my back, and I put them on, letting the fabric absorb my tears. Her life was already fading some, becoming a stream that flowed together separately from my own memories. I knew I would have a difficult time for a while reminding myself that I was *not* Braza and had never lived the life of an orphan turned almost-princess of Soiluire.

I was still Cress, an orphan turned librarian-celestial witch hybrid. I had a whole coven of good friends, all waiting for me to finish up here. Plus an adopted sister, Carly, who I was still worried about.

Braza had a best friend and sister named Ravai... Phaeron's daughter. He hadn't breathed a word of her or Keshora, but I'd *seen* how much he'd adored them. At one point, he'd doted on Braza the exact same way. Now I saw what she meant, what she feared, and why she had gone to such lengths to set me up to save him.

If we all survived this, then I would have to privately confront my feelings about seeing his former life. I was supposed to be his mate, to replace both Keshora and Morgana, but now I knew them by their accomplishments and Phaeron's love for them. It gave his slow-burn interest in me a completely different view. How did I even compare? How often did I come short in his eyes?

"I have continued to exist for several human lifetimes. It is not so bad," she answered, taking me out of my whirling thoughts.

"Stuck in one place. Never resting," I sighed, looking around at her inner chamber with new eyes. *Existing* seemed unpleasant at best.

"The last Guardian of Moongrove Library was able to take me out of the library's bounds," she said with an edge of hope to her tone.

"Then I will, too," I promised, offering her a hand up. She took it and stood, giving me a winged hug. She shrank in my hold, surrounding me in flames of black and purple shadows.

Power surged between us as the tether snapped into place. I threw my head back and screamed out a shadow-born's howl, exhilarated. The pulse of energy was unmistakable, and I felt for myself how those who could sense dimensional power would catch notice of us immediately.

We emerged from the powercore holding a sword in our dominant hand and Wren's staff in the other. The light from the tool did not damage our shadows or make them retract, as I'd seen happen with my light and Phaeron's darkness. We...*no.* I had to remind myself that I was still in charge. *I* was one coherent whole, part celestial witch, part librarian, and part shadowborn, with light and darkness swirling between my staff and sword at my will.

"Cress, tell me that's still you, kid," Madigan said. Arrayed around the chamber was a crew of her, Orthus, Geo, Áine, and most of my coven. My ghostly mother stood to the side with the cluster of my familiars, watching with a concerned expression.

"It is me," I said in a two-toned voice, mine layered with Braza's. "Plus Braza et..." I hesitated before plucking her title out of my memories. She was the second prince's adopted daughter, which made her the... "Sudairae."

"Sounds like Big P's last name," Ben commented. He had his big daggers out but a bandolier of the smaller ones for throwing at the ready over his torso.

"Title," I corrected. "Tell you about it later. It's...a lot."

Braza's shadows contracted over my skin, and through her, I sensed hundreds of monsters converging on the library. Some had two feet, an extra bad sign for us.

An alarm blared on Madigan's phone at the same time. "Incoming," she announced.

Bianca lifted her crossbow. Its loaded bolt was coated with glowing maroon. Orthus raised his hand and started manifesting sharpened crystal spikes from seemingly nowhere, and Madigan lifted her gauntleted fist to take control of them with a muttered spell. They circled over her head with slow gravity.

The fae tossed a few extra to Geo, who absorbed and reformed them with all of his quartz into a large mace to match his massive crystal shield.

"Close your eyes for a moment," Braza said in my head, using my focus and hers to comb the upper levels of the library to detect Phaeron. She knew he would enter as shadowy vapor and take the most direct route to us, solidifying in a rush to catch us off guard.

And that's exactly what he did. Her reflexes caught the strike of his sword before I even opened my eyes again. My heart threatened to stop before kicking into three times the speed. That was indeed Phaeron bearing down on me in full shadowborn form and everyone else reacting around us with shouts and fired spells.

He had one sword, the talons of his opposite hand extended into long and deadly points. It was the traditional shadowborn fighting style, to have one hand empty to weave shadows while an opponent was distracted with swordplay.

"Focus on him. Do not worry about anything else," Braza instructed. We pivoted to avoid a slice of sharpened shadows aimed to hit our back. We...I raised my left hand and blasted Phaeron with a Lux spell from the sun staff. I held the concentrated rays of sunlight out at him for a few seconds.

His talons dispelled away from the light, as did the other sneak attack he'd been manipulating from the shadows. But even as the exposed skin on his arm darkened, he didn't make a sound, not even a hiss of pain.

I struck, and he parried, the two of us engaging in a deadly dance between the fired spells and projectiles of my allies. Braza helped me find the steps to match him, her strength reinforcing my arms. Phaeron struck without an ounce of mercy. Our weapons rang with each impact, the force rattling my sword so hard it threatened to jump out of my grip.

Phaeron fought with supernatural grace to keep up with me while avoiding more than the graze of bolts and crystal spikes. My weapon skimmed his shadows and skin superficially, all made possible by the pressure we put on him at multiple angles.

Geo's obsidian form closed in from the side, shield raised. I parried another strike from Phaeron, straining as I tried to hold him steady for my gargoyle protector's charge. Suddenly, Phaeron grabbed me with tendrils of shadow, and I was hit with the vertigo of being wrenched to a different location.

For a couple precious seconds, I reeled and wavered on my feet. Thorn-studded shadows wrapped around my legs, sinking into my skin to anchor me in place. "Fuck," I muttered. A quick cast of Lux rid me of them, but the deep punctures remained, and bloody rivulets dripped down my legs.

"I will take care of it," Braza said, urging me to keep my attention on Phaeron. Her shadows flowed into the wounds, soothing and cool.

He'd taken me as far from the powercore chamber as he could carry me. The foyer of this level, with its waiting area full of chairs. I lifted one with an inexpert grab of shadows and held its legs out to keep Phaeron at bay. It caught the swing of his sword, the fabric parting like butter and the frame snapping quickly.

I flung the ruined thing at him. It clipped his shoulder, throwing off the rhythm of his footwork for a moment. Meanwhile, Braza used the telepathy of her powercore side to inform our allies of where we'd gone.

"Phaeron, stop. I don't want to hurt you," I said.

He didn't spare any acknowledgment. He seemed like an unstoppable, untiring force, while I felt the first hints of soreness and strain in my body even with Braza helping me keep up. I focused on blocking, parrying, and thrusting as darkness writhed around our feet, thrashing between his will and Braza's.

I backed into a chair and hopped up onto its cushion, spreading my wings of shadows and flapping. I put my weight behind the next strike downward. Fuchsia blood sprayed from a cut around his shoulder, quickly covered by shadows before I could determine where exactly I'd gotten him.

White shadows flicked up the side of his arm. The next thing I knew, I was landing with my ankle twisting on the unexpected arrival of stairs. I stumbled, barely catching myself on a guardrail before I could tumble down the flight we'd appeared on. Again, we hadn't gone far, but his shadowborn control was slightly stronger than Braza's. At this rate, he'd inch me up to the surface, where Myuna's monsters would help subdue me.

I lifted the staff, prepared to blast him with light. Anticipating the move, he shot out a lasso of shadow, which whipped around my left wrist and wrenched me to the side. It solidified and tightened harshly until the sun staff clattered down the stairs.

I flexed my free hand, growing shadowy talons over my fingers. Lunging at him, I moved to position myself further up the stairs than he was, taking a sharp graze on my side as he exploited the opening in my guard. Pain flared over my torso.

"*Submit,*" hissed a voice from Phaeron's mouth, unexpectedly feminine and awful.

I bared shadowy fangs and shouted with Braza, "*Never!*"

I landed a kick to the center of his chest, and he fell

backward, landing at the bottom of the stairs next to the staff, his limbs briefly still and splayed like a discarded doll's. The way he stood was also disconcerting, heaving upward like a puppeteer hadn't mastered the motion of lifting with the legs first.

I used his own trick, grabbing him in my shadows and carrying him back into the foyer, where my allies were rushing past. Ben reacted quickest and turned, launching himself at Phaeron's tail. I heard the brittle snap of bone.

"Such insolence," snapped what had to be Myuna, using Phaeron as her mouthpiece. He acknowledged another fighter for the first time in throwing Ben off and impaling him against a wall with an inky black spike.

I wanted to shout for him, but Braza suppressed me. *"He gave us an advantage,"* she said. Phaeron was off-balance when he turned his attention back to us and lunged.

Within a blink, he was slammed by a blur of obsidian and crystal. Geo had struck with his shield to the center of Phaeron's chest, and the momentum sent him crashing into a couple chairs and toppling in a boneless heap. This time, he recovered by turning into vapor and materializing again over my left shoulder. His shadowy claws cut through my back, forming several long lines of agony.

I screamed. Braza's voice in my head became white noise, and my hold on our tether faltered, making the shadows over my body flicker before they covered me again.

"We're not out of this yet," Braza encouraged.

My back ached, and it felt like most of my body was now slicked with hot blood. Yet I knew that she was right. Her shadows held together most of the damage I'd sustained so far. Power leaked into me from her powercore side, slowly knitting together the rips, scratches, and abrasions.

Phaeron's shadowy maw was open in a soundless snarl. He leapt at me and swung his free arm around my neck. The vertigo returned through multiple jumps, though I now knew the feel of his magic wrapping around me and how to fight it, my eyes closing at the right moments to stave off the worst of the dizziness.

We landed on stairs, carpeting, and tile, grappling for control all the while. He slammed me into the ground for most of our reappearances. At this rate, I'd be tenderized into submission, fractured and bruised too badly to fight back.

For one of our landings, we were in a containment room. I could've closed a stasis spell around him...but didn't. Myuna was controlling him somehow, and I was going to shake her out of him, even if it killed me and half of Braza.

As the pain mounted over my body, I started to realize that the death option was closer at hand than expected. I gained the upper hand during one reappearance and dug the edge of my sword into the shadows over his neck.

"Phaeron," I breathed out desperately. "It's me, Cress. Stop, Phaeron. Stop fighting me."

"*Oh no, pretty thing. He's taking you straight to me,*" Myuna purred. Well, it was supposed to be a smooth sound, but she had a voice like a cheese grater to my senses. "*I'll only wake him up so we can see how prettily he begs before I consume you.*" Shadows grasped and moved us to another location, and his muscular weight pinned my hips.

Braza noted the wording as we struggled. This time, I pulled him into my shadows, still trying to drag him back toward my allies. I could practically feel the lightbulb moment she had.

"Tell me you have a good idea," I said, struggling to raise my sword to block another blow. It felt like my whole body had been pummeled—I gasped for a decent breath. Under her shadows, I had to be black and blue.

"Do you trust me?" she replied.

"Down to my soul," I answered. I'd *been* her, seen her true character. There was no doubt in me when she told me her idea, and I seized it. I let her turn my body into shadowy mist, and together we went up several levels to throw off Phaeron and Myuna.

We were close enough to the surface to hear the sounds of fighting. Dust shook from the ceiling from a surge of guardian witch power, followed by either Aaron or Ajax shouting commands.

The part of me that was tethered to the powercore marked Phaeron's position as he realized what we'd done and turned into vapor. He approached our location rapidly.

I lifted and circled my sword over my head, casting the rune for the strongest light-based spell I knew just as Phaeron appeared before me. His sword and claws bit into my body as my skin heated. I'd once likened Luminare to a ground-level firework, but that was before I tapped into my celestial side.

Light erupted from my body and weapon, which I angled under his chin. Against the glare of my magic, I witnessed Phaeron's shadows blow away completely and saw his face. He was literally asleep, but his eyelids flipped open as he took the brunt of my spell head-on. For a split second, I admired the way his irises sparkled like cut gemstones before every inch of his exposed skin torched.

Phaeron stumbled back, screaming in agony and

covering his face with similarly burned and blistered hands. His sword clattered to the floor, followed by his knees as he heaved an eerily inhuman howl and rocked back and forth.

I let the tip of my weapon hit the ground, desperately hoping we were done fighting.

The sounds of battle above us faded...or maybe muted from the force of his cries. "Shit, I'm so sorry," I said. Though Braza and I still spoke together, that was wholly my own reaction.

He quieted and stole a look at me through his fingers. Those remarkable eyes I loved so much had pupils slitted like a cat's, narrowed to the thinnest of slivers.

"*Brazita?*" he asked with a hush of disbelief. She translated his foreign words through her shadows and into my ears as English. "Have I finally joined you on the other side?"

A monster released a piercing death cry above us on cue, and more dust showered from the ceiling. Phaeron's hands dropped from his burned face, and he fumbled for the hilt of his sword blindly, shaking his head with a wince. "Clearly there is no such mercy, as paradise would not have Myuna's servants."

He slid onto his feet, tail and weapon scraping the ground as he limped a step. "Phaeron, wait. You're hurt," I protested.

He huffed and struggled on. "I cannot understand your human tongue." Then, seeming to get frustrated with his body's damage, he disappeared into shadowy vapor and headed straight for the combat above us.

Braza and I both rolled our eyes with exasperation. "*That's the prince I know,*" she said before misting us up after him. She took care of telling my coven still rushing in our wake what'd happened and where to go.

In the meantime, I arrived to see our allies had been pushed back to the first-floor stairwell. The sounds and spells were like arriving in the middle of a warzone, and disoriented, it took me longer than it should've to locate Phaeron slicing the nearest unnatural in half. He released a threatening roar and threw some of his own blood toward the monsters to gather their attention.

"Shit," I muttered under my breath, lurching into motion to protect his back when he was quickly overrun. This type of fighting felt too familiar. In another life, he and Braza had fought swarms of unnaturals under all kinds of circumstances and won. The creatures threw themselves at us, sensing easy prey and meeting a swift death because of it.

What felt like minutes later, the onslaught paused, monsters freezing and then pacing away from us. Soon they were in full retreat, leaving behind a gory mess. Myuna seemed to realize she was losing servants much faster than she'd corrupted them.

Phaeron turned to me, his head tilting and expression uncertain. "We must burn the remains. Myuna can still gather energy by eating what's left behind," he said in the foreign syllables of his language, and Braza kept translating it.

I repeated his wisdom in English in a two-toned voice, drawing glances of surprise and distrust from the defenders who'd survived the onslaught. With a sigh, I released my tether with Braza, lamenting the lack of her power and support immediately. I wavered on my feet and felt my skin pull in multiple places as wounds in the process of healing reopened. "I said, we have to burn the remains." A slur crept into my voice.

Grace was the first to react. "Hate to point it out, but we're in a library," she snarked.

"Well...we made this mess. Might as well clean it up." The tired voice was clearly Aaron's by his forced cheer. His more serious twin was already kicking glass shards into a pile.

"Cress?" Phaeron eyed me top to bottom, his brow knit in confusion. He clearly still knew my name but rolled the *R* and hissed the rest, making it harder to recognize. He... hadn't realized it was me under Braza's shadows?

Maybe he was just horrifically mixed up from his whole ordeal, tortured from sleep to waking.

"And look who's back with us." Aaron, to my horror, came over to clap Phaeron on the shoulder. Phaeron winced and hissed in earnest. "Oh...damn, can I get a medic?" he called out.

Narrowing his eyes, the dimensional shook his head and gestured toward his ears. "I know. I see it now. How'd you get burned like that?" Aaron asked.

Phaeron seemed to give up and flicked out his tongue, which was now forked at the end. "He had a translation spell break," I explained for him. I inched closer, staring at his mouth in fascination. He gazed back, catlike pupils resizing.

I put on an exaggerated grin, hoping he got the message. He bared his fangs back at me and...*holy shit*, he had a mouth full of sharp teeth, reminding me of a dog's dentition. Now that I'd noticed, it was obvious that whatever the Void had done to him to make him more human had worn off, sharpening his features at unusual angles and making him that much more alien.

I remembered his many fangs from the haze of Braza's memory, but it was more real to see it in person. His expression relaxed, and he dragged himself forward a limping step, cupping my cheek and jaw. I sighed out at the familiar rasp of his calluses and even the less familiar points of his more solid, curved claws following the pads of his fingers.

He didn't speak, but he didn't have to. He was clearly somewhere between affection, admiration, and disbelief. If he could, I think he'd kiss me, then tell me off for ignoring his every warning and saving him anyway.

When the "medic," a verdant witch doctor still in his scrubs, arrived to tend to him, Phaeron cut a sideways glare before realizing why the man was interrupting our moment. He sighed out something and took my shoulder, pushing me toward the doctor.

"Wait, you first," I protested, even though I was feeling increasingly lightheaded.

He held me in front of him stubbornly. "You first," he echoed with effort.

The doctor began to heal the worst of my injuries with flashes of green and brown magic. "He will need to head to the hospital anyway," he told me in an undertone. "Actually...wow, you should as well."

I hadn't heard a doctor say "wow" before about any illness or injury I'd had. My whole body throbbed and stung with previously ignored hurts. I was going to have one hell of a full-body bruise if I didn't do as this doctor said.

I turned to Phaeron and pointed to the light outside the now-windowless library. "Hospital," I said slowly.

He frowned and shook his head, not understanding. I gestured between us, then pointed outside again.

"Allow me to assist. She wants to take you to a hospital, my prince," Braza said, somehow speaking in both our languages at the same time.

Phaeron grunted. Nice to know that sound was just a universal man thing.

18

BEN

THERE WAS a lull in the patrols of unnaturals—big fucking surprise there—so several of us traipsed to the hospital. Along with their general injuries, Phaeron had patches of second- and third-degree burns, and Cress needed a blood transfusion, so they were both in a medically induced sleep as they recovered. I checked on Lucas, just to see that he was still deep in a coma.

I'd never felt so worthless than when I was waiting around for one of the trio to wake up. I'd taken a bet with Geo on who it would be first. "It'll be Cress. She's the least injured of them," I'd reasoned.

"Phaeron, so I can knock him unconscious again for harming Cress," Geo had grumbled. I'd cast him a worried glance. He and Phaeron had been getting along pretty well until this confrontation.

That conversation had been before Geo disappeared with Wren to appear on her stream. The population of supernaturals watching was swelling dramatically each time Wren went live. Tish had set up her laptop in the waiting room to monitor the chat and donations, setting it on an end table so I could listen in with the gaggle of women I'd ended up hanging out with: Bianca, Grace, and Tish.

Geo had a presence in his gargoyle form, and his big, gravelly personality was quickly becoming a fan favorite. Wren was interviewing him as they toured the area outside, showing the blockades Ashbough Protective Services had put in. It was a little post-apocalyptic from the lingering bloodstains on the sidewalk and the way the streets were cracked and rucked up from the use of guardian witch magic.

Bianca and Grace weren't all that interested in watching, while I faded in and out of their conversation and the stream, distracted. "Why a Medusa head?" Bianca was asking about the pin the two unnatural hunters wore.

"It's not Medusa," Tish practically squeaked. Her whole expression lit up from the question. "The Furies also had snakes for hair."

"That's the name of our group within Chaos Inc.," Grace supplied.

"Because we're harbingers of *vengeance* and *death* for the wicked." Tish seemed entirely too small a lady to be a harbinger of anything. "Grace is like Alecto, an unyielding hunter of criminals."

"Unnaturals," Grace added in her rough purr, barely getting the word in edgewise.

"While I'm Tisiphone—"

"Literally her name," said her partner. Tish wrinkled her nose and gave Grace a shove, not like she could budge the more muscular shifter. "Word to the wise, don't ask Tish about Greek mythology unless you have a couple hours to spare. She was raised reciting the myths and shit."

"Weren't there three Furies?" I put in.

Tish nodded. "We're still waiting to meet our Megaera, punisher of oathbreakers."

She opened a tab beside the stream playing on her laptop. Occasionally she would go back to a random tab and type something in; she had what looked to be twenty tabs and a few programs she was multitasking between. I was rather impressed by the glimpse of how she seemed to be able to view several surveillance cameras still running in Cerris City at once.

The newest tab was for showing us her art. Most of her style was rather cutesy, but it was all about putting a modern spin on Greek myths. She'd drawn the Fury head they wore, with its snarl and spitting snakes.

We spent a few hours together until I was about to bounce my kneecap off my leg with all my restless energy. When I saw Cress's mom rush by with a medical device on wheels, I raced after her to help.

She let me shadow her, and I quickly learned the life of a nurse was *not* for me, but it gave me an outlet to distract myself. Late into her shift, one of the Crystal fae moved in front of her and stared daggers at me.

"Who's this?" he asked, jerking his chin my way.

Kathy Rollins, usually such a nice lady, scoffed and gestured for him to step aside. "Someone who's helping around here, unlike you," she said waspishly.

As the fae stared at her, the citrine-like crystals growing from his shoulders seemed to glow. "I'm keeping you safe," he protested.

"You're standing in my way," she said.

A little startled, he stepped back, and she brushed past him, saying, "C'mon, Ben, ignore him."

We helped the next patient and stepped into the hall again. There was no sign of the fae man now. "Soooo, who was that?" I asked with far more intrigue in my voice than necessary.

She rolled her eyes on cue. "Some patients set out to make your life more difficult. It just turns out that he's still doing it, but now he's ambulatory."

Maybe I'd misread something here. He'd definitely been looking at her with some interest, but she clearly wasn't returning it. "Need help with him?" I offered more seriously.

"No, sweetheart. I can handle myself."

Well, whatever. I put it out of my mind when we visited the rooms of folks I recognized. First, we saw Aurora, who showed me a gnarly row of scars that looked like tire treads on her arms and across her belly from the Jellywalker's rows of stingers. The doctors had done what they could for her, but she still froze up occasionally. She needed more time to recover from its venom and was thus bedbound.

There were more than a few guardians and fae who'd gotten seriously wounded helping out at the library too. I was glad to help them get more comfortable. They deserved that much for facing the meat grinder that was the onslaughts of unnaturals big and small.

I was starting to pat myself on the back for a job well done when we came back around to Cress and Phaeron's room. I peeked inside and gasped. I'd lost the bet—he was awake and in the process of peeling bandages off healed skin. Aware of Cress's mom behind me, I held in my "oh shit" with effort.

He'd unhooked himself from the machines without causing them to scream and settled next to Cress's bedside, still dressed in his hospital gown.

"Hey, stop that!" Kathy protested. She burst into the

room and intercepted his wickedly clawed hands as they moved toward his face.

Phaeron exaggerated a grin from within the thicket of white on his face. He gestured to himself and then held up his thumb.

"I think it's okay," I said, drawing her away from him. I still reached for a dagger to cut my finger and started drawing subtle blood runes on my arm just in case there was still some Myuna in him.

His skin was shiny from ointment, but he was clearly healed as he stripped off bandages and set them in a pile next to the chair. The docs must've given him a shot of a strong verdant witch tonic...which made me hope they did the same for Cress, who slept peacefully in the bed. Phaeron casually slipped his hand into hers and started playing with the blunt crescent of her thumbnail. Bruises had bloomed all over her soft skin and aged with whatever healing regime she'd been given, leaving them a dull yellow.

"See, Mama Rollins? All good," I said awkwardly since he couldn't speak English anymore or something. He would've charmed her right out the door if he could do more than stare at us without even a hint of compre-hension.

We exchanged a meaningful look, and she gave me a trusting nod, leaving me with him and my unconscious anam cara. I sighed, seeing this as my opening to ask him for help with something, but only if I could get him to understand me.

I pulled up the other chair across from him. He didn't pay much attention to me, whispering in his language to Cress before he bent to kiss the back of her hand. Yeah, there was no Myuna there anymore, thank fuck. I snagged Cress's phone off a bedside table—it was a miracle Geo hadn't already stolen it—and did some creative searching on the supernatural side of the web. I typed in something on a translation website and handed the phone to him.

His pupils retracted to slits, and he squinted at the bright screen, but a moment later, he hissed a laugh at my joke. His big thumb claw loomed over the glass, and I gestured for the phone back urgently before he poked a hole through it. Shooting me a confused look, he handed it back. I dimmed the display for him and came over to his side to show him how to type on the screen with all the swirlies and dots that popped up for the Soiluirian language's keyboard.

"See, fingertips," I said.

His forked tongue tasted the air, and he watched me without blinking. Okay, I had to get used to the dimensional weirdness or whatever, but he was starting to creep me out.

He carefully typed with one thumb, the very picture of a tech-illiterate grandpa struggling to text for the first time. Eventually he passed the phone back. The translation read, "I understand I have you to thank for breaking a few bones in my tail. So, thank you. Glad to see you haven't changed, even in a tiny glowing box."

Well, damn, that was a proper English translation; what a good website. I starred it for Cress and sat back down. "You're welcome, I guess. Only useful thing I did yesterday," I typed.

He read the message and shook his head. "You may have saved her life. And my actions sent her to this bed. I will never outlive my remorse."

"Hey, man, it's not like any of us can say anything. We thought you were a goner for sure."

"Goner?"

"Dead or worse."

He read that and grounded himself with a heavy intake of breath and a long blink before typing a response. "I have no business being alive. But Cress willed that I survive, so I have."

"You're kind of fucked up, huh?" I typed, then thought that was too rude and deleted it. Still, he caught a glimpse of the screen and breathed a humorless laugh, nodding an affirmative. I passed him this message: "Could you come with me and take a look at my brother?"

He read the question and cast a reluctant sideways glance at Cress before nodding again. My heart leapt up to the vicinity of my throat when he tucked her hand and stood after me, silent as a shadow as we left her to rest. Now that he was here, I was terrified of what he'd say when he took a peek at Lucas's soul.

Deep down, I think I already knew what the verdict would be. The Hungering Darkness never left survivors, right? Why would Lucas be any different? Yet I led him to the correct room, and he swept up to my little brother's bedside to take a good look.

He already had the phone and angled its face away from me as he typed a message one agonizing fall of his thumb at a time. When he passed the device back to me, his free hand landed on my shoulder, giving a firm squeeze of sympathy. "A swift death would be kindest. But there's a small chance to save him if we open Garroway's chest cavity in the next few weeks."

I felt my eyes widen as I read. Well, damn, I could get behind that. The sooner the better, even. I just wondered what the blood baron had done to earn Phaeron's blood-thirsty grin.

19

PHAERON

YOU'RE KIND OF FUCKED up, huh? Ben had no idea how right he was.

He must've alerted someone that I was awake, as a sliver of too-bright light appeared at regular intervals to check in on Cress and me while I sat with her. My body was heavy with fatigue, but I refused to close my eyes for longer than a blink.

Yet I started nodding off anyway and stirred in panic at the sensation too akin to falling backward into Myuna's control. The last time I'd slept, I'd woken up mid-combat with my mate.

I'd only gleaned what'd happened from observing those around me. Ben cradling a shoulder still healing from a blood rune on our way to the hospital. The uneasy glances from everyone, even the coven of our friends, whose eyes shaded with distrust when Cress fainted and I tried to carry her the rest of the way to a proper healing. Geo had given me a murderous look and pulled her from my arms.

For a few moments, I'd held her slight, battered form clothed in the torn rags of what had once been a beautiful robe. I had harmed her. My hands, Myuna's will. It was inexcusable.

I paced the fatigue away, eventually changing from the cheery pastel-colored hospital gown I'd woken in back into the heap of scrubbed leather folded at the foot of my bed. The chest piece of my armor, with all its careful inscriptions, was hopelessly torn up, and the gloves were gone, so I remained bare from the waist up for now.

I went to splash my face in the adjoining bathroom and inched up the light switch. As soon as the bulbs buzzed to life, I hissed from the pain that flooded my head and flicked them back off. I hated losing my humanlike adaptations already. Their world was too bright, and I could not put anyone at ease if they couldn't understand me.

I had some unpleasant conversations ahead if the magic could be salvaged. It was my duty to share news about Myuna, the presence of the Void around her—blessedly not clinging to me—and worst of all, what I'd seen while under her compulsion.

Cress mumbled something, shifting in the bed. Her hand patted the bare space next to her before she shifted to sit up with a wince. My hands were there the next moment, moving pillows behind her back and holding her shoulder so she didn't twinge her bruises too much.

"Easy, bright soul," I said, then muttered a curse. She wouldn't understand me. Laboriously, I reproduced her name like a human would say it and skimmed my fingertips over her cheek.

Her hand caught mine and held my palm to her face. I imagined she saw a yellow-eyed demon in the dark of the room, as I'd covered the displays of the machine hooked to her and the light leaking from the window with casual shadow magic. Meanwhile, I saw her sleep-softened face with perfect clarity, down to the ridge of a couple purple-edged bruises across her jaw.

"Phaeron," she whispered with such hope and longing.

She shifted her weight up and used my arm to guide her hand to one of my horns, leveraging it to drag me into a kiss. I shouldn't have allowed this, not when she was wounded and her soul was so tempting, just a nibble away…

My body heated at the merest brush of our lips; it was like emerging from the cold Void onto Earth for the first time. Warmth suffused me down to my tail-tip, and the animal in me took control. I cupped the back of her neck, drawing her in deeper. I could taste the change in her magic; it was like drinking sunshine, harmless but spicy to my otherworldly senses. My fangs nibbled on her bottom lip, my forked tongue twining around her blunt one for more.

She squirmed from the sensation. It was only natural to pin her hips and pull her closer, until the tube attached to her left arm was taut. Jostling it had her gasping, the pained sound melting to a needy whimper as I trailed sharp-edged kisses down the side of her jawline and neck.

I growled. *Mine.* In my impatience to have more of her, I pulled the needle and tape off her arm.

The machine released an ear-splitting shriek. We startled apart, and I cursed myself as I took in her kiss-swollen lips and the indentations my fangs had made on the column of her throat. I'd stopped a breath away from biting right over a half-healed bruise. Was I even thinking? She needed to rest, not be subjected to my lack of control.

Light flooded the room from someone coming to check on us. Instead of it being a nurse, the heavy footfalls and the gritty sound of his transformation betrayed Geo. He pointed an accusing finger.

"Phaeron," he rumbled. There was more, something about a "streem" and "away," but the blame was clear from just the weight he put behind my name.

I smoothed my hand over Cress's hair in apology before standing and stepping away from the bed. I coiled my tail around my legs and put my hands behind my back, head angled at an accepting angle. He had all the body language of a man about to strike. I deserved it.

Geo didn't hold back. He hit me with a fist like a brick, and the force of his blow had me tasting blood from the tear of my own teeth. I slammed into the bedside table. A lamp and her phone went flying when the cheap wood splintered under my weight.

I groaned, feeling the twinge of several bruises old and new. Cress half fell out of the bed to get between us. "Geo, no!" she yelped. Instead of stopping, he nudged her out of his way with a broad obsidian palm.

That was about the time a nurse rushed into the room and shouted. Geo's wrathful expression doubled from whatever the woman was saying. Cress was breathing a sigh of relief and picking up her phone, just to tense as she turned it over to reveal several cracks on the screen. She made a distressed noise and tapped an intact section several times, producing a whirr of static and bands of color under the glass.

The combined noise and light were too much for me. I put my arms around her from behind, murmuring a promise—"I'm sorry. I'll buy you another."—before taking her into my shadows and carrying her out of the room, leaving Geo behind to argue with the nurse.

She struggled, and I had to drop her in the hallway, the

two of us reforming out of dark mist. "No," she said, stabbing a finger at me sternly.

I gazed at her, desperate to retreat somewhere dark and safe. There was only one place to go, really. Gesturing between us, I said, "Braza."

Her face softened, and she nodded, not fighting when I took her into my shadows again. It was the fastest way to the library and the embrace of the powercore's crackling energy. Braza pulsed a feeling of welcome when she read my intentions, already formed within the powercore's inner chamber when I arrived and placed Cress back on her feet.

"I'm glad to see you whole once more, my prince," Braza said with her usual polite distance.

She tilted her head toward Cress and smiled warmly, replying in English to something she'd said. My mate plucked at her hospital gown and waved at me, stepping out of the powercore.

"She is going to get changed," Braza explained.

I couldn't blame her. I'd tossed aside the ill-fitting garment as soon as I could, too. "Will you take a look at my back?" I asked. If anyone could fix the rune that'd appeared on my skin in the Void, it'd be Braza. We called the Void's work the "mark of language and humanity" from the benevolent way it'd warped us, and I yearned to have it back.

"Lie down on the bed. Let me see what she did to you," Braza said with sympathy. I did as she bid and turned my head to watch her face, fearing the worst as her energy-formed eyes skimmed over the skin of my mid-back.

"She did not touch me," I murmured.

"And yet she harmed you all the same. I see the trauma in your soul, my prince."

I closed my eyes, shuttering my reaction. Braza knew

my regrets all too well, but I would not think about that time and inadvertently burden her further.

After a short pause, she added, "But the mark can be repaired easily enough. I shall tell Cress when it's done."

I drew breath to tell her that it would be all right if Cress witnessed her work when the first spike of pain struck me. Braza had to forcibly transform me back, her purple-black energy shoving my nails to retract into their sockets and manipulating my teeth and bone structure. It felt like she ground and broke and healed me in stages through the process.

It took fifteen minutes at most, and by the time she finished, I was panting in a damp circle of my own sweat. I pressed my fingertips into my mouth, probing at the flat line of teeth and the points of two fangs. When I opened my eyes, I perceived the glow of her magic as dimmer. The disorderly use of light by the humans around me wouldn't be so painful.

"I added the ability for you to switch back and forth at will," Braza told me.

She told me how it worked as I sat up, head tilted. "Why?" I asked.

Instead of answering, she turned toward Cress's reappearance. Her arrival came with the damp smell of soap and flowers—she'd showered and changed into clothes a little too big for her. She'd pinned her purple hair back from her face, and there was some color on her cheeks. "I, uh, thought it was wrong to keep you from your old self," she said.

"I'm flattered you found me attractive at my most different, bright soul," I replied. For a breath, I expected her not to understand.

A subtle shiver had Cress shifting on her feet. "You're back," she whispered.

I motioned for her to sit with me and looped my arm around her, tucking her into my side. "I am," I confirmed, tracing my thumb down the curve of her shoulder.

Braza was in the process of reabsorbing into the power-core to give us some privacy when Cress asked, "Have you hugged your daughter yet?"

Both Braza and I stilled in surprise. Brows slanting lower, she pointed at the energy-formed dimensional. "Have you thanked her too? Do you realize how much she did to save you? The fact that she's *here* and that she made me Guardian of Moongrove Library was all for you."

"Picking a fight as soon as we understand each other." I shook my head and stood, holding my arms out to Braza.

I hugged her jellylike body, some of my regrets leaking to the forefront of my mind before I could hide them. In binding Braza's soul to a ley line, I'd denied her access to paradise in the next life. I still wished I'd been strong enough to let her go that day so long ago.

She squeezed me harder. She *knew*. Of course she knew. Being able to read thoughts had revealed too many of the unpleasant truths that'd swirled through my mind over time.

But Cress didn't realize all the baggage that came with the decision to save Braza while also condemning her to a half-life. All she saw was the distance and damage between us, and as they were now soul-tethered, she had firsthand knowledge of what we'd lost.

"Thank you for everything you've done. Though I wish you both had not endangered yourselves on my behalf," I said.

"Into death." Braza answered with an old oath of

loyalty meant for Myuna and the royal family. *How poorly that went for us.*

I heaved an exhausted sigh and released her. I've buried too many of the women I'd loved across my long life. That Cress and Braza had both risked themselves to drag me from Myuna's talons was unbearable when I was supposed to be the noble shadowborn protector in this room, but to say that would only insult them.

"Into death," I echoed, letting it become my new vow to them instead.

20

CRESS

I ASKED what had been on my mind from the moment I woke alone with Phaeron in a dark room. "Are you safe from Myuna's control now?"

He raised a brow toward Braza, deflecting the question. "In New Salem, I was able to mitigate the hole in your soul caused by Endaeron. You were only overcome when you left the radius of my power. While I am no rival for a goddess… it's clear she has only surface-level control of you. I will be able to provide the buffer you need," she said.

Phaeron made a noncommittal "hm."

"She was able to compel me while I was in her presence. I am perhaps fortunate she did not force me into corruption," he said. He shared that refusing a direct order from Myuna had been about as painful as driving an ice pick through his skull. The goddess had gleaned information from him about the library and what a powercore was when Braza had arrived.

"Yet you were able to resist her by a fraction. That's remarkable," she said.

"It is not when she still did as she willed while I was forced to watch." He glanced toward me, a guilty look.

"Let us not split already fine hairs. You are welcome to remain here, and I will use my power to support you while we seek a more permanent solution," she said. "Why don't you go rest?"

Though purple-tinted half-moons darkened the skin under Phaeron's eyes, he refused sleep.

"You won't be taken over again, not while you're here," I said, brushing his arm in support.

He glanced toward me again, saying, "I shall retire with Cress all the same."

Braza smiled and waved farewell before absorbing her body back into the powercore. I stood on my tiptoes and looped my arms around Phaeron's neck, not missing the coy slant to his lips. "Floor negative two, please," I said.

I liked seeing him a little caught off guard. "Hmm?"

"Take me to floor negative two. I'll show you a room you can use," I clarified. We disappeared in a whirl of shadows, and I closed my eyes to keep from getting dizzy when we reemerged in the second-floor hallway, right before the elevator doors.

I laced my fingers in his, guiding him toward the original room I'd claimed before I'd moved to sharing a different one with Geo and Ben. "Maybe you'd like to relax with a shower?" I suggested.

"Implying I smell?" Though his tone was a little too flat, I could tell he was attempting to tease. I respected that he was trying for some sense of normalcy despite everything.

"Good thing you wash," I said, eyeing him askance. I'd done my best not to stare, but he was bare-chested, and I came about to pec height. He smelled more like stale hospital cleanliness than any kind of body odor, and it seemed he'd healed off the worst of his physical injuries. All that remained was the shadows in his otherworldly eyes.

"I will cleanse myself...then we shall talk," he said, slipping into the room once I showed him to the door.

I flipped the lock and patted my empty pockets. *Oh, right.* I'd dropped my ruined phone when Phaeron had stolen me from the hospital room. I imagined Geo mourning over it and stifled a giggle. Served him right for rushing in and decking Phaeron without waiting for any kind of explanation.

That phone had been the last bastion of technology between me and my three men. It'd been a fun thing to watch how Geo would change my algorithms to cat videos and "highly satisfying" type stuff, or how Ben would steal it away to leave silly or weird websites waiting for me when I needed to use the phone too.

But that left me with nothing to do after a quick trip to the laundry room to pick out a change of clothes—shadow-born black, of course—in the largest men's size that'd been left behind. Phaeron was still showering when I returned, chill mist drifting from under the door, which he'd left ajar.

I set the clothes on the inside of the threshold and raised a brow. This man was seriously taking a cold shower and singing in his own language like the deluge of icy water wasn't another form of torment. I went to remove my shoes and lie on the bed, closing my eyes while I listened to the alien syllables and soft, hissing words drifting from the shower.

It wasn't a surprise Phaeron had a nice singing voice, not when his deep, smooth timbre had the power to tighten my lower belly. I wished he would emerge from that shower wet and ready to ravish me rather than to air out the burden he was carrying.

My heart quickened when the shower shut off, as did the tune he'd carried. I heard the shuffle of fabric and the creak of the door opening, but not his footsteps as he emerged with a towel tied around his trim hips. His hair was down from its usual scraped-back tail, framing his head and tangled around the root of his horns.

Combined with a chill cast on his skin from the cold shower, for a moment, I saw the second prince of Soiluire in his prime, dressed for peace with blue contouring his high cheekbones. But it was an illusion banished in a blink. Fatigue lined his face, and he'd lost weight, evidenced in hollow cheeks and a breakdown of the perfect abs he'd once had.

"Oh, you must be hungry," I said, sitting up quickly.

"Peace, bright soul," he answered. With a flick of a tendril of shadow, he turned off the lamp behind me, leaving him backlit by the light filtering from the bathroom. He slid under the covers with a sigh, shedding the towel with his tail. "I need for little except to lie with you."

I eased myself back down and scooted closer, resting face-to-face with him. He had the uncanny way of looking right through me with those topaz eyes. They threw off twinkling sparks as he threaded his fingers through my hair, nudging my head forward to touch foreheads with me. "I have missed you far more than words could convey," he murmured.

"I should've done more to bring you back sooner," I whispered back.

He shuttered his glowing eyes for a moment, gritting his teeth. "It is I that failed you with inaction. There is something you must know."

"I doubt there's anything—"

"Your sister, Carly," he interrupted. I swallowed hard,

feeling a little ill to hear him say her name with such guilt. "She was brought before Myuna."

I broke into full-body goosebumps. "She ate Carly's soul?" I could barely put the thought into words as shocked tears pricked the corners of my eyes.

He shook his head. "She recognized Carly from the memories she'd been able to extract from me. She tore the soul from Carly slowly while demanding my compliance in exchange for her. Up until that point, every supernatural brought before her was consumed, body and soul."

I was scarcely breathing as he searched for the words to explain my sister's fate. "I struck a deal with her, to sleep if she spared Carly. She'd already corrupted your sister's soul by taking a small taste of it...but still, she returned it and revived her. I'm so deeply sorry, bright soul. Your sister is a torchbearer now, an unnatural enslaved to Myuna's will."

"That's why you were asleep when you came to the library," I realized.

"Indeed." He met my gaze, resigned for my reaction.

I glanced away from that heavy expression. "Can we save her?" I asked.

"If she is captured, I can attempt to unbind her from Myuna's will. But she has still experienced death and rebirth. She will remain an unnatural with unpredictable needs and hungers, whether or not she regains control of herself."

I couldn't help but think that Carly had become a supernatural in the worst way possible. I clung to the hope that we might still be able to rescue her and any others that were similarly corrupted.

In the meantime, I drew away a lock of hair that shadowed Phaeron's face, tucking it behind the curve of his horn. My memories from Braza suggested mates maintained one another's appearance and grooming like an act of love. "Stay right there," I said.

"What are you doing?" He gazed over his shoulder when I stood and retrieved a few things from the vanity.

In reply, I ran a brush through his thin, damp hair and disentangled it from his horns. On a hunch, I abandoned combing it out and ran my fingers over his scalp. He leaned into my touch with a low moan, and I bet he'd purr if he could. Some of the tension bled out of his body.

"I don't deserve this," he said.

"I'm glad you told me about Carly. I've been worried about her, too," I said quietly, still massaging behind his horns. "You saved her from dying. It set you on the right path to be freed from Myuna's will and returned here to me. If we can save her, we will, together. And if we can't, I will carry the guilt with you for the rest of my life. For now... relax. Let yourself recover before you try to help anyone else."

I pinned his hair back with the leather tie he used. He shifted to lie on his back. "You would care for me as a mate," he said quietly.

There was a blaze in his eyes as he waited for my answer. For all the teasing touches and whispers in my ear, the nibbles and snatched kisses...the fears born of a hunger he understood but didn't fully control, this moment felt like the tipping point between us. "Of course. I love you," I replied.

I had a moment of weightlessness as he wrapped his shadows around me, lifting my hips and setting me to straddle him on the bed. "I meant to tell you for a while, but..." I said, resting my hands on his warm chest.

He raised a brow. "But what?" he asked.

But he'd been so distant. Skirting the edges of his self-control, afraid to hurt me even though his absence was the worst pain he could inflict.

But he was so different, from a different world. Far more important than I'd ever dreamed of being. To think I was supposed to be his mate and equal.

"But we haven't fucked, even when you were in the grips of a lust spell," I settled on saying. "I thought I was, um, inadequate to you in some way. Probably in many ways."

His expression twisted into a troubled frown, and on cue, he blamed himself. "It is I that is inad—"

I swallowed the rest of what he was going to say by kissing him, holding one horn to get the angle I wanted. Just like before, the meeting of our lips seemed to obliterate Phaeron and draw out the growling animal that rested just beneath his princely manner.

He flipped us and trapped me in a cage of blankets and his body, kissing like he wanted to devour me. But he jerked away, panting. "This is a bad idea," he groaned.

With each shift, I felt the hardness of him pressed against my thigh. He wanted me, and yet...it still wasn't going to happen. I gathered myself to hear him tell me no, for him to disappear in a bank of shadows and leave me with only my hand to finish what we'd started. Moisture gathered in my eyes, and I glanced away from his conflicted face. I had to stop putting so much of myself forward like this.

He caught my chin between his thumb and forefinger, turning my head back. "It will not do to have you doubting." He pulled the covers from between us, and I caught sight of his manhood for the first time. I'd sucked on him in the dark, only able to feel the shape of him, which matched the sight. His shaft had a few nubs along the length and purplish veins, with a velvety dark gray cap at the tip, matching his lips. No other surprises—he was human-shaped.

"Cress." He pressed in close to me, our foreheads touching again. "Do you trust me?"

The tenderness in his voice stole my breath. "Yes," I managed to whisper.

Shadows unfurled around him, one particularly long tendril hitting a light switch and plunging the room into darkness. Fabric shredded, and cool air hit my chest and legs, my breasts bouncing free when my borrowed clothes parted. He lifted me as if I weighed nothing and swept away the ruined material.

His magic felt as firm as his hands. In the dark, I could mistake him for having many caressing fingers touching me all over. "Tell me to stop at any time," he said close to my ear. "But I need to have control in this bed. Is that okay?"

He pinned my wrists above my head, keeping them there with a warm coil of darkness. "I can't touch you?" I asked. The bindings flexed but held when I tested them.

"Not this night." He nibbled on my earlobe, the sensation curling my toes. Everything was more intense when I couldn't see what he was doing. He'd even covered the glow his eyes put off. In many ways, he was the night pressing in around us, here to take me. *Finally*.

"I want as much of you as I can have," I told the darkness and parted my thighs for it.

"My True Light, you have called me home." He pulled back, his voice enveloping me with warmth. One clawed hand adjusted my knee and ran a palm up the tender inner flesh of my leg. "You are my beacon to return to, and how bright you have come to shine in my absence."

I squirmed some as his touch skimmed closer to my

heated core. The darkness sighed with me as the firmness of his fingertips vanished. His shadows continued to play across my skin, drawing circles and little nonsense runes over every inch of me except the folds that pulsed with my quick heartbeat.

Was he wrestling with his control as I waited breathless for his return? I wondered if he'd created the absence of light to hide his struggles and protect me from having to see how thin his control truly was.

He cupped my needy pussy, and I breathed out a soft sound of relief. "In the madness of every moment I spent with Myuna," he said, stroking his way up my slit. "I clung to thoughts of you. If I would emerge from the ordeal as the man you recognized." One of his fingers slipped within me, and I moaned. I could feel the tremor that passed through him. "If you would still want me." In went a second finger, curling and coaxing within me.

"Of course I still want you," I said breathlessly.

"I worried I would not be the same within," he continued. He ran his lips along my throat and applied pressure to my clit with the pad of his thumb. My cry sounded ragged, too loud to my own ears. "That I would no longer appreciate the great power you carry within you. I feared the sight of you would no longer bring me joy. A true monster of hers would not crave the taste of your lips."

His mouth was there, his kiss first a chaste brush but deepening to a full duel of teeth and tongue. He trembled with fine control. The sensation of his kiss pulled away, and he withdrew from my pussy too.

"Phaeron?" I asked, flushing hot, then uncertain. "If this is too much, we can stop..."

"Still so sweet," he answered. I heard a wet sound and

was fairly certain he was licking his fingers. "I may be a touch broken. Mere pleasure cannot mend me."

"We can still try," I said.

"Yes." Before I could worry about what he was trying to imply, he was between my thighs, nudging within me. He lifted under my back, taking away the sensation of the sheets and leaving me in a cushion of darkness. And that inky night...all of it was him. His skin, his magic, his breath upon my shoulder as he sank inside of me.

His tail twined around my locked ankles, pulling my body into the roll of his hips. He drew back, adjusted minutely, and thrust again, repeating this three times until one of the hard nubs on his shaft brushed an ultra-sensitive patch within me. Back arching, I screamed at the unexpected starburst of pleasure.

The darkness laughed, a chuckle of pure male satisfaction. I imagined his smug smile, the vicious way he tended to bare his teeth when he gave in to his shadowborn side. "Oh, Phaeron." I longed to *see* his pleasure.

He didn't reply. Now that he'd gotten the perfect angle, he slowed, sawing against that bundle of nerves. Fingertips traced my face, the curve of my jaw. This was lovemaking, sure as anything. He'd not declared his love as directly as I had, but I felt it. Every tender touch and meeting of our hips said it.

He truly was mine. But I was also his, at his mercy completely.

How well he treated me, though. I came apart in his arms, seeing stars as my eyes shut tight. He stilled, then withdrew, leaving me clenching on air with a whine of denial. Even the pressure of his tail and hands vanished.

"Come back. Please," I said. It would ruin the moment, to get off without him experiencing the same.

I could hear the rasping way he drew in breath. He wasn't far, but he was perhaps on the knifepoint of his restraint.

"You are too tempting. I cannot keep my fangs from your neck if we continue," he answered after a few moments.

I wiggled my hips to tempt him anyway, and a growl drifted from the darkness. "Take me on my hands and knees, then. No need for fangs anywhere near my neck," I reasoned.

For the space of two heartbeats, I didn't think he would come back. But then he grasped my hips, and I had the sensation of turning over. He pressed his length between my lower lips, rubbing up and down and catching my clit against one of those amazing nubs. "I don't know how much more I'll be able to hold back," he whispered.

I arched my back. "Go ahead," I coaxed. "I want you to fuck me now."

He made a sound like a snarling animal and slammed home within me again. The driving power of his thrusts would've shoved me into the bed, but I didn't even know if we were on it anymore—the cushion of shadows underneath me had firmed up and kept me in the right position.

I had the biggest grin, exhilarated to feel him let loose. He released with a shadowborn's howl, holding my hips flush with his as he pulsed within me.

"Oh, I should've told you," I said as soon as he let me go and I fell into a boneless heap back onto the soft bedsheets. His magic was receding, and I spotted the half-lidded glow of his yellow eyes as he stretched out next to me.

He stroked his fingers through my hair, idly working free a tangle. "Is something the matter?" he asked.

"I'm on the pill now, so we should be safe, but next time, you should probably wear a condom."

He started to laugh. Deep, carefree rolls of his chest. "We're from different species. There won't be any babies," he promised.

"Says the man who was made humanlike on his way to Earth," I protested playfully. When he put it that way, I did feel silly.

His mirth drifted to quiet, and he didn't reply. Moments later, he was snoring.

21

CRESS

There was a timeless bubble around Phaeron and me. I slept a bit, then drifted in and out for a while. Eventually, I couldn't sleep any more, but I lay still for him. I enjoyed being in his arms, warm, safe, and glad he hadn't seemed to stir this whole time. He'd needed this so badly.

With the lights off and his eyes closed, the only light in the room was a bedside clock and a smoke alarm on the ceiling that flashed occasionally. I wouldn't have noticed it if this wasn't an underground room coated with eddies of shadowy mist that occasionally rolled off Phaeron's skin, swirling with his deep, slow breaths.

The unrestrained shadow magic was just one more quirk to love about him, and I was smitten. I drank in his presence even though I could barely see him—his night-air scent, the press of his muscles against my curves, and the possessive way his tail had coiled around my legs.

We'd fit so well together last night, and I was deliciously sore, sure to feel the evidence of his claim when I did eventually get up. My body's needs would be the only thing that'd drive me out of his arms before he woke. At least, I thought that until Braza's presence brushed my mind.

"Sorry to interject. I was not able to stall any longer," she said apologetically.

"Is something happening?" I asked. When I stirred, Phaeron gripped me to his chest tighter in his sleep.

"You could say that. There is another newcomer to the pocket dimension, and he has demanded to see Phaeron. Ben's memories show that he is Auric et Vess, an old friend. Do you remember him?"

"I think so," I replied. That sounded like the name of the Vrassorm man who'd had the idea to take the survivors of the Age of Decay off Soiluire for good. *"But is he still a friend?"*

"If he is not, he is an enemy of our enemy. The effect is the same."

Before I could ask how she could be so sure, someone pounded on the door. Phaeron woke with a growl and raised his voice in the direction of the insistent knocking. "Go away!"

"No can do, Big P." It was Ben. "Can I come in?"

"Braza says it's important. Apparently, Auric et Vess is here," I said.

He stared at me in shock. "Auric? Here?" He muttered something I was starting to recognize as his go-to curse in the dimensional language, but then he nuzzled into my hair, breathing in the smell of me with a sigh. We held tighter to one another for a moment before getting up.

I turned on a lamp and tidied the bed while he dressed in his old leather armor and answered the door bare-chested to let Ben in. I identified the scraps of colored fabric on the floor as the remains of my clothes and shook my head, going to don the black shirt of the set of clothes I'd gotten for Phaeron. It fit on me like a dress, the hem stopping mid-thigh. Not bad for the inevitable walk of shame across the hall.

I emerged from the bathroom and caught the end of a backslapping hug between the two men. I hung back a moment, oddly touched. Ben and Geo had seemed to be growing into close friends. Maybe this was a glimpse of a future where I was dating an inseparable trio. As long as Geo could finally accept Phaeron.

Ben turned and spotted me, making grabby hands in my direction. "Morning, babe." He had a hug for me too before tucking to my back and resting his cheek against mine. His clever hands slipped under the hem of my oversized shirt.

I felt him smile. "I see I was right. When Geo told me what happened, I kind of assumed." His thumbs brushed up and around where the band of my panties should be.

"He punched Phaeron for no reason," I said, still pissed that was Geo's first reaction to seeing him awake.

"I greatly deserved it, actually," Phaeron put in. His fingers traced his jaw, where a bruise was starting to bloom on his gray skin. "Your safety is his duty, and I have been a threat to it. I am surprised he's not here now."

His yellow gaze cut curiously to Ben, who I felt shrug. "We had a long chat about you after the powercore sent word you both were safe in the library. I think he doesn't know what he's feeling after seeing you and Cress fighting."

"Phaeron wasn't in control," I argued.

"Yeah, but we're talking about someone who's been a rock more hours than not lately. Just remember that he's not the bad guy, all right? He's just figuring himself out. That rock loves you as much as I do, babe, and that's saying something." He gave my bare hips a squeeze and planted a kiss on my cheek.

If we hadn't had an audience, I'd be tossing this shirt aside...hell, Phaeron had already seen us going at it, so modesty wasn't the best excuse either. The dimensional cleared his throat as I considered. "I expect you have a reason for disturbing our peace?" he prompted.

Oh, right. A living legend of a dimensional was here.

"Yeah, this dimensional man appeared out of nowhere while there was a fight with some of Myuna's creatures outside of the hospital. He made the unnaturals disappear with a flick of his wrist and said he wanted to speak with you, Phaeron. He also idly threatened to make our friends vanish one by one if we did not find you."

There was a knowing glimmer in Phaeron's eyes. "You barely need to say more. What color was his skin? Did he have one blind eye?"

"Blue. And...yeah. I believe one of our friends correctly summed up his appearance as 'creepy fuck.'"

Phaeron snorted a surprised laugh. "That does sound like Auric. Don't worry, he's all bark and little bite, as you humans say."

"You sound positively *ancient* right now, Big P," Ben commented.

He rolled his eyes. "When Cress is properly dressed, we shall go."

GEO

The blue-skinned dimensional held a cigar while seated on a granite wall next to a set of steps that led up to the hospital, smoking without a care in the world. I was posted several yards away across a concrete courtyard. My obsidian wings and wide stance blocked a second, smaller staircase right before the hospital doors. I stood next to Madigan's red-armored form and brandished warhammer.

Behind us ranged several more defenders, including Bianca with her crossbow and the rough-voiced shifter she'd come to spend most of her spare time with. We couldn't be sure this man wasn't another puppet of Myuna's and about to make a move to teleport us all in front of the goddess. He hadn't spoken up to dispel the notion, only demanded Phaeron and refused to move, creating this stalemate of wills.

A curl of shadows, distinctive on this sunny day, crossed the sky and took form next to me. I swung my head around, surprised to see only Cress and Ben take shape from curls of black and purple magic. When I looked back toward the unknown dimensional, Phaeron had already taken form and was speaking to him in the language of Soiluire.

"Oh, wow, he looks much cooler in person," Cress commented. "Also, hi, Geo."

"Hello," I gritted out.

It was a relief to see her whole and hale again, but that feeling was quickly pushed aside at my annoyance with her so willingly disappearing with a man who'd harmed her so badly. Magical influence or no, Phaeron was still the cause of the mostly healed wounds and bruises that'd peppered her body. I should've pummeled him further so he felt a fraction of the pain he'd inflicted on her.

She glowed, beaming like she held some sweet secret. A glint of her usual curious awe at learning something new about the supernatural community shone on her face as she watched the two dimensional men interact.

The newcomer spoke in a voice nearly as gravelly as mine. He'd leveraged himself to his feet with his tail alone, and I registered it as a natural weapon. It was a muscular coil compared to Phaeron's whip-thin version, heavier with a layer of back-facing spikes and a cluster of them at the end like a club. He rested it around his feet while he grasped forearms with Phaeron, bowing his head in a brief show of deference.

"That's Auric et Vess," Cress explained in an undertone. Even Madigan tilted her head to listen in. "He's from the Vrassorm tribe, the rarest of the three types of dimensionals. They usually have power over cold or the Void, and the stronger they are with either, the more potent the poison is that they store in their tail spikes."

"What is the Void?" Madigan asked.

"It's…" She circled her hand vaguely. "Like, it's the darkness between worlds. Less like space and more like a plane of existence that links universes together. It's what the dimensional peoples escaped through to come to Earth… and also what Myuna traveled through to get here."

"Fuck," Ben muttered.

"Agreed," I rumbled.

"Auric is a Vess. That's a title that means…" She seemed to search her memory. "Voidwhisperer. He sacrificed one of his eyes to the Void so he can better sense it and use it."

Auric glanced our way, maybe hearing his name. One eye was wholly a cloudy white. The other had a teal glow, with an unusual pupil like one black line with two darker blue scratches on either side of it. When he flicked out a forked tongue, he resembled Phaeron's unchanged form, complete with heavy claws and mouthful of sharp teeth.

His horns and build were different, though. He had one impressive backswept horn, and the other, on his blinded side, was cut short and resembled a tree trunk with a crack on the side. "Was the horn a sacrifice to the Void, too?" I asked.

She considered and answered in a voice combined with another woman's. "No, that's new within the last two centuries."

Both Ben and I flinched and pivoted her way. "Sorry. Did that startle you?" Cress asked in her usual sweet tone. "I wanted to take Braza out into the sunshine, and she just so happens to know this guy already."

I only relaxed when she further explained that Braza was the name of the powercore. She sounded like someone Cress trusted deeply. I'd found her judgment dubious in the past, but it hadn't been wrong about Ben...and it seemed it wasn't wrong about Phaeron, as conflicted as I felt about him.

When he turned and beckoned to Cress, she didn't hesitate to come forward. Madigan shifted to cover my post while Ben and I both accompanied her for protection.

Auric hissed something at Phaeron, who bared his teeth in the approximation of a smile while responding in a tone of warning.

The powercore's voice flowed into my head. Braza felt familiar, carrying the reassuring electrical presence I'd served for decades in Moongrove Library. *"Auric asked if Phaeron claims Cress in name only, and his response was to threaten to break his other horn if he's rude to any of you."*

My stone lips curled toward a smile. I'd gladly help if it was necessary.

Phaeron switched to English. "My mate, Cress Dark-more. Her anam cara, Ben Evenstar. And her protector, Geo."

"Charmed," Auric replied flatly. His single eye held a full sentence of judgment as he took in the four of us together. "As I was telling the prince, I'm here to wage war on Myuna the White. You lot are a hodgepodge in need of a Vess. I felt her arrival, as she ripped a wide hole through the Void and that has to be repaired. Plus, I later heard this one's silent screams trapped within the darkness and thought I'd be saving his sorry hide again." He tipped his good horn toward Phaeron.

He replied by resting an arm around Cress. "While I appreciate that you would rescue me, I'm pleased to inform you that my mate has already done so."

They had another verbal spar in their language. It seemed Phaeron won the quick exchange.

"I am Auric," he said toward the rest of us with a hint of reservation. He tugged the collar of a fine suit tailor-made to cover his thick barrel of a chest. Tattoos peeked from his sleeves and covered the back of his clawed hands. "Once a power and a threat, a leader of a resistance, now doomed to tiptoe around human-dimensional conflicts lest the rest of my Vrassorm brothers and sisters get crushed between prejudice and threat. I've saved this kid a time or two. Who knows, maybe I'll save you lot with what I have planned."

"I've known Auric most of my life. He is an elder of our kind," Phaeron supplied, and I realized he was the one Auric had called a kid. How mind-bogglingly old the Vrassorm must be to make such a claim.

"So, is joining us part of this plan?" Ben put in.

"I suppose so. On my way here, I sensed the scope of the rip where Myuna landed. If I had the proper support, I could catapult the bitch back where she came from and seal the hole behind her," he said.

Phaeron frowned. "The Void most certainly does have a lingering presence around her."

"Wait," Cress said, holding up a hand. "When my friends say you made unnaturals disappear...were you sending them into the Void?"

"That's right." He bared his fangs in a vicious smile. "They'll wander a while before its chill overtakes them, then they'll be broken down until only their voices and memories remain to haunt its nothingness forever."

"That's kind of fucked up," Ben muttered.

Cress shivered from more than just a cold breeze. "Myuna's victims don't deserve that. My sister's still out there," she said. I quickly muttered in agreement with her.

"If you intend to stay here, you will save the Void treatment for Myuna herself," Phaeron added.

For a moment, I thought Auric would step into the Void and leave with how disgustedly he looked at the four of us. "Fuckin' hell," he muttered. "Fine, you soft-hearted fools. But even the Void cannot save you if an unnatural rips out your throat."

Phaeron grinned and clapped the other dimensional on the shoulder. "I'm pleased you're here, old man," he said with affection. "I must face the judgment of this group for my own deeds, but I imagine they will offer you entry and a room if you attempt to play nice."

We turned and approached the hospital and the cluster of supernaturals guarding it. Madigan listened to Phaeron's explanation of why Auric was here, then her red helmet turned toward me. "Can we trust this as fact?" she asked.

I dipped my chin in a slow, grinding nod. "No agent of Myuna has had the presence of mind he has," I said.

"Good point," she mused. "Let's talk about your plan in more detail, Auric. I have a few augurs you should meet as well."

I cleared my throat, a sound about as pleasant as two rocks grinding together. "While you do that, I wish to have words with Phaeron."

She considered for a couple of moments. "Yeah, all right. No one's using the conference room right now."

I shook my head at Cress when she looked ready to pose a question. She'd be all right without us for a while, considering how she carried a powercore's might with her. Her gaze softened with concern as she watched Phaeron and me head into the hospital, with Ben hesitating before catching up to us.

The dimensional slowed to follow us as we took the familiar path from the lobby to the conference room that'd become somewhat of a war room. Tourist maps of Cerris City peppered the walls, each covered with different notations. One was stuck with red pins each time there'd been a sighting of unnaturals. Another marked battles and skirmishes, while a third noted suburban areas we'd tried to evacuate already.

Phaeron paused in front of these maps, his tail flicking against the carpet in agitation. He read over them for a few moments before crossing the room to have a seat at the head of the conference table. "I suspect this conversation has been due a while," he commented.

I transformed back into my human form while he and Ben got comfortable. Feelings both positive and negative flooded in, as well as the phantom sensations of hunger and thirst. I'd need to satisfy both if I intended to spend more than an hour as a human.

"Yes. We should talk about how you've put Cress in

danger," I said. My voice just didn't hit the same kind of dangerous rumble in this form, but I glared across the room at him as another way to express my displeasure.

Before I sat, I fiddled with the light switch, dimming the room and earning a grateful glance from the dimensional. I went to sit across from Ben, the three of us completing a seated triangle.

"I would not willingly harm her. I am fated to her, same as you both," Phaeron answered.

"I am aware," I gritted. I'd already expressed my frustrations about this to Ben last night, once I'd calmed down in the aftermath of finding him disconnecting Cress from the machine monitoring her vitals. "All three of us are fated to the same woman, and yet we could not be more different."

Phaeron's eyes glimmered like gemstones as he took in Ben and me. "A relationship with one man and one woman can be needlessly complicated, let alone adding in two more partners. Yet it is easy to love Cress, yes?"

"Yes," Ben and I answered at the same time.

"That's the fate part of it," Ben added.

I scoffed lightly. "Fate," I echoed. "It pales in comparison to being made for her and only her."

Ben rolled his eyes. "All right, if you want to measure dicks about this, then my soul is the other half of hers. We share a deep bond."

We both glanced toward Phaeron. "She is my True Light, the only woman capable of quelling the rages of my shadowborn side," he said. "Were she one of my kind, she'd also be a perfect biological match capable of carrying my life force and thus my child."

"So, we're all specially bonded to her," Ben said more to me, with a gesture toward Phaeron.

"But that creates the other side to being her mate. We must find a balance where we can support her while not hating one another for her shared affections," Phaeron said. "I have shared a mate before. It was not always easy."

"You have?" Ben asked.

He nodded. "With my brother. She was the first mate either of us had, before we fully developed our magic and abilities. I'm glad of the experience, as it taught me that a heart like hers or Cress's should be trusted to expand to love her mates equally. It is better for all of us not to expect her to cut herself in portions and jealously look over to see if we all received an equal piece of her."

My hands softened from the fists I had resting on the table. Somehow, he'd taken what I was feeling and phrased it just right.

"I have only seen you both as my competition," I admitted quietly. They were unpredictable and changeable, unlike myself. But that wasn't a fair summation either when Cress had already improved me just by being her.

"That is quite clear," Phaeron said. "Do you remember what I said when I offered to temper your stone form?"

I thought backward. My memory used to be crystal clear when I never took human form. But since I'd been spending more time as flesh and blood, I was starting to forget the edges of things I'd experienced. Having a human's memory was disconcerting sometimes. "You helped me to make peace between us."

He nodded. "I wished to establish some common ground for Cress's sake. I still hope to build up a foundation like that with you both. As long as we can be friends, we can focus on her despite our differences. What do you say?"

Ben's answer was quick. "I'm in." He was already in,

though. I was the one who found this difficult. My gargoyle side still saw the world in binary, so there was no "I will try" like I'd promised before.

I was the one who needed to change here. With a gargoyle's brevity, I answered, "Yes."

22

CRESS

For the next few hours, I toured the hospital, quietly showing Braza around. She was fascinated by the modernity of the facility, even though much of the beauty of the place was stripped. File cabinets and couches cluttered the first floor, turning it into a maze, and most of the windows were blacked out.

I introduced her in a one-sided way to the people I knew, speaking with her in my mind so I didn't startle anyone with a two-layered voice. I was happy to run into Mom, who was pushing a cart in the hall on floor four.

"Have they given you any time off?" It seemed like she was always running around when I had time to visit the hospital.

She shrugged. "You know what they say. Time waits for no one. I'm choosing to invest it making what difference I can."

"Have I told you lately that you're my hero, Mom?" I asked earnestly.

She ruffled my hair and moved toward the nurse's station. "I'm not that impressive, baby. The doctors around here… I'd give my left arm for the kind of healing magic they wield."

"Now you're starting to sound like…" I coughed, choking on the name. "…like Carly."

Mom's eyes flicked my way over her mask, concern creasing her brow. She'd always been able to read the shifts in my mood like her own kind of magic. I'd as good as told her there was something wrong.

"Well, you had best confide in her," Braza commented.

"Can I tell you something?" I asked more quietly.

Mom took a fifteen-minute break and drew me into an unoccupied room, where I spilled everything I knew. Phaeron's admission was enough to scare her, and Braza's supplemental knowledge seemed to make it worse. "Torchbearers were ghostly servants during the height of Myuna's power. It sounds like she's not strong enough to enslave souls like that anymore, so if we can capture Carly, Phaeron can try to remove her from Myuna's control."

"What are the chances of us finding her alive?" With her mask set aside, her face looked aged a decade, deep lines marking her nose and cheeks. Tears sheened her eyes, but she kept them contained by pure force of will. "I shouldn't think that way…but I know the men and women protecting the hospital are treating anyone touched by Myuna as a lost cause. We have the morgue filling up with these so-called torchbearers."

I felt my skin go cold all over. "Like, how many people?"

"It's grim business. I'm not sure you really want those details," she answered.

"An estimate, maybe?"

She considered me hard, and her will caved to what she saw in my face. "Dozens. The wounded guardians talk about how the corrupted animals and supernaturals all throw themselves heedlessly into fights. There are a lot of bodies left behind," she told me in a hush.

"We're lucky the hospital has a good relationship with the closest funeral home. At the moment, any body we can salvage is being stored…just in case we come out of this situation. There will be loved ones who will want a say in what happens to those remains." It was clear that was all she wanted to say on the matter. That was fine, as I was reeling.

"If dozens of torchbearers have already died in this area, Myuna must be corrupting them left and right. It sounds like she's using them as if they're disposable," I said to Braza.

Of course, I also skipped ahead to the worst possible scenario: my sister being amongst those thrown at us. I rubbed my clammy palms against my pants. Somehow, we had to save her from that fate, even if it meant snatching her out from under Myuna's watch.

"She will be pressing each new servant to bring her more and more people to consume or turn," Braza replied.

"We have to do something."

"Mom, I have to go," I said aloud, rising to give her a hug farewell. "Thanks for telling me all of this. I will find Carly, I promise."

A thread of eagerness spun from Braza, crackling with the restless energy of lifetimes stuck in one spot. *"Well, we are unstoppable together. Shall we go now?"*

I liked the sound of that quite a bit. *"Shouldn't we tell someone that we're leaving? And Phaeron…"* The only reason we'd felt safe to let him leave the aura of her powercore side was because I was carrying the other half of her with me.

She tugged on my powers, guiding me through the process of turning into shadowy mist. I may have startled Mom, passing her as a sudden breeze, but hopefully I didn't leave behind an impression of my exhilarated laughter. We reached the first-floor conference room in record time and reformed in a seat. I felt the weight of eyes on me during the dizzy spell that followed.

Looking around, I blanched as I took in the meeting we'd dropped into. Phaeron and Auric had pulled the maps off the conference room wall and were conferring over them, while Madigan and Hana had obviously paused mid-explanation to stare at my sudden entrance.

Hana broke the silence first. "Hello, Cress and Braza. We were about to talk about the ocean gate."

"Braza?" Auric echoed in disbelief.

She greeted him in Soiluirian through my lips, further baffling the old Vrassorm man.

"I didn't mean to barge in," I added sheepishly. "I just wanted to let someone know I'm going out to find my sister."

Phaeron's lips pressed into a fine line of disapproval.

"*And* I wanted to point out that A Little Wicked Coven has no job now that the library is cleared internally. Myuna is moving to take over the supernatural population. I know I can speak for my friends when I say that we can't sit idle." I flexed my hand, overlaid with purple-black claws.

Madigan propped her chin on a gauntleted fist. She'd placed her helmet aside for this meeting and shot a bemused glance toward Hana. "Well, you called it. What do I owe you?" she sighed.

"Let's call it good if you say yes. This way, you can assign them a few protectors," the augur said.

"What of protecting the library?" There was a dangerous edge to Phaeron's question.

Braza barely had to warn me. Fury blazed in his otherworldly eyes as I aired her suggestion. "You can hold it on your own with the powercore's support."

He switched languages seamlessly, the hisses and rolls of Soiluirian made crisp by his anger. "And when darkness falls and Endaeron comes for you both, I am to...what, sit idle?"

"Unless Myuna herself shows her face, you will be safe from her control this way," Braza answered in the same language.

It felt like I was double-teaming him as I added in English, "This also protects you from whatever hold the Hunger has on you."

His tail gave an agitated snap. *"He will change the subject to buy time to think of a way around our logic,"* Braza said privately.

After taking a deep breath, he said, "Let us speak of the ocean gate." Well, she'd called that. "It is surrounded by unnatural sightings and skirmishes. It's a guarantee Myuna has figured out something valuable is in the lake, but she will not know what an ocean gate is unless one of her creatures gets the opportunity to use it."

"That's only a matter of time," Hana said. "Especially with the number of unnatural hunters coming and going."

Auric loosed a displeased growl. "Those kids are pretending at being heroes."

"I know it seems that way, but they're working for the greater good out there. We simply don't have the people to rescue everyone." Madigan drummed her fingertips on the table, weighing our options with a pensive expression. "If there was a way to communicate with all of the people still trapped in their homes, we could gather them up for one big push."

"We could use Wren's stream?" I suggested.

She tilted her head back and forth with a hum. "My understanding is her audience is all supernaturals on the outside, watching for our fall with bated breath."

"Not necessarily. She's really tried to show there's hope on this side of the pocket dimension. I bet you there have been several people who've come to the hospital for protection after seeing it on her stream," I argued.

She seemed to consider it and nodded to herself. "For better or for worse. Who knows how many supernaturals were dragged in front of Myuna because they were trying to get to us?" she pointed out. "And broadcasting our plans would only make that problem more severe. Not to mention someone locking the ocean gate from the outside if it becomes common knowledge."

"I don't think they will yet," Hana said. "We'll have to talk to the mer representative when he arrives tomorrow."

I interjected before they could switch to another topic. "You're right that a lot of people on the outside are watching Wren's stream too. What if we used it as a platform to call for help? If there's a future where we try to evacuate all the people we can." My gaze landed on Auric, whose expression was cynical at best. "We cleared out the most dangerous creatures in Cerris City Library with the help of a couple unnatural hunters. They're competing, not trying to be 'heroes.'" I put up air quotes. "But there *are* people who will come help us if they know it's possible."

"I question the wisdom of dragging anyone else into this conflict, bright soul," Phaeron replied quietly. "The fewer supernaturals around for Myuna to corrupt, the better it will be for us. However a small river can help, it's not possible to comprehend her evils without firsthand experience."

"Fuckin' hell. The first thing you asked was if I brought reinforcements," Auric grumbled.

"Of *our* kind, who understand the magnitude of a soul's corruption," he said.

"Who says they won't come when they see the sudair fighting?" A sharp grin took over the blue dimensional's face. "I have an idea that will keep you away from sitting on your ass in a library. You just have to appear on camera."

"Back on Soiluire, we called this clearing a path," Phaeron said a little later, at the head of our armed group heading away from the hospital.

"We're not going to get very far on foot," Braza grumbled in my head.

We'd all kind of gotten what we wanted. Braza seemed the most disappointed, as she'd initially thought we'd be striking out on our own. It was the impulsive teenaged side of her, I thought. Traveling in a big group was much slower, but this way, we were present to keep Phaeron sane. In the same breath, he was here with me, and that seemed to put him more at ease than staying in the library.

"That's not the point of why we're out here," I replied. In a way, I knew we were being humored. We had one objective for this trip, and that was to free a torchbearer from Myuna's control. We had to see if Phaeron could do it.

Our group's spirits seemed high. Roe and her familiar, Tank, wore identical smiles, faces lifted toward the sun. Bianca and Grace were nearly attached at the hip, muffling the occasional laugh. Ben and Geo were doing much the same, actually, from where they flanked me. I was relieved to see Geo smiling again, even in gargoyle form.

There were a couple guardians and Crystal fae with us, all familiar faces who'd been assigned to the library. Absent from our group were Jordan and Auric, who'd both stayed behind to plan; Áine, whose magic was needed at the hospital; and Grant, who seemed quite shy of Wren's camera. The blonde stood at the center of our group with her phone panning the scene. More often than not, it was focused on Phaeron, a new star to the "small river," as he still didn't quite understand what a stream was.

As I hadn't wanted my hybrid status broadcast to the supernatural world, I'd left Wren's staff behind. She didn't seem to care much about its fate, still having the moon scepter tied to her hip. Walking next to her was Willow, also on her phone but for a different reason. She had our map and wore Grace's microphone to coordinate with Tish.

"We're taking a left two blocks from here," Willow said.

"Got it," Phaeron said.

Meanwhile, Wren narrated our walk and the information flashing on Willow's phone as the map refreshed in real time. "The survivors have ransacked everything of value from these stores already. This road will lead us to a location where several skirmishes have been fought against Myuna's creatures. They've wrecked enough cars here after dark..."

Phaeron shot an annoyed glance over his shoulder. I spoke up to distract him. "Just pretend she's not there. It's for the stream."

"Right. Where others can watch what we're doing," he repeated dubiously.

"A lot of others," Ben pitched in. "And they give us money for the cause."

"Well then. Once you receive your share, maybe you'll stop trying to spend my wages for me," Phaeron said.

Ben covered a surprised laugh. "Nah, Big P. I still think you need to buy a car."

"What use do I have for a car?" Phaeron put his palms up in exasperation. It was like they'd picked this argument up from where they'd left it before we were ever trapped here.

"Or a phone," Geo rumbled.

I held my breath when there wasn't an immediate reply. The dimensional flashed a smile toward me. "I've promised Cress to buy four of them. Though I still don't see why I need one."

"You do," the three of us said practically on top of one another.

"All right," he chuckled. "Perhaps our task will be brief and we can take a couple detours. I am in want of new armor."

I'd insisted on him donning a shirt for the sake of the stream. The hospital had a plain black one that fit him well enough. If he hadn't still been simmering from me suggesting he stay behind, he might've teased me about covering up. There'd been the glimmer of the idea in his eyes, at least, before he'd silently shrugged it on.

"If we can find a shop that still has something in stock," I sighed. As Wren had suggested, the storefronts we passed were completely looted. Most windows were smashed in, displays empty or turned over. We stopped at a corner mart to scavenge for crumbs, just to find a trio of ratlike unnaturals already in the process of doing just that.

We killed them without much issue, but Phaeron dragged their corpses out by their tails and lit the match to burn the pile of them on the sidewalk. "Leave nothing behind that she can consume," he muttered when Wren panned her camera from the spreading fire to his profile.

He turned away, beckoning for the group to follow him. "Now that we've encountered her creatures, we can be sure there are more nearby. Stealth is of the essence," he said.

"I'm great at stealth!" my handbook piped up next to my ear, startling me. It'd been so good on this trip until now.

I turned toward it, putting a finger to my lips. Together, we went "shhhhh."

"See, I know the routine," it squeaked smugly.

"Your shouting is going to get me killed one of these days," I whispered.

In reply, it alighted its spine on my left shoulder. "You love me, Cressie-poo," it replied, actually lowering its voice too.

Geo's wings opened with a scrape of rock. He cleared a small area and took to the sky, hopping from rooftop to rooftop above us as we headed for the place where our allies had had several skirmishes with the enemy. I knew it on sight due to the wreckage of a few cars sitting in the middle of an intersection. Judging by the number of lanes, this would be a busy thoroughfare if circumstances were different.

"Incoming," Geo announced. We bristled with spells and weapons, waiting for the space of a few quickened heartbeats before several humanoid figures poured out of a gaping car repair shop across the street, alongside many more unnaturals that used to be various animals.

I was merging with Braza's power all the while, clothed in her purple-black shadows and wearing a wolflike visage over my face. "We want to keep the people alive, if possible," Phaeron said before taking his own shadowborn form and leaping forward.

His shadows speared the nearest torchbearer, slamming him on his back and wrapping him in a layer of dark ropes. While struggling and gnashing his teeth, the man had his eyes wide open, staring at us. I could see why those who'd fought torchbearers thought they were zombies. His irises were bleached under a sheet of glowing white, unnatural and dead-seeming.

I cast Lux on my sword and joined the melee, warding away the bulbous birds dive-bombing my friends with a few swings of my light. The monsters were afraid as ever of my power, so I cast Luminaire with a warning shout, aiming to dazzle our enemies.

Monsters screamed, and torchbearers cowered, but words formed on their lips, dry whispers. "My lady," rasped one. Another begged for mercy.

I froze, my mouth hanging open for one dumbfounded moment. They thought I was Myuna?

"Shake it off," Braza warned. They quickly realized I wasn't the soul-eating goddess and stumbled back into the fighting. Something hit me from behind, and I fell face-first to the pavement, my sword clattering out of arm's reach.

A fist struck the back of my head, and stars danced in my vision. The same person who'd stunned me grabbed under my armpits and started to drag me away from the group. I recognized the first torchbearer's face. My light must have melted away the shadowy ropes that'd bound him.

Braza wanted to lengthen my fingers into talons and slash him, but I had an idea to try first. I called silently to my handbook, and it flew into my palm. I circled my fist in a figure eight and held it up, willing the Lux spell to pass through it.

The handbook flared open in my grip and emitted a spotlight of concentrated parchment-colored light into the torchbearer's face. He released me, and I stumbled back.

"Hah, take that! 'Tis I that is luminous now!" the book exclaimed.

A different figure nudged me aside. I saw the flash of Phaeron's sword, the attack checked just in time for the torchbearer's sake. He reached into midair close to the man's chest and went very still.

Braza's shadows flowed over my eyes, letting me see the knotted white ball he was pulling from the man. Phaeron passed me the hilt of his sword and took a deep breath. With both hands, he unraveled the mess of tangles the man's soul was tied in until it was a white globe being pushed back into his body.

The man collapsed in a boneless heap. I eyed him for a moment. "Did that work?" I asked dubiously.

"Later," Phaeron grunted.

The fighting was dying down around us, and he had a few more souls to disentangle. There wasn't much else for me to do except to gingerly grab one of the bird corpses by the edge of a wing to drag it toward the burn pile being formed on the street corner. Geo took it from me and lobbed it on top of the pile.

"Look, I'm a UFO!" my handbook exclaimed, hovering itself halfway open over a broken feather. A scorching ray emanated down from it, setting the feather's edges on fire.

My brows rose. "Well, that's useful," I said. I tucked the smoking feather into the burn pile for it to spread.

"Thank you. I pride myself on being *quite* useful!"

Braza cut off its Lux spell, to its great disappointment.

With our merge, I didn't feel how much power my spells drew, but she shared how depleted my natural reserves would be just from having the handbook lit for a few minutes.

"This is why we don't set random tools alight," she said. I had the feeling she'd scold me if the effect wasn't so impressive.

I turned toward the stretch of street where Phaeron had laid out six people in total. He stood over them quietly while Wren filmed him, patiently waiting for him to say something. When I joined him, looking at them with Braza's soul sight, she told me, *"The bright white color of the souls within these supernaturals is highly abnormal."* No wonder Phaeron had such a dark look on his face.

"Do you see them?" he asked me.

"I do, but I'm not sure I understand what I'm seeing," I admitted.

He beckoned for me to kneel with him by one of the former torchbearers. "Do you see the cracks?" he asked, switching to Soiluirian in a hush.

I nodded. If this person's soul was a piece of pottery, it'd been dropped from a low height and was barely holding itself together.

"That is soul damage. Myuna's work is crude. The process of binding this person's will nearly tore their soul in several places." He frowned, the picture of troubled.

"Does that mean they're going to die?" Braza spoke for me in Soiluirian.

"Probably. If they wake, it will be to great pain. All of these people will have died briefly and been reborn, so they are unnatural, Myuna's will or no. They will either succumb to their wounds or their hungers."

I thought of my sister with dread for her.

"If they are lucky, there's a small chance they will recover. In that case...we will have to study them before releasing them back into the community." When he looked over at me, I saw the serious prince, the man who'd led his people safely to another world. "Braza, we must contain them until we know where their fates land."

"Yes, my prince," she said.

"In the meantime, Myuna is probably improving on her soul binding skills. If she takes her time, the future torchbearers may have enough intelligence and presence to use their magic again," he said, shaking his head slowly. "If that happens, we will be overwhelmed."

He looked up at Wren and her camera, switching to English. "Our mission is successful. Cress and I will use shadow magic to take these people to a safe place, then we shall return to the hospital," he said.

23

CRESS

With the people we'd rescued resting in individual containment rooms and the sun setting by the time our group returned to the safety of the hospital, there was little to do but rest and wait for the next day.

Which started before five in the morning, practically a crime. Madigan flipped on the overhead light in my coven's shared room in the hospital and rapped her knuckles on her crystal-covered shoulder. "Up, all of you! We have a visitor," she announced.

We were having another odd slumber party crammed together in one room overnight. Well, most of us were. Phaeron had never settled, and Geo had remained in gargoyle form, going down to fight any creatures that sniffed around the grounds overnight.

"Mom," Roe groaned, covering her eyes with a forearm.

"A merman is asking for Willow," Madigan said.

That had the redhead's attention. Several of us moved quicker with the news and stole glances at our quiet friend. She seemed just as confused as I felt, though hope sparkled in her eyes as she murmured, "Maybe he will teach me something about how to control my magic."

"Do you know who he might be?" I asked her.

She replied with an exaggerated shrug. Oh joy...another surprise.

"We don't all have to see who it is," she protested a little belatedly when the rest of our coven was already heading downstairs.

"The sun's not even up, and he was important enough to wake all of us," Ben said, shrugging as he fell into step with Willow and me. "We'll all want to see what's up."

Madigan waited in front of the door to the boardroom we kept using for group meetings. "This concerns a matter of your identity. I'd be honored to sit beside you while you hear what this man has to say," she said to Willow.

"Of course. Everyone's welcome to be here if they want to be," she answered. She looked completely blindsided when she walked in first and the merman bowed to her from where he stood at the back of the room.

"Oh, um, hello," she said with a nervous laugh.

"Hey, it's that guy." Ben elbowed Willow, gesturing to the aquatic familiar she had bobbing over her shoulder in its own personal bubble of water. It was a cuttlefish, apparently, so skilled in changing its coloring on command that I'd never gotten a good look at it.

"You know him?" I whispered to Ben. We all filed in and had seats around the table, a full coven—plus Áine and Madigan—show of support for whatever this man wanted from Willow.

"He was at the familiar fair. You know, the one where she got a dude's number?" he whispered back.

Oh, yeah. Willow had blushed over the news of snagging a "totally cute" merman's number at the event. He was in his land form, wearing a damp wetsuit molded to his broad shoulders and carved muscles. Cerulean fish scales sparkled on his cheeks and forehead where skin met short navy-blue hair. Fins flapped in place of human ears.

There was a trident propped against the back wall. Unlike the delicate silver one Willow carried, this one was solid, built for skewering with a head marked by a few swirling runes. Mer magic.

Willow looked ready to crawl under the conference table. "Zander, what's going on?" she asked.

"I know this is going to sound unusual, especially with an audience," the merman said slowly. "Laiken, the Coral King, has sent me to find you, Willow. We strongly suspect you are his daughter."

Her mouth popped open. "What?" she gasped.

"Whoa there. On what evidence?" Madigan interjected.

He brushed a hand through his hair. "Okay, yeah, you all might be a little suspicious, and that's normal. The supernatural world watched the broadcast of the fight that led to most of the Crown Coven dying. At this point, every pixel has been scrubbed for information. The merfolk took an interest in you, Willow, and your sudden surge of power. By the abyss, even the gray color your scales manifested in the recording seems to suggest they belong to the royal line."

"Oh no," she whispered.

"It didn't take much digging to find your name and other important information. Your age and status as a half-mer are what really tipped off some of us that know the king. He tried to hide you from his enemies, but if we've found you, they have as well. For your safety, you need to come with me," he said.

She looked down at her hands. I thought she was

ducking her head from the attention on her, but then she lifted her arm. Pinkish scales covered the back of it, along with a shimmery fin of the same color. "Does this match?" she asked. The moment her focus broke so she could speak, her mer side smoothed back into creamy, human skin.

"Coral red. Royal blood runs true through your veins... Princess," Zander said, bowing to her again.

"Congratulations, Willow," I said, the first to break the silence that followed, where most of us gaped between the two of them.

"Wait, no. This is crazy," she said, interrupting the belated chorus of congratulations that followed mine. Her palms hit the table. "For those of you who don't know, King Laiken is a demigod merman who rules from...well, all you need to know is that his territory encompasses the Coral Sea and a chunk of the Pacific. He doesn't have *kids*."

"That have survived to adulthood," Zander appended. "Whatever you've heard in school, the reality is far more gruesome. All of your half-siblings have been murdered, and you will be next without protection."

She breathed a disbelieving laugh. "I don't know a place farther from King Laiken's enemies than this pocket dimension. We have more to worry about than merfolk politics right now!"

"Really? Because merfolk politics is the only thing keeping Ocean Gate 438 open. We've been turning a blind eye when groups of unnatural hunters go in and survivors come out. All because the king is waiting for his daughter to return to safety," he said.

My mouth popped open at the implications. "All because of me?" Willow asked in a small voice. "But...if I go with you, he'll close it?"

"The moment you're through, Princess."

"What if the unnaturals realize it's open first?"

Zander quirked his lip. "If things here would grow too dire, I'm sure he would close it. But only if you refuse to leave and the evil goddess is heading for the gate."

Willow was practically sparkling as she turned to me. She gave me a meaningful look, one that promised she had an idea. "Cress," she whispered. "It's my time in the sun."

"I'd say so, Princess," I replied.

A flush didn't dim her toothy grin. "Thank you, Zander. I need some time to consider your offer and what to do next," she said to him. He hesitated, looking confused by her gentle dismissal.

"In the meantime, will you help me learn how to wield some of my magic?" she invited.

WILLOW REMAINED WITH ZANDER, encouraging the rest of us to go back to sleep. I only left because she seemed to trust him and he was already holding a globe of water to begin a practice session she needed quite badly.

While everyone else filtered back to our shared room, I sat on the side of an upturned couch and closed my eyes, reaching for Braza over our soul tether. She'd left me when I'd fallen asleep, and my head seemed too quiet without her.

"Good morning, brightest of souls," she said.

"Hi, Braza. Do you want to come hang out?" The question seemed too casual, considering she was hitchhiking along in my body for this particular brand of "hanging out," but what else was I going to call it?

"Perhaps later. I sense you had an exciting morning."

I took a moment to show her the complete memory of the early wakeup and the merman's revelations for Willow. *"Do you know anything about the king they were talking about?"*

"I would ask a librarian, but..." After letting that hang for a moment, she laughed softly. *"I already know some. The affairs of mer didn't reach Moongrove Library often, but King Laiken is a particularly old figure. He was one of the last mer rulers to agree to relations with the greater supernatural community. His kingdom's wealth suffered for his decision. Such a thing breeds discontent."*

"Enough to have his family members murdered?" I demanded.

"Certainly. Up until now, he has been too powerful to kill. Not all demigod supernaturals are built the same. I can recommend some fascinating books on the lives and times of the truly godlike amongst us once we escape this pocket dimension."

"That sounds amazing." At this point, I'd even take a textbook to tuck into for an evening. I missed the escapism of reading.

"Phaeron is awake, by the way, and heading your way," she added. *"I gave him as much privacy as I could when he retired to the room you two shared the night prior."*

"Hopefully he slept," I said.

She withdrew from my awareness with a feeling of farewell. A few moments later, something tickled under my chin. Playful tendrils of shadow transformed into solid fingers attached to the Moihan dimensional who tilted my head up and leaned over to kiss me briefly.

"Do you need me to right this couch?" Phaeron asked. Though his eyes were lidded as if he'd just woken, purplish shadows were starting to color the hollows underneath them.

"Maybe if you lie down with me," I said seriously.

"Don't tempt me, bright soul. We are in public," he purred.

My breath hitched despite my concern for him, and I held up my index finger. "For a nap."

He lifted me by the hips and flipped the couch onto its feet with a twirl of his shadows.

"Showoff," I teased. The corner of his mouth lifted, but he didn't sit, not even when he placed me back down. "If you don't want to sleep, just resting for a while won't hurt. I'll tell you about the meeting you missed."

"Joy," he sighed but lowered onto the couch and held his arms out for me. He guided me so he was the big spoon, tucking my back to the line of his body. Our legs twined, and his breath ghosted over my ear. "You'll find that the older you get, the more meetings occupy your time."

"Madigan and Hana do seem to be in a lot of them," I said.

He hummed, nuzzling into my hair. I stifled a giggle at the sensation.

"Well, you might as well tell me why this one was different from all the rest," he murmured.

I told him of Willow's potential change in status as a mer princess, distracted quickly when he took the opportunity to pepper my earlobe on down to my jaw with playful nips. Hopefully this meant he wasn't angry at me anymore for yesterday's disagreement.

"I am not overly surprised," he rumbled close to my ear. There was no hiding my shiver, and I felt him smile. "Her mer side is powerful enough. Hybrid or no, it was impressive she nearly drowned several people upon unlocking that side of herself."

"Sure, but it's made her more afraid of what she can do.

I hope Zander can teach her some control," I sighed. "In the meantime, you were in a different meeting and never told me the outcome."

"Which one was that?"

"You spoke with Geo and Ben privately," I prompted.

"Oh. I think you will be pleased."

"But, like, what did you all say?" I asked. "Did you get Geo to agree—"

He patted my hip. "Be right back."

His solid form turned to shadow, and he set me to sit upright rather than roll into the space he left behind. I sighed and rested my head back, taking my own advice and resting for the day ahead. Now that Braza had pointed it out, I recognized that he was going out of his way to change the subject.

Phaeron didn't take long to reform. His shadows tickled over my skin again before becoming firm fingers, tugging my hair to fall over the back of the couch. I sat up and glanced over my shoulder, seeing he'd retrieved a comb and a brush and something else coiled in his tail.

"Don't worry. They're yours," he said. He started brushing out my hair, gently teasing out the knots.

I flushed. "It's not that bad, is it?"

"Are Braza's memories still fading?" he asked in return. "You are my mate. It's my joy to care for your needs."

He brushed on, humming a merry but unfamiliar tune. When I tried to look back at him, he pressed his fingertips to my temples and steered my head to the angle he wanted. I tried to focus on what I remembered of Braza's life, some of the finer details slipping through my fingers like water. "You used to wear dark blue on your face and horns."

"A couple lifetimes ago, yes."

"If you want to teach me the symbols...I could try drawing them on your horns," I offered.

"Soon." He stooped to kiss my temple. "I am the definition of 'at war' right now and should not wear any adornments."

"But when Myuna is dead..."

He breathed a wistful sigh. "If you are comfortable observing this part of my culture, I would love to be marked as a mated male once more."

"Of course," I breathed, sensing this meant a lot more to him than he was willing to put into words.

I barely felt the plastic edge of the comb as he divided my hair into sections. "Though I suppose you would have to source gold stain for the task. But maybe I'm over-thinking it. I'm not sure it will matter as much as it used to."

"Gold is for the king?" I guessed.

"First prince," he answered. "Paradoxically, my parents were able to wear whatever color they desired. And yet every day, they had servants paint their faces with white stain."

"Wait—"

"Hold still," he chuckled. He started braiding my hair.

"But you should be the king," I said. There was an extra tickle on my scalp from his shadows moving with his fingers. I had the feeling he was about to tie my hair into a complicated style.

"And yet I have no intentions of ever being a king. The nation that joined the tribes of my people was poisoned by Myuna's influence. I want nothing to do with it. Besides... the world has moved on while I was in stasis, and my people have too. There *is* no throne to take." He almost sounded happy about it, so I simply shrugged.

"If that's your decision. About your parents..." I bit my lip.

"I'll tell you anything you wish to know. Much of it is unflattering," he said.

"They were torchbearers?" I asked.

"Indeed. She did not turn them fully white like she did my brother, but they were the strongest followers she had. They shared animaris after an age of ruling to satisfy Myuna and earn her continued favor. The goddess was pleased to groom Endaeron, and they were quite happy to have yielded an heir and a spare on their first try. They pursued their own interests afterward."

"Does that bother you?"

"Not anymore. When I was a child, I longed for the love heaped on my brother and wondered why Myuna had over-looked me. But it makes sense now. If Endaeron had died before the Age of Decay, I would've taken his place as first prince and been corrupted by her magic in his stead. At one point, I'd have thought it an honor," he said with a scoff. "But without her blessing, I was never truly his rival when he lived. Now that he is a monster, it doesn't matter."

He was braiding the tips of my hair, so when I looked over my shoulder at him, he didn't move my head back a third time. "Still, you never should've been made to feel lesser."

He flashed a reassuring smile. "It is something I am at peace with. Almost done, by the way."

"Time for one more question?"

"As many as you desire," he answered in his effortless purr.

"What is animaris?"

"Ah." There was a wicked gleam in his topaz eyes. "As a rough translation, it is essence or life force, something my kind puts to use that yours does not. Males naturally have more than females due to how we reproduce. I know humans can get pregnant at most any time past puberty, but for my people, it is a conscious choice nurtured by both sides through a pregnancy. Animaris follows the life-cycle of the child. First, it's an aphrodisiac for the mother."

He released my braid and slid closer. I propped myself on my knees, turning to rest my arm on the top of the couch to face him directly. "How is it shared?" I asked, feeling a bit of warmth rise to my cheeks.

I'd given him a great opening to rest his fangs on my neck. His hot breath fanned over my exposed nape, and I stilled. Was this a test? Heat pooled between my legs as he drew his tongue over my skin, lips skimming my pulse point.

"Usually the same place as a mating mark," he answered. With a groan, he jerked away from me and shook his head.

He spoke while staring at my neck, which I covered with my fingers. "Anyway, once the child is made, both parents continuously share animaris to encourage growth in the womb. Since hybrids don't exist for my people, the baby usually takes after the father, as this is the stage where he's sharing energy while the mother shares nutrients. Once they are born, both parents are tethered to the child equally until they enter adolescence and their own soul and animaris is fully formed."

I beckoned for him to come sit with me, and he grew rigid, shuttering his eyes for a few long moments. "I just remember Braza was an unhappy child because of animaris," I said.

"Mmm, the lack thereof. She was small for being of the

Iorsio tribe. We never had a chance..." He drifted off with a look of pain.

"Phaeron?" I murmured.

"Children can be adopted in such a way that blood ties do not matter," he continued.

"You can talk about her. I mean, you don't have to avoid your old mate's name for my sake," I said, though my heart was in my throat.

This time, he did come sit down and drew my hands into his. "Cress, talking about past mates is unkind. Anything I tell you will make you wonder if I am comparing you or if I still think of her."

"It would be cruel to expect you not to ever think about her or the daughter you had."

That look of pain sharpened. I didn't know if Phaeron could cry, but by the defined facets I saw within the glowing depth of his eyes, he was close. "I'm sorry... I shouldn't have mentioned..." I stammered.

"Keshora," he breathed out. "Ravai. And Braza. The family Myuna purposefully destroyed. *My* family."

I gave his hands a squeeze in sympathy. "It was a beautiful one," I said.

He wet his lips, considering me for a few moments. "You would have liked Keshora. She was a kind soul. What you didn't see from Braza's memories was how heartbroken she was when her application to adopt Braza was denied. I felt it halfway across a continent, fighting in one of my old nation's constant pointless wars. Keshora loved and desired children more than anything."

He hesitated, reading my face again. I smiled some in encouragement. "That's where she was very different from you. But she was well into her hundredth year when we met, while you're just getting started," he said.

"Does that feel weird to you?" I asked with a nervous quaver.

He leaned over to touch his forehead to mine. "You have incredible potential, bright soul, and that means you will be my equal. I just get the honor of helping you reach that pinnacle. My body recognized you as my mate, my True Light, immediately," he answered. I breathed out with relief. It seemed he knew exactly what to say to make my heart shimmer. "That is destiny and nothing less. What *is* weird to me is you wearing half of Braza's power. Having you both in the same body is..." He tisked lightly.

"She gives us privacy," I said.

"She is a powercore. There is no privacy," he countered.

I raised a brow. "Okay, she's your daughter."

"One who I have failed immeasurably," he murmured. He looked over at a group of defenders coming and going from the front entrance. It was a shift change, and amongst the Crystal fae was Geo in his gargoyle form. He spotted us and started for where we were sitting.

"What do you mean? She still adores you," I said. He just had to look at everything she'd done for him lately to prove it.

"I was not strong enough to say goodbye to her. I so desperately wanted her...to live..." Phaeron cocked his head, looking at Geo strangely.

I hardly noticed, though, standing and holding my arms out to Geo. His face lit up, and he took his human form before lifting and whirling me around. "Good morning, beautiful," he said.

"Safe and sound because of you." I shared a kiss with him once he placed me back on my feet.

I expected Phaeron to have disappeared, like he so often did when I took my eyes off him for a moment too long.

Except this time, he was where I'd left him. "Take her away if you please. She must be getting tired of my stories by now," he said.

"Okay." After a pause, Geo reconsidered and added, "We will be at breakfast. Come with us and get your ration."

My astonishment must've been obvious, as Phaeron winked before Geo laced his fingers with mine and tugged me along to get some essential calories for the day ahead.

24

PHAERON

WE ATE breakfast in a waiting room with Cress's coven, as the hospital's tiny cafeteria was already packed full of defenders and staff members gulping down their rations before getting to work. The witches were quite excited. Breakfast was bacon and eggs.

Cress had gotten plenty of compliments for the formal braid I'd given her, with rows of tiny, hearty wildflowers tied just behind her ears. I was rather proud of my handiwork. She sat between Geo and me, taking slow, distracted bites while she chatted with Willow, who'd perched in a seat across from us.

"We can just announce that Ocean Gate 438 is open and ask for backup. I bet you people will come," Willow was saying. "My maybe-father won't close it unless I go through it, so why not get some help?"

"It would be unwise," I said in as gentle a tone as I could muster. I could see she was in delicate spirits, excited to contribute and help. "We need specific help. If you put a call out to the greater supernatural world, the first people to arrive through that ocean gate will be young glory seekers and a handful of demigods foolish enough to think they can take Myuna on directly. They will only feed her and make her stronger."

Willow's face fell. "But—"

"How will we even separate the help we want versus the help that arrives?" Geo asked.

"Easily enough. We don't ask for help," I said. Cress had been in the earlier meeting where we'd discussed this already and nodded tentatively. "The fewer living souls inside Cerris City, the better. If we truly wish to take advantage of Ocean Gate 438, we will evacuate the whole city, including the staff at this hospital. We'd scare the bounty hunters into returning to where they came from. No one remains except those absolutely necessary to our mission."

Dubious glances turned my way from every witch in earshot. I folded and crunched down a whole strip of bacon, waiting. The salt and fat exploded on my tongue just right, and I closed my eyes from simple pleasure. I could've eaten a whole side of bacon rather than the two sad strips each of us had been rationed.

"If all of our support leaves," Geo said slowly, "who will remain to take care of Myuna and her monsters?"

Roe, sitting close enough to pick up the conversation, pitched in, "There's no way everyone can be evacuated, no matter how far-reaching Wren's stream is. Too many people will die if you're thinking we leave too and collapse the pocket dimension behind us."

"I didn't say we flee. I'm not convinced Myuna can be erased so easily, anyway." I didn't hide the troubled twist to my mouth. "What if the fabric of Cerris City rips around her as it collapses? It will be the Age of Decay all over again, but *much* worse with such a huge population of unaware humans facing a hungry cosmic deity."

"We don't know that will happen," Roe said.

"We don't know it won't," I countered. "Auric et Vess has a plan to return Myuna to Soiluire. It will not require an army to carry out. All we have to do is get him close enough to her to manipulate the Void that clings to her like a second skin."

Willow stroked her chin thoughtfully. "Going back to getting as many people out of Cerris City as possible. We could use the stream for announcing a gathering point and avoid mentioning the ocean gate."

"Indeed. But we must be prepared to fight. We will face the majority of Myuna's forces, as the unnaturals will follow survivors or sense a big group of us and attack. When we win, we break up the flow of unwilling servants into her service and destroy what she's already amassed. She will be forced into the one thing she doesn't want to do..." I bared my fangs in a bloodthirsty grin. "To get up and fight for herself."

Cress worried her lip. "But if we lose..."

"We'd be completely fucked, right?" Willow murmured. "We'd deliver everyone left in Cerris City to Myuna's monsters."

"We won't lose. We can't," Roe said, punching her palm.

"We won't," I echoed, looking over Cress's head at Geo. He raised an eyebrow back. "We need to gather some resources before this fight."

"Such as?" he prompted.

"Armor, weapons, food, water. I would strike out on my own, but I need Cress with me," I said.

A dangerous rumble sounded from the gargoyle's throat.

"Which means you need to come too," I concluded.

"Count me in," Roe said. Not to be left out, as always. "Where are we going?"

I drew a folded map out of my pocket. I'd nicked one from a tourist display that was running low on them since most were pinned on the wall of the makeshift war room. Unfolding it, I pinched its corners with a few tendrils of shadow and floated it between us. "Highfall's Mall. Too far away for us to walk there. I know you want to help, Roe… but this is a mission for the three of us. If we run into danger, Cress and I can blend into the shadows, while Geo can fly."

"Hey, what about me?" Ben called. He sat with Wren, the two of them bent over a set of paper notes covered in basic celestial witch runes.

"And we carry Ben along to manage the stream," I added.

Wren narrowed her eyes, and Roe shifted uncomfortably at my suggestion. But we were simply too large of a group to cover the ground I wanted to see tonight.

"If you break my phone, I'll break you," Wren grumbled.

I chuckled. "We will bring back as many new phones as we can carry."

I reached down to take my other piece of bacon, and my thumb skimmed three. Cress stole a quick glance my way and covered her lips with her fingers, a subtle enough tell as to where they'd come from.

I curled my tail tip around her calf for a small caress. If only we had time for more than mere teases. *Soon*, I told myself.

Hopefully she and the other two men would be willing to go along with the rest of my plan once we were en route.

"ARE YOU SURE ABOUT THIS?" Cress asked, stealing glances upward. Myuna's foul bird creatures lined the roofs, watching our truck drive by with unblinking white stares.

Geo could've flown ahead of us and chased them off, but I needed him here to listen to my full plan. At my request, he remained in human form in the seat behind Cress. She drove. When our options were her or Ben, her caution was the preferable choice.

Our allies had lent us one of the largest flatbeds for what they thought was a supply run. Highfall's Mall was outside of the territory that'd been searched for survivors. It sat at the edge of the pocket dimension, a mega-sized structure sure to already be looted and occupied.

The truck hit a bump in the road, jostling us. I stifled a growl, already disliking the confines of this cabin. "Myuna has a special interest in you and me. If she is aware we have split off from the rest of the group, there's a higher chance she will send her strongest servant after us," I answered.

Ben said through gritted teeth, "*Garroway.*"

"You want to use me as bait again?" Cress asked dryly.

"We are both bait this time. If we are out after nightfall in a prominent public place, we can compel Myuna to send him," I said.

Geo's frown deepened. "I did not agree to this trip to put Cress in danger."

"Wait, Geo, put that aside for a moment," Ben said, turning in his seat to look at the gargoyle. "This is our chance to finally turn Garroway into ash."

The look of disapproval slowly morphed on Geo's face. He blew out a slow sigh. "As always, it seems I am the only one saying no to a reckless plan," he grumbled. "But I have wondered why we have not yet seen Garroway and the Hunger. They could decimate the survivors we've gathered in the hospital if given half a chance."

"They will once there are no easier options to steal and deliver to Myuna. She is still acting like her old, predictable self, going for the lowest-hanging fruit first," I said.

"Once we evacuate survivors through the ocean gate, there won't be many of those left," Cress said.

"Exactly. There is no better way to fight him than on our own terms."

And this time, I would snuff out the Hungering Darkness completely. I had hesitated too many times before, seeing it as the remains of my brother more than the shade that'd murdered and consumed hundreds of innocents. It was time I ripped its remaining soul in half...see how it failed to cope with such a devastating wound.

Cress smiled after a moment, saying in a two-toned voice full of forced levity, "Plus, if we have to wait for nightfall...shopping spree!"

"Everything left is free," Ben agreed.

Even Geo cracked a little grin. "Park the truck right by the doors to load it up."

And I will ensure no unnaturals disturb your fun, I thought.

Bella meowed at me, her eyes wide and concerned from where she rested belly up in the crook of my arm. "Everything's okay, baby," Cress cooed toward her familiar. The other two cats were in the back, napping with Ben's ferret. "Except...if I knew we were going after Garroway, I wouldn't have brought my familiars at all."

"We will keep an eye on them," I said. It was the only thing we could do, since Myuna was corrupting animals big and small to serve her. But they were more than just pets.

They could help Cress and Ben fight by letting them borrow an ounce of feline grace or another attribute through the familiar bond.

With the help of Wren's phone, we arrived at Highfall's Mall in a short time. Ben placed a small device in his ear and tapped his thumbs across the phone's screen. "Hey, Tish, we're here," he said, speaking to seemingly no one. "No shit? The power's out in the whole building?"

"Don't turn the stream on until we know what we're dealing with," I said to him before ghosting out of the vehicle as shadows. I stretched as the others climbed out, and Ben muttered "showoff" in my direction.

"I've grown to master a proper entrance or exit in my time," I said.

"Proper? Try dramatic," he replied. "Well, this is your kind of place, Big P. We're going blind into the dark. Tish can't find a single camera online to warn us of what's inside."

He pointed through a set of glass doors, where the insides of the mall were shrouded in darkness. "I'll do some scouting. Stay here," I said, turning to shadows before anyone could air a complaint.

I felt for the small tether of power connecting me to Braza. Neither of us had severed it, even once my free will was returned. It gave me a good idea of how far I could travel before my mind was susceptible to Myuna or Endaeron.

That thread grew taut before I was done scouting the whole complex. It was four stories of shops, play areas, and kiosks. The lights were out and the air stale. I'd expected survivors and detected none...but Myuna's creatures had infested the food court and restaurants, while her torchbearers shuffled along like sleepwalkers in the common areas. I unbound the souls of the two nearest the entryway, then dragged their unconscious bodies into my shadows.

Cress's eyes widened when I took form in the blinding sunlight and laid the former torchbearers in the bed of the truck. "Seems we have something to occupy our time after all," I said, sharing with the group what I'd seen.

"Once we take care of all the torchbearers, I could drive them back to the library?" Ben suggested.

"Perhaps. I don't like the idea of splitting up further," I said. The first batch I'd unbound from Myuna's will still rested in their containment rooms without waking. These victims had a similar level of soul damage, unfortunately. Early victims of the goddess's sloppy work.

Cress drew her sword and handbook and set the edge of her blade alight. It'd be a beacon for any unnatural the moment she stepped into the mall. Geo nudged his way in front of her after transitioning to gargoyle form, holding his tower shield and a mace made from his quartz spikes. And Ben announced he was turning on the stream, placing the phone in a sling over his chest.

"Yeah, I hear you," he muttered while he drew blood runes up his arm. "I don't need you chattering in my ear, Bianca... Uh huh, fuck you too. For those early watchers, hi, it's Ben. Today we're going extreme shopping."

I shook my head, bemused by the whole idea of streaming. "Ready?" I asked.

Cress, now wearing the purple-black shadows of Braza's power, nodded first. She wrapped a concentration of darkness around her blade to dim it.

I hissed toward Ben for quiet and pointed at the nearest shopfront. A sheet of what looked like chain-lengths covered up the entrance, except a huge hole had been ripped through the metal. Dozens of white eyes turned our way from the bowels of what'd once been a restaurant.

Geo charged, catching the first lunging rat-creature with a swing of his weapon. It died with a piercing squeal, and I hung back, hearing the death cry echo further into the enemy-infested mall.

Footsteps pounded their way toward us. I raised both hands, warping the shadows into grasping things. Three more turned supernaturals threw themselves into my snares. I made quick work of unbinding their souls and was about to carry them through the shadows to our truck when a flash of green brushed the back of my hand.

Stinging pain followed the line of a two-inch long cut. I swirled into the shadows, passing through a second shot of green magic while searching for the culprit. A verdant witch clutching a wand stooped just behind a counter, her white eyes roaming for where I'd gone. I reappeared behind her, and she froze as my claws tugged her soul free.

I clucked my tongue as I inspected the loose knot her soul had been tied into. Just as I'd feared—Myuna was figuring out how not to destroy her victims utterly during the binding process. We'd have to be more careful to weed out intelligent torchbearers. There were countless hiding spaces in this mall for ambushes.

The others were waiting for me when I returned with the verdant witch's unconscious body. *"Trouble, my prince?"* Braza asked privately.

I answered her aloud for the sake of the group. "Perhaps this location is too infested with Myuna's victims. That last witch still had access to her magic. Imagine if there are many more like her... We will exhaust ourselves clearing out the mall before nightfall."

"I think we should try it," Cress said. "Imagine if we

gained control of the mall and used it as a rendezvous point for survivors."

I shrugged and gathered up the unconscious torch-bearer to deliver her to the truck. In the meantime, Cress talked to Geo and Ben. The former expressed a desire for us to leave before nightfall, while the latter wanted a good fight.

The familiars were distracted by a game of chase around their witches' feet, with Flit outpacing them. He used me as an obstacle when I took a knee, scaling my leg and squirming when I caught him and placed him on the ground.

"I know you can understand me," I said. Four sets of eyes blinked up at me, quite keen for a set of animals. "Your task is to stay close to your witch and avoid capture at all costs."

Flit bobbed his head and moved to stand by Ben's feet. Bella purred and brushed my leg, tail up, while Jin meowed in response. "They're saying they understand," Cress translated.

"Let's see how we feel after a couple hours of this, then," I said, standing.

The beast of shadows and teeth hiding just under my skin relished the idea of a true fight. I would've eagerly taken on the challenge ahead of us on my own if it weren't for the hole in my soul and the consequences that came with it.

Cress lit the way for Ben and Geo while I prowled at the edges of her magic. I had to turn my head away from her radiance. It made my mouth water. Another reason to despise the Hungering Darkness, for infecting me with this desire to taste my mate's soul. It was truly relentless.

I pitched my frustrations into the intermittent fights

that followed. It took less than an hour for us to travel to the top floor and clear it, though I spent a significant amount of time afterward forming a burn pile of slain unnaturals and filling the truck bed with unconscious torchbearers. One of us would have to return to the library sooner than expected.

Chill wind kissed my face, and I risked a glance at the sky as clouds skidded over the sun. An angry gray storm flowed toward us from the horizon, moving impossibly fast on magic-kissed gales. With that realization came a pricking sensation over my scalp. The ghost of white talons trying to burrow into my skull.

The Hungering Darkness was coming.

25

CRESS

"Totally chic, don't you think?" I asked Braza, eyeing the dress displayed on one of the last standing mannequins in a storefront. We were taking a quick break while Phaeron cleaned up the mess we'd made of the unnatural nests we'd stomped.

"*You should try it on. Dark colors look nice on you,*" she answered in my head.

"Maybe if we get a chance to shop." I practically pouted. Maybe it was my entitlement showing, but I'd hoped the mall would've been relatively empty and untouched. A shopping spree in a mega mall with just my men and Braza? *Yes, please.*

"Are you talking to yourself again?" my handbook asked, fluttering in for a landing on top of my head.

"Quiet. There are still monsters," hissed Jin. I stooped to scratch her behind the ears, and she loosed a soft purr, leaning into my fingertips.

"Is the kitty mad at me?" my handbook asked in a loud whisper.

I put a finger to my lips, and again, we went "shhhh" at the same time.

Braza crackled with electric surety. *"Something's wrong."*

I lifted my weapon and spun, looking for the danger. Ben and Geo stirred nearby, alert within moments. Over the sound of my breath, I could hear the calls of unnaturals on the levels below us, plus the sound of claws on tile. "They're on the move," I murmured.

Phaeron took form from shadows just as I was smothering my blade's glow. A crazed glint flashed in his gemstone eyes, his teeth bared in a snarl. Braza reacted first, throwing out a wave of energy that suffused him within moments.

He flinched and grasped his head. With my weapon dimmed, he was nearly one with the dark mall around us. "Endaeron is almost here," he growled.

A winged shape dive-bombed us. The creature, a former seagull with a puffed-out chest like a water balloon, released a shrill scream. It exploded with a wet sound when Geo smashed it on the flat of his shield. "Myuna is not content to wait for nightfall," he rumbled.

"Much as I want to fuck up Garroway...we're outnumbered," Ben pointed out.

Thunder rumbled overhead. Rain began to aggressively patter against the ceiling.

"I moved the torchbearers we rescued to the entrance foyer," Phaeron said. I heard the rasp of his sword leaving its sheath. "It's too late to retreat."

"Then it's time we stood and fought." Despite everything, Ben smiled. There was a sound of glass cracking, and then he had purple liquid on his fingertips, using it to paint a bold eye symbol between his brows.

Geo took to the air with a heave of his obsidian body.

There was an outraged series of shrieks that followed, accompanied by the sound of groaning metal. I encouraged Braza's shadows over my face, parting the impenetrable darkness to spot what he'd done. He'd dropped his considerable weight in the middle of the closest escalator, buckling it in half and stranding the torchbearers that were halfway up its stationary length.

Dozens of hands grabbed for the gargoyle, dragging him off balance toward the seething mass of unnaturals.

"He can handle himself," Braza reassured me. A split second later, he'd taken to the air again, shaking off a doskalo-like creature trying to cling to his ankle. It dropped for a hard landing a floor below.

Every prickling length of her shadows had gone taut with awareness, pressing into my skin with an electric sense of danger. The Hungering Darkness was somewhere close, its presence swirling over our heads in search of an opening.

"Go hide," I whispered to Jin, who scampered away but not too far, hunkering down with the other familiars. I could still feel my connection to her, the ferocity I could borrow if I needed it. Bella could grant me her enhanced senses, while Milo preferred to lend his feline grace. In a pinch, their contributions could change the momentum of a fight.

"Geo!" I shouted. We needed him here, with us. He was in the process of destroying the other escalator, set a few yards away from the first. It wouldn't stop the unnatural infestation below us, but they would have to find another route to the top floor.

White shadows took form right in front of me. Garroway moved like a blur, striking my sword right out of my hand with a full-strength snap of his own blade. The

Lux spell sputtered out, throwing our surroundings into dim murk. The relentless gray storm overhead prevented any natural light from interfering.

Phaeron charged him with a shadowborn's roar, shattering the air with his fury and the ring of metal on metal. I sent out a tendril of Braza's shadows to retrieve my sword by its hilt and turned to Ben. The mark on his forehead glowed a faint purple. "Can you see with that?" I asked, pointing at it.

"Kind of," he answered.

"Good enough," I said, then leapt forward in full shadowborn form to join the duel of black and white shadows.

Phaeron had been edged back from the combination of Endaeron's power and Garroway's vampire strength and speed. He attacked with bladed shadows, distracting Garroway for a key moment. I slipped my weapon into the vampire's guard, spraying dark blood from a slash just above his ribs.

But the rip of flesh began to knit together. Skin and blood reattached before my eyes, a sickening sight that reminded me of how a blood witch healed from a mending rune. In seconds, all that was left was the blood on his skin and the rip in his clothes.

He'd turned to glare in my direction. "Cress, at last. How I've grown to despise you," he said in a two-toned voice. White shadow flashed in my face, forming thorny tendrils that bound my upper arms to my chest.

"The feeling's mut—"

His magic ensnared and moved me; I squeezed my eyes shut just in time, struggling out of his shadows. We'd traveled down a level, and I was a few feet above the ground when I freed myself of his magical grasp. I crashed to the unforgiving tile with my arms still pinned to my side, pain flaring through my hip and leg.

What felt like a hundred sets of eyes turned hot attention toward me. Unnatural creatures and torchbearers alike leapt the moment I landed. Panicking for a moment, I released a shout of alarm, only drawing more attention to myself. Braza took over to help and made shadowy claws over my fingers, which I used to cut through the bindings he'd left on me. They dissipated into white wisps before fading, leaving bright spots over my vision.

I stood and drew my sword, squaring up against an onslaught of monsters. As I debated fleeing, an obsidian figure swooped in for a landing and faltered, lost in the dimness of our surroundings.

"Light," he ground out. I cast a quick Lux on my sword, and the monsters winced. Geo kicked the closest raccoon-like creature away before it could sink its teeth into my shadows and flesh. He lifted his shield and spread his wings, blocking a handful of torchbearers and their grasping hands from reaching me.

A warning jolt of pain radiated down from my jarred hip when I moved to cover his back. *I shall repair you. We must rejoin the prince before Endaeron tries to take his mind,"* Braza said with urgency. We both noticed the duel of black and white above us, occasionally punctuated by the flash of a silvery throwing dagger or a hint of Ben's blood magic infusing a strike.

No one was fighting alone, at least. I helped Geo with waves of light and shadow, shooting out darkness with many sharp edges to strike at the creatures surrounding us.

I cowed the torchbearers by blinding them with a flare from my weapon. They babbled, begging Myuna for mercy as they clawed at their eyes.

"Your goddess says stand down," I ordered with as much authority I could muster. A family of four—two adults and two kids of different ages—the nearest white-eyed people, dropped their hands and stayed in place, looking confused.

Geo hesitated before pivoting, showing no mercy for the twisted animals still throwing themselves at us. The blunt force of his fighting style crunched stretched bones and strained tendons. It left a graveyard around him, shattered bodies tripping the torchbearers that were still trying to get through him to me.

We could try to save them, unlike the animals. As long as Phaeron survived this fight, he could unbind their souls. "I'm going up! Come with me!" I shouted to Geo before falling into the shadows, letting Braza control the magic that turned us into particles.

In a blink, we cleared the guardrail one story up, just in time to see Garroway catch one of Ben's daggers and reverse its course, embedding it in his chest. I heard the sucking gasp he took as he fell backward.

"Stay alive a bit longer, little Benjamin. We have unfinished business," Garroway said in a two-toned drawl.

Ben bared his teeth with another gasping breath. He probed at the wound and wrote the rune for healing on his skin with a shaking hand. I placed myself between him and the possessed vampire, sinking into a guard stance.

"As do we, blood baron," Phaeron snarled.

He reengaged Garroway's attention, lifting his sword to check the vampire's next strike. Several new rips decorated his shirt, most over superficial wounds that leaked his fuchsia blood. The worst one was just under his armpit, where it would cause him trouble in an already difficult fight.

In life, he and Endaeron had been fairly evenly matched with swordplay and shadows. But in death, Endaeron had the advantage of Garroway's preternatural healing and other attributes to help him when he was outnumbered four to one.

I prepared to leap back into the fray. Braza pulled at my awareness, asking for a few more moments as I tested my wounded leg. Her power had turned the lingering ache into a smaller pinch of pain.

Garroway tilted his head. "Ah, yes. So we do. My lady is quite displeased to have you off your leash—"

Phaeron's attention drifted for a split second before he disengaged in a swirl of black shadows, which stirred in the wake of Geo arriving like a battering ram. He checked his momentum with stony wings and slammed shield-first into Garroway, sending him straight through a glass storefront.

I lined up just a step behind Geo as he and Phaeron faced the ragged hole together, forming a wall of muscle and rock. But the Hungering Darkness didn't emerge as a corporeal vampire, instead escaping as a curl of white shadow.

"Behind you!" Ben called in a strained voice.

I whirled around just in time to see Garroway's sword descending toward my head. He'd taken a page out of Phaeron's playbook of tricks to use his shadows to appear in a blind spot. The first to react properly was Phaeron, who caught the swing of the weapon with his own.

His shadowborn form bared its lengthened fangs. "You will not harm my mate," he snarled. "This is the end, Endaeron."

I called on Jin, borrowing from the core of fury she held for the creature that'd killed her first witch. That fierce desire for revenge filled me. I moved with sinewy grace to dance between them as the two men reengaged their stalemate. Phaeron pressed the attack, and so did I, wounding Garroway when he wasn't able to hold us both off at the same time.

When the vampire's sword strayed too close to me, he met the edge of Geo's shield or the swing of his mace. My stony protector moved with me rather than the two nimble swordsmen, covering any avenue that might lead to my harm.

Garroway's wounds were beginning to stick, his vampiric healing overwhelmed by his mounting injuries. It was a matter of time before he started slowing, bogged down by pain. He wasn't going to win this fight, even with Ben recuperating. A flash of understanding lit his blood-colored eyes before he turned to white mist.

"Is there any way to stop him from running?" I asked Braza.

"Patience, brightest of souls. Turn off Lux for a moment."

I did as she suggested, shaking the lingering light out of my weapon. Now that I wasn't actively fighting, Geo shouldered in front of me, shield raised for whatever came next.

"Lick your wounds, then. Coward," Phaeron spat, watching Garroway circle overhead, just beyond our reach.

"As I was saying." Without physical lungs, the dry rasp of a voice speaking telepathically had to be the Hungering Darkness. *"Myuna desires your return. And she is practically salivating for the soul of the purple-haired witch."*

"She can have neither." Phaeron bristled with power, more and more darkness answering to his will. Without the light of my weapon in the way, he beckoned a wave of shadows. A tide of blackness swarmed over the curl of white shadow and dragged it back to the ground. Upon impact, it became Garroway again, struggling against several loops of inky rope binding his body and forcing its way into his mouth, nostrils, and eyes.

"Why must you struggle against the inevitable?" hissed the Hungering Darkness, independent of its host body's choking and writhing. White light flared around Garroway, and Phaeron staggered, clutching his head.

Braza forced a steady stream of power into him through the invisible tether between them. Geo spread his wings to block me from going to him, rumbling dangerously when Phaeron turned. White flared over the yellow in his eyes.

"You shall not harm her," Geo said.

"Just one taste." The psychic whisper was chilling when I realized Phaeron was compelled by it.

He echoed, "Just one taste."

Garroway was getting to his feet, shaking off the choking shadows. White shadows made extra fangs around his victorious grin as Phaeron evaded around Geo's wide stance, rushing straight toward me.

I backed away instinctively from the visage of a predator on the hunt. Before Phaeron could lunge through the remaining distance between us, Geo grabbed his shoulder, fingers digging in hard as the dimensional struggled and bit him, though his shadowborn fangs slid ineffectively off the gargoyle's stone arm. Already, his form softened at the edges, threatening to slip into the shadows and out of Geo's grasp.

"This isn't you. Come back to me." I was begging, fumbling for the mark of protection he'd left on my wrist. I touched it and breathed his name.

Phaeron froze, tilting his head. It was impossible to read his expression under the black shadows that made up his shadowborn form. The white shadows that blazed through the holes for his eyes flared brighter. Was that the Hungering Darkness digging in, forcing his will into my mate's skull?

I circled my thumb on his mark, breathy with fright. "Your True Light needs you."

A snarl of rage left his fanged maw. He drew on his magic for a burst of strength and ripped away from Geo. The gargoyle fumbled and cursed viciously, rushing toward me.

I lifted my hands defensively, shadowy claws out, and braced for impact. No matter how fast Geo was, Phaeron could relocate himself in a blink. But instead of going for me again, Phaeron had turned around and sunk his teeth deep in the white shadows over Garroway's shoulder.

There was no mistaking how he jerked his head to the side, tearing at the Hungering Darkness like an animal. My mouth dropped open in shock. "Oh, fuck," I whispered, fearing the worst for him.

A cloud of white magic enveloped Phaeron. He was a horned shadow crouching within the heart of it, unmoving.

Garroway staggered to the side, clutching his head and his bloodstained sword. He looked around and took in his surroundings, mouth twisting into a sneer. "Well, then," he muttered.

He turned and fled in a blur of speed.

PHAERON

I tore the Hungering Darkness down the middle, just like it'd done to Braza's soul so long ago. When I'd envisioned myself destroying it so utterly, I hadn't dreamed of using my teeth or swallowing a mouthful of the vapors that spurted from the wound like blood.

With that taste, I was damned. So many of my people had started an addiction to the rush of energy and memory within a soul with just one bite. It became a craving that couldn't be slaked except by death. There was no coming back from it once one of us has destroyed the soul of another.

I gave thanks that instead of drinking in the spice and sunlight of Cress's soul, it was what remained of my brother's spirit tearing between my teeth. His memories suffused my mind as the white magic keeping him stitched together failed.

I would've expected him to taste of blood and grave dirt, as painful deaths were the only thing he'd wrought ever since the Age of Decay, but Endaeron was not an ordinary soul, not even when it was only a portion of him left behind. A smooth alcoholic taste suffused my mouth; it was Endaeron's favorite blend, something we'd left behind on Soiluire...akin to an aged whisky.

I felt my awareness fall deeper and deeper out of my body.

A jolt passed through my mind. I opened my eyes, finding myself in a distantly familiar room with that whisky taste on my tongue. And next to me, a figure I'd forgotten yet never could. Endaeron, alive, taller than me. He was ivory-white horns to feet, broad with icy wings shot through with silver blood in his veins. Gold stain limned his forward-facing horns and the angles of his face.

He was in his prime, the First Prince in his suit of white fabric, with the golden symbol of a shadowborn on the breast. Though technically, it was "lightborn" in his case, with his white shadows.

I stilled, and my breath caught. "Brother," I said, like this memory would turn to speak with me.

To my shock, he did. His face tilted down, his white-lined eyes meeting mine. "Brother," he echoed, deep and sure. "Our time is short and your needs are great, so I have selected this memory for you to witness before I fade."

I became aware of the scene around us in a blink, dropped into it as a bystander. Endaeron stood by Myuna's right hand, with me inserted on his other side. In this memory, she was in the form of an Iorsio tribe female, seated on a massive throne in one of her many private rooms. A Vrassorm woman knelt before her, her skin nearly as pale as the goddess from what she witnessed within a globe of black Void energy.

"Well? What does the Void whisper of my future?" Myuna asked in her awful multi-layered voice.

The woman was a Vess, with one cloudy eye and the other quivering with fear. "I need to consult with it f-further, my lady. S-Sometimes the Void can be so cryptic..."

A tight smile twisted Myuna's mouth. "I insist. Surely you do not doubt your goddess's ability to understand a prophecy?"

"My lady, it is unwise to probe the future out of fear," Endaeron said.

As a dimensional, her eyes glittered like diamonds as she swung her attention toward him. I tensed, but she didn't notice me. Of course not. This had happened on another planet, in another age where my brother still lived.

Even seated, she loomed over him. "Do I seem fearful to you?"

"Fear comes in many forms. It would be disconcerting if you were looking for any other reason," he answered.

She propped her chin on her fist, stirring a circle of light with her other hand. "So long I have known you, and yet there is still so much for you to learn. My ascension is soon."

He was the picture of happiness. "Yes, my lady."

With a flick of her wrist, that circle of light spun toward him, popping against his cheek like a soap bubble. "And you shall ascend with me. To ensure our success, why not harvest the Void? Why not have its greatest wielders tell me what could go wrong?"

She laughed, a great shriek of wailing souls. The Vess flinched, as did I.

"*I didn't know what she meant, Phaeron.*" My brother's voice was in my head as the memory continued to play out.

"You were the one closest to her. You never asked for specifics?" I asked aloud. My voice echoed hollowly in the vault of his memory.

"*Just watch.*"

Hands curling into fists, I did. The Vess had extinguished the Void in the room and gathered her skirts to kneel before Myuna. "Please, great goddess of light, spare me in exchange for the knowledge I have found for you within the Void."

"So there will be something to interrupt my ascension. Speak freely, my child. I will reward you for your candor." Myuna wove light between her fingers as she spoke, easing into her throne more. It seemed to put the Vess at ease.

She closed her eyes and spoke with the echoing power of the Void behind her. "A tide of souls will wash Soiluire clean."

Myuna's fingers froze for a moment. Her secret was

there on the tip of this female's tongue...there for Endaeron to unravel.

So why hadn't he?

"You shall swell with great power and hold everything you desire in your palms."

Light pulsed under the goddess's skin as she leaned in, a grin spanning the pit of her mouth. "Go on," she purred.

"But this planet shall be your last." The Void giggled around the Vess. She bowed her head nearly to the ground as the pulse of Myuna's light heated the air. "Another shall ascend to rival you, and she will bring about your end."

The goddess wasn't pretending to be at ease anymore. She stared at the Vess with white-hot fury. "*Who would dare?*" she thundered with the voices of hundreds.

Dread tingled along my scalp as Endaeron whispered to Myuna, patting her lustrous arm. Of centuries of memories, *this* was what he'd chosen to show me...

"It's okay, my lady. You were right to ask for a warning. Now we can handle it," he soothed.

"Who?" Myuna whispered to the frightened Vess.

With a swallow, she forced out the rest quickly. "She who would mate the son of night and fight you alongside his daughter. She will defeat you before you have a chance to spread your influence on a new world."

No. It couldn't be, I thought. A sick feeling rose in my stomach as I eyed the patterns on Endaeron's horns. He'd worn these particular marks late in his life, with his last mate...around the time Keshora and I welcomed Ravai.

This was why Myuna had targeted my mate and daughters.

"And that is all the Void whispered?" Myuna asked.

"Yes, my lady."

With one intake of breath, Myuna had the Vess's soul in her mouth. The body slumped pitifully to the ground.

"Myuna!" Endaeron exclaimed, shocked. "She was only doing as you asked!"

The goddess's skin shimmered from the infusion of power. "As always, you shall breathe no word of this, as you yet live," she stated. "This Vess simply...disappeared." She lassoed the woman's discarded form with the rope of light she'd woven, consuming it whole to leave no evidence behind.

Endaeron stared at her in defiance. "Eating those who bring you bad news isn't going to solve your problems, my lady," he said through gritted teeth.

"You're right. There is still one problem I will have to preemptively consume," she simpered.

The scene smudged into darkness. Endaeron and I hung in the Void together, surrounded by shadows. "I did not know, at first, that she thought the son of night was you. I would've done more, I swear," he said.

"You could not speak of it," I replied sharply. In a tunnel of endless black, there was nothing to look at besides him. Nowhere for my bottled-up rage to go except for straight at him. "You stood by a goddess of entropy as her champion and helped her fool our people. How do you like your *ascension* now?"

"I was as much a victim as you were. Maybe more, if we must measure our suffering." He met my snarling with calm, his palms up. Though a human gesture, we observed it too.

I sensed that he was flimsy, just a memory of a memory. To scream and rail at him would be futile. He wasn't able to do anything about Myuna now. And he had willfully armed me with a piece of knowledge I needed time to chew on.

I drew back my claws and fangs. "Say what you will, then," I invited more quietly.

"Myuna groomed me from birth for something far worse than taking up a throne. She had two options, but she used to talk about how your darkness stung her when you were the babe she picked up first," he said. "She never forgot that you slighted her when you were minutes old."

My lips pulled back in a sneer.

"Your shadowborn soul was too pure for the seed she planted in mine instead. She made me...like her," he sighed.

"That is quite apparent from what you did as the Hungering Darkness."

"You don't understand. I was her seedling. The only soul she would take with her once she wiped out Soiluire completely." This vision of him was starting to fade around the edges, the sounds and colors of reality pressing in around us. He growled, baring a mouthful of teeth. "Stay with me a little longer."

"I'm trying." It was like straining to hold on to the edges of a dream. No matter what, my body wanted to wake up.

"As a nascent god of entropy, my remains will be built like her. There is a hollow within my core. Search it. Maybe you can do some good with what remains."

I swallowed past a lump in my throat, not trusting my voice. I simply nodded.

Sorrow filled his eyes, which gleamed like milky diamonds. "I'm sorry, brother. Even if I had years rather than moments to atone..."

"Endaeron, no." He was nearly gone, and my composure fell apart as I envisioned what would come next for him. What remained was too shredded and warped to find the next life. This was my last chance to speak to him at all before he became dust. "I—I forgive you! I only wish you peace."

"It would bring me great peace...to fix one thing I did wrong..." Fading in earnest, he extended to me a spark of bright white. "Take what is left, freely given."

I let him place it in my palm and drew him into a one-armed hug. The ghost of his wings closed around me before I was suddenly in the shopping mall, surrounded by the stench of blood. I knelt on the ground, my mouth still tasting of Soiluirian whisky.

A spot of warmth was now clenched in my hand. I turned it over and gaped. It was a teeny piece of a soul that was white with lightborn shadows. I sensed Endaeron within it, with no lingering hint of Myuna. Grief tightened around my eyes. "Is this truly all that remains of you?" I whispered.

Freely given, I could do whatever I wanted with it. I could snuff it out, warp it so the last part of Endaeron felt pain before it faded away. It wasn't large enough to exist on its own for long.

I waited to feel hunger, to salivate over consuming this soul energy. I'd bitten the Hungering Darkness, after all. The cravings were said to be immediate and life-altering. But there was nothing of the sort...

Only new mourning squeezing its way in with the old. That was *Endaeron,* and he had given me tangible hope to dance on my fingertips. A patch for the hole in my soul. A way for a small portion of him to live on in me if I chose to accept it.

I pressed that piece of him to my chest. It attached to my soul like a magnet, flowing to the spot where it was needed to make me whole again. Tension bled out of my body on a wave of sheer relief.

The ghost of the best of my brother remained, and I felt it all: a hint of his confidence and savvy. His boisterous laugh, his optimism, his love for women and drink. There was even a bit of his strength, skill with a blade, and honor in knowing when to use it.

To turn *him* into a monster like her, Myuna had had to crush and destroy nearly everything about him. That was the true tragedy of Endaeron et Myudair, his only other remains the white residue scattered around my knees.

I rifled through it with my hands and senses alike, scattering husk-like pieces of souls sucked clean of their energy and color. The moment my claws touched them, they disintegrated. But one piece was larger than the rest, freshly torn away from its rightful home. Young, male, a hint of carefree emotion twined with blood witch magic.

I tucked it into a ball and held it protectively. Without a vessel to hold it, I needed to get it back to Lucas right away.

26

BEN

THERE WAS a particular look on Garroway's face. One that said he was going to bolt before he actually did, running full pelt away from the four of us.

Oh no you fucking don't, I thought, struggling back to my feet. The mending rune had made sure I wouldn't die from the sucking chest wound he'd given me, but that didn't mean I was ready to run him down.

"A little boost?" I asked Geo while Cress disappeared in a swirl of Braza's shadows to give chase.

Geo reluctantly turned his attention away from the vapor of white shadow still enveloping Phaeron. "Yes," he said, running at me with his wings flaring out. He lifted me by the hips, and I clung to him with my arms. We took to the air and gained ground on the retreating vampire.

"You want to double back for Big P?" I suggested.

"He can handle himself," Geo rumbled.

I wasn't so sure. But then again, he was an indescribably old being from another world, while I was squarely twenty with a deep grudge for the vampire trying to escape his rightful death, so I didn't argue.

Garroway snaked his way around some of the unnatural creatures and enslaved supernaturals. They had found another way to the top floor but had frozen in place, white-glazed eyes staring out at nothing. "Eerie," I muttered to myself.

Of course, when I could've wished for the monsters to attack someone and drag him off, they didn't bother.

"The Hunger must be dead," Geo commented.

But it wasn't a mission accomplished. Not yet.

Static crackled in my ear, and I nearly ripped off the tiny mic taped to my ear. Bianca, Tish, and Wren had spoken on and off during the less dangerous parts of our trip, just to go silent with the big battle. "...Ben? Ben, you there?" Tish asked.

"Oh, thank fuck. The stream is back," Bianca said a moment later. "You okay?"

"Mostly okay," I answered. The mending rune had closed the worst of the wound, leaving a raw edge of pain below my collar.

"Want to tell the audience what happened, then?" Wren prompted.

"Just...give us a few minutes," I said, flustered. If they'd missed *all* of that battle, then I didn't have the breath to explain it.

Light was starting to pour in from the dirty windows overhead, courtesy of a few gaps in the storm clouds. They appeared to be receding as rapidly as they came on...almost like they were magically created.

Below us, Garroway struggled within a trap of black and purple shadows. His ankle was caught in a thorny loop of them, and he bared his fangs in a frustrated grimace while glancing up at the sky. If the freak storm was fading, that meant he was stranded here with us and a whole bunch of monsters until nightfall.

Sounded like my kind of party.

Geo dropped lower to the ground and released his hold on me, giving me a running start. He flapped his wings hard before coming down on Garroway with his full obsidian weight. The vampire gave up trying to escape the shadow trap and rolled his ankle at a brutal angle to avoid getting crushed.

The snare disappeared, and Garroway straightened, favoring his broken foot. He came face-to-face with Cress, her head and hair bare of Braza's power, though the shadows curled around her hand and glowing sword. He recoiled and pivoted, but he was boxed in by Geo and me.

"Oh no. Nowhere to run," I mocked, flipping a dagger between my fingers.

"All right, I admit it," the vampire drawled, slowly raising both hands. "You've got me. How much will it take for us to part ways peacefully? A million each?" He flashed his most charming spider smile toward Cress. "Two, perhaps? I can have the funds wired to your bank account tonight."

Cress tilted her head, pretending to consider. "I think for many, Garroway," she said, tapping her chin with an elongated shadow claw, "your death is priceless."

Face morphing into a snarl, he turned and pointedly met my gaze. The force of his vampiric compulsion reached for purchase within my mind, but I was beyond used to his tricks after a lifetime of them.

"Fucking shank him already," Bianca muttered in my earpiece.

"With pleasure," I said, already in motion, signaling Geo. I snapped my fingers, casting a level-two celestial spell. A new trick just for him—a series of exploding stars right in his face. Geo clamped onto Garroway's upper arms to force him to take the brunt of the magic. Stinging burns broke out all over the vampire's exposed skin.

"The magic I was supposed to have," I said. I pictured the spiked rune that made the spell possible, about to snap my fingers to set it off again.

"You insolent—" Inky darkness slid over his mouth, cutting off anything else he might say. His eyes bulged in their sockets, and he thrashed, struggling in futility to break Geo's hold. Shadows had twined around and through his legs, rendering him completely immobile.

Geo nodded, and Cress gestured. He was all mine.

I sheathed my dagger. My fingers shook with the sheer force of my anticipation. "Doesn't feel good, does it?" I asked, daring to step into his space and stare him down properly. "To be silenced and held down. At the complete mercy of another person."

Something like fear lit in his bloody gaze, along with a pleading softness that said, *"Maybe three million?"*

"I don't want your blood money. I don't want your contacts or your resources or even your pocket dimensions," I told that expression, hoping to see that light of hope die when he realized he was about to pay for his sins.

His eyes widened, and he made a muffled shout. It wasn't until Phaeron spoke that I realized he'd snuck up on us out of the shadows. "There's one thing *I* want before you go on."

I nearly jumped out of my skin. "Goddamn, Big P. We've got to put a bell on you," I muttered.

"I would not wear it, Little B," he said.

I stepped aside for him, figuring he had a few things to say to Garroway after his time under the tender mercies of him and Myuna. Phaeron looked like he'd rolled in flour, something white and powdery smeared on his face, horns, and clothes. Otherwise, he seemed…fine? Maybe better than fine, with some new confidence in how he held himself. Cress eyed him closely, and he winked back at her before reaching for Garroway.

He unbuckled the sword strapped at the vampire's side with one hand and the aid of his shadows. More muffled sounds came from Garroway, along with a futile thrash of his whole body.

Phaeron fastened the sword to his belt and tipped his head my way. "Sorry to interrupt. Might I help? Though it looks like you all have it well in hand."

Well, that was the gist of my grand revenge speech anyway. I glanced up at the peaceful blue sky left now that the storm had passed. "He needs to greet the sun," I said.

"I'll carry him," Geo rumbled.

"And I'll keep him bound in shadows," Cress said in a two-toned voice.

I saluted them playfully, and together, they took him down to the bottom floor. Phaeron offered his free hand, the other curled in a loose fist. "Little B?" I asked.

"If you must call me something silly, am I not permitted to do the same?"

"I think…" I grinned up at him and took his hand. "I'm finally rubbing off on you."

"Frightening." He grinned back, baring his fangs, then turned into shadows slower than normal, giving me plenty of warning to close my eyes before we were jerked to another location.

When I felt tile below my feet again, I jumped back in surprise with a shout of "holy shit!" A massive rat-shaped unnatural scurried toward the doors we'd entered the mall through, joining a stampede of monsters and people alike. They hadn't bothered with the mechanism of the doors, instead going straight through the glass in the middle.

Cress, Geo, and a viciously struggling Garroway stood just to the side, while Phaeron and I had landed amidst a group of stragglers. I palmed a dagger, but these unnaturals weren't interested in fighting anymore. They ran like their life depended on it.

"She's taken control of them. She knows we'd kill them otherwise," Phaeron remarked. He casually grew shadow talons and ended the lives of a pair of rat creatures that brought up the rear. Whatever good cheer that'd come over him faded quickly as he dragged the corpses outside by their naked tails. "They took the torchbearers I unbound from her will. And the burn pile."

"Looks like we're not going to be invited to do another supply run anytime soon," I snarked.

Unfortunately, this was being recorded on stream, which meant Roe's mom was going to be *pissed*. The truck was destroyed—the wheels popped by ragged slashes, the doors and hood torn clean off. Truck guts littered the front of the mall. Here, a half-shredded seat; there, a chunk of metal that could've been part of the engine torn straight from the front.

"Roe is going to be so mad we didn't bring her," Cress whispered.

Phaeron had ditched the rats to help pick up and bind Garroway instead. He had the ankles in one hand while Geo had the shoulders. The vampire resembled a worm with how he was bound in two layers of shadowy ropes and reduced to squirming as the two men carried him out of the shade of the building.

"Right here's great," I said. They dropped him on the

wet pavement, and I made sure he was face-up to greet the sun properly. His skin was already starting to redden as rays kissed his face.

"That looks like it hurts," I taunted the vampire, squatting by his head. Phaeron lingered close by, weaving shadows back into place when the sun threatened to fray away the ropes that bound Garroway.

"In your moment of greatest need, where is the goddess who declared you her right hand?" the dimensional added with a low chuckle. He was watching for Garroway's death nearly as avidly as I was. Did that make us a fucked-up pair?

I pulled the phone out of its sling, swiftly killing the stream and pulling the mic off my ear before Bianca could cuss me out. The public didn't need to see us gloating over this.

Black spots broke out over Garroway's face, the skin charring and becoming eddies of ash on the breeze. "I want you to remember how many people you killed like this. Burning in their own agony, often from the inside out," I said with a sneer.

The shadowy gag was wearing away, poorly muffling his screams. He jerked, trying to roll over and hide from the unforgiving sun. Obsidian hands seized his legs, slamming him back onto his back. Geo nodded toward us and backed his shadow away. He put his arm around Cress, who watched from a healthy distance, a concerned frown on her face.

I pinned the vampire's shoulders down, careful of any snapping fangs as the heat damage accelerated. "Better enjoy the coolest moments left," I said with malicious glee. "Hell is hotter still."

His skin and facial hair caught fire, his whole body

going concave as he entered the last stages of burning to ash. Garroway's screams faded to one last moan of agony before only char remained of him and what he'd been wearing. The wind started to break apart the man shape left around the burnt clothing when Phaeron and Cress withdrew their magic.

I snapped a picture and texted it to Bianca. Instead of the stream of abuse I expected, she merely texted back, "Wish I could've seen it. :("

The excitement was fading about as fast as it'd been to kill Garroway out in the sun. "It was too easy for him," I texted back before pocketing the device. Any death would've been too easy, though. What would've really satisfied me, when he was the reason I'd lost my mom and childhood? When Lucas was still in a coma in a hospital we were about to evacuate.

There was an awkward silence between the four of us. Well, they had just helped me murder a man, no matter how deserving he'd been. I didn't know what to say after it was done, either.

"Shopping spree?" I suggested.

Cress breathed a disbelieving laugh.

"No," Geo grumbled.

"Stay if you wish. I need to borrow Little B," Phaeron said.

Cress covered her mouth, trying to contain a string of tired giggles. "You're really calling him that?"

"Yes, and I will bring him back shortly. I owe you all phones, after all." Phaeron glanced toward the wreckage of our transportation. "We'll need to steal another truck, I presume?"

I handed Wren's phone over to Cress. "Here. Call

Bianca. She knows how to hotwire a car. I'm sure you can get tools from the mall somewhere."

Geo raised a stony brow. "And if the unnaturals return?"

"They won't," Phaeron said confidently. He rested a hand on my shoulder.

"Wait, you never told me why—" And we were off in a puff of shadows.

By the time Phaeron released me, I was about to throw up over his leather boots. We'd arrived in a hospital room in what felt like no time at all. Dizzy, I fell toward the nearest trashcan and fumbled it under my chin to dry heave until my stomach felt better.

"Sorry. Time is of the essence," the dimensional said. He offered me a hand up once I set the trashcan aside.

We were in Lucas's room. The steady hum of machinery beeped around his still form swallowed up in white sheets.

Phaeron turned toward him too. He leaned over my little brother, presumably staring at his soul. "Such a long possession by the Hungering Darkness has left him quite damaged. But he is the last victim," he murmured. "And a chunk of his soul remained in the belly of the monster."

I choked on a breath. "You're going to save him?"

"I cannot make any promises," he warned. "But my soul was just made whole, and the process was...easy. The missing piece knew exactly where to slot." He untucked Lucas from his hospital sheets and drew aside the collar of the gown. I went to the other side of the bed, watching with my heart beating erratically in my throat.

Phaeron opened his fist and placed his palm flat against the skin over my brother's heart. A jolt passed through Lucas. His fingers twitched; his legs shifted. He was waking up!

Above the ventilator strapped to his face, his eyes flared open. The irises were a shade of gray one small notch off from white and swam around in a panic as he spotted the two of us standing over him. "Lucas," I breathed.

He clawed the mask off his face and started screaming. Dragging his nails over his cheeks, he nearly scratched furrows into himself before I caught his wrists. "It's okay. You're in control. It's okay," Phaeron was saying.

"Look at me," I begged as Lucas continued screaming his lungs out.

The door into the hall slammed open, and in rushed Mama Rollins at the head of a trio of nurses. Thank fuck she was here—anyone else would've seen what was happening and immediately assume the worst.

"Use some magic. Check him," Cress's mom barked toward the fae nurse behind her.

Phaeron slipped into the shadows and reappeared at my side in moments, giving the green-skinned woman space to work. "Lucas, you're okay," I said, giving his wrists a shake. "You're in a hospital, and you're safe."

"You are your own person, free of the Hungering Darkness," Phaeron added.

The title seemed to catch his attention. Lucas relaxed back into the bed and looked around again in earnest. Green tinged his skin from the fae nurse's magic. She was quickly checking him head to toe.

"Ben?" Lucas rasped. He hiccupped dryly, his face creasing like he was going to cry. "Ben, I'm so sorry, I didn't mean to run off like that."

"Shh." I looped one arm under his shoulders,

awkwardly bending down to hug him when he was still hooked up to several machines. "It doesn't matter. All I care about is that you're finally back."

I looked up at Phaeron. "Thank you," I said, properly teary for my brother and me both.

He dipped his chin in acknowledgment, a hint of something like grief and longing passing over his expression. "I'll give you some privacy," he said.

27

GEO

CRESS and I exchanged a glance the moment after Phaeron and Ben disappeared in a swirl of shadows. "I don't feel like committing grand theft auto right now. Do you?" she asked.

"No," I answered.

"How about this? I'm going to go find us something to eat in the mall, and then we can go back to the library."

"No," I said again. Her eyelids fluttered. "I shall come with you to find something to eat."

"But you can't see in the dark," she pointed out.

My shoulder blades ground together when I shrugged. "And you control light. You're not going back in there without me."

She tilted her head back and forth before unsheathing her sword and casting Lux upon it. With no need for us to hide anymore, the shadows she'd worn over herself like a coat seeped back into her skin.

With a surprised sound, she glanced down. "Oh, hi, Flit. Ben left without you, huh. You can hang out with us for now," she said to the ferret standing on one of her shoes.

She lifted him with her free hand and placed him on her shoulder. He draped across the back of her neck and settled with a little huff.

"You'll have a lot more fun if you take your human form," she suggested to me before tiptoeing over the glass shards littering the way back into the mall. Her three cats stood clear of the wreckage, waiting for her.

I crunched straight through them, lifting her by the hips to set her outside of the destruction wrought by Myuna's creatures. She turned with a crease between her brows, undoubtedly to tell me to stop treating her like a doll, but I was already halfway through the process of shedding my wings and stone skin.

I swallowed her complaint with my warm human lips against hers. She sagged into me with a muffled moan.

Banding my arms around her, I cuddled her and rested my chin atop her head. "Why is it so important we retrieve some food?" I asked. She was tired and bloodstained, with rips in her clothing. I was sure she had wounds that needed tending.

My stone heart thrummed in my chest. I would ensure she received proper care with my own hands, even if I had to carry her out of this dark mall before she was ready to leave.

"I would give my left arm for some junk food, Geo," she said matter-of-factly. She removed her handbook from the holster on her hip. "*The Librarian Witch's Handbook*, scan for junk food that hasn't been spoiled."

"Aye, aye, Captain!" it squeaked, taking flight from her palm. It flapped away into the gloom ahead.

She took my hand and tugged me along, holding her gleaming sword in her free hand. "Are you sure about this?" I asked.

"I'm feeling okay. Promise. Besides, when was the last time I had you to myself?" She had a cheerful bounce to her step. "And it's always a treat to see you outside of gargoyle form."

"It's always a joy to be with you," I answered.

She ducked her head with a giggle. "Aw. I love you," she said.

There was no mistaking the rush of warmth that suffused me head to toe, loosening muscles and joints from their rocky stiffness. Those three words were more efficient than a full-course meal or any cup of coffee in reviving the man in me. "I love you too."

After a couple seconds' pause, I added, "We should locate your junk food quickly." The longer we delayed, the more likely one or both of her other men would return. I might've agreed to share her, but that didn't mean I wouldn't hoard every second of her undivided attention like the gold it was.

She smiled and led me to a directory, which helped us map out all the probable stores to visit. As we headed to the closest one, a shadow wound around her feet and released a rasping meow. "Okay, okay. Jin wants to take a ride on your shoulder," she said, motioning to the black cat.

I bent down, and Jin jumped the rest of the way, little razor claws digging into my skin. It was the most pain I'd felt all day, a fact that made me feel guilt over the bruises and scrapes Cress had sustained from her fight with the Hungering Darkness.

"Greetings, small feline," I said, nearly knocking her clean off my shoulder trying to pet her. She purred thunderously and dug in to remain in place, rubbing her face against my fingers.

Jin perched on my shoulder like a mini gargoyle as we

started finding the kinds of things Cress wanted to bring back with her. The first store was dedicated to selling records and movies, with a small subsection full of chips, candy, and cans of soda in bright packaging. The unnaturals that'd overrun the mall had torn into some of them, but Cress's face lit up nonetheless when she realized there were a few rows higher up that were left untouched.

We left with two sturdy shopping bags full of junk. She had the biggest grin on her face, so I refrained from asking if this meant we were done. "Let's make a pile of loot," I suggested.

"Of what?" she giggled. "Did you hear 'loot' on the Internet?"

"Yes," I admitted.

"Well, I agree." She whisked away the two bags behind a still-sealed security gate in a swirl of shadows.

I don't know how long we spent in the gloom of the mall, combing several stores for their goods. We did not find any new phones to claim, alas, but by the time Cress and her familiars grew tired of walking, we'd amassed enough junk to ration some to everyone. Well, if Cress wanted to share. Once we gathered up all the shopping bags and boxes, the first thing she did was tear into a container of chocolate-dipped cookies.

She crunched down on one, and I watched the pleasure crease her expression at the taste of chocolate. She offered me the box, where the cookies stuck out like straws, but I only took one to commit its taste to this memory. It was sweet and crisp against my teeth, the chocolate studded with crushed almonds for that extra kick of flavor.

"Good, right?" she asked.

I smiled dreamily at her. "Fantastic."

We worked our way through the cookies slowly, as she

relished each one. Only when she was down to the last one did she wave it around to punctuate what she said. "I was thinking I could take all of this and you back to the library with Braza's shadows."

I frowned. "I would be happy to assist you."

"Yes, but this way, you don't have to go back to gargoyle form. I'll drop the familiars back at their room and then..." She winked.

Hmm, now that was quite tempting. It wouldn't be a long flight, but I'd lose the certainty that I was a man, rather than a rock, with any time in my other form. I'd gotten a grip on my emotions and loosened my fingers enough to properly scratch Jin under the chin, two bench-marks amongst many that had to be achieved each time I became a man again.

So I said yes and allowed her to enfold me, the familiars, and our loot in a layer of black-purple shadows. There was a tugging sensation, and wind ran along my skin and through my hair before we arrived in a familiar room. Cress appeared next to me and sighed as the shadows flowed away from her body, disappearing like mist.

The familiars were no longer with us, so she must've released them from her magic before letting me go. "First, my feet are killing me, and I stink. Shower?" she offered.

I heard the weight of fatigue in her voice and resisted the urge to carry her there myself. "Only if I get the privi-lege of joining you."

"I thought that was a given," she said. She backed in that direction, shedding clothing as she went. My mouth went dry as I pursued her, also undressing along the way. Just the sight of all that soft skin had heat flooding to my groin.

She leaned over to turn on the shower and stood in a

graceful arch, lifting her hips to jiggle the globes of her ass for my appreciative gaze. Shooting a coy smile over her shoulder, she stepped into the stream of water and then let off a less than dignified screech. "It's cold!"

A tentative laugh ground out of me. "Turn it up," I suggested.

"I did! Fuck," she sighed. "Guess there's no more hot water."

I stepped in behind her and drew the curtain. The water was punishingly chill, dampening my earlier excitement. Well, we both needed to wash, and she had cuts and scrapes on her body that I intended to clean before she leapt out of the tub. I pulled her into my body heat with one arm and grabbed the soap, lathering up my hands.

"I'll go quick," I promised before rubbing the suds into her shoulders and arms. As soon as both of us were soaked with cold water, I turned so my back took the brunt of the stream. Icy mist rolled around us.

Despite what I'd said, I found myself worshiping her body, hands molding to her curves and brushing tenderly over new hurts. I gave her breasts an admiring squeeze, and she leaned her head back on my shoulder, damp hair tickling my chest. "I was hoping we could..." she said tentatively.

"Soon," I rumbled. Definitely not here, while she was standing on aching feet and cringing away from the cold water. I knelt to finish cleaning her long legs and helped her balance for a quick scrub of her soles.

Her teeth clicked together when we switched places, and she slid the bar of soap out of my palm. "My turn."

I breathed out from her touch, which was as soft as she was. After being hard and unfeeling for so long, simply being touched was its own pleasure. I closed my eyes as

Cress stroked the lines of my muscles in a path top to bottom. She was finished before I wanted her to be, shutting off the water with a sigh of relief.

She passed me a towel and tousled her hair with another. "You haven't relaxed like that in a long time," she murmured.

"That's the magic of your touch," I answered.

She hummed, drying herself off thoroughly with a few shivers along the way. "Geo," she said, tossing the towels aside and coming over to rest her palms on my chest. I rubbed her back, feeling the chill she carried on her skin. "I think you need to start taking longer breaks from your gargoyle form."

"My duty is to protect you." I answered without really thinking. "Well...you are my duty, of course. And I am the only gargoyle in this entire pocket dimension. Thanks to Phaeron's tempering of my stone, I have yet to be injured. While you..."

She glanced down at her body, touching the reddened skin around a set of scratches on her side. "This could have been much worse. What I'm saying is, it's okay to take a breather from constant vigilance. I appreciate everything you've done. But..." She leaned in to press a kiss above where my stone heart rested. "I need you like this sometimes."

A little tremor passed through me, a shockwave emerging from the brush of her lips. I couldn't deny the rightness of what she was asking. Her heart was big enough to encompass me along with her other two men, but I needed to occupy that space. In this, I needed to bend, to be flexible.

To be soft, when all I'd ever been was hard and unyielding.

"I need you, too," I murmured. "Touch me."

"Where?" she asked.

"Everywhere."

Her palms ran up to my shoulders, rubbing outward down the line of my arms. With a gentle nudge, she started walking me backward. "Everywhere, hmm? I'm going to take you literally."

I nodded. Good. I was always literal.

She traced new pathways over my body, taking her time without the obligation to hurry us out of a cold shower. I backed into the bed and lifted her to sit astride my lap. Her lips and tongue followed the trails set by her fingers, and by the time she was halfway down my chest, I was hard as obsidian, jutting into her hip.

One of her hands slipped down to cup my erection, and I held in a gasp. "I'll take care of you last," she promised before reaching over for Wren's phone resting on the bedside table. I watched her through lidded eyes as she scrolled through a music app and put on a slow and smooth instrumental that played a little tinny through the small speaker.

She used the pace of the music to slow down and leave no inch of me untouched. I slid my fingers through her damp hair, finding what I'd asked for had swiftly turned into the sweetest torture as she skimmed her attention around my cock. She kissed her way down my thighs. That was about all I could take. "Cress," I moaned.

Her brown eyes flashed to my face. She'd put on a playful expression, but she had to know. "I...I was not speaking literally," I said.

She covered her mouth with a hand, eyes creasing at the corners. "No?"

"No," I confirmed.

"This is a first," she said, skimming her palms back up my thighs. I throbbed for the touch she was so close to delivering. "Are you sure you want me to jump straight to the end?"

Her fingertips skimmed closer. "Yes," I practically begged.

While she didn't laugh, mirth danced in her eyes as she rose between my legs and licked her way up my shaft. She cupped my tightened balls, rolling them between her fingers. I moaned her name, grateful when she took the crown between her lips and sank me further into the heat of her mouth inch by inch.

She didn't hold back. Her mouth was torment and relief, keeping me in place so I could only reach her shoulders and back. I was possessed with desire for her, to caress her as she had touched me.

"Maybe not the end," I said, tugging on her hair. "Come join me on the bed."

A furrow appeared between her brows as she slid my cock back out of her mouth. I helped lift her up and lay her out on the bed, bracing myself above her to take in all that soft skin turned golden by lamp light. A body I was made for. My hands, shaped for her curves. I started at her hips, running up the dip of her belly to the swell of her breasts.

My lips, shaped to mesh with hers. I reminded myself to inhale as I kissed her, as her mouth so often stole my breath. Our tongues met in a heated tangle.

My stone heart, animating me to her service. It throbbed in my chest, full to bursting with the satisfaction of this moment. I cupped her cheek, meeting her gaze briefly. How had one person so efficiently become my purpose? I'd already changed for her, flexed when I didn't think I ever could.

Cress was my everything.

I was still kissing her when I ran my palm down her thighs, moving her leg to open her for me. Rubbing my cock between her folds, I reluctantly pulled back at the last moment to ask, "Condom?" I regretted that I didn't have one handy.

Her hands pulled me back, one at my hip, the other hooked around my neck. "No," she said.

I smiled, grateful I got to see her expression as I sank into her. My cock, formed to fit her perfectly. Her kiss-swollen lips hung open as I sank into her to the root. We communicated like how I used to. "Good?" I rumbled.

"Yes," she gasped.

"Okay." But it was more than merely *okay*. Being inside of her was simply *right*.

I braced my weight on one arm, still touching her, a gentle counterpoint to the way her body rocked with my thrusts. The texture of her skin, the way her breast jiggled in my palm; the muscles low on her belly shifted as she lifted her hips to mine; every piece came together to form the whole of her pleasure.

She came with a velvety clench on my cock, arching into me. I savored the brush of our sweat-slicked bodies together. As much as I didn't want this to end, I was close, and her leg twitched from taking my thrusts during that sensitive time after her peak. I let go, spilling in a rush of liquid heat and settling still hard inside of her.

It only took her a few minutes before she asked, "Again?"

And I answered, "Sure."

28

PHAERON

At the dawn of my life, a set of scholars had taught me what it meant to be a prince. A straight posture was a requirement; composure, a necessity. I had to achieve perfection. I'd caught glimpses of the ideal prince within me, though *perfect* was always an impossible standard.

Shadowborn were instinctively drawn to dark, quiet places. We'd evolved on a planet shaded by eternal night as protectors, there to eliminate unseen threats so the rest of our kind could thrive. I was meant to have a territory to patrol, unceasingly seeking out the next fight until my True Light called me home and into her arms.

There was also the rage, a trait inconvenient and inferior to my station. Yet it so often simmered under my skin, reminding me not to remain in one place for long. I'd tried to heed my tutors and snuff out its sparks and heat, but it remained part of my core being, the blame of its reoccurrence straddled somewhere between the instincts of a shadowborn and the inferiority of a second prince.

I hated when there were witnesses to when I lost

control. I always sought solitude to hunt and exist without the judgment of society or man.

But first, while balanced on a knife's edge of self-control, I looked for Cress and found her scent lingering in Highfall's Mall, twined with Geo's earthen tang. She alone had the power to ground me.

But they'd left the mall by that point. I was the only living person in the whole complex.

Alone.

I took form far from the battlefield where the Hungering Darkness fell. My chest rose and fell in shallow gasps for air. I was too hot; my clothes and armor were too tight. And even with no man-made lights shining overhead, the numerous panes of windows high above made this mall too *fucking* bright.

Shadows erupted from my skin while I screamed a shadowborn's howl. Magic and power answered my call, and I wrapped myself in a cloak of night and became a destructive creature with a wolflike head and a trailing tail of spikes. My fingers lengthened into foot-long talons, shredding sidings and tile like ripping paper.

"Myuna!" I raged. Every uprooted sign and display could've been her, thrown, shredded, and ruined.

I pictured her paranoid expression, the rage and fear that'd twisted her face from the Void's wisdom: *"She will defeat you before you have a chance to spread your influence on a new world."*

But the narrow-sighted monster had set her sights on what was before her, not the scope of what the Void knew. A prophecy from a Vess was supposed to be taken with a cynical ear, for it was most likely the madness and the laughter speaking through them.

I continued my rampage, imagining tearing her throat

out with my teeth. Did goddesses bleed? Or was she simply a hollow vessel, a stretched-out form of clay that would deflate from a mortal wound?

She'd trespassed against me personally, worse than I could've ever imagined. My wobbly memories conjured Keshora, and my pace faltered a moment. I squeezed a guardrail over the three-story drop to the bottom of the mall, leaving behind an impression of my hands.

Keshora, as I knew her, was a weaver and a mother. A proud but unlikely second princess. I'd returned from war to find that, in my absence, she'd given her heart to two girls, *Ravita* and *Brazita*. When I tried to imagine their nicknames in her voice, only the throbbing of my heartbeat filled my ears.

"She who would mate the son of night and fight you alongside his daughter."

I made a sound of pain low in my throat. It was ludicrous. Myuna thought the Void's prophecy would be crushed into dust as long as she killed Keshora and Ravai, two women who'd never been a threat to her.

"It wasn't referring to either of them," I mumbled, as if the truth would bring them back.

Unlike the wreckage I'd left behind me, I damaged the railing purposefully, creating a ledge for me to sit and dangle my feet and tail over the perilous drop. My power receded in tufts of smoke, exposing the rawness of my expression. What I thought was anger twisted and revealed itself as chest-cracking grief, which pounced the moment I acknowledged the truth.

My brother was dead.

My family was murdered.

My world was destroyed.

And my people were scattered and endangered, unlikely to unite as a kingdom again.

At the center of it all sat Myuna, gorging and laughing in her death knell of a voice. Fear and revulsion shuddered through my body. If the Void's prophecy was to be believed and her assumption of my identity as "the son of night" was correct, then I was a key figure to her end. But the one to wield the sword would be Cress, aided by Braza. I was two crucial steps from setting that destiny into motion.

I inspected my hands. Blood and smears of white-ish powder clotted under my nails and in the creases of my skin. One step would be easier than the other. I had no doubt Cress would agree to carry my mating mark, but I still needed to cobble together a proper gift for her.

And Braza... I cursed under my breath. I'd ruined that relationship with careless, unguarded thoughts. We'd had powercores on Soiluire, but she'd been the first I'd known before her transformation. Though she had become *other*, it'd been tactless to shout in my head that she wasn't the daughter I remembered and marvel at how strange she'd become upon shedding her body.

I couldn't remember the last time she'd called me Father, a consequence I deserved and one that would not be reversed with a simple apology. I would produce a grander gesture for her for the right reason. Not just to kill Myuna, but to give Braza back the life she deserved.

"Well," I said, scrubbing my cheeks to rub away the self-pity, "idleness is the enemy of progress."

I fixated on my new mission, becoming a spirit that popped in and out of being only to take what I needed. Clothes were last, for when I cleansed the filth of battle from my skin. First, I sought abandoned shops for rare spell reagents. The couple I found were already ransacked, most items of value taken.

No matter. I was chasing another memory, a ritual few supernaturals would remember and fewer still would approve of. I filled a box with powders and tonics that'd been overlooked on their shelves and tucked in a few potions of a vibrant hue of purple that matched Cress's hair. I'd noticed earlier that some of the strands were reverting to a dark brown, a sign she needed to renew the dye.

There was one reagent no shop would sell, and I found myself browsing the guardian witch sections of each one I visited, looking for a suitable replacement. The best I could find was the scale of an earthen dragon, and that was lucky, as it was hidden under something else in a nearly empty display case. It wasn't much on its own, just a matte disc the color of dried mud, but I felt the latent power within it as it sat across the length of my palm.

The most powerful supernaturals in this world were those that took a dragon's shape. As unlikely as this scale was for the task I required of it, it would do if I did not acquire a better alternative.

Evening was beginning to touch the sky as I considered what to find next. Traditionally, I should present Cress with a gift made by my own hands. But I didn't have time for that, not with Myuna breathing down our necks. I would make her something she'd cherish if we made it back to the safety of New Salem and Moongrove Academy.

In the meantime, I sought comforts for her. As night fell, I encountered more unnaturals stirring from their nests. They met a swift death as I emerged from the darkness with each sighting. It felt good to have two blades in my hands again, though most of Myuna's creatures required little effort to slay.

The occasional roaming torchbearer added hours to my quest, as each time I unbound a soul, I ended up with an unconscious body that needed to be carried to Cerris City Library. I felt Braza tracking me coming and going, though she didn't try to talk to me as I added a few people at a time to spare containment rooms.

Past midnight, there were no more unnaturals to kill. I sensed the wrongness of that fact when I dared take form in a beauty store. Chill dread creeped up my scalp while I busied myself with inspecting labels. There was a baffling amount of makeup products, lotions, hair care, and serums in this store.

I stilled halfway into my search and turned in the direction of timid footsteps. There was a soft gasp and a scuffle. Human sounds.

"Hello there. I won't hurt you," I said.

"That's exactly what a monster would say." She sounded young, and I caught myself rolling my eyes despite the circumstances.

"None of Myuna's creatures speak coherently. That's how I know you are not one. You may apply the same logic to me." I glanced down at myself and hoped she wasn't a shifter or vampire, able to see the state I was in through the dark. My shirt was in tatters, and I still bore the grime of battle, new and old. "Would you like me to take you to a safe place?"

"I thought I had a safe place." She was peeking around a display of nail polishes, and I caught a glimpse of her aura, that of a witch who hadn't picked an affinity yet. I drew a layer of shadows over my torso when I noticed she was aiming a phone light in my direction.

"Oh! You're the dimensional from the stream. Are you here to rescue me?"

I tilted my head, bemused, and fibbed, "Yes." I would take her to the hospital no matter what. She needed to evacuate with the rest of the survivors we were protecting. "But before we leave, I need some advice."

The girl ended up being an employee who was living in the back room of the shop alone. She was more than happy to help me load up on things Cress probably wanted. I left with a couple heavy bags of various products and her in my shadows, plopping her on the front steps of the hospital and disappearing the moment she turned to thank me.

I returned to the library to deposit the bags next to the other items I'd found, finally turning my attention toward making myself presentable. First, a shower. I luxuriated in the cool water even though it ran off me in the various colors of blood and battle. I was cleansing my wounds a second time when the feeling of dread returned.

Power intensified in the air, and I clutched my skull, wailing from the pressure bearing down from all angles. It lasted for all of a minute before abruptly disappearing. I shut the shower off, breathing heavily.

There was no questioning that Myuna had done something awful. But what could it have been?

My thoughts strayed to Carly. I could only hope she hadn't harmed the girl further with whatever madness she was undertaking now.

Braza tentatively brushed my mind. *"I know you're probably resting..."* she said.

"My next rest will be when Myuna is dead," I replied.

She had a way of holding her silence in a way that felt disapproving.

"I shall come to you shortly." I didn't need her to be

concerned for me, even though I muffled a yawn at the thought of sleep.

"I shall be ready," she murmured.

The fatigue I was running from threatened to catch up with me as I dressed in the set of too-tight clothes that'd been left here earlier and prepared what I was going to say in the mirror. I had to keep moving. Though I did pause by the bed to catch a breath of the scent lingering on the sheets. The perfume of Cress's arousal and my magic, intertwined.

My body ached for hers. I'd make her my mate on this bed now that my soul was whole.

I shook my head sharply and turned into shadows, leaving before I could fantasize about it further. Taking form in front of the domed powercore, I forwent the formality of bowing and asking permission to enter. Braza was already formed of black and purple energy in the middle of her small space, hands on her hips, tail flicking as she took a good look at me.

I didn't give her a chance to speak before I swept her off her feet and into a hug. Whatever she was going to say rolled into a squeak of surprise, then she hugged me back, curling her wings into a looser second embrace.

She fixed her luminous powercore eyes on me, a little furrow in her brow. She was undoubtedly searching my mind for an explanation, but the rehearsed words had evaporated away already. I was, perhaps, more fatigued than I expected. I held her more firmly, enough that her body dimpled and static tingled on my skin.

"I'm sorry," I said in the language of our people.

"About—"

"I'm sorry, Brazita," I corrected myself.

Her breath caught. Though I didn't think she needed to

breathe, some gestures transcended death and ascension into a new form.

"Recent events have forced me to look at what I have become, and there is much I would change," I continued. "Starting with my failures as a father. I have much to apologize for, but I hope we can repair the damage between us."

Her smile echoed a brightening of our surroundings. The immediate joy and relief were unmistakable. "I would like that more than anything," she murmured. She angled her head, and I met her halfway, our foreheads touching. A sign of trust and affection for our race blessed with sharp horns.

There was an echo of Cress's chastisement in my ears, once uttered in this small space. *"The fact that she's* here *and that she made me Guardian of Moongrove Library was all for you."* Braza had been trying to reach across the gap this whole time.

"I want to apologize too, for holding you in containment for so long," she said.

I shook my head. "I've already accepted your reasoning and come to peace with the missing years. If I hadn't been contained for that period of time, how would I have met Cress? Your actions guided my destiny."

She wiggled, and I realized I still had her held up off the ground. I placed her on her feet, and she beamed up at me. "You're happy with her," she said knowingly. "It's time."

"Tomorrow." I was pleased at the approval I felt from the electric currents of her power. The tether between Cress and Braza made them close in their own way. No one was cheering on Cress more than my adopted daughter. "But first, I have to tell you something."

A hint of wariness touched her voice. "Okay."

It was easier to show her. I took her hands and closed

my eyes, letting the memory of Endaeron's last moments float to the front of my mind. Reliving the Void's prophecy was no easier a second time, and it was tied up in other thoughts Braza undoubtedly skimmed from my mind.

Her energy-formed fingers were starting to feel warm in mine as she took from my body heat. She was silent for a while after witnessing what I'd seen and concluded about Myuna's actions afterward. I only hoped she'd picked up that I would've come around and apologized to her with or without this glimpse into the past.

When she finally spoke, it wasn't about the prophecy at all. "What you're planning to give me is illegal by supernatural law."

"But do you want it?" I asked.

She glanced away, lip caught between her teeth. "Every gargoyle forgets their past life," she said.

"A purposeful flaw, I imagine. Otherwise, the supernatural world would be flooded with witches chasing immortality." I squeezed her fingers, surer than ever that I wanted to try to do this for her. "I have Geo, who may allow me to study the spells keeping him animated, and an abundance of time. I would make the body perfect for you so you can have the life that was stolen from you so long ago. No human law will stop me from trying, only your word that you wish to continue on as a powercore."

She took in our surroundings, releasing a sigh weighted by centuries of unceasing service. If I thought I was tired, all I had to do was listen to her to know what true exhaustion sounded like. "I...I do want to be alive again. But how will we hide a female gargoyle? And who will power Moongrove Library?" she asked.

"We'll figure it out. Besides, you switched places with the powercore in this library, now empty save for temporary containment of torchbearers. There's never been a better time for you to go missing." I nodded slowly to myself, seeing it play out in my mind's eye. "We will blame Myuna, and this library will remain empty until another power source can be found. In the meantime, I'll hold your soul in a suitable temporary vessel."

I pulled the dragon's scale from my pocket, and she took it to inspect. "This isn't a purified fae crystal," she said skeptically.

"It is the best I could find for now. I have faith it will contain your soul long enough to give me time to source a proper gargoyle heart," I said.

In answer, she gestured overhead at the powercore above us. "All of this is my soul now."

I glanced up with a thoughtful hum. "Perhaps I should find you two. One for each half."

Though I'd never been involved in making gargoyles directly, I knew the magic-washed stones chosen for their hearts were selected for the lattice structure within. If I phrased the question correctly, maybe one of the Crystal Court fae would be willing to sell me two without realizing what they were for.

"I shall write down everything I remember about gargoyle creation. Between us, we can figure out the spells and materials. Once Cress and I defeat Myuna for good, we will have all the time in the world." The smile she offered was fragile with hope.

I'm sure mine was as well. "There are a few last things I need to retrieve from the city. Perhaps when I return, we could sit and talk for a while?"

"I'll be here," she said wryly.

29
CRESS

GEO and I took the luxury of a slow wakeup with Wren's phone between us, watching highly satisfying videos of molding kinetic sand and hydraulic presses at work. Then the device buzzed continuously and threatened to jump out of my hand. It was Ben texting in bursts from someone else's phone.

Geo groaned in denial, and I made a sound of agreement. The outside world was about to steal us both away; I knew it.

I pieced Ben's message together and read it in a frenetic pace in my head from how short the individual texts were. "Hey, babe, where are you? Have you seen Geo or Phaeron? You have to come to the hospital! My brother's awake! He's doing good, and I want to introduce you guys. Sorry, did I wake you? I've been waiting all day for you to steal a car and come back! You're okay, right?"

Someone had to teach this man to text all his thoughts in one message.

Wait, Lucas was awake? I gasped and reread that particular message. "We have to go!" I exclaimed.

"What? What's wrong?" Geo asked, sitting up at full alert.

I grinned and showed him the message. "We have to say hello to Ben's brother."

His silvery eyes widened. "That is quite remarkable," he murmured.

I stood to get dressed, reaching out for Braza in my head while I tugged on my clothes and attempted to text Ben back all at the same time. *"Good morning, brightest of souls."*

"Guess what," we said at nearly the same time.

She already knew my news, that some miracle had occurred to wake Lucas from his coma. There was a playful jolt to her energy today, as if she knew exactly how it happened and was looking forward to me figuring it out.

"I've spent the greater part of the early morning with my father," she said.

I didn't miss the change in title. My jaw dropped, then a delighted smile formed on my lips. *"You two made up."*

"We did. I'll let him know where you and Geo are going. But for now, we're catching up."

I knew all he had to do was set his pride aside and apologize. She'd wanted to repair their familial relationship so badly.

"I'm happy for you," I said while humming an upbeat tune out the door and to the elevator. Geo was just a step behind me, resting an arm around me while we waited.

"Thank you. By the way, did you feel the anomaly last night?"

"The what now?" I asked.

"Myuna's power surged for a short time last night. Perhaps if we'd been merged, you would've noticed it." She sounded troubled. *"I'm hoping you can speak with the seers to figure out if they know what she did."*

"Of course." I had a question for Hana, which meant I'd probably be pestering her with several of them to get a halfway decent understanding of her answer. Though I hadn't forgotten the very literal hint she'd given me about Phaeron's "slumber," which I'd completely overthought.

Without the convenience of shadow travel, Geo had to take his gargoyle form to fly us to the hospital. There were no signs of unnaturals on the streets, nor any white-eyed birds staring from signposts and rooftops. I rubbed my arms, more unnerved by the lack of Myuna's monsters with the knowledge that she'd done something big last night.

We could've had a leisurely late winter stroll free of threats and kept Geo out of his stone form. He shed it upon landing and took a moment to breathe and pinch the bridge of his nose. Once he'd recovered, he jerked his chin in hello to the bored-looking defenders on duty around the hospital's perimeter on our way inside. Several hellos were called back to him.

I hesitated between seeking out Hana or Ben first. The decision was made for me, though, as the dark-haired woman was sitting primly on a couch in the foyer, her signature secretive smile in place when we made eye contact.

"You have questions," she said.

"I do." I turned to Geo, brow raised curiously.

"Tell me if you figure out anything concrete," he rumbled. I wasn't too surprised, since he cared more about actions than possibilities. He took Wren's phone to return to her, and I slid onto the couch next to Hana.

She gestured for me to speak and stacked her hands patiently. Though she'd mastered the mysterious air of an augur, I wasn't sure if she knew the faces of the demons I wrestled with: the first time I'd come face-to-face with death. Her daughter Lanie's unseeing eyes, her motionless body sprawled in a pool of her own blood. And in the aftermath, Hana had gazed into the future for me...

"You told me once." I took a ragged breath, feeling myself get choked up. "You told me that I'd avenge Lanie."

"And so you have," she said. The knowing look hadn't left her face yet.

"But I didn't kill the Hungering Darkness. That was Phaeron," I said in a small voice.

"Ah. Didn't I tell you that I saw you vanquish a creature, standing over it with three men who adore you? That *did* happen." Her aura lit with gray, centered around her head. "I see it, even, but the monster you four watched die was the vampire, not the Hungering Darkness. Fairly accurate as far as a gaze into the gray is concerned."

I felt the chill of goosebumps. What she'd told me and what happened still didn't quite match up. How often had her augury been a shade off from reality?

"I see," I said neutrally.

She turned her dark eyes my way. They reflected with gray magic deep in her pupils. "In this, you have fully avenged my daughter. The blood baron's legacy is dust, and the unnatural remnant who attacked her is no more."

"What about my sister, Carly?" I leaned in, yearning for some hope. "Have you seen her future?"

She maintained her mysterious poker face. "I have. There are good outcomes and bad, as sure as everyone else's fate at present."

I wrung my hands. How intensely vague of her. "Will we cross paths before she ends up in a morgue?" I asked in a smaller voice. With everything that'd been happening, I missed Carly more than ever.

"You will," she confirmed, then cleared her throat and

clearly picked another topic. "I see now that you are on the verge of discovering your potential."

I set my spine under that prophetic gaze, wondering what exactly she was seeing when she inspected me. "What should I do?" I breathed.

"The hour of our final confrontation with Myuna grows near. She has chosen a new champion and embedded a seed of entropy in their soul. In this, she has learned from us and plans to raise a larger force than ours. We must broadcast our evacuation plans before it's too late for the majority of Cerris City's survivors," she intoned.

I held my breath, committing every word to memory.

"Pool your resources, and you will find the key to our victory." She nodded slowly, and between one blink and the next, the gray magic left her. Her shoulders slumped, and she muffled a yawn. "And speak to Phaeron. We can spare you both for a day while the rest of us prepare."

"Fuckin' hell. That was a damn good prophecy." We both jumped when the gravelly voice spoke up behind us. Auric et Vess had appeared out of nowhere silently, just as Phaeron usually did. Maybe it was a dimensional thing.

Hana recovered first. "How long were you listening?" she asked.

"I heard the whole thing from the other side. The Void frothed up nicely for you. It speaks to you, hmm?" He was inspecting her closely.

"Augurs see the future," she corrected.

"Fascinating," he remarked. "Where I live, there are no human augurs. Only my kind." He tapped the angular cheekbone below his sightless eye meaningfully.

"Perhaps the madness would be less if you saw, rather than heard, its wisdom," she said.

"If only the whispering stopped that easily." He flashed

a multi-fanged smile before his one good eye trained on me. "Hey. Resources are usually pooled in a circle, if you catch my meaning."

I felt my lips press together. If anything, it felt like he'd just said something random to confuse me.

"Eh. The sudair will know, if you don't figure it out." He made a dismissive gesture.

"Well, thank you both for your wisdom," I said, standing. I tucked away the tidbit that Hana had looked into *the Void* to see the future. I could wonder about the implications later.

Hana waved farewell while Auric said a gruff "Bye, kid" before turning his attention back to her. I went to Lucas's room first, but it was empty, the sheets on the bed in an untidy pile to the side. While I stood in the threshold, I caught a hint of Ben's laugh and followed it to a waiting room jam-packed with people.

My coven and friends were mixed with a group of healthy survivors. At the center of it all was Wren, phone in hand, interviewing a teenage girl.

Ben stood toward the edges of the gathering and waved me over. He had a hand resting on the handle of a wheelchair, where his brother sat, head lolled back. I was caught for a moment by Ben's big, carefree smile. It was rare to see him without that signature smirk, but he was obviously carrying on over some story for Lucas's benefit.

Geo was nearby, keeping careful watch as always. He flashed me a quick wink, and I brushed my fingertips up his arm on my way by him. The contact had him shivering with awareness.

"Cress!" Ben's teeth were practically sparkling. "Come meet my bro, Lucas."

"Hello, Lucas." I held my hand out for a shake, and he

gripped my fingers loosely. His smile was slow and shy, and he looked me over with unusually pale eyes. We'd met before, though I doubted he remembered it, as he'd been deep within the possession of the Hungering Darkness.

The real Lucas peered up at me with slow blinks, as if he were still waking up. He was nothing like the young man I'd briefly met; his weakened body was lost in his hospital gown, and he looked like he'd been dipped in bleach from his ghostly skin tone and how platinum his overlong hair had become.

A little line of concentration marked his forehead. "It's a pleasure to meet you." He spoke slowly, almost stiffly. I wondered if it was difficult for him to talk after a monster had been speaking through him for months. "Ben has nothing but praise for his anam cara."

I felt a blush touch my cheeks. "We definitely complete each other," I said, sharing a glance with Ben before returning my attention to him. "How are you doing?"

"Better...I think," he said, speaking in short bursts. "It's frustrating. I'm not a blood witch anymore. There's no easy recovery ahead."

"Not a blood witch anymore?" I echoed in surprise.

"Yeah, blood runes don't work on him anymore," Ben confirmed. The shadow of troubled thoughts passed over his face. "Big P might be able to take a look at him and tell us what happened to his affinity, but earlier, he restored Lucas's soul and dipped. No one's seen him since."

He told me about the scrap of soul Phaeron had been holding after killing the Hungering Darkness. How Phaeron had pressed it to Lucas's chest and woken him when modern medicine hadn't done a thing.

"Oh, shit," I muttered. "Ben, he'd just killed what was left of his own brother. No wonder he disappeared."

He scratched the back of his head, lips quirked. "I know. The man needs a hug and a medal. Can you make him reappear so we can give him both?" he asked.

I touched the mark of protection on my wrist, drawing breath to say Phaeron's name when I noticed motion on Lucas's hospital gown. "Isn't that your shoulder mouse?" I asked. The cute little albino mouse was climbing up to perch on Lucas's shoulder instead.

"My brother's familiar, it turns out," he chuckled.

"Wow, that's—" I jumped at the sudden pressure of hands on my waist.

Phaeron's fingers seemed to form first, but it was unmistakably his presence behind me and his breath in my hair. "You called?" he asked. I felt a rush of warmth between my thighs from his smooth voice suddenly washing over my ear.

"You know, on second thought, wearing a bell won't save our girl from getting jump scared by you, Big P," Ben said casually. "Where'd you go?"

"Here and there," Phaeron answered, and the girl Wren interviewed suddenly pointed at him.

"It was him! He found me last night!"

The dimensional's presence behind me vanished the moment Wren turned her phone toward us. I waved awkwardly, as did Ben, and a moment later, Lucas too. Geo gazed stoically at the lens.

"Anyway," Wren said, rolling her eyes before focusing the camera on the girl again.

"Do you see her expression? In the dictionary under 'crestfallen,'" Ben quipped in a whisper. He started to wheel Lucas's chair toward the hallway, and Geo followed.

The moment we turned a corner, Phaeron reformed a

pace behind us. "She was about to say where I'd saved her from. I've got to keep some secrets."

Ben raised a hand, wiggling his fingers. "Air of mystique."

I snuck a glance over my shoulder. Yeah, he hadn't slept again. But he'd washed the white residue off his skin and had found a black sweater and dark wash jeans that he looked comfortable in. He was relaxed, laugh lines creasing the skin around his yellow eyes. "Something of the sort," he agreed.

Once the five of us were in Lucas's room and the door was closed behind us, Ben turned the wheelchair toward Phaeron. "I was hoping you could take a look at his soul. Blood runes aren't working to help him heal."

"One should not expect another to walk through hell unscathed, Little B," Phaeron answered but crouched down to be on eye level with Lucas. The young man seemed to be mustering himself to speak while Phaeron tilted his head, inspecting his soul closely.

Ben edged closer to me and took my hand when I reached for him. Our anam cara marks brushed, setting off a spark of awareness, and I squeezed his palm. I missed him. Now that I'd had a night with Geo, I craved two more, and they had *Ben* and *Phaeron* written on them. My body hummed for more of Ben now that he'd shed the manacles of guilt over his brother's condition.

"Did you know there's a white streak in your...darkness?" Lucas's weak voice drew my attention back to him. He gestured vaguely in a circle.

Phaeron's pupils narrowed to slits. "You can see my soul," he remarked.

A white streak? How alarming. He met my gaze over Lucas's shoulder, eyes shining with pain for an unguarded moment before he schooled his expression. "Endaeron repaired the damage he caused me with the last bit of himself. I assure you, I am whole," he said.

Wow. When Braza reassured me that Phaeron was safe, she hadn't mentioned this. I couldn't imagine how difficult it was for him.

Phaeron crooked his finger at me, gesturing for me to squat next to him. "What do you see of her soul?"

Lucas blinked, his gaze going unfocused, before he flinched away from me. "Like...looking into the sun," he mumbled.

Phaeron smiled wide enough to show the edge of his fangs. "Perhaps we shouldn't blind the boy."

I took the hint and returned to Ben's side, leaning against him companionably.

"Well, I admit that this is unique. No human has seen my soul with their own magic," the dimensional continued. "While your soul, Lucas, is still taking a new shape after what you've experienced. It's said that extreme trauma can cause changes to a witch's affinity. What I see is that you've been altered by a minion of Myuna without becoming corrupted. Time will tell if you'll be able to find a way to draw on soul energy, as I suspect that is your new affinity."

Lucas breathed raggedly, looking moments from a panic attack. "I don't want to eat souls," he said between gulps of air.

Phaeron laid his hand over Lucas's, pitching his voice to soothe. "No one's eating souls here. Perhaps you will find a ghost willing to share if you help them move on to the afterlife, or no consistent source shows up. Witches channel magic through common origins that can be found most anywhere. You've simply been altered to draw upon a much more uncommon supply of magic."

"Well, fuck," Ben muttered.

"And when you're feeling stronger, I will teach you what I know of souls. I already have a few ideas of what you might be able to do. You're not alone, okay?" Phaeron continued, patting his hand when he earned a slow nod.

"You're in good hands," Geo said. I smiled to myself at the unexpected praise from him.

Lucas needed rest for the moment, so I flagged down a nurse while my men helped him back into bed. Mom answered the call button and drew me into a brief hug. "Thank God you're still all right. Did you know your demo —" She caught herself at the last moment. "Dimensional boyfriend is the reason Lucas woke up?"

"Pretty amazing, right?" All I could do was beam. Even with Lucas having an uncertain future with his magic, that was worlds better than being in a vegetative state. Phaeron had done this without any expectations of praise, which meant I needed to be the one to sing it for him.

He glanced over his shoulder like he sensed us talking about him. "One good turn deserves another." He crossed the room in a few strides and reached out to take my hands in his. "Now if you all will excuse me, there's something I need to show Cress."

I met his slitted gaze. "You don't mind if I steal you away, do you?" he purred more quietly. I had a feeling... well, a *hope*, I knew why he wanted a moment alone and agreed wholeheartedly.

30

CRESS

Phaeron whisked me away in an embrace of shadows. By the time I blinked away the dizzy spell that followed my sudden relocation, he'd placed me on the couch in one of the library's private rooms. It was his room at this point, with the tatters of the clothes he'd shredded off me still lying beside the bed and his night-air scent lingering around us.

I took a deep breath and released it in a happy sigh. That smell clung to his skin, magic and man combined.

It took me a heartbeat longer to realize there were bags cluttering the floor by my feet. Phaeron had an odd expression, something like chagrin tugging at his dark gray lips as he looked at them. He was about to apologize about something, so I stood and kissed him before he could.

He cupped the back of my neck and stroked down the sensitive column. His lips caressed mine at a slow, measured pace, at odds with the frenzy that usually lit in him at the brush of my mouth. It was such a small tell, but also an immediate neon sign that suggested something had changed. He was in control, just as he'd promised, his soul healed.

So that meant...maybe this really was the moment he'd claim me in the ways he'd promised. Pulling back, he met my gaze. Warmth danced in the topaz facets of his eyes, and I stood mesmerized by them.

"Can I tell you something?" he murmured.

He could tell me a lot of things with that voice of his. By his serious tone, I had the feeling this wasn't a sexy kind of something and sobered myself. "What is it?"

He smoothed his thumb down my cheek, tender despite the weight of what he was about to share. "My brother showed me a memory as he was dying. A prophecy of Myuna's fate that he bore witness to," he said.

"Was it an accurate prophecy?" I asked, huskier than I intended. The roughened textured of his callused fingers brushed featherlight down my jaw and the tender skin over my throat.

A hint of pain sparked in his gaze. "It was told by the Void, so it has the chance of being accurate one day. Listen to this and tell me if you think you know who it speaks of..." He took a breath and intoned it from memory. "Another shall ascend to rival you, and she will bring about your end. She who would mate the son of night and fight you alongside his daughter. She will defeat you before you have a chance to spread your influence on a new world."

There was a knot where my heart should be, beating erratically against my ribcage. "Wait...no," I said. He tilted my chin up so I would see the way he was looking at me. "It couldn't be me."

"It could be you," he echoed.

I considered the prophecy's wording again. There was one step I hadn't taken, one close enough that I felt my toes resting on the precipice, itching to take the plunge. My heart thudded. I *wanted* to be the one to kill Myuna. Why would I back away from my destiny just because a dimensional had seen it in the Void?

"Keshora and Ravai died because of that prophecy. Myuna has been sure of my identity as 'the son of night' before I even knew what Earth was," he continued, like he mistook my pause for doubt.

"It's a self-fulfilling prophecy. Myuna is causing it to come true because of her reaction to it," I said. If only he could feel how much I wanted to take care of her menace once and for all. Not only for my own sake, for things to go "back to normal," but also to give him the closure he so clearly needed because of this goddess who had ruined his old life. "She meets her death *here*, in a new world, at the end of my sword."

He released me and stepped away, working the buckle of his belt. Was he getting naked already? *He went for that fast!*

Phaeron pulled his sheathed swords free from his hips and sank to his knees in one graceful motion, laying them at my feet. He cupped my right hand with both of his, brushing a kiss over my fingertips. "Cressida Rollins Darkmore," he began. "From this moment forth, I swear my blood, blades, and magic to your service."

There was adoration in his gaze as he said this oath. I reminded myself to breathe, caught up in how special it was to see such a private glimpse of his culture. Of course he wouldn't immediately undress and take me to bed. He was an old-fashioned prince first, and I loved that about him.

"You have captivated me from the moment we met. For what is a soul but a manifestation of a person's core truth?

How radiant you are, my True Light in the purest sense. I swear to be your Shadow, a loyal protector. The one to come running to fulfill your *every* need." He ended this with a suggestive lift of his brows, and I shivered with awareness.

But he wasn't finished speaking. He gestured to the pile of bags by the couch. "Though I have little by way of material wealth, I have found for you a patchwork gift. I hope you will accept a more proper offering that I will make for you by hand when we are again in a period of peace."

I wanted to say that he didn't have to give me anything, but this was a dance I was just learning the rhythm to. Perhaps all shadowborn made their mates custom gifts. Ah, shit. I didn't have anything to give him in return. "Phaeron, it's okay, I—"

"Let me finish," he whispered. "If you accept me as your mate, it would mean everything to me and my new life here. Your family and friends will be mine too. Your other mates will be my brothers. But you, Cress, shall be the only goddess of light I answer to. Will you wear my mating mark openly, without regret?"

He waited expectantly for my answer, and I bit my lip. I hadn't gotten him anything or prepared any fancy words. If I was going to be a good mate, at least I could try to offer the latter. Phaeron watched my expression and smiled wide enough to show his fangs, amusement creasing around his eyes. "A simple yes or no will suffice," he added.

"Yes," I rushed to say. "Of course it's a yes. I've wanted this since..." A dark containment room in Moongrove Library. I pictured the viciousness of his desire when he let it off the short leash of his self-control.

I would've walked out of that room as his mate if circumstances allowed, but there hadn't been a moment between us yet where he could fully trust himself. "You don't want to take a bite of my soul anymore, right?"

"Not in the slightest," he said. He took my free hand and pressed a kiss to the mark of protection on the inside of my wrist. There was a prick of pain, soothed by the brush of his tongue, and then that bit of magic was gone.

"Hey!" I protested.

"I will replace it with something better," he said. His hands moved to my hips, nudging me closer. A coil of his tail drew his weapons out of the way. "With the mating mark, I will always know when you need me, and in what way."

"Will it work the other way around?" I asked. He flicked open the button of my jeans, dragging the zipper down with the tip of his claw.

"I only know one answer, based on the experience with a different human mate. Shall we see what happens with us rather than look to the past?"

"Okay." Cool air hit the damp fabric between my legs when he nudged my jeans down, and I trembled with anticipation. It was finally happening. I could have Phaeron without fear of his control snapping at the wrong moment.

He hooked his thumbs through the thin straps of my panties. "I think I'll begin my worship of you here," he said, dragging them down ever so slowly.

"You should try me in your other form," I suggested. My cheeks heated as he paused and tilted his head, considering what I'd said.

Then a grin split his face. "Naughty witch. I know what you want," he teased. With a murmured word in his native language, his features shifted into the alien angles of Soiluire. He flicked his forked tongue out with a wink.

I nodded eagerly. When he'd been stuck like this, I

couldn't help but wonder what he could do with that tongue and how the rest of his body differed under his clothes. Maybe he'd indulge my every wicked thought as soon as today.

Solid shadows unfurled around us, helping him angle and anchor my legs. His claws dimpled my skin where he held me spread open for him. He laved his way up my inner thigh and peppered the path with grazes of his sharp teeth. I was already moaning for him before he reached my aching center and delved between my pussy lips with one stroke of his tongue.

I nearly jolted off him from the shock of pleasure. That tongue was a lot longer than I expected, and its forked end fluttered over my clit just so. His answering growl vibrated through me, his grip tightening. I felt him mumbling, and it became English halfway through, "...Don't move, Cress. My horns."

He tilted his head an inch to the side, and the hard point at the end of his spiraled horn jabbed in a sensitive spot close to my ass. "I won't," I yelped.

He answered with a Soiluirian purr and tugged my thighs just a bit wider. Now I noticed the ridges of his horns against my skin and the occasional brush of the tips, but with me as still as I could bear, there were no more unwelcome pokes. Only the glide of his tongue and lips as he feasted on me.

I would've expected him to need a bit of time to get used to his old body since he'd been modified to be more humanlike centuries ago, but he used that tongue like he'd never been parted from its length and flexibility. By the time he wiggled it up my channel and stimulated every inch, I was trembling in place.

Shadows held my hips steady, and when he noticed

how close I was, he circled his mouth to mimic how I'd chase the high of pleasure. His horns were the most natural handhold, so I clutched them with both hands as I came hard, back arching and toes curling.

He cleaned my pussy with slow, sure strokes and a rumble deep in his throat. It seemed he genuinely liked the taste of me, and I flushed pleasantly at the thought. When he retracted his magic and placed me back on my shaky legs, my bare soles hit the carpet, and I glanced down, impressed. He'd worked off my shoes and bunched-up jeans while I was otherwise distracted, leaving me bare from the waist down.

For the moment, he remained on his knees, licking the glistening remains of my pleasure from his face while adjusting the bulge that tented the front of his pants. His toothsome grin put his usual viciously pleasure-filled smile in context. This was who he was, the wolflike shadowborn that lurked below his princely manners.

"You're incredible," I told him.

He shifted, blunting his sharp alien features back into humanlike ones. "What was that?"

I pulled off my shirt and bra. "Come and get me," I invited instead.

His gaze brightened with predatory interest. It wasn't really that far from the couch to the bed, but I walked backward to the edge and sat while he prowled after me, shedding clothes on the way. He slid his arms on the bed and leaned in to cage me with his body.

I breathed in his presence, the earthy scent of night that clung to him like a cologne, and felt his soft skin and dense muscle as I caressed his chest. Several lifetimes of fighting scars patterned him, faded by time but still notable to the touch.

He was so close, the heat of him resting between my legs. "This is permanent, Cress. You'll wear my mark for as long as we both live," he said against my lips.

"Are you asking if I'm sure?"

Instead of a kiss, he rested our foreheads together, gaze soft on mine. "You must understand this is a lifetime of devotion I promised you. Some may find that..." He circled a hand, searching for a word. "...intense."

Maybe it was. By most metrics, our relationship had been a whirlwind, but I didn't need more time. No matter how unlikely our pairing was, we fit together. "We're meant to be, literally light and dark," I murmured.

He brushed a hand through my hair, breathing out his lingering tension. "You complete me, bright soul."

The next thing I knew, he was lifting me to carry me around the bed and laying out so I straddled him. His shadows reached for the bedside lamp. "Could you keep it on? I want to see you," I said.

"Not the request I expected." But he retracted his magic, his pupils slitted in the golden light. His hair pooled over one shoulder, dark and glossy as ink.

I ran my nails over his chest, earning a soft, approving hiss. "What *were* you expecting?" I caught his throbbing length between my cheeks, rolling my hips to tease him through my slick folds. One of the hard bumps that gave it unusual texture caught against my sensitive flesh, feeling like the press of a fingertip.

He bared his fangs in a grin. "I will fulfill anything you desire. You need but ask."

"Well, I was curious..." I drew out another stroke against him.

"If I've learned anything on Earth..." He rested his

hands on my hips, nudging me onto the crown of his cock. "...it is that curiosity is utterly human."

I sank down onto him slowly, savoring how he stretched me. "Is your dick any different in your other form?" I asked.

He held me flush against him, head tilted at a coy angle. "Let's find out," he purred. In a few seconds, he'd transitioned to his alien form and rested lengthened claws ever so carefully on my skin. Something else had changed about him, but I felt it inside me as a slight thickening when he was already a snug fit.

I lifted and popped my mouth open with a shocked cry. The discovery was immediate, an unusual but intense starburst of sensation. He watched my reaction with a pleased expression as I sank onto him again for more. Like his vampire-like fangs were remnants of a whole mouth full of them, the few nubs on his length were a hint at the full texture he had in this form.

He stimulated every inch of me even on the way down, hitting that sensitive inner patch for a gush of liquid warmth. His shadows piled pillows behind him, and he propped up his shoulders, crooking a finger with a literal smolder in his eyes. I saw the Iorsio tribe in him, a hint of yellow flame, as if he didn't already have the most beautiful eyes on this world and the next.

I leaned in as he'd beckoned and felt him shift, taking control. His fangs grazed my lips, his kiss hungry but measured. With one hand, he helped me ride him as fast as I could stand without coming on the spot. He cupped the back of my head and ran gentle pressure down my jaw with strokes of his thumb.

My body tightened as I sped toward release...and then he slowed and stopped, holding my hips to his. Huffing out a frustrated breath, I wiggled, and that release slipped away one second at a time. "Phaeron," I groaned.

He took his time shifting back to his humanlike form. "I made you something like a promise before...this." He gestured to encompass the room.

"You did?" I couldn't think of anything. Not when he'd thoroughly scrambled my brain and was still nestled within me, hard as iron.

"Mmm. Perhaps it will come to you soon."

He caught my lips, this time hardly holding back with only two fangs to navigate. During that savage kiss, he started to move again, reawakening my body. But this time, I ached for that release I'd been denied and started to tremble as we approached it again.

I halfway expected him to stop again when I was close but breathed a vicious "Fuck!" when he did.

"Now, now," he teased, a growl edging his tone. He wasn't unaffected by his own game.

I worked my jaw, finding it harder to talk. "What was the promise?"

He shook his head minutely. "Trust me, you'll remember," he rumbled.

When he thrust again, the rise and fall of pleasure to frustration took even less time. "Please," I breathed. He wanted me to beg. Oh! He wanted me to beg him to bite me.

One day, you will carry my mating mark. You'll beg for it.

I felt his cock kick within me as he clamped down on his release too. He met my gaze and sighed, filtering a few locks of my hair through his fingers. Speaking Soiluirian, his cadence rose and fell in waves. Like music or poetry. Words of love. Words to soothe.

"I trust you," I answered. My tongue felt too big for my

mouth. "I love you. I want to carry your mark forever. On my skin and my soul. I want to be yours. Please, Phaeron."

His hold on me tightened. When he lifted me and thrust deeply, I knew. We were speeding toward the end this time. He skimmed his lips down my neck, and I was wound so tightly even his hot breath was erotic as it washed over my skin.

"It will hurt, but you will barely feel it," he promised. He used his free hand to angle my head, placing his fangs in just the right place, in the hollow where neck and shoulder met. I was already unraveling, coming so hard my eyes rolled back.

He inhaled and then bit me. I screamed, pleasure and pain flaring and entwining for several heartbeats before he exhaled. He'd swapped a tiny piece of our souls, and I felt the pressure of memories that weren't my own all crowding in as my body surrendered to unconsciousness.

31

CRESS

Like when Braza created the tether between us, I experienced Phaeron's memories as if I were him. Yet a tug in my gut reminded me I wasn't a Moihan male, as if I wasn't quite sleeping under the layer of his recollections. I existed as a tagalong for the journey through his past.

The pieces of memory were snippets from a very long life. Yet what I saw defined who he was.

Shadowborn. Soldier. Prince. Lover. Father.

His earliest memories were of shadows, curling and billowing between his small hands. They were always there behind the beacons of a goddess of light otherwise present on a world saturated in a deep shroud of night lit only by distant, cold stars.

What he truly remembered of childhood were bits and pieces of an ancient whole. Finely tailored suits reduced to shreds because they fit too snugly. The shadowborn rage, overwhelming in a boy's body.

He associated his Iorsio mother with her disapproval, her pursed, white-stained mouth.

His father, however, let brief glimpses of sympathy

through the cracks of his stony visage. Phaeron and his twin had taken after him, after all, beget of the strongest shadowborn to ever serve Myuna.

It was his father that'd put him into physical training early, and from there, he discovered his first love...a weapon in his hands.

The sword did not require manners or doublespeak, nor did it look at him with weighty expectations. It was straightforward, something to master. He learned with one, then two swords, moving through forms and stances until his fingers bled and it all became muscle memory. He honed himself to a fine edge of mastery made of blade and shadow.

Like any other weapon, he was put to use. His birth nation was constantly at war, conquering and expanding in the name of Myuna. The softness of his teenage years dulled as time progressed. One of the only constants he had was his brother. Early on, they would trade battlefields: from court to bloodshed and back. Phaeron preferred bloodshed at first, but he did his duty as a prince as was required.

The first half of his immortal lifetime was divided into eras, each corresponding with a different mate. Phaeron had shared his first female, Hisulet, with Endaeron. The royal family and courtiers viewed their relationship as perfect, as Hisulet was Vrassorm and a noble groomed for the tasks of royalty. She'd loved them both but had eventually bent to the whims of the court and carried Endaeron's heir, with a second on the way, when she'd taken a drink from a poisoned cup. Once she was buried, Phaeron sought cold-blooded revenge while his brother and nephew continued to mourn.

His parents shuffled him to war for a longer period of

time, which suited him fine at first, especially when he crossed blades with his second mate, Baeri. She was shadowborn and Moihan too, a fierce warrior from a rival nation that'd played cat and mouse with him over the course of several battles. When they came together, it was not sweet and gentle, but a whirlwind of claws and snapping fangs. He carried the scratches down his back with pride.

Baeri woke something cruel in Phaeron. He took pleasure in his strength and skill, fighting for the end result of victory and his mate's approval. Together, they had a streak of victories that won Myuna uncontested control of an entire continent. Enemies began to lay down their arms when they saw him across the battlefield rather than risk having their immortal lives torn apart.

Baeri had died as she'd lived, suffering a truly violent and instant death right next to Phaeron. He returned to the capital alone, ready to receive accolades, but instead was handed orders to lead his army overseas for continued conquest. Eyes still burning from grief, he'd refused and drawn Myuna's ire, which reflected in the court's response to him, especially when Endaeron left to fulfill the goddess's wishes instead.

Phaeron met his third mate soon after taking to his old diplomatic role, marking the shortest time between losing a beloved and discovering another. Solirin was an Iorsio tribe debutant, young and doe-eyed, who trembled when he first tried to touch her. To have a female fear him was so strange that he'd taken another look at himself and his reputation. For her, he trimmed his claws and polished his manners, slowly coaxing her trust and affection with gentle touches, poetry, and flowers.

They spent over a century together. It was a time he remembered fondly, as it was the closest he'd come to retiring his weapons for good. Then they decided to have a child, and Solirin passed in the midst of a difficult birth. He'd gained a son, Sennvold, but lost his True Light. This would not be the last time he raised a child alone, and his son took after him in more than just looks. When Phaeron returned to the battlefield, his boy was his squire and eventually a full-fledged shadowborn warrior.

Now that Phaeron was older, he saw the rashness of youth in Sennvold and the exhilaration of the fight in his fourth mate when their paths crossed in a war camp. Theda was Moihan too, but not shadowborn; instead, she was an experienced axe maiden who'd fought for Myuna only because her country had been conquered. Their pairing was benefited by experience. His newest mate went to war for the challenge and glory, not to gloat over how many kills she could etch into the runes on her armor, as vicious Baeri had done.

They grew tired of fighting together after several campaigns. Phaeron spoke of retirement more and more, suggesting Sennvold could take up the mantle of general with a few more decades' experience. He was done fighting because Myuna told him to. If she did not accept his decision to retire with his mate, they would disappear. He knew where to take her.

Days before they were to return to the capital, Theda was assassinated, taking a blade that'd been meant for his back. He grew bitter with regret that she'd pushed him out of the way. There was no one else for an endless drudgery of years after her death, as if fate was saying that he'd outlived too many of the women in his life and did not deserve another.

His memories skipped ahead, coming back into crystal focus with the ringing of claws on metal. Phaeron rapped the ends of his swords, peace tied in their sheaths, as he waited one cold evening at the mouth of a cave. Not just any cave, but Shenmaw, an underground town and home to the secretive Vess.

Restlessness shifted under his skin. I felt a shade of his discomfort and the weight of darker thoughts and emotions. It felt like he was here because of the despair, loneliness, and heartache that filled him, though he longed to melt into the night as the passing seconds wore his resolve away.

He had announced to the Vrassorm male keeping guard that he was there to see Auric et Vess. The leader of the voidwhisperers was not usually one to be summoned casually, but Phaeron had minded their rules and kept to the line in the dirt he was not allowed to pass.

I was surprised when Auric arrived. He was nearly unchanged this far in the past, except he had two intact backswept horns and his navy-blue hair was long and woven elaborately into braids. The stain on his face glimmered purple, tracing jagged lines over his skin and horns.

He still had a spiked tail, tattooed blue skin, and a clouded eye, the other teal with a scratch-thin pupil. Phaeron tensed as the other male inspected him, tension threading the air between them.

Phaeron broke the silence first. "I have come to take you up on your offer." He was ready to disappear. Slowly, he inched his chin down in a show of respect for the elder Vess. Here in Shenmaw, Auric was the ranking male, practically a king of the tiny population he kept protected underground.

Auric also held a precarious political position as the leader of an order separate from Myuna's nation of worshipers. Shenmaw was within her territory, clinging to a technicality for its neutral existence. It was close to uninhabitable, reportedly close enough to a rip in the world that the Void's madness twined through the air like a physical force.

None of the devout wanted to experience the Void that way, and they weren't invited at any rate. As long as Auric sent a steady supply of Vess to predict the future for Myuna, Shenmaw was allowed to govern itself.

A smile broke across Auric's face. "About time, kid. Leave your goddess at the line and enter." His voice was also the same, a deep rumble from his barrel chest.

"Myuna does not dwell in my heart. I am no more than a tool to her, a blade," Phaeron said with venom.

Auric turned, motioning to the guard, who resumed his post in front of Shenmaw's opening. "Then you are welcome here. Come," he said over his shoulder.

Phaeron followed, and time blurred. I felt his surprise as he walked Shenmaw's spacious corridors for the first time. Many single-eyed Vess practiced their magic here, but there were others from all walks of life. The one thing they had in common, he knew, was they all spurned the goddess of light to live in the pitch-black depths of the earth.

I felt his loneliness deepen. There were families here, and the sense of loss within him grew more biting. "Will you look into the Void for me?" he asked.

"That's what I do, kid." Auric stole another glance over his shoulder. "But this is the first time you've asked. What are you trying to find?"

"Hope, perhaps," he murmured.

Auric grunted. "The Void contains little of that. Come eat with Geryn and me."

Phaeron resigned himself to the cross-examination about to occur with Auric and his mate. Later that evening, when their young children had been put to bed, he sat with them, nursing a cup of spicy-sour broth that was common amongst the seers. It helped clarify the sight and sounds of the Void, apparently. He couldn't stomach much of it.

He shared his news and his request. He'd only just buried Sennvold, the last of his family. It was an honorable death for his boy but an unbearable loss all the same. War had finally ruined everything he'd held dear, and he felt...so alone. He found it hard to say the words, gazing into the depths of his soup rather than meet their eyes.

Auric's hand on his shoulder was about as welcome as the sharp edges of shattered glass. But his only words of comfort were, "The Void cannot soothe your pain, nor will it give you an immediate answer. You would be better served by reaching for community rather than the unknown."

"A promise of future peace would be enough. I have been unmarked for so long now..." Long enough that he'd forgotten the relief of a True Light's soothing touch. He needed something to anticipate, something to hold on to. Desperately enough to truly anger Myuna, should she know he'd gone to Shenmaw and ducked into the one place her all-seeing light did not reach.

Geryn glanced toward Auric. She was also of the Vrassorm tribe, but not a Vess, her belly well rounded with child. "He could stay here for a while. We have the space."

"If it pleases you." Auric gave her a tender smile. He wouldn't invite another male into his mate's space unless she approved. She'd be bedding down soon to rest for the last months of her pregnancy, exhausted by the needs of the growing child.

Phaeron masked his discomfort with a sip of broth. "I don't mean to impose, especially not at a delicate time."

Geryn smiled warmly. "Nonsense," she said with a dismissive wave of her hand.

So, Phaeron stayed and eventually learned the peoples' many reasons for hiding from Myuna in Shenmaw. He let his own resentment of her fester, created by her wars and the thousand cuts of indifference she'd led her followers and his parents to inflict upon him.

Auric took Phaeron on days' worth of tours deep with discussions on magic and meaning. He showed Phaeron how easy it was to call upon his latent soul magic here, so close to a rip in reality, implying with his knowing smirk that he should practice with it. The Void must have informed him of a possible future where he needed it.

Soul magic was akin to a party trick on Soiluire, though Myuna took a shine to those who had true skill in it. Most of them became torchbearers...except for Phaeron, ever the forgotten shadow to Endaeron. Still, he made a mental note to practice glancing deeper into others, stealing fleeting looks at their souls.

Long before he ever saw the rip in reality, his conversations with Auric and Geryn steered him toward airing how deep his burden had become. "Without a family of my own making, I'm not sure of my purpose anymore," he murmured to his friends, who listened well. "I have grown weary of what I once enjoyed. Why fight and perpetuate the cycle of tragedy?"

He only wanted *peace*. The desire echoed back to me full definition. He yearned for it within himself.

When he finally accepted this truth and began to feel his pain ebbing, Auric took him to see the Void. It was in a cavern deep within Shenmaw, where the blackness of the Void leaked into reality. Their surroundings distorted in the narrow corridor, and Phaeron felt the chill of the space between worlds for the first time.

Its laughter immersed him, and he growled, swinging his head around, looking for the threats mocking him. He kept a leery eye out, fearful of the alien presence of the magic and how it dug into his senses.

Visions played across the walls. Faceless figures drifted in and out of focus, interacting with Phaeron's shadow in various ways. Creatures dying, spraying blood from a slash of his sword. Females laughing, giving him the charmed looks he once strived to earn. Laughter. Screeches. Demonic, warped noises that could've once been words.

He hunched and covered his ears as the whispers pushed in, too many to be understood.

"You have to ask it to focus on what you want," Auric advised over the cacophony. He took him by the arm and guided him to the site of the rift, where the visions and sounds were at their most real.

The Void responded to Phaeron's thoughts, a blessing when he'd have to scream over the echoes as they intensified in the small, cavernous space. He wanted to know there was a future for him, that the piercing loneliness he contended with each day would pass.

The chill in the air intensified, prickling over his skin like ice needles, and answered. Half or more was madness and distortion, but Auric was there to wave away the worst of it.

The future immersed him. Voices of all kinds spoke his name. Male, female...kind tones, needy ones, furious intonations. Auric and Geryn swirled in with them before stopping abruptly.

I didn't recognize any others at first, but woven into the tapestry of sound was Keshora and then Morgana. And...my voice. Ben and Geo were there too, and all our friends and eventually Auric once more. Phaeron didn't realize there was a change of worlds and languages. The Void presented us all as the same: those that would cross his path in the future.

Phaeron raised his head, letting his eyes slip closed. My voice had caught his attention, and his lips curled slowly. *Definitely a lover,* he thought, picturing me as a curvy Moihan female.

When he opened his eyes again, the Void showed him children. Delicately clawed hands holding an infant that could've been Ravai. A scramble of insanity that Auric quietly dispelled for him. Then toddler Braza shyly meeting his gaze as he placed her on a countertop.

Phaeron reached out, scalding his fingertips on freezing cold Void mist. He hissed and flicked his hand, only regretting that he'd disrupted that particular vision. He longed to hold them with a fierceness that was nearly painful.

The two girls reappeared, older. He watched them from the edge of a field, soaking in their laughter as they played within the shadows, using them to jump around trying to tackle one another.

Optimism for the future rekindled in his chest. Those were the only sweet laughs within the whole Void so far.

"It could be a turning of the millennia before this happens," Auric said. The visions became nonsense once he relaxed the fist he'd been holding at his side.

The scene was just changing. There was a third child, who he only caught a fleeting glance of. Phaeron ended up shrugging, embracing the knowledge that there might be more family further into his future. But I could've gasped, creating a dissonance that completely shifted the course of his soul memories.

TIME SPED BY. For the next age of his life, he'd stayed with the Shenmaw rebels until he became one as well, before returning to the capital to cross paths with a new mate, Keshora, and fitting ill at ease into his old life and the weighty expectation that he return to fighting in Myuna's name. He'd had a spell of contentment and a family he lost along with everything else in the Age of Decay.

I saw him with Morgana next, and yes, he'd loved her dearly. It wasn't as hard as I'd expected to watch them together after seeing him in love five other times. He viewed his first human lover as both fascinating and fragile. In their short time together, he'd figured out how to elevate her to demigoddess status just so they could be together into eternity.

Phaeron's memories jarred forward. He'd woken to a world changed, damaged librarian witch runes fading to black on the ceiling above. He'd been locked away for two hundred years by Morgana, a huge rift that betrayed the vows of their mating.

"Why?" he'd asked in a pained whisper.

The emotions were still real, as recent as an echo. He'd later stood before her ghost and heard her reasons, but her memory was tainted now, a complicated blip in time for him. She had picked him up at his lowest and helped him acclimate to a new world. Her presence in his life was once hope, a promise that he was not alone in this strange world, where his people were feared and hated. Now that she had found her purpose in death, he could wish her well and allow them both to move on.

But in sealing him in stasis, she had cut him off from everyone and everything that'd still mattered to him. He had essentially risen from his grave by waking up. That it was an accidental side effect from a blood baron's plot to unleash the Hungering Darkness made it worse. He could've been lost to time in that room.

My heart twisted as I watched him struggle, his stark retread of a lack of a *purpose* now a resonant note in his memories. When he wasn't blacking out from the Hungering Darkness's attempts to control him, he sat in an alley with a homeless man, sipping the cheap alcohol he kept in a paper bag. I barely recognized David, a bear shifter Phaeron had later introduced me to, under a layer of hair and grime.

The alleyway served as a resting place when he failed to find a sense of normalcy in the modern world. Lanie had just died, and he saw me in his mind's eye, all grief and ugly tears and incorrect conclusions.

He had no place on Earth. No people, no mate...nothing but the ear of the shifter next to him, who drank to muffle the pain of his soul damage. He spoke in depth about a place called Aurora Heights, where shifters rejected by their mates gathered for second chances.

"Why don't you go to this place?" he'd asked.

"I dunno, man," David slurred, knocking back the rest of a nearly empty bottle. He looked into its depths, and his expression darkened. "I guess I keep expecting someone from my sleuth to come find me."

"Your family?" Phaeron guessed.

"Yeah. Maybe they're just ashamed of me now. My perfect match rejected me...so there has to be something wrong with me." With a shrug, David placed the empty bottle aside and transferred the paper wrapping to a new one. He turned the cap toward Phaeron.

"While you yet live, there's nothing to stop you from finding a new path." As he spoke, he used his shadows to remove the cap with an effortless twist. His shadowborn abilities...reduced to a party trick.

Yet David barked a laugh. "You're like a fortune cookie, man."

His eyes narrowed. "What is a fortune...cookie?"

David just laughed harder. He seemed to think Phaeron was hilarious for some reason. They shared the bottle, and Phaeron cringed from the first few sips. Had distilleries not improved while he rested in stasis?

"You know, like from Chinese joints." Sometimes he took pity on Phaeron and tried to explain. "You break the cookie open, and it tells you your fortune. Sometimes they're all mystical like you are."

"The cookie tells... You know what? Never mind." He leaned back, his head full of fuzzy warmth.

There was nothing to stop him from treading a new path of his own. To become someone else again, continuing to adapt and grow even though it felt like the twilight of his immortal life. He saw me again when he closed his eyes, this time walking side by side with Lanie. We'd been dressed nearly identically, something my seer friend had done on purpose.

Phaeron was sure she'd been targeted because of me. My proximity to his release meant it was a miracle the Hungering Darkness hadn't immediately killed me and eaten my soul to soothe the edge of its starvation. But if it had a sniff of me, then it would hunt me tirelessly until it was my eyelids he was forced to close.

As the only one who could go toe-to-toe with his undead brother, he had a duty to try to protect me, even if I hated him in those days for assuming *he* was the monster.

I'D LIVED MOST of the memories that passed by next. Phaeron didn't find much purpose until he was kneeling in the dirt, bleeding out from protecting me and my friends from our ill-fated first fight with the Hungering Darkness. As Áine healed him back from the brink of death, he'd asked, "Do you see now that I am not a monster, bright soul?"

My shaky "yes" had meant much more to him than I'd ever expected. There was a chance we'd make amends, even become allies, now that it was understood that we had the same enemy.

He began to think of me as lovely and often triggered his otherworldly sight to see my form haloed by my soul. Light was anathema to a shadowborn...but not the kind I put off. My soul flickered around me like liquid gold, an eternally flattering light source that limned my cheeks and put a shine to my purple hair. My brown eyes turned honey-toned and sparkling.

He'd been admiring me for longer than he'd admitted to. I was soft and rounded compared to the females of his own species, confusing his attraction. Fate reminded him that it was my voice to bring him back from Endaeron's control twice, helping him shake off his cravings to bite into my soul since he admired it so.

As early as the evening he'd walked me to my dorm room, he'd known I was supposed to be his next True Light. From then on, he'd taken the duties of my Shadow and gladly stepped into the role of training and spending time with me and my friends. Tempering Geo's stone form and protecting Ben with his presence were merely a part of it.

With the tug of hunger in him every time he glimpsed my soul, his role as protector was all he felt he could offer. That didn't prevent the little touches and teases as both of our feelings deepened, but each was a test of his control. One slip, and he'd hurt me beyond repair...but he couldn't bring himself to stay away.

If I could've caught a breath, I would've at the feeling of yearning that deepened in him with time. He'd ached with unfulfilled need so acutely each time he denied both of us more. Enough to have a spike of shadowborn rage toward his oldest friend when Auric called me "a mate in name only."

I saw a closed-door conversation between him, Geo, and Ben; then the memories took a single step back in time from his diplomatic request for peace between my three men. "It is easy to love Cress" in a conference room became the soft slide of covers against his naked body and my slight form so close to his.

"I have missed you far more than words could convey." Underneath the tender whisper was the horror he'd barely staved off, the control Myuna had failed to fully exert over him. He'd refused to give in to her with me on his mind, my name on his lips. Knowing he would one day return to me sustained him and kept him awake, aware, and alive just long enough to save his life and soul.

I'd comforted him and run my fingers through his hair, blunted the disjointed edges that existed within him after his torture at her hands. But it was my reaction when he'd tried to pull away again that'd tilted his self-control straight to possessive desire.

I will not go quietly into eternity without lying with you, he'd thought.

That had truly been lovemaking in the dark. My skin glowed to his sight alone when I was surrounded by his shadows, and he'd touched my face, enamored by the sight and the utter trust I'd surrendered to him.

From that night on, I was fiercely *his* and the one to complete him in his new Earth life. I was his mate, his future, his purpose, and his much-longed-for peace.

32
CRESS

I woke feeling more loved than I could imagine, drifting on the safety of my mate's feelings through a rough return to wakefulness. My skin ached like I'd been sandpapered top to bottom, and I couldn't lift my head from where it rested under Phaeron's chin. The pain radiated from my shoulder like a pinched nerve.

Well, as he'd explained, we'd just swapped a tiny piece of our souls to create a permanent bond between us. Maybe this was a taste of what it'd feel like if he'd taken a bite out of my soul as he'd craved until very recently. His brother had given him a very important gift: the opportunity to start again without being impaired by soul hunger.

Phaeron was out cold underneath me, his breathing evening out to the slow and steady cadence of deep sleep. At some point, my memories must've transitioned straight to dreamland for him. I couldn't really be upset about it. Compared to the pieces of his life I'd seen, mine must've been brief and mundane.

No one could really rival an immortal prince from another planet for interesting life experiences.

Knowing he needed rest pretty badly, I moved off of his chest carefully. I'd been out long enough that my legs had regained most of their feeling. I tucked a layer of covers around him and took slow, measured steps toward the gifts he'd gathered overnight.

He'd known to raid a beauty store, and I could've wept when I saw moisturizers and makeup again, especially the expensive brand names I wasn't able to afford. But I put it all aside, shifting through bags of nice clothes and a box full of bottles and what could be random odds and ends.

For Braza's gargoyle form. I simply knew about it now and would help him do what it took to give her a new body. It was incredibly important to him... She was family.

He'd taken several different models of new phones and accessories as well. I fished out the one with the newest hardware and a sparkly case, putting them aside to set up soon. Ben and Geo were going to be overjoyed when they got new devices too, *and* they'd stop taking mine! Win-win.

Lying flat at the bottom of all this stuff was what I was looking for. "My precious," I murmured, pulling out a new, quality sketchbook and a premier pack of colored pencils. I thumbed through the blank pages and opened the pack as quietly as possible, stealing a glance at Phaeron's sleeping form to ensure I hadn't woken him.

I ran my fingers over the rainbow of pencils I'd freed and smiled to myself. It wasn't much, but I could give him something back. I gathered up the art supplies and laid a loose blanket over my naked body before propping the sketchpad on my legs and getting to work. I scribbled away with my tongue caught between my teeth, recreating something from Phaeron's memories before it faded and smudged like many of Braza's recollections had.

With him sleeping away, I had a chance to take my time. I hadn't drawn a portrait like this in a while, but I was a woman possessed. It took full form, and I was rubbing a cramp from my hand when Phaeron finally stirred.

The phantom sensation of panic gripped my chest as he shot up, looking around. When he found where I'd set up, he tilted his head. I realized I was feeling his emotions—in this case, his confusion. "I didn't want to wake you. You needed to sleep," I said.

"Silly female." He sounded groggy. He rubbed his face, glancing down at his clawed hand and flexing it. "All I need is you."

My heart fluttered. I quickly placed the pencils back into their slots and flipped the sketchbook closed, taking it with me. As soon as the blanket fell, the rising burn of his lust kindled across our mating bond, and my sex ached for him in response. I placed the sketchbook on the bedside table and let him pull me back into bed, though he cupped my stiff neck so we didn't jostle the place he'd bitten me.

When we lay face-to-face, he swept my hair back to look at the wound and blew cool air over it. "My mark is developing well," he said, proud. I realized I hadn't taken a moment to look into a mirror at it, and he responded like he knew my thoughts. "You can inspect it later, once it's set."

"How..." I drifted off when I realized that was the wrong question to ask. It was magic from his world, undoubtedly stronger on his end of things. "This really is intense, huh?"

He nodded. "It will fade some with time. But I will always know your needs so I can fulfill them." He stroked his thumb over the curve of my cheek, and I felt him admiring me. I could only mirror him, appreciating seeing him at ease. He really was handsome in a striking way, different yet familiar. Still a man despite every extraordinary circumstance.

"What did my soul memories show you?" I asked.

"A true understanding of who you are." He held me to his chest when he felt how that answer made me nervous for what, exactly, he'd seen. He spoke tenderly in my ear. "Relax, bright soul. I should be the fearful one, with how many terrible decisions I have had to make and live with. You probably saw the worst of me."

"With your shadowborn mate...Baeri," I murmured.

Pressing his lips together tightly, he nodded. "We were too young to understand the damage we caused. I am glad I am not that person anymore. You could say I've been someone different with each of my mates, versions of myself tailored to them," he said.

"I saw them all briefly. If you'd told me before this that you'd had six women before you met...I mean, you've lived so long..." I stammered, drifting to a stop when he pressed his fingers to my lips.

He took my breath away just by looking at me and pushing his tender feelings into my headspace. "They mattered to me in their time. The memories should have shown you that I've had to move on far more than I've wanted to."

"No one should have to bury so many wives," I agreed quietly.

"Each funeral was more difficult than the last. Fate seemed cruel for sparing me, yet it has led me to you. You've swiftly become someone I cannot live without." He took my hand, laying it over his chest and the steady beat of his heart. "I have no desire to exist on Earth without you. Whatever length your life shall be, I will be glad to go along with you when you depart for paradise."

"Phaeron," I said, shocked.

"Too honest?" He was completely serious. This wasn't just him expressing devotion, but a kind of world weariness I could barely wrap my head around.

I got a little teary. I'd just seen how much loss he'd endured and didn't want to picture a time where he was gone. Seeing my distress, he kissed me, slow and loving, while his hands traced my curves. "Don't worry," he said into my lips. "I will find a way for you to enjoy immortality with me first. I want a long, long time with you."

I wanted that too, as long as we could also have Ben and Geo with us. "I agree. I hope you can retire from fighting like you've wanted to for so long."

"Yes," he murmured.

"What do you want to do instead?" I asked.

The sparkle was back in his eyes as he imagined the future. "Mmm, I've found joy in teaching others. I would continue to pursue that and await the day you give me children to raise." He mentioned it casually, like a logical extension of our relationship.

"This is not to say I will hang up my weapons forever. Anyone who challenges our family will find my blades as keen as ever. Besides...most of your friends are unmated women, and I will continue to protect them as they grow into their powers. Maybe it's old-fashioned by Earth standards, but it is only right."

"There's my prince," I said with affection.

"Yes, yours," he purred. "But that's enough about me. You were wondering what your soul memories showed me."

The anxious butterflies took flight in my belly again at the reminder.

"First, I need you to understand that I am not 'more

important' than you in any way. I am a prince of nothing and wish I never had the title since I've seen it has intimidated you. We are equals. Okay?"

"Okay," I answered. He rewarded me with another kiss.

"To put your mind at ease, I saw your early childhood and the abusive rages of a man your mother made the decision to leave. May I kill him?"

"What?" I practically yelped.

"I didn't think you'd agree to that," he said, sounding a little disappointed. "You survived growing up with very little, doing your best with what you had, and took a job early to support your mother and sister. Discovering that you're a witch was a twist of good fortune until it came with the baggage of political plots and assassins. One of your biggest regrets is misjudging me and my intentions at first."

That was an understatement. He kissed the apology off my mouth before I could say it, as I'd started to do with him. "I could have stayed and done a better job convincing you of the circumstances," he murmured.

"But you were depressed," I added.

I reached out and brushed my fingertips over his cheek. He closed his eyes, tilting his face for more. "Incredibly. Yet I found it within myself to go on," he said.

"I'm glad."

He breathed a soft sigh. "Me too."

"I saw you talking about it with David. Did you ever find out what a fortune cookie is?"

He cracked open one eye to squint at me. "He wasn't making that up?"

"No, he just explained it really badly," I said, muffling a laugh at his disbelief. "They're folded around a slip of paper that holds a generic statement about the future."

"Hmm. Would I do a good job making fortune statements?"

"I think so."

"David also thought most of the things I told him about my past were from video games." I got the distinct feeling his thought at the moment was *whatever those are* and had another chuckle over that. "Thank you for reminding me of him. I'll have to check on him when we return."

"Maybe he's moved on to Aurora Heights," I said.

He shook his head. "Wanting your family to wake up and see how they've wronged you is one of the strongest desires one can have."

"Spoken from experience." At this point, I was exploring the curl of his horn. It was built solidly, hard and smooth, thinning at the pointed end.

"They never saw me. I found more fulfillment in moving on and being the father I'd never had." He took my wrist and placed my hand on his cheek again, nuzzling against my palm.

"Speaking of which," we said at the same time.

"Jinx. You go first," I said.

He already had that uncanny way of looking right through me, and now I'd armed him with insider knowledge of the depths of my soul. "I think you will make a great mother. Your circumstances are going to be much different from your own childhood."

"I do want kids one day." But he'd touched on something that went deeper, which I hadn't said aloud to another person. "I've had a strong role model. My adopted mother is my hero."

"But you haven't known a positive father figure. You've been afraid of marrying a male like her ex-mate?" The concept seemed to puzzle him.

"It's a human thing. I don't want to give any kids of mine a father like that. And"—I held up a finger—"I realize it's a silly fear when I know now I'd make a dad of Ben, Geo, or you. None of you are like that."

"The babe would have three fathers. Practically tripping over us." He rubbed my belly with quiet longing.

"I have a little gift for you," I said, seeing that it was time to show him, before I could embrace any last-second doubts that he'd find it a meaningful mating gift.

He reassured those nerves. "You don't have to give me anything. You are gift enough."

"It's in the sketchbook. There was a memory... You looked into the Void," I said clumsily.

His pupils narrowed. "I have only done that willingly a handful of times. Was Auric there?" Shifting to lie on his back, he reached for the sketchbook.

"Yeah. It was the first time, I think," I supplied.

"Then the Void was as honest as it can be," he commented.

He flipped up the front cover and looked at the portrait I'd made. The kid was unmistakably Phaeron's son, I thought, if a shade like his mother too. Lighter gray skin; straight, dark brown hair, and slitted dimensional eyes cooled to orange embers. He could've been ten, with the points of his horns starting to emerge from his crown and a layer of baby fat that could give way to high cheekbones one day.

Maybe I was wrong and Phaeron had already met this boy and said goodbye to him without it appearing in his memories or regrets. But the way he froze with a sharp inhale, the phantom of his emotions cycling between surprise, realization, and yearning erased my doubts.

"Is this...?" He reached out to touch the paper.

"I think so," I answered in the same hush.

He set the sketchbook aside and rolled onto me, framing my face and peppering it with kisses. I felt his joy like my own but winced when he put me on my back. My neck was still quite tender. "Thank you," he said, touching foreheads with me. "I don't know how, but...it must be possible."

"We'll figure it out," I promised.

"Someday." He went for the mating mark next, licking the tender space and blowing another cool, soothing breath over it. "Would you like to try my animaris? It might overtake the pain of this setting."

"Sure," I said but swatted him when he bit me none too gently. *Ow.*

The new wound stung for a few seconds. "You're responding to it fast." He gave my hip a squeeze, watching my reaction closely.

Warmth replaced the pain and swiftly met my bloodstream, spreading from there. It hit my heart and radiated out from my chest. A pleasant flush was soon buzzing through me head to toe. He palmed one of my breasts and tweaked the hardened bud, grinning as I nearly arched off the bed. I felt so sensitive all of a sudden and tingled from the brush of his skin on mine. "Phaeron," I moaned.

He hardened against my thigh, responding to my sudden surge of need in kind. "Is this normal?" I asked breathlessly.

"Completely." Despite how he throbbed against me, he pinned my hip, making no move to claim me. "I only gave you a bit. It should wear off...about now."

I did notice it fading. I still ached for him, though, and that was all me, jumpstarted by his animaris. I touched my shoulder. The mating mark tingled with discomfort, but there were no open bite wounds. "It healed me," I said.

He nodded, saying, "I gave you a tiny amount of my life force. It'll fix up superficial wounds and bruises, but it's meant to excite you. Now that you know what it feels like, do you want more?"

I checked myself on agreeing enthusiastically, wiggling underneath him. "Depends. Are you going to deny me again?"

He lifted my hips and thrust with little preamble. Back arching, I moaned hard; it was a relief to feel him fill me again. "I have not the strength nor will to deny you anything," he growled.

"Then I want more. A lot more." I tilted my head, and he kissed his mark before biting down.

BEN

I drew the short straw to go find out where Cress and Phaeron had gone, to deliver a message. I was a bit grumpy about it, but they were probably fucking, and there were only a few safe places around to do that.

She'd been making bedroom eyes at me, damn it, and he'd stolen her away before I could. I was jealous. It felt like it'd been ages since we'd had some bonding time...and I didn't want Big P biting my head off for interrupting them with the news I had to share.

The run to the library was uneventful, though. I didn't have to worry about unnaturals. According to our spy extraordinaire, Grant, there were no more animal unnaturals because Myuna had eaten them all to cast a huge spell that was bad news for us. Because of it, the torchbearers seemed to be waking up from their zombielike state and practicing their magic again.

"Just knock," I told myself as I navigated the wreckage of the first floor and took the stairs down. "The worst that can reasonably happen is he tells you to go away. Again."

And I would not. We needed Phaeron in full tall, dark, and terrifying mode to help us plan the upcoming offensive, and the meeting was scheduled for tomorrow. He needed to know that before he got back to hoarding our girl in his shadow dungeon or whatever.

I didn't worry for long that he'd taken her someplace new. The scream I heard came from the same room where I'd last found them. As expected, it sounded like they were having a good time. I rolled my eyes and knocked.

No answer.

I tried again. *Knock. Knock. Creak...*

The door seemed to have unlatched and opened on its own. "It's Ben?" Cress was asking.

"I can wait for you guys to, uh, finish," I said, peeking inside anyway.

Shadows obscured more than their outlines, but the slap of skin on skin was pretty distinctive. My pants got tight fast from her breathy moan. "Ben," she called, sounding more than a little lust-drunk.

"You can be here if you help pleasure our mate," Phaeron added in a tight growl.

"Oh! C'mere, Ben," Cress cried out.

"Don't threaten me with a good time," I said, jolting into the room and locking the door again behind me. Phaeron retracted his shadows and helped lay Cress down at the foot of the bed. She was giggling and flushed, watching me strip avidly with eyes more dilated than normal.

He sat behind her, waiting with impatient flicks of his tail. But I didn't pay much attention to him, more worried about what was going on with her. "You okay, babe?" I murmured, bending down to kiss her.

"Better than okay. Touch me," she demanded, meeting my lips with open-mouthed passion. Phaeron also answered her need, running his palms up the back of her legs and squeezing her ass.

While I moaned and met her tongue for tongue, he said, "She's under the effects of my animaris. She consented to it."

I broke off the kiss with a, "Your what now?"

"An aphrod—"

"His sexy venom," Cress interrupted.

I felt my face light up. Oh, I was going to have fun with that. "Just full of tricks, aren't you, Big P?" I teased.

"An understatement, Little B," he replied in kind. "But enough talk. Join us...or don't." He lifted her into his arms and kissed her with the same level of passion she'd hit me with at the door.

Like hell I was going to choose not to join them. I climbed onto the bed behind her, smoothing my hands down her back and leaning in to kiss her unmarked shoulder. There was a new pattern of dimensional magic on the other shoulder, looking like fancy scrollwork stretching a couple inches in a circular pattern around two points where he'd obviously bitten her. Maybe that was where the "sexy venom" thing came from.

His mark on her was a light gray, unlike the pair of black and purple bat-like wings over her shoulder blades, where Braza had tethered to her. The magic was dormant, the skin pebbling with goosebumps in the wake of my touch. I could get used to her being this responsive. I loved hearing how much she enjoyed having us both kissing and stroking her all over.

I'd gotten used to navigating around an extra pair of hands with how often she preferred to have Geo and me at the same time. Phaeron cheated, though, using his shadow magic to leave lingering touches on her legs and arms where we weren't concentrating much attention. I focused on stroking her hips and belly, feeling her quiver between us, almost like she'd come from touch alone.

My fingers dipped toward her overheated core. Fuck, she was already soaked. "Ben, wait," he said, cupping Cress's cheeks. "Look at me, bright soul. Ben's here now. You're about to have us both."

"Oh, yes," she said dreamily.

"Any preferences?" he asked.

She leaned back to look at me over her shoulder. "How do you want me?" she asked huskily. With those lidded bedroom eyes on me, I would've said any way she wanted, but it was clear she was offering it back to me since they'd been at this a while.

"You know I can't resist that pussy, babe," I answered.

Without missing a beat, Phaeron put in, "And you've made quite the mess of me."

"Oh no, we can't have that." She leaned back further into my arms, threading her fingers into my hair as our lips met for a hungry kiss. I took the opportunity to shape the familiar curves of her body with my hands.

As impatient as he'd been to have her again, Phaeron sat back and watched us with an approving growl. When she pulled away with a lingering graze on my bottom lip, he stood and helped her balance on her hands and knees, using his tail to prop her up around the middle. She moaned into his cock when I ran mine through her slick folds.

"Hey, Big P," I said, reaching for his tail. "Could I borrow this?"

With a wave of his hand, he made a cushion of shadows for her middle and held his tail at an angle for me to take. The bunch and flex of muscles under the skin suggested he could've done this for himself, but I was in the business of pleasuring Cress right now, so I teased her with him, drawing a few inches of tail over her pussy.

She moaned into his cock as it sank into her mouth. He cupped the back of her head, testing her with a couple shallow thrusts. "She's going to love this," I said, grabbing her hips and sliding myself home within her easily. She jolted and arched back to meet my hips, fists clenching on the bedsheets.

He waited to see what I was going to do, which was place the tip of his tail at the entrance of her ass. It was perfectly shaped for such a task. "Good." His usually smooth voice was little more than a rumble as he slid the first inch within her and twisted it. "Then she'll enjoy all three of us at once someday."

"How the hell is that going to work?" I asked. I was more focused on staying steady for her despite how she came hard, making me ache to spill early.

"I have a few ideas," he said.

"Of course you do."

"Jealous of something, Little B?"

"Yeah, actually. I wish I had a flexible tail for situations exactly like this one," I said. He was keeping pace with me with it, driving several inches of tail into her. If her mouth wasn't occupied, she'd definitely be screaming right about now.

"I have to have some assets to please her with, besides my wit," he said.

Cress breathed a distinct little "hehe," giggling like she did when I coaxed Geo into bantering with me in bed. Maybe whatever venom he'd given her was wearing off, as she was clear-eyed once he and I finished and lay out on either side of her.

Phaeron touched the mark on her shoulder. "More?" he asked.

"Wait, wait," I put in. "I came here to tell you two something."

"Can it hold on for a couple hours?" she asked.

I scratched the back of my head. "I guess?"

"Awesome, because I want to ride you both for at least that long before letting reality in again." She tilted her head for Phaeron. "More animaris, please."

33
GEO

I APPEARED on Wren's stream to deliver an important message. She'd wanted me in stone form, where my grinding tones and deadly serious expression would lend us credibility with the remaining survivors in Cerris City.

I looked into the camera and said, "We have discovered an exit to the pocket dimension that Myuna and her forces don't know about. All survivors and noncombatants will be evacuated through this secret exit in one week's time."

I listed the four new rendezvous points Ashbough Protective Services was opening up now that we knew Myuna had consumed her poorly shaped monster creatures. The seers had balanced out all possible futures for the evacuation and decided one week would allow us to gather as many of the dwindling population of survivors as possible while the twisted goddess would still be mastering the fine control needed for the unfamiliar magic of her torchbearers.

According to our changeling, there didn't seem to be any movement coming from Myuna's throne. She was deep in meditation alongside a handful of the most powerful supernaturals she'd managed to bring under her sway. We were still outnumbered three-to-one by her torchbearers, and that number could still grow before we moved a large group toward the operating ocean gate.

Hell, if we messed this up, her forces would grow *because* of us. I made it my new, temporary duty to help locate survivors and bring them to safety. For the rest of the day, I flew loops around the furthest reaches of the city as a scout and guard for anyone I came across.

It was my pleasure to serve. Cress would be happy I'd used my time wisely, and it helped me feel productive. I had no doubts Phaeron and Ben were, quite literally, fulfilling my primary duty, and...I came to terms with it on my long scouting flights. Logically, I knew I could not be with her all the time. There was work only I could do here and wouldn't if I had to choose between it and protecting Cress.

I glowed with the pride of a job well done the next morning, having personally saved a dozen survivors and left a single stray torchbearer in quartz cuffs and a medically induced sleep in one of the hospital's rooms. I stood in the foyer, waiting in human form, a few minutes before the big meeting when they arrived in a swoop of shadows.

Phaeron had transported them with his hands on Cress and Ben's shoulders. Her face lit up when she saw me. "Geo! I have something for you," she announced.

I found her elation to be infectious, cracking the first smile out of my recent stint in gargoyle form. "Oh?" I asked.

She took the back of my hand and placed a cool plastic box in my palm. "Your very own phone. Brand new." She beamed as I looked from it to her and released a single, grinding laugh.

"Now I will never break yours again," I said.

"Look, he's smiling. That's practically bursting with joy," Ben laughed, reminding me he and Phaeron were still there. The dimensional hung back a step, wearing an expression that could only be described as besotted as he watched Cress.

I nodded in approval and bent to kiss her. "Thank you," I said.

She lingered close, hands resting on my chest. "Of course. Ben's going to get us all signed up on a plan together, and then you can watch cat videos to your heart's content."

"Soon." I had a pang of regret to end this moment, but the meeting was about to start without us. I pocketed the new phone for the moment. "There is a lot that still needs to be done. Some decisions were made in your absence yesterday, and other things need an expert's opinion." My gaze flashed more deliberately toward Phaeron.

"I enjoyed my respite quite thoroughly," he replied. And judging by the lack of dark hollows under his eyes, it seemed he had finally rested. Good. He'd be ready for the tough challenges ahead. "After the meeting, perhaps I could trouble you for a moment alone, Geo?"

"No problem. I want to show you to a torchbearer that needs your attention anyway," I said.

He dipped his head and led the way to the meeting, which started up the moment we settled. Madigan stood over a spread of maps pulled down from the wall. Today, we were joined by the usual group of decision makers: the two Crown Coven members, Hana Graygazer, Auric et Vess, Madigan's husbands, plus Roe and Grant.

Auric greeted Phaeron in Soiluirian, who replied in kind, taking a seat next to him. I glanced over at Cress, who shrugged. Without Braza, we had no hope of knowing what they were actually saying, but Auric's guffaw and hearty slap on Phaeron's back seemed fairly universal.

"Fashionably later than me. Nice," Roe said, fist-bumping Cress.

"Hello, you all. Welcome," Madigan said at the same time. "We are gathered to plan our methods of attack. We've just set the hourglass over and have less than a week to evacuate civilians and noncombatants before it's too late."

"What do you already know of Myuna's recent actions?" Phaeron asked.

She mentioned the consumption of most of her unnaturals and the way the torchbearers were seeming to wake and use their magic at her direction. He nodded, speaking up at the end of her narrative. "I've come to understand that Myuna is not the only monster of her kind. She intended to create another being of entropy in my brother and planted a seed of corruption in his soul. It was why the Hungering Darkness was so exceptionally awful while also being like her.

"It is more than likely, with its death, she has chosen to ascend another, who is helping her control her torchbearers. Such an expenditure of magic would be quite difficult for her in her current state without a sacrifice." His yellow gaze cut to Grant. "Do you know who she ascended?"

"No. I just know she's sitting around with five of her strongest minions right now. It could be any one of them," he answered.

The others nodded. At some point, he must've shown his changeling nature to everyone else in this room. Soon it wouldn't be much of a secret at all, if we survived the coming fights.

"If we can kill the ascended torchbearer, Myuna will be at her weakest. She will be so distracted by her hunger that we could bait her into a trap. Auric will manipulate the Void to send her back to rot away on the remnants of Soiluire," Phaeron said.

Hana's grave voice cut through his confident tones. "We will still need someone to stand toe-to-toe with her while he works."

He frowned, shaking his head. "Even weakened, she is still akin to a goddess..."

"A point we can come back to," Madigan interjected. "We have exchanged a few messages with the Coral King. He's willing to send his myrmidons to help us defend the ocean gate as long as Willow Frost is among the evacuees."

Cress shifted uncomfortably. "Has Willow agreed to this?"

Roe turned to her with a guilty little look. "Most of our people are leaving with her. She's going to be okay."

"Who is going to stay, then?" she pressed.

"Well, you, Ben, and me. Wren wants to stream the battle, but we want to avoid that. We're going to be using deadly force against the torchbearers. It's the only way we'll survive," the redhead replied.

Cress paled, while Phaeron nodded in grim understanding. With him as the only one capable of unbinding the souls twisted to Myuna's service, he could not physically save them all. With no further protests aired, Madigan finished outlining the rough sketch of our battle plan.

We would lure Myuna's torchbearers and chosen ascended to the lake where the ocean gate dwelled and fight to the bitter end to evacuate nearly everyone. Then, Auric would take the remaining fighters through the Void to Myuna's chamber directly.

"The smaller the group that remains, the less likely I lose someone along the way," he added.

"Comforting," our leader said dryly.

"He speaks in jest," Phaeron said, rolling his eyes. "His control of the Void is masterful."

"Why joke at a time like this?" I asked. Everyone but me seemed to turn to humor when up against such serious events.

"What better time?" Auric countered. "The hour of Myuna's death approaches, as foretold long ago, by a Vess as dear to me as a sister. She gave her life to tell the dread goddess she would be defeated by the duo of Phaeron's mate and daughter." His one good eye fixed across the table at her, glowing teal. "And now we have Cressida et Sudaira and her tether to the powercore, who, in life, was Phaeron's adopted daughter. She is only missing one thing. Have you figured out what you need to do next yet?"

Color touched Cress's cheeks as most everyone turned their attention her way. "It slipped my mind," she admitted.

"I believe the wording was..." he drifted off with a glance at Hana. "*Pool your resources, and you will find the key to our victory.* Right?"

She nodded. Phaeron seemed unsurprised, saying, "I remember now. I saw the conversation in Cress's memories and your heavy-handed hint as well. You believe a mating circle will truly be a solution here?"

Ben sucked in a gasp, while I felt as blank as Cress looked. I went ahead and asked the question for both of us. "What is a mating circle?"

For once, this room filled with all these big personalities was pin-drop silent. Ben was the one to break the silence, albeit with a nervous shake to his voice. "It's like marriage, but for a group, sealed with cupid magic."

Cress's eyes widened. "Marriage?" she echoed.

I drew breath to reassure her. The saying was that one could be married to their duty, after all. I wouldn't have minded binding myself to her forever at that moment.

"It is crazy enough to work." Phaeron disappeared in a whirl of shadows, taking form again behind Cress's chair. He rubbed her shoulders and bent to whisper something into her ear.

"It's a lot to ask of you all. We can find another way," Roe blurted.

"I would appreciate an opportunity to discuss this with my mate and her potential circle," Phaeron said, a steely edge to his voice. "Without an expectant audience."

It was Prince Orthus who responded first by pushing back his chair and standing. "For such a lofty request, it is the least we can do," he said, gesturing to the room at large. Madigan nodded and turned, going with him to be first out the door.

Soon, we were alone, and Cress was pacing the room. "Why is us all getting *married* such a big deal?" she asked.

I stood too, wanting to hold and comfort her while she balanced herself on the edge of panic. Ben did the same. "There's more to it than the marriage part, babe."

"Allow me to explain," Phaeron cut in, shooting him a warning look. "The point of a mating circle is empowerment. The more mates one person can bind into the circle, the more powerful they become. With us bound to you, Cress, you will be able to take from a pool of our magic, attributes, and resources. Imagine having my shadows and skill with a sword, Geo's impenetrable stone skin, and Ben's channeling ability. Plus your tether to Braza."

I imagined it, and judging by the way her steps faltered, so did Cress. "She would be unstoppable," I said with wonder.

"No wonder we're the plan," Ben said, running a hand through his overlong hair.

Cress shook her head slowly. "Is all that possible?"

Phaeron walked into the path of her pacing, cupping her face. "Yes, it would be possible," he said, stroking his thumbs over her cheeks. "And it would allow me to share my immortality with you, Geo, and Ben. It is the next step for our relationship anyway...merely so early as to scare you."

"I'm not scared," she said slowly. When he raised a brow, she blew out a breath. "Okay, maybe a little bit."

"Until this meeting, I was not sure how you and Braza would accomplish such a feat," Phaeron admitted. "But perhaps the four of us, plus the might of a full ancient powercore, can match a starving goddess. Before we decide anything, there is one huge downside I will remind you all of."

"It's permanent?" she guessed.

"Surprisingly, no. You could disband the circle once you have slain Myuna," he said. "It ties our fates together as one. If any of us die, so do the others." There was an odd note of relief in his tone.

"Victory or death," I said.

He grunted in agreement. "As it always has been. If we go this route, we will be the ones to distract Myuna while Auric weaves the Void to trap her and drag her back to Soiluire. I would not put you in such danger if there was any other way." There was a distinct *but* at the end of his statement.

There probably wasn't another way. None of us could fight Myuna alone without being consumed.

"Are you willing to do this?" she asked Phaeron.

Without hesitation, he said, "In time, I would have begged for the opportunity to share eternity with you. So what if it is a little early? I love you dearly enough to share you."

"I love you too," she murmured. She drew up to the tips of her toes to share a kiss with him before turning to me next. She took my hands, looking up at me. "What about you, Geo?" she asked.

"Now that I know it's possible, I want it more than anything. You can always use my magic to keep yourself safe," I said. After a couple moments, I thought to add something, and she waited with a knowing look until I did. "I already recognize you as my only love, my duty and devotion. This is merely a formality."

She started to blush again. "Even if you have to share me?" she asked in an undertone.

"At first, I found the others unworthy of your attention," I said honestly. "In time, they have become tolerable."

Ben, who waited a few steps away for his turn, scoffed. "Tolerable. C'mon, Geo. You can say we're friends at this point."

"We'll be family yet," Phaeron added.

"Even...more than tolerable at times, yes," I ground out. "I have bent for you, Cress, made myself flexible to change." For a gargoyle, it was akin to admitting the impossible, yet I was more than that now. I was a man because of her.

She reached up to kiss me next. "Thank you, Geo. I know it couldn't have been easy."

"Yes." An understatement. I released her, reluctant to see her turn away, but she needed to talk to Ben.

She met his eye, and he smirked. "Why'd I have to be last? Now I have to follow up what they said," he snarked.

Cress looped her arms around his shoulders, pressing closer to him and dropping her voice. "Because I think you're the only one as scared as I am over how big a step it is," she murmured.

As they put their heads together, Phaeron caught my eye and angled one horn toward the door. "Now is as good a time as any to give them a moment," he said to me. "Call to me when you have a decision, bright soul."

"Okay," she answered over her shoulder.

I led him out, heading for the room where the torch-bearer I'd captured yesterday was resting. "I have a large request," Phaeron said once we were alone in the elevator.

I felt a sudden, oily surge of trepidation. "What is it?" I asked.

"I want to give my daughter a new life, and one of the only ways to accomplish that safely is through making her a gargoyle." He clasped his hands together. "Will you assist me?"

Though I was happy he didn't mince words, it was perhaps the boldest request he could make that didn't involve Cress. We arrived on the correct floor as I answered, "That is highly illegal."

He didn't say anything else until we entered the torch-bearer's room. She lay on the bed, arms cuffed over her chest by my quartz, ankles tied to the bedposts. Though I was assured she'd be kept asleep until Phaeron could see to her soul, her eyes were open, unblinking, and glowing white from within.

Sitting by her bedside was none other than Lucas, who withdrew his hands from her arm when we came in. "I was just—"

The torchbearer lifted her head from its pillow at the sound of the door latching closed behind us. An overwide smile split her face. "Phaeron et Sudair." It wasn't a normal human's voice, but the screaming echoes of dozens of wailing souls all speaking in chorus.

That had to be Myuna speaking through her. But Phaeron didn't reply immediately, instead taking a ragged breath and stopping short with his eyes narrowing to tiny slits.

"You took something from me, Phaeron et Sudair. I felt you kill my beloved Endaeron," she continued. Lucas clapped his hands over his ears when she laughed, and that awful sound seemed to jolt Phaeron back to himself. He reached out with a lash of shadowy magic, lassoing it around the general shape of the torchbearer and pulling.

Myuna's laugh faded, and the woman's eyelids began to fall. "So I took..." Myuna rasped. "...something from...you."

She went silent. He took a rigid breath from between his teeth and noticed Lucas's attention, moving his hands slowly to untie what Myuna had done to this victim's soul. Coming to her bedside, he reached down and returned it to her with a hand on her chest.

Then, in a tone laden with agony, he said, "I know who she ascended in my brother's place." Pressing his palms into his eyelids, he made a sound of anger low in his throat. "I should have been more like you, Geo, dedicated to duty over pleasure. I should have rescued her before..."

"Who are you talking about?" I demanded.

"Carly," he gritted out. "She picked her out of spite. Who has had time to impress Myuna otherwise?"

Tentatively, I laid a hand on his shoulder. "You can't be so sure."

"Myuna has little left to harm me with. And she meant harm, even with that threat." He dropped his hands, looking over at me with eyes that gleamed internally like yellow gemstones. His slitted pupils dilated with his surprise when there was a gasp from the bed behind us.

The former torchbearer was trying to sit up, looking around in a panic and thrashing against her restraints. "Where am I? Who the fuck are all of you?" she demanded.

We both turned to Lucas, who looked embarrassed. "Sorry, ma'am. I didn't mean to wake you. Uh, again," he said.

"What did you do?" I asked.

"Her soul is..." Phaeron scrubbed his eyes. "Young man, I think you need to come with me. All of you, in fact."

Despite how he said her soul was miraculously stable, Phaeron still placed the woman in a stasis room and asked Lucas for an explanation. Ben's brother was less sickly today but still needed to sit down shortly after arriving in the library from the sudden jerk of the dimensional's shadows.

"I dunno. There were a lot of cracks in her soul. It felt like my magic could do something for her, and the next thing I know, she's awake and..." He pinched the bridge of his nose. "I'm dizzy."

I walked away and returned with an armful of Cress's

beloved junk food and soda. Lucas looked like he could've wept when he saw what I was offering him. "Finally. Flavor," he murmured.

As he tore into a pack of chips, Phaeron drew me a few paces away. "He healed her soul. I've never seen anything like it," he whispered.

"His new affinity is powerful," I stated.

"Potentially the miracle we need, with all the torch-bearers we have saved," he said. "However, a week is not long to master a unique power. Especially considering…" He gestured over at Lucas, who'd abruptly passed out with his hand in the chip bag.

He went to return him to the hospital, taking the junk food with them with a promise to hide it from the nurses. I waited with the patience of my stone form for him to return, knowing he would want to speak in more depth about what he'd revealed in the elevator.

I considered what I knew of Braza. A considerable amount, considering she was the powercore to my home library and tethered to Cress. She'd told me as much as she remembered of Braza's life after experiencing it close to firsthand. But did she deserve a gargoyle form and a second chance?

Did anyone? I was here, after all, first animated by an honored witch I was nothing like.

When the shadows writhed in front of me, I was already saying, "I do not know the secrets to my own making."

He answered as he took form. "The secrets are within you. I acknowledge that I am asking the world of you, but you are my only hope to make a gargoyle form for her possible. I need to study your heart and the magic that made you."

I stiffened. He'd taken my heart out before to say his goodbyes to Morgana, but this was something entirely different.

"I understand she means a lot to you," I said. By the shift in his expression, that was an understatement. "You realize she will not be the same person, yes? If you wish to pass her off as a gargoyle that has existed since creating one was legal...she will need the body of a man. There are no female gargoyles."

He blew out a breath, nostrils flaring. "I cannot make changes to the spells unless I see them first. Perhaps it is folly, but I need to see for myself if it is possible."

I considered whether it would be wise to aid him in veering so far from the right side of supernatural law. What shifted my opinion was knowing that Cress would approve. She did have a deep connection with the powercore and expressed her regrets that Braza's life had been cut short so traumatically.

Phaeron waited for me to come to some semblance of a decision. With a sigh, I said, "She could pass as a half-gargoyle if her body is formed with it in mind. One of my friends has a daughter, and she inherited some of his features and a temporary version of his stone form."

A smile started to tug at his lips, showing the edges of his fangs. "You would help me?"

"After we join Cress's mating circle, yes," I said.

He breathed out with relief and stepped forward, reaching out. "You will be as close as family on that day, if not sooner. Come, clasp arms with me, brother."

Now that was a change in tone from the hostile way we'd met. Cress had led me down this path, though, where I suspected he and Ben would both become my closest friends in time. Because of her, I had a future where I *had* friends.

We gripped one another's forearms with a new sense of kinship.

34
CRESS

After how intense Phaeron and Geo could be, it was nice to sit with Ben in the quiet conference room. We held hands, our anam cara marks brushing with the spark to remind us that we were connected. He'd left a mark on my skin too, but one first made of deep friendship that we'd turned into something more.

We chatted around the subject, calming down together, before he finally sighed and said, "I never thought the fate of anything would hinge on me getting married."

"Me neither."

He snickered, and I giggled, which snowballed into a laughing fit for us both.

"I don't even know where we're going to find a cupid for the ceremony!" he chortled.

"Imagine if we could make Dr. Aurina do it," I said, picturing her embittered face. That airbrushed bitch had tried to steal Phaeron's affections, and I was angry about it anew now that I'd experienced the intimacy of his mating bond.

On second thought, I didn't want her anywhere near him again.

"You know, Ben, we could do a lot with forever," I added more seriously.

He sobered up as well. "I know. But it could be about as long as one week if one of us gets eaten by Myuna. At the same time, it sounds like we will all get *homphed* by her if we don't make a mating circle."

"Homph?" I echoed.

He smirked. "Thought the situation warranted some onomatopoeia."

I laughed again and shook my head at the same time. My cheeks were starting to hurt in the good way from all the fun I'd been having within the last day. To think I could have this every day for the rest of a—hopefully—very long life with my men.

All I had to do was slay an interstellar dread goddess first. No pressure.

"I love you, Ben," I said. "Let's do this and see if it's so bad."

He squeezed my hand. "I love you too. And something tells me it's not going to be bad at all."

"If it doesn't work out, we can disband it after we kill Myuna," I continued, worrying my bottom lip between my teeth.

"Nah." At some point, he'd swapped the smirk he wore like armor for a more genuine expression. "It's going to be amazing. You kidding? First hending I'm going to do is steal your celestial magic and piece it together with mine. Maybe together we make one celestial witch."

I was a little surprised that was what he'd go for, but maybe he was right. He'd practiced and ended up with a better basic grasp of the spells than I did, and I was the one with the light in my soul. Come to think of it, my birth mother's ghost hadn't appeared much lately. I should've practiced harder with her.

"Good luck with that," I chuckled. "Should I get Phaeron and Geo to come back?"

"Nah. Let them figure some of their shit out first. C'mere, babe," he said, patting his lap. We cuddled together for a while, to my less than subtle sigh of relief. I'd definitely overdone the animaris yesterday. It'd healed most of the lingering soreness I'd otherwise have, but I was content to have my lady bits relax after sharing so much passion in a short time with him and Phaeron.

He took my device and worked on setting up a phone plan with four lines. I rested my head on his shoulder and watched him type in a card number straight from memory. "I always forget it's a 'Ph,'" he said, going back and fixing his spelling of Phaeron's name.

"You have this memorized?" I asked, raising a brow up at him.

"Yeah. You think he knew how to set any modern stuff up? I got him a bank account and credit card and made sure he paid all the bills for our place." He shrugged underneath me. "Now he's making our cell plan payment. We can change the name on the account later."

"Out of curiosity, do you know how much money he has?" I asked.

"Let's see." He navigated to a bank's website and logged in. Snickering, he added, "Nice."

Phaeron had $969.47 to his name. "Fuck, we're all broke," I said, covering my face. "You, Geo, and I have nothing."

"Maybe Wren will share that sweet, sweet stream revenue," he suggested. "People have been throwing money at her, and she doesn't know what to do with it. It's not like we need it right this moment."

"I'll get a job once we're out," I sighed. Much as I've started to consider Wren a friend, I doubted she'd be in a position to share much of her streaming money. Considering how we'd openly admitted we would have to start killing torchbearers and Myuna's new ascended, it would only be right to distribute the money to the families affected.

"No, no," Ben said. "We make Phaeron and Geo get jobs. What says eternal devotion better than working a nine-to-five for the two broke college students in your mating circle?"

I laughed, covering my face with my hand. "Oh, Ben, you're awful."

"I'm just saying!"

"I thought you weren't a student." I poked his belly where he was ticklish.

He tried to bat me away. "I am conveniently a student right now."

There was a knock on the door, swiftly preceding Auric poking his head into the room. "You kids done having your moment?" he rumbled. I sucked in a startled breath. "Good, because I brought you a cupid."

He held the door open for a woman to walk in. He'd said "cupid," but I wondered if he meant angel, as she had a set of feathery, off-white wings and the same kind of flawless face as Dr. Aurina. Her lips formed a perfect blood-red bow in a heart-shaped face, and her pink hair fell in ringlets down her back.

The only thing that made me think something might be off about her was the shapeless white robe she wore, along with a collar of blue lace. She held herself still like a frightened deer when he reached over to unhook the collar from her slender neck.

"You will be able to stay here once you perform the ritual for me. Don't worry, you're amongst good people," he told her in an undertone. It was the kindest I'd heard the old dimensional sound, other than in my secondhand memories of him with Phaeron.

With a nod, she made a shaky smile. "T-thank you," she whispered.

Ben and I exchanged a glance. "Well, go on," Auric said in his usual abrasive manner. "Call your mate."

"How are you so sure I've agreed to join a mating circle?" I asked. He gave me such an unamused look that I nearly regretted even that small challenge.

"I hate stupid 'what if' questions. Call your mate," he repeated.

I put my hand over the mating mark on my shoulder. It was already prickling with awareness, like Phaeron could sense how much I wanted him to act as a buffer between Auric and me. He was able to send me a feeling back, like a cheerful "Be right there!"

"I called him," I chirped. I made introductions with the cupid woman while we waited. She had a soft-spoken, musical voice and seemed to have little interest in small talk but told me her name was Crissina.

Phaeron and Geo arrived through the shadows after a few minutes, taking form behind where Ben and I sat. Phaeron ran his fingers over his mating mark, and I felt a streak of possessiveness in him flare as he squeezed my shoulder.

"Where did you come from?" Geo asked Crissina.

"I found her," Auric answered.

It was still a little disorienting to feel Phaeron's suspicions rise separate from my own. "She was in Cerris City?" he asked.

"No, but once she does me the favor of securing you lot into a mating circle, she's going to stay to be evacuated like she was here all along," Auric said. "Let's just say she is leaving a bad situation."

Phaeron frowned. "Ah. Well, thank you," he said to her before turning his attention to me. "You've both decided?"

"Let's get married," I said with a lot of cheer and a pinch of nerves for seasoning.

Crissina shifted her wings with the silvery sound of her feathers rubbing together. "Um. Do you have a private place to go afterward?" she murmured.

"We do," Phaeron said.

"Come along," Auric said, turning toward the door. "I went ahead and invited some witnesses to the establishment of your mating circle."

Something told me "some" witnesses meant it would be the whole hospital, and as I walked out hand in hand with Ben on one side, Phaeron standing on my other side, and Geo behind us, I saw I was right. The maze of upturned tables, chairs, and sofas had been hastily moved aside to make space for us in the foyer, and several friendly faces lined the second-floor landing, hooting and waving down at us.

Arrayed in a waiting semicircle was my coven and our closest friends, plus Mom, who looked like she'd just hastily pulled her mask off and changed into street clothes. She came forward and pulled me a step away from my men. "What's happening, baby? They announced that you're going through some kind of marriage ritual to save all of us?" she asked, one shade away from panicking.

"Relax. It is meant to be," said my birth mother's ghost

as she formed next to Mom and sent tingles up my arm as she attempted to hold my other hand. Mom had no idea she was there, as only Phaeron and I could see her. And Lucas too, I supposed. He was with my coven, leaning against Roe heavily.

"That's right, Mom," I said, squeezing her hand. "It's... well, it is a big deal, but it's not a sacrifice. I love these three men."

Eris dabbed at her eyes with the corner of her sleeve. "One glance at you all, and I knew it would lead here eventually," she said.

I smiled briefly at Eris before meeting Mom's concerned gaze. She'd be worried about me being coerced into this or moving *way* too fast, and I wasn't sure how to convince her otherwise. Compared to me, she barely knew my men.

Well, there was little to do except tell her everything. "I'll be right back," I said, tugging Mom into a private nook behind where Áine was weaving branches and blooming vines together, creating a makeshift trellis of flowers. She beamed up at her creation proudly.

In the meantime, Phaeron snagged Eris's attention, coaxing her away for a few minutes of privacy for us. "Mom, I know this is going to sound crazy," I prefaced. The truth came out in a rush about mating circles, my tether with Braza, and our plan to defeat Myuna. It was a lot, and I'd had a bit of time to accept it all, while I left her reeling and holding the side of her head.

"Your sister's not here to see it," she said in a sad hush.

My heart hurt at the reminder. "I wish she was. But we can't delay until we find her."

Mom's expression twisted with worry. "If...if any of them don't treat you well after this, they have me to answer to," she said, drawing me into a crushing hug. "I understand why you have to do this, but it is *very* sudden."

"It is," I agreed.

"But you're going to kick Myuna's pearly white butt, huh?" She held me harder, enough to restrict my airflow.

"Yeah," I gasped out. "In theory."

She loosened her hold enough for it to become a normal hug. We swayed together for a few moments before she whispered, "Can I tell you something crazy too?"

"Of course."

"You know that fae man who keeps following me?"

"The really annoying one?" I asked.

"Yup. We finally had a conversation past him trying to 'protect' me," she said, making air quotes with one hand. "He believes I am his fated mate."

I sucked in a breath so hard it was a wonder my lungs didn't explode.

"And if you can...get magically married to three men...to save us all from a soul-eating goddess," she continued with a few rapid blinks, "then I think I just might accept his invitation to go on a date."

"Mom!" I practically shrieked, bouncing on the balls of my feet. Most of my coven and all of my men came running to see me clutching her with an open-mouthed grin. "Guys! Everyone! My mom is going on a date!"

They whooped, which caused our watching audience to do the same. A big blush overtook Mom's fair cheeks.

"I knew it," Ben said under the general din of the crowd.

"Is he a worthy male?" Phaeron asked. "Perhaps I should inform him I will rearrange his insides if he acts like her last partner."

"Maybe that is too extreme for a first date," Geo suggested.

Phaeron nodded slowly. "The second date, then."

I gave Mom one last squeeze. "I think it's time," I said.

"Wait! Promise me you'll have a normal...ish wedding in a couple years," she said, clasping her hands under her chin.

"Absolutely," I said. "You're going to walk me down the aisle, and Carly is going to be my maid of honor. We have it planned, remember?"

A hint of tears sheened her eyes. "How could I forget?"

She took her place in front of my coven next to Jordan, unknowingly having my birth mother on her other side, who was also holding back from weeping. "Right here," Crissina whispered, pointing to a place for me to stand.

She sprinkled magic around me, the sparkles matching the off-white of her feathers. She repeated the process three times, having Ben stand about a yard to my right, facing me. Phaeron went to my left, and she gave him a wide berth as she dispersed magic around his feet. I glanced over my shoulder to see her place Geo behind me.

"Are you four ready?" she asked.

"Yes," I said amongst a masculine murmur of agreement.

"Then let us begin." She raised her hands and spread her wings. The particles of magic around my feet danced to a personal breeze, spiraling upward slowly. She went to stand before me. "State your full name."

"Cressida Rollins Darkmore," I answered.

"Are you here of your own free will?"

"Yes."

She spoke with the familiarity of an old ritual. "From this moment forward, these three men will be bound to you upon their agreement and admission of free will. You will become the strongest member of your circle, its core figure. As such, you must protect and cherish those who have joined you on this path. I sense three is the limit of what you can bind to you at this time."

"That's fine by me," I said. I couldn't even imagine needing the intimacy of such a close relationship with any other man.

"Very well." A hint of some emotion touched her perfect lips before she went to Ben next. She had him state his name and agree that he was here of his free will as well. But what came after that was different for him. "Do you agree without regret to bind yourself to Cressida Rollins Darkmore's circle?"

He looked over at me, a shy sort of smile on his face. Gone was his usual smirk. "I do," he said.

She dipped her head in a brief nod. "From the moment of your binding, you shall be known as Benjamin Darkmore."

Then she repeated the process with Geo, seeming puzzled when he stated his full name as Geo, like she expected more. He accepted his new name, Geo Darkmore, without complaint.

Finally, Phaeron, who quietly told her his title before she could announce it. "Phaeron Darkmore et Sudair," she repeated at the end of his part of the ceremony.

"Humans have been trying to give me a family name for centuries," he murmured. "I am glad to accept yours, bright soul. Also...brace yourself."

Crissina spread her wings again, and the particles of her magic began to form patterns and loops midair. More sparkles leaked from her palms to fill in the gaps of the complicated lattice of cupid magic which connected us. She drew in a deep breath and began to sing in another language, the words flowing out of her like an angel's call.

"Body, heart, and mind," Phaeron translated in a low voice. "I bid these souls entwined."

The audience murmured in awe as the magic shimmered to the cadence of her words. There was more to the song, but I barely heard it as the binding portion began, and I forgot who I was in the sudden crush of power, magic, strength, and knowledge that flowed into me.

For however long it took, I knew what it felt like to be my handbook, stuffed as full of foreign facts and magics as I could take.

I was Ben: young, limber, and irreverent. His power tasted of blood in the back of my throat and felt like possibility. Anything a body was capable of, his magic could do.

At the same time, Geo: solid, focused, and steady. I had the sensation of my skin being cool rock, impervious to all but the slow weathering of elements.

And also Phaeron, but he was a reprieve on the edge of where I could've been overwhelmed. I'd already seen the depths of his soul yesterday, yet his magic felt like raw power in my veins.

Just when I thought I couldn't take it anymore, Crissina's angel voice dipped, and all I'd experienced and all that I was moved on through the circle. Ben knew what it was like to draw librarian witch runes with a silver sword. Geo clutched the strength of my emotions tight to himself. Phaeron focused on the skills he could glean, how to cut and sew and apply makeup like a modern human.

And just like that, the song was over, and the sparkling magic suffused us. While I figured I'd be sneezing cupid dust for days, a small portion of the ambient magic went to my three men. I squeezed my chest, feeling a heaviness that hadn't been there earlier.

"Ladies and gentlemen, the Darkmore circle," Crissina announced, and the foyer exploded with applause.

I looked around, dizzy and off-center all of a sudden. Sound was coming in and out, like I was hearing from one of my men's ears as well as my own. The clinical lighting around us seemed too bright. Geo put his arms around me to steady me as I wobbled.

"Smile and wave," Phaeron instructed in one ear. "We're leaving as soon as you blow a kiss so we can consummate the circle and stabilize its effects."

"Thank you for doing this for us," Ben said, probably to Crissina.

I did as Phaeron said, hoping I didn't make anyone concerned if they noticed my sudden disorientation. I found Mom and Eris and blew them the kiss, then closed my eyes to be whisked away into darkness.

35
CRESS

Phaeron placed me back in the same room we'd just been sharing with Ben. "I'll go get the others. Just rest a moment." He felt concerned for me, which was about as defined in my mind as if I were the worried one.

"Okay," I said.

He vanished back into the shadows, and it was a relief to be alone for a few minutes. I rested my head back against the couch, waiting for my ears to stop ringing. The dizziness would probably return when it was just me and my men, but I sure hoped it wouldn't be so bad after we consummated the mating circle.

I was a married woman now. Just thinking about it gave me butterflies. How'd I get so lucky as to have this experience, even if it was in the service of taking down a larger threat? Now that we were bound together in the same circle, I would not need to pick and choose my affections. I'd keep all three of them close.

Supernaturals often formed groups with multiple people, especially with notable someones like Dr. Aurina and her five partners or Madigan and her three husbands.

It'd been on display during the Mabon feast as well, when family units had included children and multiple spouses to a single partner.

And I was that core figure now. Me, someone who, only a year ago, had no idea the supernatural world existed. Once we ended the threat Myuna posed, I would get to spend my days with three incredible men.

They arrived, and I felt the shape of their thoughts as I teetered to my feet. Ben reacted first, catching a hold of me around the waist before I could fall. He was wondering, *"Is Cress all right?"*

"I'm fine, I think," I said, though he hadn't spoken aloud.

Geo observed our surroundings and noted the bags of gifts and the fading smell of sex from the night prior. *"I knew it,"* he thought.

And Phaeron was considering how to change the mood in the room, noting how tense we were. *"My mate will not know peace again if we don't stabilize the circle. How can this be romantic if those two males keep standing there gawking at her?"*

"I was admiring her. She's shining," Geo said in a defensive tone.

I looked down at myself from their concentrated attention. "Oh *nooo*," I exclaimed, pulling at my shirt. "It looks like I drowned in a glitter factory!"

Geo and Phaeron exchanged a glance. They didn't understand, but Ben pulled a sympathetic face. "This is never coming out," I explained. "Is it in my hair? On my face?"

"No, and yes," Phaeron answered. "I believe we're meant to...smear it around. It's cupid magic." Though unsaid, I felt him imagining us skin to skin, the sparkles absorbing into us because of shared pleasure.

I flushed with heat at the thought. "Shall we see how much of me it covers?" I invited.

Judging by the arousal suddenly leaking from all three of them, that was a major *yes*. Phaeron had wanted to change the mood, and it seemed he had with one lusty thought.

Kind of like animaris, spreading through the bloodstream once it hit the heart. His gaze flashed with awareness, and he wondered if I wanted another bite. And while I did...no, it wouldn't be right for this moment to let my body take over.

He nodded. We'd just had a full conversation in the space of a few moments... How surreal. I toed off my shoes while Geo murmured, "What even is animaris?"

"Phaeron's sexy venom," Ben said.

The gargoyle's brow furrowed. "His what?"

Phaeron barely cracked a smile, but now I felt him using all of his impressive self-control not to die laughing.

I giggled for him, and that, plus the shimmy of my hips as I slipped out of my jeans, had their undivided attention. Ben started to help me. He'd gotten a thrill at hearing my *"sexy little laugh,"* and then all three of them were reaching to pull my clothes away faster. A few seams popped in the frenzy to get me naked.

"I think it's safe to say all of you sparkles," Geo remarked. I saw hints of creamy, glimmering flesh, but their mouths and hands were on me. Ben tilted my head up, our lips meeting, breath heating, tongues and teeth clashing.

Geo's broad palm splayed over my lower back, holding me steady. He tweaked one hard nipple between his fingers with practiced care, and that was him laving up the soft plane of my belly.

I knew it wasn't Phaeron, since the sharp edges of his fangs were working their way up my inner thigh. He braced my shaky legs as he snuck a taste of me, projecting a feeling of smug satisfaction.

Their emotions, thoughts, and desires came together for a moment. They gave, and I took, but I didn't just want them to please me. I tugged at the back of Geo's shirt and fumbled for Ben's pants, needing to feel their skin on mine, wanting to give back.

"Whatever you want, babe," Ben groaned once he pulled away from my lips.

Clothes hit the ground, and claws pressed into my skin in warning not to move. Phaeron dove in eagerly for a feast, suckling on my clit and sharing how I tasted with the other two men. That wasn't playing fair. Ben and Geo throbbed with need as they revealed their bodies—and a bit of cupid magic on their chests, I noted vaguely. I jolted with a moan when a smooth tail ran between my pussy lips, twisting to get the first few inches slick.

"Fuck," Ben said. There were grunts of agreement. "Your body is putting off 'fuck me' signals that I can feel now."

Phaeron maneuvered my legs around his horns after giving my clit one last lick. He lifted and shook his head briskly, focusing long enough to take us all in. "If you stay like this, Cress..."

He outlined a simple enough plan to account for all our limbs and their general bulk. Despite some crowding, it seemed like the soundest way for me to have all three of them at the same time. We agreed enthusiastically as a unit, and I coaxed Ben and Geo in closer with a shiver of anticipation.

Phaeron shaped the curve of my hips and ass, and I glanced over my shoulder when he reappeared there with an eddy of shadows. I thought, *"You're still wearing too many clothes."*

"Patience," he answered. The slickened tip of his tail brushed the edges of my hot core again before pressing into my ass with intention. My mouth opened on a gasp, and Geo took me by the jaw, turning my head toward where he stood beside me. His quicksilver eyes glimmered with love, and we kissed for a long moment.

Ben's hands were on me too, squeezing my breasts and gripping my waist above Phaeron's clawed fingers. His cock throbbed against my lower belly until I took it in hand, stroking my thumb through the slick at the tip to draw it over his velvety shaft. I soaked in the sound of his moan.

My lips left Geo's when he stepped away reluctantly and went to stand on the bed. I looked over, measuring the distance from my lips to his shaft. I was a little too short to do more than lick the underside, but that just might be perfect.

Phaeron's hands slipped under my ass, lifting me, and Ben caught my knees, guiding my legs around him. With the boost and some quick shuffling, I turned my head again and kissed Geo's blunt tip. Flicking my tongue out, I tasted his salty essence and started to take him into my mouth. The tail in my ass flexed, wiggling a little deeper to curl my toes, while Ben was rubbing against my clit and getting ready to slide inside of me.

If I thought being shared between two guys was intense, it didn't hold a finger to the focused attention of all three of my men. I sank into the feelings of their shared affections and desires, which only built as the tension between us pulled taut.

"Take her," Phaeron demanded. He trembled with desire, holding me to his now bare chest as he continued preparing my ass with slow pumps of his tail. The other two barely needed the invitation. Ben pushed the first few inches into me while I sucked more of Geo into my mouth. We moaned together when their pleasure was a separate sensation yet as bright as a starburst when mixed with mine.

The synchronized way they claimed me broke. Ben slammed home, his hard lower belly grinding my clit. Fingers threaded through my hair, Geo claimed my mouth with more care. I gripped what I couldn't fit my lips around and moved my head in counterpoint to the thrust of his hips. The echoes of sensation between us felt incredible but overwhelming, and yet I only wanted more.

They adjusted, finding a new balance that was insistent, gentle, and teasing all at the same time. Phaeron didn't use any shadowy tricks, not with three sets of hands making sure no sensitive skin went untouched. His claws left light scratches under my ass, a little pain to ground me in the here and now.

I was beginning to feel a tug of magic between Ben and me, stronger than the sparks of our anam cara marks. Little did I know that I was shedding cupid sparkles by the moment, a minor detail compared to how it felt to join with him. The snap of his hips drove me higher and made it clearer that a tether of sorts was forming between us.

I only noticed Phaeron was moving when his tail slid free of my ass, an absence quickly filled by the nudge of his hot length. He'd disrobed the rest of the way and hadn't jostled me a single time. His sudden entrance pushed me into Ben, my legs gripping him harder. When I came, it was like a detonation—no, an implosion. My eyes rolled back in my head, and I came close to losing consciousness.

Ben came with me, and *snap*. Something fell into place between us in the radiance of bliss. I could feel him in a magical sense, a presence woven with shades of maroon and gold and tied to me by fine strands.

With a jerk, I returned to myself and noticed a warm liquid rush between my thighs when Ben withdrew, panting hard. My legs had gone limp, but Phaeron held me up and pressed to him by the hips. *"Take her next, Geo,"* he thought.

Geo pulled free of my mouth, grunting an agreement. His eagerness pulsed within me like a second heartbeat. He wanted to step down from the bed and hold me, which he did, guiding my arms around his shoulders. He supported me under the thighs, helping Phaeron push me between them with effortless strength. *"A muscle sandwich. My favorite."* It was a quick thought, but it didn't go unnoticed.

Phaeron chuckled close to my ear. "Is it?" he growled. He rolled his hips, pushing deeper into my sensitive ass. I'd have been weak-kneed if my legs weren't already jelly.

"Mmm, yeah," I moaned.

Geo settled himself in the circle of my legs, brushing the thick head of his cock between my slick lower lips. He took himself in hand and claimed me next. I could tell he wanted to take his time, yet it was difficult for him not to spill immediately from the tight, hot squeeze of my pussy.

Cupid magic smeared between us, bright against his dark skin. I watched it disappear as that feeling of connection built between us with each slow, powerful thrust. With my back pressed to a firm chest, my core rocked from his pace. My pleasure mounted to match his quickly, as

Phaeron stroked into me the same way, following him like an echo.

Ben tugged my hair to grab my attention. With a little reach, we could kiss, and his lips were a gentle and soft counterpoint to my body's utter claiming. Unhurried compared to Geo's tightening hold and the couple body-shaking pounds of his hips before he came and I followed a moment later.

With a second *snap*, Geo and I connected, and his presence, glittering with multicolored shards like the quartz in his gargoyle form, slid into place next to Ben's. My eyelids sagged, and darkness clustered at the corner of my vision before I drifted back to full consciousness with the sensation of my mating mark sparking with warm sensation.

Phaeron suckled on the swirls of ink he'd left on my shoulder. *"Come back to me, sweet mate,"* he thought.

"I'm here," I croaked.

Ben had stopped kissing me to watch the force of that second orgasm. He helped hold me up when Geo had to stagger away to take a moment to recover.

The cock buried in my ass throbbed insistently. Phaeron's claws dimpled the skin around my waist, and he panted while he licked his mark. "One more," he said.

"One more, babe," Ben said.

I nodded, echoing them both. I could do one more, even though I'd never come so intensely twice in a row. Phaeron jerked at the end of his next thrust, growling like the roll of thunder.

Ben's clever fingers pressed between my thighs, thumb circling my clit. He curled his fingertips within my pussy, searching inside me by touch. I leaned into him to take the force of Phaeron's next push. Judging by the way he shook with restraint, he had one more left before he came.

Another pair of hands rejoined us, landing on my breasts to stroke and tease. Geo rubbed my painfully puckered nipples. I moaned hard—he nipped my free shoulder just as Ben found the ultrasensitive patch within me that lit up every inch of my sensitive skin.

My head fell back with Phaeron's last thrust before he came and I followed with a little extra coaxing. He was already there, like our mating bond intertwined with the tether of fine strands, ensuring his shadow-black presence was bound to me in both ways. The sensation of his pleased rumble followed me into the bliss that followed.

The cupid magic entwined us all together and faded out once Phaeron and I completed the circle. My men were all permanently connected to me now, and while I rode the high of my last orgasm, I felt like I *could* take on an eldritch goddess and win. I was an unstoppable force of blades, shadows, and obsidian.

But I was also loved by three men, who I equally adored. That sensation of affection and satisfaction hummed through our mating circle, shared by all four of us and made stronger for it. I could've stayed in the embrace of this feeling for days, if not longer.

I drifted down from this feeling far more slowly. When I came to, I became aware that we'd all moved to the bed at some point. All three of my men were touching me, waiting for me to stir. I blinked a few times, relaxing into the sensation of being surrounded by them, and not only in the physical sense.

Where I could reach into the depths of my librarian and celestial witch magic, there were now three more strands. Their magic orbited mine, just a little extra reach away. I could borrow shadows as easily as the piece of celestial witchery Ben held in his aura. They were contained and separate from me now that the circle was stable, and that was already better than the crush of their emotions, senses, and thoughts all at the same time.

"Welcome back," Geo said. He was propped on his side, still hard but patient about it, like he always was. I felt his arousal first, but it pulsed all around the mating circle. It seemed heightened emotions were still shared between us.

I wasn't going to leave this bed for a long while. Not that I minded.

36
CRESS

Ben shared that it was common for those newly tied in a mating circle to disappear for several weeks before rejoining polite society. I understood exactly why. I'd had all three of my men in every possible way, often all of them at the same time, and had lost track of when and where I was. Without sleep, hours passed in a timeless blur.

When we started wanting non-carnal experiences, we did so as a unit, with a collective "Shouldn't we be doing something else?"

As we prepared to get out of bed, Phaeron figured out how to borrow from me. I felt a tug on my magic from the strands that connected us and sensed a request coming from him. *"Can we trade eyesights and knowledge of technology?"*

I agreed and felt a shift between us, soon covering my eyes from the assault of the lamp lit right next to the bed. While lying next to me, he wove a tendril of shadow between my fingers, forming a blindfold of sorts. "You see why I expected to go blind on your world," he said.

I heard the rapid clicking of his thumbs on his new

phone's screen as he set it up, then he turned the haptics off.

"Yeah. We're getting you sunglasses," I declared.

"Should've done that a while ago," Ben commented from the other side of the bed.

"We've been a bit preoccupied," Phaeron said. "Hmm. This was a lot easier than I expected." He gave me back what he'd borrowed, and I glanced over to see his pupils narrowing to slits as he looked at the phone screen he'd dimmed until it was nearly black.

"You should ask Geo for tips," I suggested. The gargoyle grunted from somewhere on the floor. He was retrieving clothes, the most determined of us to leave this room today.

Phaeron nodded, staring at the screen with utmost concentration. "Geo, why is the..." He seemed to wrack his brain. "...browser named after a hunting expedition?"

"It takes you on an adventure through the Internet," he answered.

"Ah, yes. An apt name."

Ben and I started to crack up in sync. The next thing I knew, tendrils of shadow coiled under my back and rolled me off the bed. I sprawled on the carpet with a squeak of surprise. Judging by the nearby thud and curse from Geo, Ben had been pushed off too, on top of the gargoyle.

"Let's get moving," Phaeron said, turning into shadows and reappearing at the foot of the bed, where he started to dress himself.

I reached out and plucked away Phaeron's sense of balance. There was a hint of resistance, but it seemed I didn't need to ask to take an attribute from him. One moment, he was shrugging on his shirt and looking for his pants, and the next, he was tripping over his tail and stumbling.

I gaped for a split second, then rose with his usual grace to my feet. "You're right. We should be practicing," I said.

He hissed a laugh. "Fair play, bright soul, but I need that back."

He already had his balance returned by the time he finished speaking. I didn't know how to hold on to it for long, as it was naturally his soundless predator's prowl instead of something I had practiced.

We dressed successfully without ripping the clothes right back off and relocated to the other room we'd claimed. We sat in a circle facing one another, our various weapons in the middle: my sun staff, Geo's crystal shield and quartz hammer, Ben's daggers, and Phaeron's swords.

"It would be ideal if we got to a place of trust where any of us could pick up these weapons and wield them like the original owner," Phaeron said.

"How do we do that without crippling someone else?" I asked. My mind drifted to how easily he'd blinded me with a taste of his usual photosensitivity. I was worried this would be more difficult than just taking attributes from one another. We still needed them to function.

"Practice," he replied. "And a clever mind, perhaps. Much as I would like to see you face Myuna carrying one of my swords and Geo's shield, there are factors at play other than skill."

I had a feeling I knew where this was going. "I can't lift his shield. It's too heavy," I admitted.

"Therefore, you will need to borrow some strength, as well as two separate skills from either of us," Phaeron said. "Three separate attributes to channel continuously from us to you. Lose your attention on just one of them, and everything gets fumbled. In the meantime, we will fight by your side and share what you don't need between the three of us. We'll all have to learn a fine balancing act."

I nibbled into my bottom lip before steeling my resolve. We hadn't joined a mating circle just for the hell of it. First, it was time for baby steps. We started borrowing from each other and testing what we could do while seated and relatively at ease. What we shared turned out to be more aligned to quirks of personality and small skills and attributes.

I worked up a headache concentrating, trying to hold on to a portion of Geo's stoicism. I'd quickly learned that something so integral to who someone else was was almost impossible to keep in full. But Geo had patience in spades, so I could borrow some without immediately losing a hold of it. Designating how much, exactly, was where I needed a lot more practice.

While I didn't have much trouble reaching out and plucking something from them, my men struggled more. They had to reach through my magic to one other, a process that was tedious for all of us. They were bound to me, though, so it made sense that I controlled the flow of the magic.

I was concentrating so hard that I missed a flash of emotion between Phaeron and Ben. The dimensional pinched the other man with little flickers of shadows and they glared at one another.

The next time it happened, Ben's arousal sparked through our bond, closely followed by Phaeron trying to resist feeling the same way. "I can't help it," Ben said, swiping at the shadows before he could get pinched again.

"Think about something else, then."

"Something unsexy," I suggested, picking up on the problem. "Like Myuna."

Phaeron's burst of hatred was strong enough that we all felt it. There was an echo amongst us, a shared distaste for the goddess who'd tortured him and threatened the lives of those we loved. I thought of Carly's uncertain future, worried for her continued absence, and Phaeron and Geo tensed.

This seemed to dampen Ben for a while, but it wasn't long until I felt his attention running up and down my form in appreciation. I was no longer holding on to a portion of Geo's steadiness, and while it was a relief to feel like myself again, I didn't need the sudden tingles of awareness when I was trying to focus.

Yet all three men had turned their attention toward me within a breath. *Here we go again,* I thought, sure we were going tumbling back into bed for who knew how long.

The next moment, Phaeron and Ben disappeared in a swirl of shadows. Some time passed without them, during which I kissed Geo and then pushed at his chest when he tried to draw me in closer. I murmured, "We really shouldn't."

He rumbled an "indeed" with great reluctance.

The dimensional returned sans Ben. "He'll rejoin us shortly, once he's cooled down," he said. I felt him tug on my magic in request, as he was practicing by borrowing bits of my knowledge to learn more about modern culture from what I knew. I sent him memes, and his nose wrinkled at that bunch of nonsense out of context.

"Where'd you put him?" I asked.

Phaeron shrugged. "A cleaning closet."

I had a hearty laugh before explaining what a horny jail

was to him and Geo. "It's not usually a literal place, but I guess we've got to make an exception," I said.

It was a lot less funny when I got distracted by the flex of Geo's muscles that evening while we were still practicing and ended up the second member of the circle to go to horny jail. At least I knew where Phaeron had found a janitor's closet—on floor negative one behind a door that'd been locked earlier.

I spent maybe ten minutes breathing in the cleaning product fumes before deciding I was definitely, most assuredly not horny anymore. The guys had called it quits without me and greeted me with a scavenged dinner and their caressing hands and...yup, we were in bed again.

Madigan arrived the next morning with her own mating circle in tow, and our real training began. "We gave you guys a couple days to get used to it. Sorry it couldn't be longer," she'd said.

Had it really been two days? I figured it had, considering how tired I felt when not in bed with my men. We definitely had not had enough time to get used to this, but by necessity, we had to move on.

Their arrival started the clock on four last days of practice before we would help escort a crowd of survivors to the ocean gate. The knowledge was like a bucket of ice water over my head. As much as I wanted my men, we were using up precious time, and a lot of lives would be on the line soon.

The first thing they did was separate us into different containment rooms for a one-on-one talk. I was with Madigan, face flaming when the first question out of my mouth was, "Will it always be like this?" She'd barked a laugh and hugged me, knowing exactly what I meant.

"Yes and no. It takes a while to get used to sharing strong emotions. But men outside of your circle will be entirely unappealing. And vice versa for your men. The stability of your shared relationships becomes quite comforting."

"That's a relief," I said.

She patted my shoulder reassuringly. "When I was just coming into my power and circle, another woman took me aside to teach me everything I could do as the core of a mating circle. If you think I got to grow my reputation as Mad Ash without a significant amount of my men's help, you'd be wrong," she said.

"Every circle is different, of course. The secret to my success is that the members of my circle specialize in similar magic. We all manipulate earth, stone, and crystal with strength-based runes," she explained. "Over time, we've figured out how my men can send me three different pieces of their magic and muscles so I seem unusually gifted in guardian witch spells.

"What I see in your circle is that you have one man specializing in each of the three measures of power level. If you can take something from each of them, it would boost your own power level significantly, to the point where you could hold off someone as strong as Myuna for a short time. It would take a lot out of all of you to maintain it for a prolonged battle, but we'll work up your endurance as much as we can."

We ended up chatting for hours, with my handbook floating nearby, recording every piece of knowledge Madigan shared. Milo curled up in her lap, purring, while my other two familiars spied on happenings around the library.

Bella had ended up in the room with Phaeron and Orthus, projecting happiness from all the belly rubs she was getting from the dimensional. I'd almost forgotten he liked cats and Bella in particular. There wasn't an equivalent pet from Soiluire, as far as I could tell.

Meanwhile, Jin had avoided the ongoing conversations and was watching the powercore ripple with shadows and the points of purple-black claws. She was fairly sure Braza was practicing with her shadowborn magic within the confines of her living space.

Armed with the knowledge of those who'd gone through this before, we rejoined one another in a large room on floor negative five, fully equipped with weapons and armor. Phaeron had acquired a new leather chest piece from his nightly wanderings, though it remained free of the runic etchings of his original.

A set of his gifts had been from the same store, and I wore them to get used to the weight and movement of the celestial witch robe partnered with a pair of dark pants built for my heavy librarian witch belt. It was an expensive ensemble due to the magic woven into the cloth, a concept that immediately fascinated the side of me that'd wanted to go into fashion design before meeting my men had set me on another path.

The stars and tiny crescent moons stitched into the robe formed celestial runic shapes, making it resistant to heat and light. When I donned the matching gloves and lifted the robe's hood over my face, I'd never get a sunburn again, but more importantly, they'd dampen a fraction of Myuna's light magic when we finally met to fight.

My men and I squared off against Madigan and her

circle. "Hit me as hard as you can," she invited, fully encased in her red crystal armor and resting the head of her warhammer on the ground. "I guarantee you I won't break."

"None of us will," Orthus agreed.

Aaron, the less serious of the guardian witch twins, pointed to the shadowy claws lengthening over Phaeron's hands. "We do bleed, though."

"I shall be gentle," he replied. He'd drawn one of his swords and taken up a guard stance, opting not to use all of his combat skills for this fight. There was some reluctance in him that I immediately understood. He didn't want to harm our allies, even for practice.

I tried not to let his emotions into my headspace too much. First, we had to share magic. I looked toward Ben, who traded a part of his blood witchery for a portion of my celestial witchery. He carried his father's staff, Evening Guidance, intending to practice with it first.

I held out my finger for Phaeron to prick with one of his talons and winced before drawing the blood rune for strength on my arm.

"Not like that," Ben said, taking gentle hold of my hand to draw it a second time. With a squeeze on the pad of my finger, he drew out enough blood to etch the rune for energy right below it. There was a surge through my muscles, and I itched to use them, practically vibrating in place.

Geo offered me his shield. It was a massive slab of crystal, but I buckled it to my arm and lifted, amazed when it came off the ground smoothly with the help of the blood magic runes. He gave me a measure of his endurance, necessary for taking hits in the thick of battle and continuing on without tiring.

Lastly, Phaeron drew his other sword, offering it to me hilt first. "A weapon of two worlds, yours to wield," he murmured.

A sense of wonder that didn't belong to the circle suffused me. Braza slid into my mind, her electric presence further augmenting me in a way that felt as familiar as sliding my feet into a pair of shoes. Together, we admired the shining length of metal, polished to gleaming, with words in the dimensional language etched up the middle.

"He reforged his Soiluirian blades with Earth silver upon learning how deadly it is to unnaturals," she told me privately. *"This blade is Flame. It's the shorter of his two swords, made for his left hand."*

"Thank you. Your swords are named?" I asked.

He nodded, tapping the gemstone set into the end of the pommel. It was a gleaming yellow with orange under-tones, shades I'd seen in his eyes countless times. The other had a red and black stone. "Shadow and Flame, to reflect myself," he explained. "As long as you have my skill to wield it, I believe Flame suits you better."

"And mine as well," Braza said through me, creating a two-toned echo to my voice.

"Between us, she will be unstoppable," he said. He lent me some of his considerable knowledge of swordplay, honed over endless years at war.

Madigan picked up her warhammer, slinging it up at the ready. "All right, let's see what you all can do," she said. With a grin, she swung the massive weapon at me.

For all the skills of others swirling in my head, I still panicked and held up the shield, taking the full force of the blow. The crystal rang and vibrated my arm, and there was dissonance in my head. Geo thought I'd done a great job, but Ben and Phaeron would've sidestepped, and Braza was annoyed, wondering why I'd taken such a slow attack head-on.

I lost control of the connections with my men just like that, and the shield tipped forward, threatening to take me toppling over with it. Several masculine shouts sounded as Phaeron caught me and Orthus did something with his magic to make the shield lighter.

"Let's try that again," Madigan suggested.

And thus began the first session of us practicing combining our skills under pressure.

PHAERON

We had little downtime as a unit from the moment Madigan and her mates started helping us train. My shadowborn side liked that—we were moving closer to our goal, even if we weren't leaving the library yet.

Cress's coven and friends moved back into their rooms by the second day of our training, many of them helping by testing Cress's concentration with their varied magics. She was figuring out how to channel for longer and flinching less when spells or weapons came her way.

I tried not to be too territorial when she spent much of the evening before bedtime in a communal area with her friends rather than her mates. She needed community and, sensing my mood, dragged me in to spend time with them too. As we chatted, she rested in the circle of my arms, where she belonged.

According to them, things were as silent as the grave up on the streets. But that meant Myuna was also practicing her magic, testing the bounds of her army's control through her new ascended.

"When will you tell her your suspicions?" Braza asked. Now that we'd exited the bedroom, she was privy to all my thoughts and worries again.

"I don't know." I still hoped I was wrong, but it made too much sense. Selecting Carly for ascension was akin to the twist of a knife. She was also the only target we'd hesitate to kill, making her the best strategic choice, as Myuna's control would falter with the death of her chosen assistant. *"There's one more factor I'd like to consider. Why present Cress with a problem and no solution?"*

Lucas was here. He was growing stronger by the day, and the unusual ripples that suffused his soul were flattening, smoothing into a new whole to represent who he was after his ordeal. I had to see what his new magic could do, and that would only be possible if I witnessed how he'd healed one of Myuna's victims. If his magic reliably mended the cracks and traumas that resulted from soul ties, perhaps he could help me remove a seed of corruption planted in Myuna's chosen ascendant, regardless of whether it was Carly or someone else entirely.

"Promise me you're not going to go after Carly on your own," Braza said, nervous.

"Of course not."

Grant was the only coven member not here. I intended to shake him for information on a certain blue-haired teenager once he returned from his spying.

Cress leaned her head back to look at me, and I took the opportunity to kiss her sideways. "Penny for your thoughts?" she asked.

Between our mating bond and our connection in the circle, she'd feel my restlessness without a doubt. Maybe even that I was having a conversation with Braza and plotting over some of the finer details before the coming confrontation. "Aren't pennies worthless?" I asked.

"Well, your thoughts aren't," she said.

I leaned in, whispering in her ear, "What if I was mentally undressing you?"

Braza's presence in my mind faded in an instant, and both Ben and Geo faltered mid-sentence to turn their heads our way. Blushing, Cress reached up and tapped me on the nose. "You know what this means," she whispered back. "Horny jail."

I tugged on her sleeve, exposing the edge of my mating mark. Giving it a lick, I felt her tense and bite her lip to cage in a gasp.

"Oh no, horny jail," I teased, stealing her away to the closet with me on a wisp of shadow.

It was much later that night when Geo and I sat at the base of the powercore and he allowed me to pull his crystalline heart free from his chest. I began the painstaking task of writing down the runes that encircled his heart, borrowing most of Cress's drawing ability to diagram it.

I hadn't had to ask for permission, since she was sleeping off our visit to the closet. It seemed the magic would continue working even if one member of the circle was unconscious. That could be helpful in a pinch.

I used her skill to write down and study the numerous chains of spell runes that led from the heart back into Geo's body next, noting them down on a separate page somewhere in the middle of Cress's sketchbook. Braza's electric energy watched over my shoulder. "Do these match what you can remember?" I asked her.

"They are animation spells. None concern the identity of the soul inside of the heart," she replied.

We both had the same translation spell, which made these human-made runes something I could read and understand. Unfortunately, she was right. At some point, I'd started copying down the same threads of runes—his heart was like a central nervous system while he was in gargoyle form, connecting to each limb, muscle, and tendon.

I manipulated these threads with care, relying on my shadows to keep from tugging one free of its connection by accident. They were intricately wrapped and would only unravel from each other so much before there was tension. The edge of a shadow brushed the strand of runes they were all wound around, and a fission of pain ran from it straight to my fingers and down my arm. I jerked away with a hiss. That'd felt like trying to grab a bolt of lightning.

"Let me try, Father," Braza said. Her powercore presence pressed into the gaps where I'd threaded my shadows.

In the meantime, I inspected my new wound that ran from fingertip to shoulder, branching in the patterns of an electric shock. I noted it at the bottom of a page. Geo wasn't entirely helpless even while his heart was exposed in gargoyle form. That magic had to be guarding the most important runes keeping him animated.

I flipped the notebook back to the first page while Braza hummed and shifted around the magic, murmuring to herself. The portrait Cress had drawn from my memories gazed back at me. Our son. She saw much of me in the boy, but in this quiet moment, I noted how he was human in his smile and the curve of his ears.

The Void had seen a future where he lived. I was struck breathless by hope, no matter how unlikely it seemed that a witch could carry a dimensional child to term. If we lived and Myuna died, he could exist. Perhaps Cress would agree to name him Teziel, meaning victorious. I had met many good males with that name in my time.

Braza tapped on my thoughts, and I glanced up. *"May I see?"* she asked politely.

"We have no other secrets. This is certainly not one," I replied.

She took in the drawing and squealed in delight. *"He looks just like you both."*

"He was foretold by the same vision that showed me you and Ravai," I told her, faltering for a moment. "He is still an idea, a kind daydream before I remember I live in this unforgiving world now. I do not seek to replace you, Brazita."

Her tone implied a smile. *"I understand. You might have a future with both of us. I was able to inspect this."*

She pushed an image of the central link of runes connected to Geo's heart. I flipped back to my sketches and added these runes, heart thudding hard in my chest as she sent two more memories from different angles. It was a woven braid of several spells concerning control, identity, intelligence, duty, and the protective spell meant to electrocute anyone who tried to tamper with them.

I smiled to myself. Given time, I would unravel each of these runes into their component spells. My clawed finger followed the path of the identity spell, already spotting where it was written for the soul in the crystal heart to forget its past life and start again with a baseline of the duty that it was entwined with. There was a significant chance I could make this work.

Once I placed his heart back in his chest, Geo shuddered and shifted back into his human form with a grind of clashing rocks. He coughed up a plume of dust, then ground out, "Well?"

I clapped him on the shoulder. "I'll have my daughter back because of you. Words cannot express my gratitude... but perhaps you would welcome an idea that will elevate you in the eyes of our mate."

He straightened slowly, having spent this whole time hunched over with his heart exposed. "I'm listening," he stated.

37

BEN

"THAT ONE CASTS STARSEAR, A LEVEL-FIVE SPELL," Cress's handbook informed me when I held out one of the pieces of paper attached to Evening Guidance. My father had stored a trove of spells on the staff, and I was still trying to figure out which were useful. Most were priceless, spells I'd find nearly impossible to replace once they were used up.

At my core, I was still a blood witch, but I could still cobble up enough celestial witchery with Cress's help to channel these spells. Very few witches, even those in varied mating circles like mine, had the ability to switch between affinities. I was *rare*. But that didn't mean I was powerful, and I crammed every second I wasn't training with Cress or sleeping. It was the evening of our third day of serious training, with one more to go before we joined the push to save everyone we could.

"Starsear is commonly a spell for celestial witches with a star alignment. Like you, bub! It makes one gigantic star-shaped, uh, thing, that explodes," the handbook continued cheerfully in its squeaky toy voice. Now that it had identified the spell, it flew a curlicue over my head.

It then shouted a dramatic "KA*BEWM*!" and flopped out of the air with the clap of its pages snapping closed.

I snickered. I couldn't help it. Ever since the mating circle ritual, I found it as amusing as Cress did.

She peered into the room I'd claimed for the evening, and my cock twitched just at the sight of her. *Down, boy.* Sharing lust with two other dudes was ridiculous. Especially when I was usually the first to get distracted and thus sent to the closet.

"Is everything okay?" Cress asked.

"Just demonstrating how devastating Starsear is," the handbook whispered from the floor.

She came in to pick it up and gave it a little toss so it would take flight again. "Everything's fine," I added.

"Well, good. I thought you might want to know that Phaeron is having Lucas experiment with his magic."

I clenched my fists. Lucas had barely begun to recover from his coma. There had to be a damn good reason he was being pushed to use his nebulous new magic, no matter how powerful Phaeron thought it might be. "Where?" I demanded.

We walked to the row of containment rooms for the former torchbearers. One was unlocked, and inside were the two men, standing over an unconscious body resting on a narrow cot. Phaeron watched Lucas nearly as closely as my brother stared at the woman.

Lucas had his hands held palms out toward her until the door latched behind us loudly and he startled. He turned our way, then a wide smile split his pale face. "Hey, big bro! Guess what," he said.

An ugly gasp sounded from the woman he'd been working magic on. She leveraged herself to her elbows, looking around with rapid breaths causing her chest to heave. Phaeron nudged Lucas our way and bent to speak to her in soothing tones.

Lucas came over and dropped his voice to a whisper. "We've figured out how I can gather more energy for my affinity. It turns out that helping others with damage to their souls gives me the power to help more people." He beamed with pure relief. The idea of inflicting hurt to acquire soul energy had really triggered him.

I gave him a quick once-over. "And you're feeling all right?" I asked.

He considered himself, finger to chin in thought. His nod was slow in coming. "I think so. You know how it was hard to activate blood runes when we first took our affinity? It's like that. The more I practice, the faster and easier it is. And Phaeron's been a great teacher." With a glance over his shoulder, he shrugged. "Though he tends to disappear a lot."

The dimensional in question had left behind shadowy smoke in place of him and the woman Lucas had healed. I wouldn't be surprised if he'd taken her to one of our safe houses to wait for the trip to the ocean gate.

"Does he jump scare you when he comes back, or does he save that for Cress?" I asked.

"Oh, I think he reserves that for me," she said. "I'll just be minding my own business, and everyone else goes quiet. And I ask myself 'He's behind me, isn't he?'"

The shadows twitched behind her, taking shape into Phaeron. There was a mischievous gleam in his eyes. "He's not always standing behind you. That would be ridiculous," I said, biting the inside of my cheek to keep from giving him away.

"Yeah, well..." She drifted off and glanced over her shoulder, yelping when he took that moment to grab her.

Lucas made a *blech* face when their play wrestling turned into kissing, and I elbowed him. "Hey, she has a sister," I said in an undertone.

There was one benefit to the bleaching he'd gone through. He clearly blushed up to his ears when I embarrassed him. "Ben," he complained. "I'm some kind of soul witch now. I don't have time to think about girls."

"Pretty sure you'll be back to that in no time," I teased.

Phaeron cleared his throat as he pulled away from Cress. "I did have a goal for us to reach this evening," he said, gesturing for us to follow him. "We have containment rooms to clear, and then I have some news to share. Grant has returned with our last glimpse of information on Myuna's machinations."

"Oh, where is the spy extraordinaire?" I asked, following my brother and Cress as we all headed for the next containment room.

"At this hour, resting," he answered. Somehow, he also sent me a thought in my head through the magic of the mating circle. *"I'd prefer to tell our circle something privately. I've already bribed Grant to keep it to himself until tomorrow morning."*

"All right," I murmured. I'd have to ask him how he did that. He seemed to be figuring out what this magic could do a lot faster than Geo or me.

Cress's eyes narrowed, like she knew he'd done something, but she didn't comment.

"Anyway, these last few torchbearers are more recent victims. Myuna's power runs deeper in them...nearly embedded in their souls. I was able to remove her control, but her corruption remains," he said to Lucas. "I would be quite keen to see if you can help them."

Lucas squared his shoulders with confidence. "Leave it to me," he said.

I guessed I was turning overprotective, as I earned an annoyed look over his shoulder when I said, "Just don't overexert yourself, okay? I don't want you leaving this pocket dimension wheeled out on a hospital bed."

"I'll be fine. Trust," he said.

I stood aside with Cress, who watched them with shadows of black and purple flickering over her eyes. I'd seen it enough to know that Braza was lending her soul sight so she could watch what was going on.

"Their souls are still bleached." She leaned over to whisper to me, gesturing to the two unconscious people on either ends of the containment room. "I see the corruption as swirls of brighter white. Lucas is trying to get a hold of it to pull it out."

Sweat visibly beaded Lucas's forehead. He concentrated, flexing his fingers like he could grab and remove Myuna's influence as easily as pulling a weed. As the minutes rolled on, it was clear it wasn't that simple.

I ended up behind Cress, cuddling her to my front while she watched and updated me occasionally on how he was doing. His success was obvious from her gasp before she said, "He's holding the corruption separate from that person's soul. It looks like he's absorbing it."

"Is that safe for him?" I asked, looking between her and Phaeron.

The dimensional watched intently before nodding toward me. "In this case, it seems power is power," he said.

"A *lot* of power," Lucas murmured. "I don't even know what to do with it."

"How fortuitous, for I have a plan that hinges on that feeling," Phaeron said.

Blinking, Lucas moved on to the next person to remove their corruption too. "I mean, sure. Whatever you want. You saved my life, after all."

There was a heaviness to his reaction and response. "We shall face many soon that we will not be able to save. But there is one person who we must, who is corrupted more dangerously than anyone in these containment rooms. After seeing how your magic works, I believe you are up to this task."

"Who?" Cress asked. The spike of dread from her hit me like a sucker punch.

"I suggest you gather up Geo and head to a private room. I will tell you the news and my plan as soon as we finish up here," Phaeron promised. "You will want to be sitting down for this, bright soul."

CRESS

Phaeron didn't hide the truth from me—he'd suspected for days that Myuna had ascended Carly. It hurt, but he'd had a reason to keep it private as he sought a solution for the situation first.

I could hardly breathe. Grant had spotted her commanding torchbearers separately from the goddess while wielding a staff formed of white light. Carly was bleached more severely than Lucas, according to the changeling, overriding even the magical blue dye in her hair to render her fully white, like Myuna had once done to Endaeron.

"She is still alive, so there is hope we can pry the seed of corruption out of her before Myuna transforms her into a second Hungering Darkness," Phaeron was saying.

At some point, I'd tuned out, curling into a ball with my chin on my knees. Ugly tears and sobs ripped from me despite being pressed between Ben and Geo, who tried to comfort me with tender touches. "She picked my sister on purpose," I croaked.

"Indeed. She wanted to hurt us," Phaeron said more quietly. He stood apart, watching my breakdown, shame radiating from him. "Apologies will not suffice, I know. I failed her when she was brought before Myuna the first time and did not attempt to rescue her before... I did not know she was capable of turning your sister against us quite like this."

I sniffled, scrubbing at my face. "How could you have known?"

It was personal. It had to be. Myuna had to realize the prophecy she feared most was on the cusp of coming true. Phaeron's mate, assisted by his daughter, was coming to cut the bitch's head off. And like a cornered animal, Myuna had struck out in the only way she could. She'd put us in a situation where the easiest victory was closed to us. Neither Phaeron nor I would sacrifice Carly, but if we didn't, her torchbearers would kill our defenders and friends with free access to their magic.

My grief twined quickly with a new burn in my chest, hatred blazing to life like I'd never felt before. There were few people I'd truly wanted to kill, but they were the villains of my life. Those who were now deceased, Garroway or Blaize Starsurge, for what they'd done to me, my family, or to others. But Myuna...I would commit any kind of violence necessary to ensure she joined them in hell.

Understanding seemed to glimmer in Phaeron's gemstone eyes. "Do you want to hear my plan to fix this?" he asked.

I nodded, and he shared it. We'd prepare one last containment room layered with librarian witch runes and powered by Braza. Lucas would remain behind in the room to await delivery of Carly, though he'd have a fallback in putting them both into stasis if removing her corruption was beyond his abilities.

Geo had already agreed to be the retriever. He didn't flinch when I turned a look his way. "You could've told me about this too, you know," I grumbled.

"My apologies," he said in that grinding way that suggested he'd been in gargoyle form recently.

"In the meantime, I will be storing the second half of Braza's power in this," Phaeron added, withdrawing a dragon scale from his pocket and handing it to me.

It was ringed with runes on its front and back, currently a dormant black. "It just needs a librarian witch's blessing before it can hold a soul and hook into the spells that would reanimate it in a gargoyle's body," he added.

"Wait, what?" Ben asked.

"He copied the runes from my heart last night," Geo supplied. "I shall explain the situation to Ben."

He drew aside a confused, scowling Ben to the other side of the room while Phaeron sat next to me to walk me through the blessing. It needed a kick of librarian witch power, something I did easily enough through drawing a rune over it with the tip of Flame, which functioned just as well as any of the other silver swords I'd used for spell-casting.

The scale crackled with power, each of its runes glowing from within with purple light. "I knew the scale could do it," he said. He picked it up and held it to my ear. It thrummed at a deep frequency, awaiting an occupant.

"What about the other half of her soul?" I asked.

"For right now, you will have to hold it within yourself. After we kill Myuna, I am assuming it will be a simple thing to acquire a crystal heart from our Crystal Court allies. Prince Orthus seems the sort who would give it freely, even if he knows what it's for," he said.

Though we were in private, Braza made herself known with a crackle of her electric presence over my shoulders. *"I assume you will have to draw upon a significant portion of my power to fight Myuna. If it all comes from the half attached to you, brightest of souls, you'll barely notice me clinging to you while you all seek a second heart."*

"Hmm. Who are we lying to, then?" I asked.

Phaeron dipped his head in acknowledgment of the unspoken intention. "Most everyone. The death of a power-core is a monumental event, nearly unheard of, but Myuna will be an easy scapegoat for Braza's disappearance. From there, it will take years to construct her gargoyle body with the proper intentionality that will be required to hide the suddenness of her second life from this modern world."

My brow furrowed. That would be nearly impossible, considering most everyone had a social media trail that started with their parents photographing them in diapers. "We should at least get Madigan and her men in the know. My coven, too. They're good at keeping secrets."

"Agreed," Braza said. *"I'll want some friends who know who I am."*

With a sigh, Phaeron rubbed his face and thought it over, replying after a while, "Yes, perhaps with the assistance of a fae deal. Grant's identity has been the only well-guarded secret amongst us."

"I'm sure Áine would help us with that."

I trusted her a hell of a lot more than Grant, even though he'd done nothing to earn suspicion other than exist as a changeling from a dangerous court. His scouting and spying had really come in handy, but sometimes I couldn't help but wonder what his ultimate angle was and who he served back in the Autumn Court. Áine didn't have that kind of potential baggage behind her intentions.

"She would. And while no plan is foolproof, I will do everything in my power to return your sister." He took my hand in between both of his and searched my face for forgiveness.

I smiled back sadly. It was clear he sought the kind of absolution I couldn't offer him. "Carly will forgive you when she's returned to herself. I'm sure she knows you were as much a victim as she is. Hell, judging by the other torchbearers we've encountered, this whole time may be as memorable to her as a long nightmare."

He brought my fingertips to his lips to kiss. "I hope so, bright soul. She is family now. The thought of her warped into undeath like my brother is unthinkable. I have to save her now, like I wish I could've saved him then." He released a ragged sound of pain.

"We will," I said. We had to. My sister deserved nothing less.

38

CRESS

My sister's fate had me throwing everything I could into our final day of training. I stood toe-to-toe with Madigan, the two of us brawling like juggernauts with the combined backing of all of our men. As evening fell, I covered myself in healing blood runes to recover from all my various hurts and spent what was left of the night before the battles ahead with my coven and friends.

We'd taken over the staff break room in the library, dragging in extra chairs from elsewhere to fit everyone. Roe was rolling a water bottle between her hands, looking pensive. Her moods were usually contagious, and considering she seemed concerned, tensions were high until one of the Furies, Grace, arrived and plunked a few wine bottles on the table toward the back of the break room.

"To take the edge off," she said, starting to rummage in the cupboards. "Surely this place has got some cups."

"Hey, not to spoil your fun, but most of us are under-age," Grant said.

She shrugged and started taking down an assortment of

plastic cups. "I won't snitch. It's the end either way. Might as well enjoy it."

The other Fury, Tish, was already set up in a corner of the room with her laptop. She glanced up from the screen and paused mid-typing. "Besides, that's about enough for one glass for each of us," she tittered.

Phaeron stood to help Grace pour and distribute. "On the eve of big battles, I'd drink with my men and discuss what we'd do *when* we'd win. It helps to focus on goals, not fears. We all have lives to return to once Myuna dies and we leave Cerris City at last," he said.

"That sounds like a good idea. Who'd like to go first?" Roe asked, accepting a cup partially filled with wine and taking a careful sip. She winced at its taste.

Bianca was the one to break the silence. "First things first, I am going to fight to the bitter end. I'm not running away through the ocean gate."

"You're not?" I asked, surprised.

"No way." She toasted me with her cup. "I haven't run from a fight yet, and tomorrow won't be the exception."

"There was that one time before Samhain—" Ben began to say.

"That was different," she interrupted. "I didn't actually want to fight you."

"Uh huh." He turned down a cup of wine. "You can have mine, Big P. You seem bougie enough to like wine." When Phaeron's brow furrowed, Ben added, "He doesn't understand slang, you guys. His translation spell is a bit literal."

The dimensional's eyes narrowed. "It translates intention well enough."

"Mating circle life. Yuck," Bianca said lightly.

"Fuck off," he answered her in the same tone.

"I'm going to, actually." She glanced away, fidgeting

with her fingers for a moment. "I guess this is your official notice that I accepted a position with the Furies as their third member. I'm going to hunt unnaturals professionally with Grace and Tish." The mountain lion shifter nodded stoically, while Tish beamed.

Ben blinked in surprise. "No shit?"

"None. I can't stand the idea of going back to school, and that's where most of you guys are headed." She wrinkled her nose in distaste. "So, I'm going to go do what I'm good at—killing monsters."

I nodded. She'd been spending a lot of time with those two women. It only made sense that she'd join them. "Good luck," I said.

"Thanks. And best of luck replacing me, of course. Now that Wren's made our coven famous, there'll be tons of witches that will want to take my place," she said with a flip of her hand.

"Hey, she mentioned you by name, Wren. What's next for you?" I asked.

The blonde sighed into her cup. "Well, apply for college loans, first off." She laughed alone, a nervous chuckle. "I'm going to reinvent myself, maybe go off on my own like it's the old times to seek out a new experience to name myself after. I'll have to continue streaming something too, with all the followers I've built up."

"You don't have to be alone," Roe said.

Tish glanced down at her computer, clicking around. "And I'll help you with your stream. I'm having a blast being a mod. Your fan group is popping off right now!"

My brows rose. "You have a fan group?"

"Yeah, but they're going to get bored of me once Myuna's dead and such."

"Nonsense!" Tish chirped, to an echo of agreement around the room.

Wren loosened her shoulders from a rather un-Wren-like hunch. "You're right. It'll be fine...great, even. What about you...Roe?"

Now it was the redhead's turn to look nervous. "Well, I hate keeping secrets," she blurted out. "I made a deal with a fae a few months ago, and I, uh, I'm gonna have to take off for a while to back up my end of things."

Áine's deerlike ears pinned back. "I immediately do not like this. Who was the fae? What was the deal?" she demanded.

It looked like Roe was going to hold her breath until she exploded. Her gaze tracked across the crowded room to Grant, who opened and closed his mouth a few times before scuffing his foot on the floor.

"If I show you my true form, Áine, do you promise not to get too mad?" he asked.

She whipped her head around, nostrils flared. No one smelled a fae deal like one of the fair folk. "I agree," she stated slowly and watched as Grant melted away, replaced by his changeling form. Her mouth fell open in shock.

Áine hopped to her hooves, pointing at him. "Changeling!" she barked. "And to think I *trusted* you!"

"I can explain—"

She spoke over him, panning the room in disbelief, but it seemed the only ones surprised were her and the Furies, not including Bianca. "Did you all know about this? Every time he disappeared..."

"He was spying for us. Áine, please. I'm sorry you're learning like this." Roe got up and hugged the faun, who stood there trembling and not returning the affection.

"You made a deal with him?" she asked in a low voice.

"An Autumn Court changeling, one of the *enemy*. Roe, how could you?"

"I can explain," she said, echoing Grant.

Áine pulled away, crossing her arms and taking her seat at an angle. "By all means," she said with gritted teeth.

"Well, we needed his help around Samhain, when Garroway and the Hungering Darkness went to ground," Roe began slowly, her voice shaking as she spoke to the faun's turned back. "He revealed himself first to a small group because he was tired of pretending to be boring-as-toast Grant Norwood."

"To be fair, my sponsor also wanted more information than I was gathering. He suggested that I be your friend," Grant put in.

"Yeah. So, the deal was of friendship," Roe said, nodding. "He would spy for us and do whatever we needed for free, and in exchange, I would visit the Autumn Court with him to compete with other fae nobility for the crown prince's hand."

Áine's cold shoulder thawed almost immediately. "What?" she asked, looking over her shoulder at Roe in disbelief.

Roe smiled sheepishly. "He said I didn't have to take it too seriously."

The faun turned a glare on Grant. "Well, *changeling*, how about you explain why you'd ask for something like that of my best friend."

I sensed that Ben wanted some popcorn. Most of us watched this play out, heads turning back and forth between the three of them. I had to admit, I was curious about the competition too. But the Autumn Court...helmed by a bloodthirsty queen who once sacrificed countless lives to the old Mother Tree that'd anchored the pocket dimension where Northern Supernatural University and the rest of New Salem resided. That was too dangerous a place for Roe to go alone.

"All right," Grant said, flicking his green and orange braid over his shoulder. "Long answer or short?"

Our friends shouted their answers, punctuated by Áine's eye roll and drawl of, "Tell me everything."

"Everything, cool. So, I'm Ambrose." He put a hand on his chest. "That's part of my true name, I mean. Before Roe and I shook on our deal, I told her the whole thing, so she can order me to dance myself to death if she wants. I'm the crown prince's body double and have spent most of my life learning how to be him."

"He's the mysterious sponsor," Roe said.

Ambrose sighed, his dragonfly wings shifting and layering over one another tightly on his back. "Prince Soryn asked me to seek out potential brides in the ruins of the Fall Court. Little did I expect to find it a bustling metropolis and for my cover story to tie me to the most important coven of witches in the whole of Moongrove Academy. I've been winging it for a while, pun not intended."

Phaeron felt badly for him, which echoed over our circle. "Your spying has been invaluable to us," he said.

"Well, thank you. I've been keeping Soryn alive for a few years, since I came of age and earned permission to impersonate his lordship. Believe it or not, I can't take the shape of folks above a certain power level threshold. I've never been Geo or Phaeron." He pointed at the two men with his thumb. "And trust me, I've tried."

"Don't try anymore," Geo grumbled.

"It's all good. I need your permission and blood to ever be able to," Ambrose said. "Anyway, there's a somewhat likely chance that Soryn is still alive without me. He doesn't actually want to get married, but he does want to end his mother's curse. Most of you are familiar with the old Fall Court's bloody past, I presume?"

Áine scowled. "I was the one who told most of them."

"Well, she made a deal with one of the Unspoken Ones long ago to have the power to augment her first Mother Tree with the blood of sacrifices. A side effect of that deal was true immortality. But she's kind of...rotting." Ambrose flinched as he said it. "Like, she has enough enemies that she's been assassinated a few times, but her body just gets back up and continues on. And as more time passes and she doesn't fulfill her end of the bargain, the more Autumn Court denizens get afflicted this way too."

Phaeron tilted his head. "Unspoken One...as in a death fae?"

"Yup. Thus, the undeath. He's getting impatient. Soryn is gathering allies for what we're calling Turning Leaf, a movement to remove both the Autumn Queen and the Unspoken One so our friends and family members can rest in peace and we can finally make amends to courts we've wronged." Ambrose nodded toward Áine, who seemed to finally be listening and accepting what he was saying. "In the meantime, Roe is considered royal fae by technicality, so I'm going to look like I'm doing my job by bringing her home to star in the next bridal competition the Autumn Queen puts on for Soryn. And there's your long answer, Áine."

"Hmph. I'm coming with you," she said to Roe.

"Wait—" she began to protest.

"I'll hide my Spring-ness, promise. If you're going to be in a bridal competition, you're going to need a fae you trust," the faun huffed.

"Sounds like a party. Can I come too?" Ben asked. Both

of them said a quick no at him. "Okay, fine. But how is Roe fae anything? She's human. Right?" He eyed her as if waiting for her to drop a glamor too.

"The Crystal Prince is one of my fathers. Technically, that puts me in line for the Crystal Court throne," Roe answered. "But if the bridal competition is held in typical fae style, Prince Soryn shouldn't even look twice at me. I'll be in and out before you know it."

Ambrose glanced away from her. From his expression, he thought otherwise. He shook his head, schooled his face, and said, "And as for me, I'm hopping through the ocean gate wearing Willow's face tomorrow. Girl, if someone tries to kill me, you owe me twice over."

"Sorry. It might happen, given the history." Willow ducked her head shyly under the room's concentrated attention. "I, uh, wanted to stay and fight. My control has gotten better."

I raised a brow and glanced around. "Who here is leaving through the ocean gate tomorrow?" I asked. Only Ambrose raised his hand, though he'd shifted to look exactly like Willow. Her reedy form was engulfed by his clothes.

"Really?" I asked in surprise.

"Furies finish what they start," Grace said.

Roe held up a fist. "You know I'm not going anywhere. I got your back."

Wren held up her phone in echo to the redhead. "Someone's got to record you defeating a goddess. We just won't stream any fights with torchbearers if we can help it."

"You're all the best. I thought...well, I thought you'd want to be safe," I said. "But I guess none of us will be. Not even Ambrose. Would you go back to being yourself, please?"

He transformed to his changeling form and made a dramatic bow. "It's still Willow's turn to talk," he said.

"Well, what I do next depends on how much danger Ambrose finds. I might go find my place in my alleged father's city or hide from the mer if it turns out a lot of them want to kill me," she said, scratching the back of her head with an uncertain tilt to her lips.

"Play it by ear," Roe suggested.

"Yeah. I guess that covers everyone but Cress and her circle. What's next?" she asked me.

"Um…" For all my fantasizing about the white-picket-fence life with my three men, I couldn't imagine returning to my quiet dorm room with the empty bed where Lanie used to sleep. My life had grown too large and busy to fit back into that box, even though I knew I needed classes and a degree to eventually get an ideal job. "I'm going to debate whether to tell NSU that I'm a hybrid witch so I can learn more celestial magic. And hopefully move out into an apartment big enough for my circle."

"Staff quarters," Ben suggested. "You and Geo can move in with Big P and me."

Phaeron released a skeptical breath. "Implying I'm still employed at Moongrove Library. I intend to resign anyway, as I'd rather cut off part of my tail than work for Dr. Aurina any longer."

"While he searches for a job, I intend to be gainfully employed with the SPDI. I've been texting my old friend, Marl." Geo held up his own phone. "He's a fellow gargoyle who's served for decades. They're always looking for durable talent."

Amusingly, I felt a dissonance between Phaeron and Ben's reactions. The former nodded in approval, while the latter balked at the idea of Geo becoming a member of the supernatural police. But it suited him, I thought. Criminals would rue the day they crossed Officer Geo.

"Officer Darkmore," Phaeron whispered behind his hand, in response to my thoughts.

Right, they had my name now. I kept forgetting.

"Well, I'm going to be a student," Ben said. "Just throwing that out there. I'll major in something useful and even go to class."

"I'll believe it when I see it," I said, a sentiment most of the coven echoed.

I looked down at my cup of wine, left untouched where I'd rested it on my thigh. Most everyone had finished their taste of alcohol by now. Taking a sip, I recognized that it was a milder wine, both bitter and sweet notes mingling on my tongue. Kind of like this moment, a bubble of peace right before the uncertainty of tomorrow. Sweet, but bitter with the knowledge that we might lose anyone who'd chosen to stay with us until the very end.

39
GEO

We woke early and traveled to the hospital to join a meeting of fighters. Those staying behind to battle Myuna and her torchbearers filled the foyer, where instead of gathering to witness a mating circle ritual, all attention was on Madigan explaining how the upcoming battle would go.

The acoustics of the room caused her hearty voice to echo up to the people lining the second-floor landing. "We want to stir up Myuna's forces and cause them to meet us at the lake where our ocean gate lies. To generate as much motion as possible, you have been divided into five teams to escort noncombatants from either the hospital or one of our four safe houses."

A few glanced my way as I gave a grinding nod. I was in my stone form, placed prominently behind Madigan as the leader of team four. While I flew there, most of the team would be driving, and then we would approach the battlefield on foot, as our assigned safe house was closest to the lake.

"You have full authority to use lethal force on any torchbearer you meet today. They will certainly be doing their best to kill us," Madigan continued. "We are outnumbered and outmatched if our intel is accurate and they are able to use their magic and wits against us."

A hush of voices followed her declaration, some astonished looks being passed around. Many of those staying were the Crystal fae and guardian witches of Ashbough Protective Services, who had been spending their time defending our territory until the recent lull in activity. They knew about as much as the handful of doctors and nurses who'd dressed themselves in distinctive colors for battle-field triage.

"However, we do have the element of surprise. King Laiken has promised to send myrmidons to help us defend the ocean gate. These will be fresh and rested merfolk right next to their element. The tide of battle may easily turn to our favor, pun intended." She paused for a moment, waiting for a few groans amongst the crowd.

"While we engage the torchbearers, our noncombatants will flee to safety through the ocean gate. I know it may seem counterintuitive, but we want as much torchbearer attention as possible while our civilian count dwindles. It's a bait and switch, folks. We will be teleporting using dimensional magic the moment the gate closes and the myrmidons leave." She glanced over at Auric, beckoning him over.

"We're not mentioning the Void?" Cress asked quietly. She held hands with Ben a couple paces away, where they stood with the cluster of their coven.

Ben shrugged. "I still don't think I understand what it is," he whispered back.

Phaeron wasn't present to attempt to explain it again. To get the last librarian witches to leave their posts at the library, he'd promised to personally defend Braza. He'd rejoin us with her powercore half safely secured in his dragon scale later on. The only person who would truly remain at the library was Lucas, awaiting a delivery of Carly in one last containment room.

Hopefully his unusual new magic could do something for her. Cress would never forgive herself if we lost her sister, especially this close to the end of everything.

"All right, listen up," Auric said gruffly, cutting through the crowd's murmuring. "Many of you haven't met a dimensional that looks quite like me. I specialize in, ah, teleporting. My magic will look like a heat mirage or sometimes blue and black mist. You will want to be ready to disengage from any fight and cluster up, else I'll end up leaving you behind. The actual relocation will take three seconds, if that, and you will feel an intense chill on your skin. Questions?"

He didn't pause. "Good. During the second half of our plan, I will drop us all in the audience chamber where Myuna has been sitting this whole time. She...teleported here from my old home world and left behind a hole, so to speak. My goal once we arrive is to send her back through that hole and sew it closed so she cannot return. It will take me a while to harness enough power to make it possible."

"What are we doing in the meantime?" shouted a Crystal fae from the second floor.

Madigan gestured up at him and answered, "We expect a smaller force of elite torchbearers will remain behind with their goddess. Those of us who choose to fight will hold them off from Auric as he works his magic.

"As for Myuna, no one is to engage her recklessly. Any attempts to do so may result in the consumption of your soul or the possibility of being turned into a torchbearer and against your friends. Only Cress Darkmore and her circle will approach her, and then it is only to distract. This way forward was seen as the most successful path by the Graygazers."

She turned to Cress, who flexed the powers Braza gave her to make purple-black shadows slide into being and dance and eddy around her when she raised an arm to wave. "Thank you for your bravery," Madigan said.

After a tense smattering of applause, Madigan opened the floor to questions. She went over fine details before dismissing the meeting for us to head off and put the plan into motion. I gathered team four, which mostly consisted of friends, both from Cress's coven and the defenders who'd helped us clear the library of its monsters.

"Madigan would like a few of our cars to whip through the city streets en route for maximum attention," I stated.

Ben and Bianca both lit up. "Race you," she said.

"You're on!" he exclaimed.

Cress raised a brow but shook her head rather than say anything. She'd probably been planning on carrying Ben in her shadows. Instead, she turned to Grant and Willow, making an offer to them in an undertone. They disappeared with her into the darkness, and as the rest of us finished coordinating transportation, the merman who'd originally come here for Willow walked up to join us.

It took me a moment to remember his name. Zander. He was dressed in what I assumed was a myrmidon's battle armor, gleaming plates interlocking over his chest like over-sized fish scales. One over his heart was etched with a symbol of jagged coral. Those plates continued over a leather kilt that looked like it was designed to wrap around the weak point where fish tail met man's torso in his aquatic form.

He carried along his heavy trident, using its blunt end

like a walking stick. "Where's Princess Willow?" he asked, eyes narrowing as he took in our group.

"She's taking a safe route to meet us there," Ben answered for me. He knew I was practically incapable of uttering direct lies in my stone form.

"Is there such a thing as a safe route?" the mer warrior asked skeptically.

Ben smirked. "Let me put it this way. It's less dangerous than Bianca's driving."

She shot him a venomous look. "We'll see about that. I'll meet you on the road." We split up, most of the team following them when they headed off to claim a vehicle, while I emerged into the early morning through the front doors and spread my wings. Flying might've been slower travel than the maximum speed of a car, but nothing could beat the feeling of soaring across the sky.

I knew the way from my trips scouting or performing search and rescue. The safe house was a dance hall, where an overflow of healthy noncombatants had been living ever since Myuna had consumed her unnatural creatures. The survivors were now out in the parking lot, many clustered in family groups. Some of them held suitcases or sacks of belongings; others had the clothes on their backs and clutched weapons, ready to fight for their freedom.

Spotting Cress's purple head of hair, I came in for a landing nearby and checked my momentum with heavy strokes of my wings to land without cratering the asphalt. "Willow?" I asked the brown-haired girl next to Cress, who ducked her head too readily.

"Nope," replied the changeling in his voice before switching to speak in her usual wispy tones. "She's wearing a set of Crystal fae armor over there. I assume she'll take some of it off before she gets in the water and sinks like, well, a stone.”

I glanced in the direction he pointed. Her thin outline was bulked out by the hard facets of the armor, and it did look too heavy for her.

“Oh, I put a glamor over her trident,” Ambrose added. The graceful weapon seemed to resemble the kind of hammer a guardian witch would wield. If anyone checked her aura, the deception would fall apart, but no one would be looking in the midst of battle.

“Did she make a separate bargain for such services?” I asked.

“Curious?” he countered with a lift of a brow. “As a matter of fact, no. I want to see King Laiken’s palace and politics for myself. It seems like a shoo-in for a hellhole worse than the Autumn Court, but maybe I’m biased.”

“Perhaps,” I muttered.

“I mean, there shouldn’t be undead there,” Cress pointed out.

Ambrose smacked his lips. “Guess it’s hard to get worse than that.”

We lapsed into companionable silence, some of the survivors around us drifting close enough to eavesdrop. Ambrose practiced some of Willow’s typical poses and expressions as if he were limbering himself up for a performance as her for the foreseeable future. I wondered what he planned on doing when he was asked to demonstrate her powerful water magic.

Well, a problem unrelated to the challenges ahead. While I pushed away any squirmy feeling of nerves with ease as a gargoyle, Cress tugged some of my stoic calm to wrap her own emotions in a dampening blanket to keep from bouncing on the balls of her heels or pacing as we waited.

The sound of wheels screeching on pavement had all of us looking up. Two cars came zooming into the parking lot, engines purring as they came to an abrupt stop and fighters piled out. "Incoming!" shouted a guardian witch coming from one of the vehicles.

A third truck struggled along, its side gouged by massive claws. I loaded a quartz spike in my right arm, lifting my palm and waiting to sight the creature that'd done such damage in one long swipe.

Weapons unsheathed, and magic ignited around me. We all heard it coming, the *thump thump thump* of heavy paws.

A shifter in full grizzly bear form charged into our midst with an ursine roar. Its tiny, round eyes blazed with Myuna's white power, and spittle ran in rivulets from its open jaws. Each stride was punctuated with its pants and grunts.

It noticed Cress mid-stride and changed course to head straight at her. The same guardian witch jumped in the way and raised a portion of asphalt to serve as a shield. With agility that belied its bulk, the bear edged around the chunk of road to slam its paw into the witch. He crashed to the ground with the crack of his stone armor hitting concrete.

Shadows wrapped around Cress, making her a purple and black version of Phaeron's shadowborn form, complete with tendrils trailing after her to emulate a pair of wings and a tail. She stepped forward to meet the bear shifter at the same time I fired my primed spike. It cut into its thick hide, emerging through its shoulder.

Left arm failing to take its weight, it skidded to the ground. An ordinary shifter would've bellowed in pain, but it was eerily silent as it struggled to its paws and accidentally shoved the spike further through its body. Several spells ripped into it as it lurched forward, gaze still focused on Cress with murderous intent.

She hesitated when it fell again nearly at her feet. "You have to do this," she said in a two-toned voice, but I had the feeling it was Braza speaking.

"He's crippled. We could still save him when Phaeron arrives," she said in response to herself.

The bear used its back paws to launch at her, stretching out in one last-ditch effort to tear out her throat. I moved to shove her aside, and my hand met shadows when she reflexively turned to vapor and reappeared a couple feet away. Its bulk hit me, staggering even my gargoyle form. I dropped my shield and caught its head, ending its life with a harsh twist to save her from the task.

The bear dropped, head rolled askew. In death, it shifted back into the limp form of a naked man, his body covered in the same wounds he'd sustained as a bear.

"Let's get moving," I rumbled to get attention off the body.

Eyes averted slowly from him, back to me as I issued instructions. The survivors moved into a cluster as I told them to, with fighters forming a protective ring around them. I picked up my shield while consolidating my quartz into a club for the fight ahead and walked at the front of the group. Cress and Ben moved into place a step behind me.

We took a back road, circling around the bulk of an abandoned strip mall. The ground sloped downward, and we ran into a fence that bordered this side of the lake.

It was a mer-made thing, crystal-green water rimmed by imported sand. There was no visual sign of an active ocean gate from here. It would be in the middle of the lake, where the water was deepest, connected to a network of similar gates for aquatic folk to move through freely.

I looked for any hint of movement on the lake past the placid ripples from a breeze. The myrmidons had to be scouting the area, awaiting us. We were relying on them, after all. There would be no reaching the ocean gate without the help of an oceanic witch or one of the merfolk.

Another team emerged from the tree line several yards away and headed toward us. Now that our allies were arriving, weapons were drawn, defensive lines were established, and traps were set around the perimeter from pointed stones to sand stirred into a mire.

Civilians were placed behind the wall of defenders, backs to the lake. We wanted to look helpless to draw out the torchbearers in force, but Cress and Ben shared a feeling of unease that infiltrated our circle as more and more people joined us. All was quiet, save the murmurs that built as we waited for some sign of movement from the lake.

"The hospital's team hasn't gotten here yet," Ben commented.

"Do you think they're taunting torchbearers?" Cress asked in a two-toned voice.

He exaggerated a shrug. "Hurry up and wait to find out."

Wind stirred the crystals that formed my hair in gargoyle form. It would've been a beautiful spring day, the sky clear and blue, if this calm lakeside wasn't about to become a battlefield. Even the trained Crystal fae and guardian witches started to shift and rub at their armor as time passed.

There was a splash of water, and many of us turned to look. A dark-skinned mermaid emerged from the lake, dripping streams of water from her armor and a battle trident clutched in one maroon-finned hand.

"Is the princess here?" she demanded. The coppery fish scales on her cheeks caught the light when she turned to Zander and Willow emerging from the crowd. "Good. Let's go. King Laiken is expecting her."

The real Willow, still concealed in heavy armor, turned to stare meaningfully at the changeling that was taking up the center of attention as her. "Um," Ambrose said, scuffing his foot. "Everyone else first. I won't go through the gate unless you help all these people."

Willow nodded in agreement behind him.

The mermaid bared her teeth in a bloodthirsty grin. She snapped the butt of her weapon underwater, a swirl of bright blue magic emerging from it as a ribbon that sped away deep into the lake.

I wanted to say the surge of relief within me was from the mating circle. Cress breathed out with it as figures breached the water's surface. Merfolk of all kinds were here. I recognized the finned and sharp-toothed horses as shapeshifted kelpies, along with the long, sinuous form of a single sea dragon shifter.

The combined power of the mer began to part the lake, creating a narrow path that led deeper and deeper through the silt at the bottom of the lakebed. It revealed the ocean gate, a pair of columns carved from cerulean stone with a sheet of magic that looked as thin as a soap bubble stretched between them.

The dry path expanded wide enough for two people to walk side by side, and that was when the maroon-scaled mermaid nodded toward the fake Willow. "It is safe. Send your people through, and I will remain at your side to protect you, Your Highness." Her warmth faded as her eyes landed on Zander. "Good job finally doing something useful for our kingdom," she added to him tightly.

His gruff response was drowned out by Madigan and others shouting, "Form a line!" With her arrival, heading up the group that'd traveled here from the hospital, the trap was fully set. The first survivors rushed to the safety promised by the ocean gate, disappearing the moment they touched the gate's bubble of magic.

A handful of guardian witches helped maintain calm and stopped the shoving that resulted when most of the survivors saw the truth: salvation was real and in sight. That didn't stop several screams, most shrill with the panic of children, when a less friendly shifter announced itself with a roar, followed by the howls of several wolves.

These shifters were sighted first, each torchbearers with flaming white eyes that prowled the line of the fence, growling. "There are so many," Cress muttered.

They came from sidewalks and backstreets, forming a crowd in minutes. While our guardian witches fired volleys of sharpened stones toward them, Myuna's turned guardian witches nullified the rocks into dust and crumpled lengths of metal fence like balling up paper.

I had to acknowledge that she and her chosen ascendant had practiced well. These torchbearers moved like they were in charge of their own bodies and actions, though many faced us in torn and stained clothes, wielding makeshift weapons. They may have the numbers, but we were more prepared to fight.

As they fanned out and the shifters prowled looking for weaknesses in our defensive lines, each of the torchbearers began to speak at the same time. In the past, when Myuna wanted to talk to us, she used her discordant voice straight through her victims. These men and women used their own voices, forming a monotone chorus.

"Where is the son of night? All this trouble, and Phaeron refuses to face me?"

"Release your hold on these people, Myuna!" Madigan shouted back at the crowd. She flashed a quick look over her shoulder, where survivors were still fleeing through the ocean gate, now a coordinated line with fighters and mer placed at regular intervals to shove civilians along.

A flat chuckle sounded from the chorus. "It seems we have not been properly reintroduced. Myuna has sent me to crush you in her stead," they said. The crowd tremored and parted for a petite figure.

Cress gasped, and I felt her vertigo secondhand before Ben steadied her and murmured in her ear. Across the short stretch of beach stood Carly, a white apparition standing ramrod straight. Myuna's light glowed from her irises, a subtle difference to set her apart from the blank white stare of the torchbearers who surrounded her. She held a length of pure white light in her hand as if it were a celestial witch staff.

"Carly!" Cress screamed.

It was so unusual to see Carly turn such a hateful look toward her sister. But as Phaeron had said, this wasn't her, but a twisted version with any good qualities sanded away. Myuna's ultimate vision was to turn her into another soul-consuming monster, and with that came the death of who Carly used to be.

"My lady has seen potential in me above all others. I am an ascendant now, the one who commands the goddess's legion." Though Carly's lips moved, it was the torchbearers who spoke for her. "However, we do not need to fight. Surrender Phaeron and Cress to the lady's mercy, and the rest of you may run to safety." The crowd gestured dismissively as a unit.

"Carly, this is crazy! You're the one who should surrender to us. We can help you," Cress called. Tears clustered in her eyes even as the shadows around her stirred, ready for the fight ahead.

"I don't need your pity anymore. I am more powerful now than you could ever imagine."

"I've never *pitied* you! You're my sister, no matter if you're a supernatural or not. Come with us, and we'll get the corruption out of you." She shifted to the side, shouting around the bulk of the fighters who moved into position, bracing for a fight.

A cold smile crossed Carly's face. "Look at you. Now that I have power, here you are begging me to let it go." She lifted her staff of light, and the torchbearers shifted, preparing to fight. "If you will not surrender, I will take you to Myuna by force."

"There is no sense in arguing with her while Myuna is treating her like a puppet," I gritted out. With a nod, Cress called upon the shadows, letting them wrap around her and releasing an unearthly howl.

In answer, Carly pointed with the staff, and her people surged forward, meeting us fist for fist and spell for spell. I flared my wings and took up a defensive stance in front of Cress, assuming rightly that several white-eyed shifters would be going for her throat directly.

She threaded her shadows around my bulk, striking at vulnerable openings as a pair of wolves and a tiger shifter tried to maneuver around the shining surface of my shield and the swing of my club. They learned I was a living wall. No force Myuna had called up could get past me to hurt my love.

But for every enemy we downed, two took their place. Ben fought at Cress's back, relying on his old combat training with daggers in hand and blood runes drawn. Cress channeled some of my durability into him, trading back to me some of his agility.

If the torchbearers showed any hint of emotion, they might've been surprised at the speed I countered attacks and swung back, or how spells designed to gouge and burn flesh only grazed Ben.

I tuned out the screams of the dying and of panicking civilians as our allies were inched backward under the onslaught of the torchbearers. It was only when the possessed guardian witch that'd crossed weapons with me twitched and spoke did I take a moment to listen.

"Too cowardly to fight, son of night?" The torchbearers were everywhere, speaking slightly off sync mid-combat.

I didn't bother trying to find Phaeron, knowing he'd be an elusive curl of smoke until it was time for us to trade places. The librarians must've finally passed through the ocean gate for him to have revealed himself.

When he'd first suggested the plan we were about to engage to save Cress's sister, I hadn't thought Carly's corruption would run so deep that she would seem to willingly turn on us. But he'd told me everything to expect. That name, *son of night*, was all Myuna. There was every possibility Myuna was watching and manipulating this fight through her ascendant, which meant the tirades and threats would begin now that she'd noticed Phaeron's presence.

"Did you know I used to look up to you? I thought you would save me when Myuna first held me," Carly continued, the confession too raw to be anything but her own. "How foolish of me. Like any shadow, all you're doing now is tiptoeing around. Look at what happens when you pick the light."

A ray of white radiance blasted from her direction at the back of her forces, reflecting off the lake's surface. It appeared to be a direct hit, as Phaeron slipped out of his shadow form and crashed into the water. He emerged, sputtering, on the back of a nickering kelpie.

I caught a glimpse of the dwindling number of civilians. The other side of the battlefield was full of the drowned corpses of torchbearers who'd crossed the maroon-scaled mermaid and her forces. But instead of pressing their advantage, they began to retreat toward the water with changeling Willow at the back of the procession of noncombatants.

I fought on. Though the mer had helped, they wouldn't stop the onslaught of possessed aiming for Cress. It did not take long for Phaeron to emerge at my side, drawing his sword. He was soaked through, looking pissed but unharmed.

"Go," he said. Black shadows swarmed down his arms, forming talons over his fingers.

"You don't want to do the honors?" I confirmed.

"You are better suited for the task. I will make amends with the girl when she is back to her senses."

I nodded and sucked my quartz club back into my arm, reforming it into the tool I needed. I flared my wings further, careful of where my allies were standing, and lifted off the ground with a heavy flap. Phaeron moved into the place I'd been after a second flap took me airborne and sailing over the heads of the combatants.

Carly realized what was happening when I landed with a thud before her, letting the force of impact knock her off-balance. She bared her teeth and turned the staff toward me, shooting out a superheated wave of light. My obsidian body sizzled and heated as it absorbed the magic, but stone could be heated hundreds of times without sustaining any damage.

I took a step forward, and she scrambled back. Whipping the staff, her next attack was a spinning disc of white light, which I deflected with a lift of my shield. "You cannot harm me. I was tempered to fight the Hungering Darkness, whom you are not," I rumbled.

Her breathing quickened, a glimpse of the scared teen girl under the overwhelming influence of Myuna's magic. "Get away from me," she yelped, this time without a monotone echo.

"It is for your own good," I answered, grabbing her wrist and smacking the staff out of her hand with a bash of my shield before I purposefully dropped it on the sand.

A set of quartz handcuffs emerged from my hand, sealing around one wrist. We wrestled for her other hand before I managed to grab and secure it. Carly screamed at the top of her lungs when I seized her and took to the sky.

The screaming faded as the air thinned. I sped through the sky as fast as my stone body would allow, pumping my wings with urgency. My destination: a single containment room and the young man waiting to see if he could do anything to help her return to herself.

Carly whipped her head around suddenly, hitting an unnatural angle that caused her neck to crack. "*Unhand my chosen ascendant now,*" she said in the fully wailing cacophony of Myuna's rage-filled presence.

I met her glowing white eyes. "Or what?" I asked.

"*I flood her with my power,*" Myuna answered. A flourish of light pulsed from Carly's body, lighting up her skeleton to shine through her skin for a moment. "*To your simple mortal mind, she will die. She will become something greater than Endaeron ever was, capable of consuming even your rock-encased soul.*"

She inspected my expressionless face, the threat hanging between us. Here was the moment Phaeron admitted he was not strong enough to face.

So, I did it for him, saying, "Bullshit."

The answering bellow was deafening. "*Do you not care for this girl at all? Would you not mourn if she died?*"

"There's no need for mourning," I stated. "You are not powerful enough to do more than bluster."

"*Hmm. The prophecy only concerned the son of night, his mate, and his daughter. It never mentioned a man of stone impervious to magic. Who are you?*" Myuna asked.

"My name is Geo."

"*Geo. I look forward to consuming you whole.*" Her presence left Carly, who fell into a limp faint in my arms.

40

CRESS

WHEN GEO CARRIED CARLY away and she screamed, so did the torchbearers. It was the scene of a horror movie, with the gore washing into the lake as the water flowed over our feet. The mer had retreated with who they thought was Willow and closed the dry stretch to the ocean gate. Eddies of pinkish foam splashed over the battlefield.

When the echoes of screaming faded, the torchbearers dropped weapons and spells, eyes glazing over to blank, zombielike stares. Phaeron placed his sword aside and grabbed the soul of the nearest one, untying it from Myuna's control.

"Do you see what to do?" he asked in Soiluirian.

Braza answered affirmatively from my lips.

"Madigan!" Phaeron shouted. The woman's red-clad head turned his way. "Carly's lost control!"

"Arms down," she shouted. Her fighters echoed the order and took the cue to stop fighting, watching with unease as the torchbearers that were still alive went limp and some collapsed bonelessly with the one controlling them gone.

I let Braza take control for now, and she turned on her soul sight. I was disoriented by the sudden double-images overlaid behind everyone, their souls appearing like auras except larger and with more vivid and varied colors. But she knew exactly what she was looking at and what to do. While she worked, my suppressed thoughts came back up from where I'd buried them during the battle.

That'd been my sister saying those awful things. I couldn't get her hate-filled stare out of my head, aimed directly at me. Even though I knew, logically, she was as much a victim as the torchbearers we'd had to kill, it hurt. She'd suffered and become this shade of herself...a servant brainwashed to believe Myuna's side was just.

"If we can remove the seed of corruption planted in her soul, she will return to the girl you know," Braza said privately.

"That's a big if." Though Lucas had been able to save the less afflicted souls, who knew if he was powerful enough to erase the full and malicious intent behind Carly's deep corruption.

Phaeron had been able to confirm that Lucas had rescued those people from unnatural status and returned their souls to the state they'd been in before encountering a dread goddess. There were no others with magic twisted into a new form, like Lucas, but also none so severely changed as Carly. *"If she remains unnatural, then what?"* I asked.

Braza sighed deeply. *"Another big if. She may have to be contained in a library, depending on if she develops a hunger for souls. Otherwise, she would be monitored for the rest of her life and fed bits of powercore energy to stave off any possible cravings. In the best possible scenario, Lucas removes Myuna's influence completely, and Carly becomes fully human again."*

After the pain of having her soul warped by Myuna...

well, I hoped my sister would be okay to return to her normal self. *"Now that I have power, here you are begging me to let it go,"* she had said. But I didn't know if that was her deepest wish twisted by corruption or a true reflection of how she felt within.

"While there is no harm in speculation, we have one last fight ahead of us," Braza said, cutting into my thoughts. Our allies helped move the unconscious torchbearers we'd saved first, dragging them away from the lake. Then came the dead, pulled out of the water before they could sink into the waves.

Though many of us had been hardened against such a sight after the awful fights that'd occurred with countless unnatural creatures over these long months, fighters and medical personnel alike wept over several of the fallen. The air had changed. We were all that was left in the whole of this pocket dimension, other than Myuna. And I was afraid more would be sacrificed to see this through to the end.

I looked around for my men, coven mates, and friends. Phaeron was a few feet away, wringing water out of his hair. For a few moments, I saw him with Braza's soul sight and paused. *Son of night* became a lot more literal all of a sudden.

Phaeron's soul was a rich, velvety black, with a flicker of white that arched toward the top. The patch of Endaeron looked like a crescent moon at the right angle, and I'd expected the piece of my soul we'd swapped with his mating bite would look the same way. Yet instead, my light came through in pinpricks, making it look like his soul had been carved from a starry night.

I blinked, and the sight was gone. He'd noticed my stare and tilted his head. "What has you so spellbound, my heart?" he asked.

"I've never seen your soul before now." I searched for a way to describe it other than *pretty*, considering how he could wax poetic about my own. "It's like a peaceful night. One I could get lost in."

There was a flicker of interest in his expression before he pressed his lips together tightly. "Tell me more soon," he said, edging closer and showing me the rune-etched edge of the dragon scale. Braza shivered within me in recognition of the holding place for the other half of her soul. Her emotions felt a lot like anticipation and hope for her fresh start.

He slipped it back out of view as Auric approached us, growling. "The more time we spend dawdling, the more prepared Myuna will be for us," he snapped in Soiluirian.

"I told you. I don't want to go until Geo is with us," Phaeron said.

"This is not what we agreed to. You told me we were killing the ascendant, not trying to save her."

I glanced away from them, pretending not to understand. I looked around again for all my friends. They'd come together, everyone alive if a little scuffed. Ben had his back turned to Bianca, who was applying a healing rune for him on a gash over his shoulder blade.

Phaeron spoke to Auric much more patiently than I would have. "Plans change. We did not expect to save any lives today, yet we have. Peace, old friend. Myuna will be rotting again on the planet she destroyed before you know it."

"She deserves to die a true death. Her soul ripped to shreds, unable to enter any semblance of the next life," Auric said in a tone of pure acid. "I wish I were strong enough to do it."

"You will still be responsible for ending her reign of

terror here before it begins. We could not send her through the Void without you."

"That still does not bring back Geryn. Fuckin' hell, even if Myuna dies today, that does not give Geryn or any of the other lost souls a single ounce of rest," Auric muttered.

Phaeron rested a hand on his shoulder, and his sympathy and understanding flowed across the mating circle to me. They remained that way for a few minutes, until Madigan and her men checked in with us about the plan. "Geo should be back any minute now. Once he is, we will empower Cress and be ready to go," he said.

Madigan nodded to me, and nerves fluttered in my belly. They intensified with every beat of my heart as it sank in: this was truly it. Either my circle held off Myuna long enough for Auric to send her through the Void, or we all died. Not just my life and those of my men were at stake, but also the lives of almost everyone I cared about.

"It'll just be like what we practiced," I murmured to myself.

My friends came over to cluster around me. Ben seemed to pick up on my headspace immediately and wrapped his arms around me for a quick hug. "Just think. In a few years, we're going to be talking about that one time we fought a goddess," he said.

"And won!" Roe exclaimed, staggering me with a slap on the back.

I looked around at them all, still amazed everyone had stayed to fight, other than Ambrose, who'd engaged in a different kind of battle halfway across the world in King Laiken's undersea court. Willow had shed the heavy armor disguise and stood in the lake up to her knees. Water wove around her delicate trident, forming spheres that rotated around her body like moons to a planet.

I felt such an overwhelming surge of gratitude seeing even my most gentle friend ready to fight with us. "You all are the best," I said, swiping under my eye. "We're going to do this... We're going to get through this together."

Ben reached out and squeezed my hand, static brushing our anam cara marks. "Together," he agreed. I managed a tense smile for him.

When Geo landed a few minutes later, he found me between Ben and Phaeron, his discarded shield gleaming at our feet. I met his quicksilver gaze with anticipation, and he shifted into human form to cup my cheek in a warm hand.

"How is she?" I whispered.

He pressed a kiss into my hair. "She is with Lucas now. Though Myuna blustered, she didn't do anything to harm her," he said.

I flung my arms around him, sighing with relief. "Thank you."

He hugged me back, squeezing gently. I looked up to see a meaningful glance pass from him to Phaeron. "What did Lucas say?" the dimensional asked.

"That Myuna's corruption is very distinct inside her soul. He promised to do his best to remove it," Geo answered.

"Once she is gone, his task may be easier," Phaeron mused.

An impatient noise nearby had Geo stiffening and turning to glare at Auric's darkening face. I put a hand on his arm. "It's all right. We should get moving," I said to my men, who nodded.

After days of practice, we had found a pattern of sharing our magic and abilities that worked best. First, Ben and I shared our witcheries, with him taking my celestial side and me taking his blood runes. I cut myself on my sword and lifted my sleeve to paint the runes for strength, agility, and speed on my skin before putting a tiny healing rune over the cut to close it fast.

Next was Phaeron, whose knowledge of swordplay mixed with Braza's shadows and magic to lend me the skills of a shadowborn.

And finally was Geo, who changed back into gargoyle form and gave me as much of his endurance and stoicism as possible. He bent and offered me his crystal shield.

"We're ready," I told Auric in a two-toned voice.

He grumbled in his native tongue as word traveled through the group of fighters. We gathered in a tight semi-circle at his direction, and the weight of many expectant gazes seared into my back. *I can't mess this up. I won't.*

When he raised his arms, shimmering magic in shades of sapphire and gray spread from his feet, flowing around us. It moved like mist, getting under the layers of my clothes to chill my skin. I stayed by Phaeron's side as the Void closed in around us. He'd done this before, walked the endless nothing for what could've been an eternity, and come out on the other side okay.

It was over in the time it took to blink twice. We went from a bloodied beachside to the remains of the audience chamber where Myuna sat upon the dais, towering over us in her glowing white splendor. When we first came here before the Crown Coven, I'd thought the chamber was beautiful, with the artful display of the seven affinities of witch magic. It'd been built to impress all seeking an audience with the highest coven in North America.

The battle and resulting occupation by a ravenous goddess had wrecked it. Auric had dropped us in the middle of the long path that led to the dais. Instead of a placid pool with splashing sculptures to our left, there was a crater littered with shattered cement debris. Dried blood stains turned much of the sides brown.

To our right, the carefully cultivated soil with its verdant display of flowers and herbs was turned over, finger-shaped furrows marking where huge hands had combed all living matter free of its home. The domed roof overhead had long lost all of its glass, with the metal frames hanging and looking like they could fall at any moment.

Myuna wasn't the only one here. A dozen figures stood below the dais, their heads jolting up as she noticed our sudden appearance. Her shocked gaze moved unerringly to Phaeron and me standing together, and she opened her mouth to scream. Though Braza quickly plugged my ears with shadows, everyone else covered their ears to block out some of the unholy sound.

"*You stand before Myuna the White, the reaper of worlds!*" she shrieked. Her voice shook me to my core, resonant with power, madness, and countless souls crying out through her cavernous open mouth. "*Throw down your weapons and prostrate yourself for my mercy, or face the end!*"

Despite Geo's steadiness grounding me, my heart still thumped hard against my ribcage as I stepped forward, raising Flame until its tip pointed at her chest. "Myuna!" I shouted. After the deafening force of her, my voice felt like it was emerging through water. "I, Cressida Rollins Darkmore, challenge you to a duel!"

My arm trembled as Myuna observed me with a sneer. I only had to keep her occupied for a few minutes, long enough for Auric to do what he needed to. Strains of laughter danced in and out of my ears, a chorus of disembodied, mocking voices. The mist of the Void seeped and spread in freezing eddies toward the dais. Bluish mist rolled over our feet, gathering in the pits and valleys of the broken concrete.

Braza flared her power, wrapping me in shadows of black and purple when Myuna eased off the dais, standing to her full height. "It is *you*. No matter how much I tried to twist fate, this moment has arrived all the same." She reached toward the sky, harnessing a beam of light and holding it, shimmering and pulsing, in her hand. "It seems I must destroy you myself to be free of this wretched prophecy. I will fight you, she who would mate the son of night. And to keep all of these friends of yours busy, they will fight my followers."

Each of the men and women behind her had flares of cold white light in their eyes. Most dashed past Myuna at a full run, weapons lifting. One, a near-naked man, rippled with a shifter's transformation and expanded rapidly. Crimson scales coated his elongated neck, and ridges grew over his back. He spread leathery wings and roared, blasting a superheated wave of flame directly at me.

Myuna smirked, firelight flickering over her milky eyes. "Oops," she said. I felt her attempt at being playful in the headache that rushed through me when I became shadows and reemerged a few yards to the side.

We hadn't come here to fight fair, so I wouldn't expect Myuna to either. It was in her very best interest that I get "accidentally" turned into a smear of ash. I raised the crystal shield, shouting, "Let's see if you have better aim than him!"

For a moment, her gaze was unfocused. Sounds of battle raged around us, and I waited tensely for what she'd do next. *Just keep her attention. Don't let her get any closer to souls she could consume.*

"I got it!" I heard Roe announce. She ran as fast as she

could in her orange crystal armor, intercepting the dragon shifter's head. As he inhaled to breathe another gout of fire, she nailed his jaw in an uppercut, and Myuna stirred, her mouth gaping when the dragon bared his fangs.

She took a step toward me, and I retreated, facing her back to the rest of the group. I would soon be pinned between the dais and the far wall, but my breath was turning to smoke with each exhale. The Void was so close I could practically taste the madness and its taunting words hanging just out of the range of hearing. The mist was thickening up, turning the air gray and dense. It muffled some of the sounds of combat around us, making it truly seem like it was just Myuna and me locked in a duel to the death.

Myuna flipped the ray of light around her arm, its point now forming a spear that jabbed at my face. Braza's power blew away from my body when I leaned to the side, feeling the sear of intense light so close to my skin. When I whipped a set of sharp shadow tendrils toward the goddess's exposed arm, they dissipated into nothing moments from contact. Braza cursed in my head. *"Her power is a counter to mine. Try using Flame."*

I flowed into the first form of a fighting style that'd barely seen the light of Earth. When Myuna jabbed for my heart, I deflected her light and shoved with my shield, following through with Flame to cut a jagged line into her forearm.

To my horror, her skin split open in bloodless, hanging chunks, as if she were made of papier-mâché. I caught a glimpse of her hollow, black insides before the rip closed on its own, the skin flowing back together in moments. There was no sign I'd hurt her at all, not even a grunt of pain.

"Do you see now what it is to face a goddess?" Though

she'd pitched her voice to whisper, it still boomed over me. She grabbed her spear in both hands and drove it downward toward my skull. With the sear of light so intense, I barely gathered enough shadows to move sideways and reappear a few feet from the impact of her impossible weapon.

She checked the momentum and swung to the side, hitting me against the shoulder. My robe took some of the blow, but white-hot agony burnt and crisped my skin underneath it.

My hold on my men's powers wavered when I needed them most. Phaeron's fighting techniques slipped from my fingertips, leaving his weapon feeling awkward in my hand. *"Focus, my love,"* he said over our mating circle. A moment later, he pressed the lost knowledge back into my head.

"Keep moving," Braza urged. There was no way to easily paint a healing rune on myself, given the location of the wound.

I took to the shadows before Myuna could try to skewer me again, regrouping up on the dais. God, it stank up here, like fear, piss, and rot all smeared in a ghastly mix.

"We just need to disarm her. That spear is too intense," I said, hoping she'd get angry when she saw me standing so close to her throne. Her legs had left indents in the tile and metal from sitting there for so long.

In one way, I was lucky. Myuna was uncertain of where I was for a moment, her white eyes roving points through the Void mist. When she spotted me, she hurled her weapon at me, and it disappeared in a burst of sunlight when I ducked aside.

"What is the meaning of this Void magic?" she boomed.

I groaned in a mix of agony and dismay when she held her arm toward the sky and a new shaft of light began to form in her palm. She swept it in an arc, clearing away some of the mist that'd been creeping in to surround her. Through the cold gray buffet, she approached me with her hand still raised, the weapon in her hand sputtering in and out of existence.

That was it. She couldn't get unfiltered light with the interference of other magics. "Phaeron!" I screamed, unknowing of how he was doing in the fight below. He read my intentions and responded immediately, creating a thick cloud of black shadow to blot out the encroaching sun.

The only light in the chamber now was from Myuna herself, her sickly white radiance doubling in intensity when the sunlight faded from her hand completely. She clenched her fist with a furious bellow. "If you insist on interfering, then I will have every head in this room in addition to hers," she announced.

Her body warped, arms stretching out of their sockets first. She became longer, thinner, a towering eldritch horror with sharp talons of light erupting from her fingertips. Black slits opened in her torso, over her arms and legs and even her forehead and cheeks. Mouths. Countless sucking mouths.

"Oh god, oh shit," I said under my breath. I lunged forward and dove into the shadows, emerging inches from her grasping hand as it tried to close around the nearest ally—a doctor helping a badly burned guardian witch. They stood back at what they'd thought was a safe distance before she proved that whatever she was made of was stretchy enough for her to reach anywhere in this chamber.

Her hand bounced off my shield, which rang with a discordant note. I slammed into the doctor and rolled off him, cracking my head against the floor. With a groan, my gargoyle-enhanced endurance fled, and my body erupted with pain all over.

I looked over in dismay at Geo's crystal shield where it'd landed a yard away. It vibrated intensely enough to spread a web of cracks through the inside of it. If I was lucky, it could take one more blow before it shattered into crystal confetti. But first...I reached for Geo across the mating circle and felt him meet me halfway with the endurance I lost.

Bolstered by him, I stood and felt a shiver wrack my figure. It was *so* cold all of a sudden, turning my sweat to ice against my skin. Auric stood behind the wall of our fighters, which I'd crossed violently with Myuna's slap. His brow was knitted with concentration, his mouth forming whispers only heard by the Void. The densest gray and blue mist unspooled from his hands as he seemed to will it into existence, plucking it from beyond.

His one good eye met mine, and the mist parted for him so I could read his lips. *Bring her over here.*

In the freezing presence of the Void, only the burn on my shoulder remained a throbbing, angry patch. It twinged as I raised Flame and took up a guard stance. Myuna lumbered toward me even now, her massive body seeming slower than it was. She lashed out a hand to grab me, and I stepped aside, only to spear her hand into the ground with Flame as the stake.

She howled in fury and pain, shaking the whole complex. A chunk of metal fell from the ceiling, landing amidst my allies with a deafening crunch. I didn't have time to worry if everyone was all right—she leapt and snapped her stretchy body to rubber band to the location where her hand was pinned. She grabbed me with her free hand.

Hopefully Auric could deploy that trap fast, as the

sucking mouths along her body were dangerously close to everyone else. Myuna loomed over me, black mouth gaped in a victorious smirk. Her booming voice shook me further as I gasped for air in her crushing grip. "You see now that you cannot win." Black spots crowded the edges of my vision when first Geo's magic slipped from my grasp, then Phaeron's and Ben's.

The shield slipped out of my nerveless fingers, shattering with the delicate tinkling of small pieces of glass. I *did* see the nothingness of the Void enveloping us both in its freezing embrace, the gray and blue mist condensing into a bubble over her head. She was too busy gloating over her impending victory to notice the precise moment we slipped into the space between worlds.

"No prophecy can spell the ending of a goddess such as I." Without the acoustics of an audience chamber, her many voices rang hollow. "How foolish I was...to believe..."

My vision was fading. I gasped for air, and painful prickles coursed over my skin head to toe as I just couldn't find any to fill my lungs. Myuna squeezed me instinctively now as she turned her gaze to the Void, a dark nothingness in all directions.

"This cannot be!" she thundered.

In one last act of defiance, Braza spoke to her, mind to mind. *"Soon you will know only the rot of Soiluire, and I hope you choke on it."*

Her pale irises refocused on me, the prize she crushed in one hand. "You insolent—no. I shall know the taste of you *first.*"

Myuna lifted me, and I fell face-first into her mouth's pit.

41

PHAERON

Familiar shadowborn rage coursed through my body as Myuna's minions rushed us. Eleven supernaturals, all possessing strong magic or powerful, enchanted weapons. And the last of the dozen... I fixed my gaze on the dragon shifter that'd tried to incinerate my mate.

And on Roe as she recklessly ran ahead of our defensive line to punch said dragon in the face. I swore under my breath and burst into shadows, racing after her. With Cress occupying Myuna's attention, it was my duty to nullify the second-worst threat here.

The dragon raised a taloned foot to crush Roe, flinching at the last minute as my shadowy claws punched through the scales over his sole and loosed streams of blood. While fire dragons ran hot, his blood shouldn't have steamed as much as it had under normal circumstances.

Insane chatters of laughter accompanied the Void's chilling touch. Its mist surrounded me gleefully, frosting the dragon blood I flicked off my shadows as I regrouped next to Roe.

"Defensive magic, now," I ordered her. All we'd done

was annoy the massive shifter, who, to our luck, was moving much slower than he should, dragging under Myuna's control.

"Got it," she said. Luckily, there was plenty of debris lying around that answered to the magic of a guardian witch. She cobbled together a wall of cement, rocks, and tiles.

Our opponent turned one blazing eye my way, sucking in a deep breath to feed the inferno at the back of his throat. I disappeared into shadows when he was already breathing out, to keep the gout of fire away from Roe.

Reappearing by his hindquarters, I lashed solid shadows into knotted ropes between his legs and tail. "Hey, ugly!" Roe shouted, accompanied by the sound of rocks cracking against scales. *Fuck.* The bold female had a death wish.

And I was acting on Cress's wishes too much, trying to ensnare the shifter to lead him into a moment of weakness, to save him and his soul. She'd taken much of my sword skills, and it seemed I'd gained her empathy. A dangerous emotion, given the stakes. I should've shoved my sword through his skull and been done with it.

Instead, I ripped my weapon through the wing membrane looming nearby, which flared with his shift of attention. I accompanied it with a shadowborn's roar of challenge, hoping he would realize Roe was not the opponent worth his flames. He swung his head on his long neck, lifting his wings and looking at me over his shoulder.

That's right. Come this way.

I shifted my stance, suddenly more confident with the sword in my hand. Cress had lost the skills she'd borrowed from me, which created a ripple over our circle and mating bond. I closed my eyes for a critical moment. *"Focus, my love,*" I encouraged, sending her back what she needed from me.

A solid force slammed into my waist. I was thrown several yards from the impact, only seeing the dragon's turned hindquarters and the tail he'd struck me with. I cushioned my landing with shadows, skidding to a stop and making an exaggerated groan to tickle his prey sense.

Light exploded in the chamber, filtering through the gloom of mist starting to surround Myuna. Someone screamed, though it echoed a hundred times with the rest of the voices the Void wanted us to hear. Still lying on the ground, my gaze flashed to the dais, where Cress crouched behind the crystal shield, her face turned to the ceiling.

"What is the meaning of this Void magic?" the goddess boomed, swatting the mist aside. I bared my fangs. As powerful as she was, she couldn't do much more than hold Auric's magic at bay. The Void had never answered to her command.

She was gathering rays of light, her hand held in that direction. "Phaeron!" Cress screamed, reaching out to our mating bond. She needed my darkness, and I gave her nighttime, reaching upward too and blasting all the shadows over my form and every ounce of magic I could muster to block out the sun and cut off Myuna from its power.

The goddess's furious bellow resonated with ghostly laughter. "If you insist on interfering, then I will have every head in this room in addition to hers," Myuna thundered.

I was sure she would turn her wrath on me and hissed, welcoming it. The dragon was in motion again, lunging at me, a crimson blur with a snapping, ember-filled mouth. With my power occupied helping Cress, I didn't dare try to dive into the shadows to avoid him.

I rolled to my feet and leapt, sinking my claws into his scaled neck and climbing. He tripped from the snare I'd tied through his back legs, his bulk going down. The jarring impact of his body hitting the ground nearly unseated me, but I remained clinging on his neck.

"Are you okay?" Roe shouted.

"Fine! Hold his head if you can," I called back. I searched him frantically with soul sight, locating the aura of his soul between his shoulder blades, where his wings met prominent flight muscles clothed in platelike scales. It did not encompass his whole body, remaining the same size as it would be if he were in his human form.

I dove for it as he started to stand. There was an abrupt jerk of his head and neck; Roe's grunt of effort was eclipsed by the sound of flame igniting. I had moments before he incinerated her and so I hooked my claws into his soul and heaved for all I was worth. It didn't want to come free, emerging nearly torn from my efforts.

When I had his knotted soul between my hands, he slumped to the ground, drooling burning liquid. I tisked under my breath as I got a good look at it. No wonder it'd been a challenge to remove. Myuna had tied it into two knots, a sign he hadn't gone to her control easily.

My hands were shaking. It was cold, bitterly so. The Void's presence made it nearly impossible to untie both knots, and it took all my focus to do so for a few crucial moments.

Cress's alarm and pain tore through me. I gasped for air, dropping the soul back into its body.

Myuna had my mate in her hand, crushing her with overlong fingers. The Void swirled around them both, forming a dense bubble of blue-tinged mist that closed into a cage while the goddess gloated.

And then they disappeared together.

My mating bond intensified with agony, urgency, and distance all at once, a shrill tone at the back of my head. Sunlight returned to the chamber as I ripped my power back, appearing where Myuna had stood and pulling Flame from the ground.

There were a few torchbearers still standing. They'd gone limp without Myuna's presence, staring around at us with blank white eyes.

I took my shadowborn form and let my shadows hold my swords. With one leap, I was before Auric. I grabbed the front of his suit, dragging his stout body up so we were face-to-face. "Send me after her," I snarled.

"It's too la—"

"Right now!" I shouted at him.

"She's already halfway to—"

Pain flooded down my back, and my fingers clenched, tearing his clothes. He slipped out of my grip as I bent over, breathing heavily.

Cress!

My bonds to her pulled taut. Energy flowed from me into the endless nothing, a tether of pure life force. Something—*Myuna*—guzzled the power greedily on the other side.

"If you've ever valued our friendship," I rasped, "you will open the way."

Figures crowded us. "I'm going with you," Geo rumbled.

Ben helped support me upright. His face was dangerously wan, but his tone brooked no argument. "Me too."

Instead of wasting his breath, Auric drew the Void's presence back. Cold mist enveloped his fingers, and it was the work of moments to open a rip in reality and expand its yawning black mouth wide enough to fit us one at a time. "I will leave you in the Void if there's any sign of Myuna returning here," he said, deadly serious.

"Fine," I said. I flexed my hands, and my magic retracted, placing my sword hilts in my palms.

Auric shouldered between the rip and me. "I will reverse part of the spell so you can find her."

"I'll find her. No one should follow, though," I growled. He nodded and stepped aside for Geo, Ben, and me.

On the other side, the rip was an oval of brightness in a world of encroaching cold and nothingness. "Whoa," Ben murmured, bending to try to touch a ground that wasn't there.

"Stop fucking around. Follow me, and stay close," I snapped, following the call of my mating bond. Ben recoiled, shocked, but did as I said.

I'd be able to find Cress even in the endlessness of the Void. Nothing, not even the whisper of voices and visions, would stop my forward charge.

I didn't dare disappear into shadows to move faster, considering the other pieces of Cress's heart ran to keep pace behind me. Without me, they'd be lost here in minutes and then reduced to laughing echoes. If one of us died, we'd all haunt the Void for eternity.

Instead, I spread my magic, forming a shadowy bubble of relative safety from the Void's madness. The visions and whispers were held at bay from its radius. As long as Ben and Geo didn't listen too closely or stray to chase a vision, we stood a chance of making it to Cress in time.

"What is this place?" It was Roe's voice. I flinched at the sound and glanced over my shoulder. It was the real her. She'd retracted her crystal armor into its pendant and sprinted to join us alongside Wren and Áine.

My blood ran as hot as liquid flame. "You should not be here," I said harshly. "I thought I made it clear that *no one should've followed us!*"

Roe puffed along, shrugging off my anger. "Cress is my coven mate, and I wasn't about to leave her behind...no matter where the hell we are." She had a chipper enough tone, like a run through the Void was a Saturday morning jog and not a dip into a location of near-guaranteed insanity and death.

"Don't worry." Wren's voice was a lot more labored. "The blue dude cut everyone else off. It's just us."

I grunted. It was the least he could do after banishing my mate to the Void with the likes of Myuna. If we survived this, he'd be lucky if I didn't gut and fillet him for the oversight.

And if we didn't...

"*Phaeron,*" called a voice from the Void. I didn't turn my gaze, knowing an apparition would be there to try to tempt me from my path.

"*Come back to bed.*" A whisper of Soilurian from a long-lost lover.

A couple of my companions startled and made confused sounds. "Ignore everything you see and hear. It's all fake," I advised over one shoulder.

Easier said than done sometimes. I saw a small figure at the edge of my vision, a gray-skinned boy. His orange eyes glowed in the darkness, and he waved for my attention. He was a smiling, happy kid dressed in human clothes. Gritting my teeth, I turned away from him. As much as I desired a family, he was only a manifestation the Void thought would distract me.

Nothing would prevent me from getting to my mate, though. I felt the currents of magic around us shifting and Cress's presence coming toward us as Auric reversed his spell, as promised. She was no longer halfway to Soiluire, where she'd perish long before we'd manage to find her. In fact, we were drawing close enough to hear the echoes of distortion from what had to be Myuna's voice.

My pace faltered, and I nearly tripped to fall into nothingness. Between the numbness brought on by the cold and the suction of magic and life force, I was fading faster than expected. Geo and Ben had to be faring similarly...but we would limp to Myuna if we had to. She could not have the considerable power of our mating circle, plus the half of Braza's soul Cress carried.

Still, we slowed, and there was some relief between Ben, who *was* limping, and Wren, whose breath sawed as she clutched her side. I strode unerringly toward the glow of white light marking the first landmark in this place of nothing.

Myuna was thrashing around, occasionally screaming in her chorus of agony shriek. At first, I thought it was from a Void feeding frenzy, but her belly bulged and roiled, jerking her hollow body around as if she were a ragdoll.

It looked excruciating. I grinned, finally speeding ahead of the group when the rest of the way forward was obvious. My boot met her shoulder, knocking her prone on her back. "Indigestion?" I sneered.

My mating bond tugged straight downward, toward her stomach. Cress was in there, fighting back. Before Myuna could consume me next, I drew one of my swords down her middle, splitting open the gaping blackness within her.

From the nightmare of her guts, human fingers emerged. I grabbed my mate's hand to lift her free, gasping in shock when I got a good look at the light blazing from her.

CRESS

Myuna's guts were like a portal to another world. Braza and I fell and fell and fell like we were on our way to some kind of twisted Wonderland.

"Good going, getting us eaten," I thought to her irritably. Without the crushing grip of the oversized goddess, I'd begun to breathe again and consider whether it'd be possible to condense into shadows to escape from between Myuna's lips.

But Braza was not responsive, nor were her shadowy powers. I was leaking a trail of black and purple and began to fear the worst when I saw it. Was it Braza's lifeblood? Were both of us already dead and I hadn't felt it?

Eventually, I landed face down on a soft heap, and intense pain ricocheted through me. *Fuck, definitely not dead yet.* I hurt all over, especially over my burned shoulder. My clothes fell right off me when I moved my arms to lift up to my knees. That expensive robe, reinforced with magic, disintegrated into threads before my eyes.

My naked skin blistered and reddened, and it was excruciating to experience. I'd taken an acid bath some-where on the way down—Myuna was *digesting* me. "Well," I said from a raw throat. "Hell of a way to go." I took heart in knowing Myuna would die eventually, starving to death on the planet she'd already destroyed. My sacrifice wouldn't be in vain.

But my *men*. When I died, so would they. I wished I knew how to sever the mating circle so I could do it here and now. If only they could keep going, to escape Cerris City and enjoy a blissful, Myuna-free life.

Phaeron wouldn't go on without me even if I figured out how to save him, though. I felt him like he was still with me, the mating mark on my shoulder pulsing with flashes of hot and cold prickles.

Maybe someday, someone would discover the dragon scale he carried with the other half of Braza's soul. She could live on... I mean, I didn't know for sure about that. Could half a soul as big as a powercore continue to exist without the other half? It was an unheard-of situation. She'd be the first and only one to attempt it.

Shadows sputtered around me, lacing into two thin wraps for my breasts and hips when I gestured. *"Braza?"* I projected hopefully.

"Cress," she answered. Her voice was faint. *"Touch the souls."*

What? There was nothing here but us. I looked up first, seeing the white-lined layer of Myuna's stomach. Then down...ugh. What did I think I'd landed on? Those were... souls, I guess. Parts of them, sucked dry of everything except for a paper-thin layer.

There were heaps of souls everywhere I looked, mountains of the remains of the dead who'd passed the same way I was about to. My gorge rose, and I gagged, swallowing down the taste of vomit before it could burn my throat any worse.

Fuck, that's disgusting. Still, I did as Braza commanded, putting my palms down beside my knees. The ribbons of her leaking magic reversed course, flowing downward and out like a wave.

The nearest souls twitched. Each caught a spark of magic from Braza, and their colors quickly shifted from black and purple to skin tones. Souls inflated with new purpose, glowing from within and erasing major features with an internal shine.

These husks turned into souls once more. *Ghosts.* Hundreds, then thousands, and then more, all of the damned turning eyes limned with light toward me, the only one still alive amongst us.

"Um, hi," I said to the nearest person, a human man who must've died quite recently. He stared at me without any comprehension. Most of those around us were tall and horned, similarly blank, but further back in the crowd were smaller, furry shapes and others with scales and spiky fins. Just how many worlds' worth of different people had Myuna consumed?

"Make way," said a female voice. She spoke in Soiluirian, but some vestige of Braza translated her words. "That is my daughter! Make way!"

The souls murmured, a sound like a distant crowd, but parted for the liveliest one. A glowing gray figure pushed her way to me, her red eyes like liquid rubies. "Brazita...no. You are not her."

Keshora et Sudaira's kindly face fell with disappointment. Something broke between Braza and me in that moment, and she flowed free of me, standing beside me in shades of black and purple. "It's me," she answered.

By some miracle, I understood, and tears pricked my eyes when both souls crashed together for a strong hug.

A third figure piled into their embrace with a girlish laugh. "Braza!" Ravai exclaimed, her voice high, on the cusp of breaking to the deeper tones of adulthood.

"Ravai! Wait, how are you here?" Braza asked. She

looped an arm around her sister, holding both of her lost family members close.

For a moment, Ravai looked baffled by the question. "I... oh. Uncle took my soul and carried it to the goddess to eat." She looked around at the silent audience of souls, blinking twice. "I guess I've been here ever since."

My heart broke for her and everyone else who'd formed mountains of husks within Myuna's stomach. There had to be billions of victims here. The foundation under my feet was shifting as more and more souls stood back up, briefly reanimated to bear witness to this reunion and my eventual death. *Think, Cress.* There had to be a way to escape.

"She's been using your power as her own," I said, mostly to myself. Thousands of eyes blinked. Ah, shit. Most of them were from Soiluire and had never seen a human in their lives. I tested the thread of connection between Braza and me and tried to repeat myself in their language.

Keshora was the one to answer. "That's right. I watched for an age as more and more of my people came here before the true end came..."

Cutting herself off, she released Braza and stepped toward me. Her pupils narrowed as she lowered toward my shoulder, inspecting the mark there. "You have mated my male. Who are you?" she asked suspiciously.

"Oh...ha haaa," I stammered. Maybe Myuna's stomach acid didn't have to kill me. Keshora, for all that I was promised that she was nice and gentle, looked ready to tear my throat out.

Braza put her hand on her arm. "Mother, please," she coaxed. "You have been dead quite some time. This is Cress, his new mate from the world we traveled to."

"It's nice to meet you. I've heard...well, I haven't heard much," I said, apparently deciding to put my foot further down my mouth. "Braza speaks well of you. And Phaeron had a very difficult time overcoming your death."

Keshora's eyes gained facets as she made a sound of pain deep in her throat. A set of hands seized mine, feeling as soft and pliable as jelly. "What about me?" Ravai blurted. "How is he? I've missed him so much!"

"He's..." I didn't know how to answer her questions, considering my impending death.

"Take a look at her soul," Braza whispered to their mother in the meantime.

I squeezed Ravai's hands. She had infectious energy, and I wished I had more time to get to know her. "Your death is something he still can't bring himself to talk about. I think he's missed you just as much as you've missed him."

It seemed I was here just to cause his old family pain, as she made the same dimensional noise I associated with their way of crying. She pulled me into a hug while she wailed. "I'm sorry," I said, squeezing her tight.

"Thank you for bringing him comfort. And for being a good friend to my sister." She glanced toward them. "She wouldn't speak up for just anyone."

At this point, Keshora and Braza were deep in conversation. It seemed the older dimensional was relaxing, at least, listening and nodding as Braza fell into the tones of explaining something as quickly as possible.

When she was done, Keshora breathed out slowly and squared her shoulders. She turned to me. "You are still alive," she stated. "Your soul is made of light, just like the creature I once revered as a goddess. For the ages I have rotted here, she has used up every bit of what made me who I was. I had no choice in this because there wasn't a choice."

She stepped forward, putting her clawed hand over my

marked shoulder. "But now there is one, and I choose you." When nothing happened and we just blinked at each other, she put pressure on my skin. "You may be a strange being yourself and not a goddess, but you may use what is left of me all the same. Make me anew in your light."

The spark within her dimmed a fraction, while I started giving off a hint of a glow. I glanced down at myself with a gasp.

"Oh, me too!" Ravai exclaimed, putting her hand on my other shoulder. "Make me anew in your light!"

Another soul's hand landed on Keshora's shoulder, and she flinched. But power flowed from her into me. Yet another soul joined him, and then a dozen more, and then a hundred, a chain reaction spreading through the lost souls as they gave me what they could in the name of salvation.

I filled from within with light, growing stronger and stretching the limits of my magic to find it a well filling itself with pure power. These people gladly fed me what they could. It wasn't that they knew me, but as a unit, they decided I was better than Myuna and worthier than the monster that'd originally consumed them.

I became strong enough that my skin healed of its burns and blisters. "We have to get out of here. And the only way out...is through," I said, pointing at the wall of Myuna's stomach. The chain of souls moved with me, all of us beginning to hammer at her from within. The material of her skin stretched and morphed around our fists like wet clay.

A force slapped the other side of her belly, sending me tumbling backward, and many others went flying. That must've been her hand. So, she felt us in here. I hoped it was painful to have a roiling sea of spirits hitting every wall of her stomach. The Iorsio tribe souls even took flight and slammed into the sloping roof of this inner chamber.

A terrible, distorted noise vibrated her skin. She must've been saying something, but for once, those she'd damned did not scream out through her mouth, but hit her with more ferocity than ever.

The only thing that stopped us momentarily was when the whole chamber rolled. Myuna must've flopped onto her belly, as she pitched all of us forward. The spirits weighed no more than a feather each, but I still felt crushed by the sheer number of them until they started regrouping and hitting her again.

Soon she was rolling around constantly, churning us in a whirlpool. Many spirits brushed past me, only adding their magic to mine in the process. I caught glimpses of more alien souls than I ever thought existed, nameless creatures of races long snuffed out by Myuna. Their power and sorrow filled my magic to overflowing.

There was no pain when I was flung into one of her stomach's walls anymore. The material was bound to tear eventually under our onslaught. Legions of souls rose to join us, stretching the limits of her insides in our revolt.

My marked shoulder itched intensely. I felt Phaeron when I touched it... He was close? But that was impossible. Auric would've sealed the way behind Myuna, not risking any chance of her returning.

With our next onslaught, I had the sensation of movement. We could've been curving Myuna's spine or tugging her around or...I don't know. There was nothing to see in here but the countless furious spirits now given the freedom to do something against their murderer. All I could tell for sure was that she was *definitely* screaming.

We were flung one more time. I got up and launched myself at her again, just to see the tip of something sharp breach the top of this chamber and drag down. There was a sheen of darkness between us and...more darkness beyond. But a pulse of urgency in my chest had me reaching through the darkness for the spray of cold beyond the humid depths of Myuna's guts.

A leather-clad hand wrapped around my own and pulled. I drew in a breath of chill Void air and met Phaeron's gaze. He was in full shadowborn form, practically vibrating with the fury that came along with it. The sudden surge of my mating circle's heightened emotions hit me like a punch to the gut.

They were all here, and a few of my friends besides, all gaping at me as I emerged like the sun, fully naked and blazing with light from within.

42

CRESS

Souls fled out from behind me, a gilded flood of them. One, darker than the rest, kept to my side. It was a relief to see Braza, even though it was strange that she and I were only tethered by the merest thread. She reached into Phaeron's shadows while he stared at me in disbelief, retrieving the dragon scale and diving back into Myuna's torn belly without him seeming to notice.

"How dare you. She was delicious," the goddess grumbled. She probed at the slash across her midsection, pushing the flaps of skin together, but they did not sew into a seamless whole like the last time I'd wounded her. Souls held the wound open, and thousands of them escaped by the second, flowing into my body. I felt their presence like a pressure within, my form stretching to accommodate so many different pieces of others and the power they wished to lend me.

Finally, Phaeron gathered his wits. "Cress, are you all right?"

"I think so." I had the voice echo now, the power of

thousands or more coming through me. "You might want to step back."

He hesitated before turning to Roe and the others, herding them with shadows and gestures. I flexed my hand, willing my new power to give me a sword to match my new stature. A hundred souls surrendered part of their energy for me to have one form for me, the hilt perfectly matching my enlarged hand. The blade was made of pure celestial magic, glowing golden.

Myuna stumbled to her feet and gathered her own magic, creating the shaft of a white-glowing spear and flipping its blade up. She straightened with a wince. "You have...stolen from me. It is no matter. We will still end it here, in these moments past the prophecy. You defeated me..." She coughed up a dribble of black tar, smearing it across her white cheek. "And now I will defeat you."

All the while, the flood of souls from her stomach did not abate. As I grew, she diminished, my light dwarfing hers. "Big words. Let's go," I said, lunging at her. Our weapons caught and rebounded. She stumbled backward, wailing in earnest and stirring up the Void to scream with her.

I clenched my teeth and tried to block out the awful cacophony. Amidst the wailing were voices I recognized. Roe called my name in desperation, and I pivoted, only seeing darkness from where the shout originated. The Void wasn't going to watch this battle quietly, it seemed.

I struck out at her again, opening a wound in her side that closed itself quickly. Now it was obvious she drew on the life force of those within her to mend so fast or to strike so hard. A dozen souls had to give up their power to help me heal just as swiftly when the next thrust of her spear jabbed its point through my thigh.

Our gazes met. We were of the same size now, meeting somewhere in the middle of her impossible stature and my ordinary human frame. There was a new emotion there, something I don't think Myuna had felt for a long time.

Fear.

She attacked in a flurry of blows, all the while stoking burning rays of light from the holes of several mouths that formed on her torso and arms. Inspired by her changing it up, I summoned a ball of concentrated light and threw it at her, shaking the Void with the resulting explosion and knocking Myuna off her feet.

The Void echoed the explosion with a set of gleeful cackles.

"Ka*bewm*," I whispered for my handbook, which was hopefully flying in distressed circles somewhere on Earth, awaiting my safe return.

I swung my sword downward, intending to lop off her head. But it was still me, and I wasn't borrowing anyone else's sword skills. The blade dug into her back and shoulder blades, creating a cut that seared itself open with blackened edges. The dark matter that seemed to hold her together internally was exposed.

"No," Myuna groaned, lifting up and grabbing a huge handful of glowing souls that'd escaped when she hit the ground. She ate them again, struggling to swallow with several painful gulps as their fists made round outlines against her throat.

I kicked her weapon out of her hand, and it disappeared into wisps of light. Holding the tip of my sword to her neck, I echoed her with a smirk. "Do you see what it is to face a goddess?"

Her lips spread across her gaping mouth in a grimace.

"You are no goddess," she thundered in her loud but diminished voice.

"I'm starting to realize that you never were one to begin with," I replied, lifting my weapon for one last strike to end this.

"You are no goddess," the Void trumpeted.

Myuna launched herself at me, her mouth stretching even wider and sucking hard. I felt an obscene tug on the souls within me as she knocked us both to the ground. We grappled, her punching, me trying to stab her, and rolled a couple times before something lassoed her around the neck and dug in with ebon hooks.

It looked like shadows and vines braided into one massive rope. At the other end heaved Phaeron and Áine, plus Ben, Geo, Roe, and Wren anchoring behind them. But further back, feeding shadows to make the rope as sturdy as possible, was a team of horned spirits.

I pushed Myuna and watched with a grin as the vines grew new tendrils to encircle her neck completely, with shadows following their path to reinforce them. She gripped the rope with both hands, gasping and thrashing, still leaking more and more spirits. For once, she was quiet, and my ears rang as I stood over her with sword in hand, wondering where to stab her to truly end her awful existence once and for all.

"You are no goddess," the Void echoed again, quieter this time.

"Shut up," I muttered, my brow drawn in concentration.

I opted for the heart, thrusting my sword downward clear through her chest. With one last jerk, she went limp, save for the flaps of her stomach, where her victims continued to escape. I gazed down at her still face. "It's over," I said with the relief of a destroyed world's worth of souls.

The rope around her neck faded, the vines withering away to brittle stalks in an instant. I was reaching down to tear her belly open further when her body flared with white light. A white figure emerged and lifted up, floating inches above the corpse.

I jumped backward and faced it, sword raised. It looked like a soul and perhaps Myuna as her original race, a spiky-finned creature with a mouthful of razor teeth. Her clawed hands darted out, catching my wrists.

"It is the turning of an eon. You are worthy where I no longer am," she said, putting something in my palm.

It was massive and white, pulsing with power and a slimy feeling. *Hunger.* It looked like she'd shoved her heart, stabbed straight through the center, in my hand. It was fleshy and ribbed with swollen veins and, impossibly, still beat outside of its body. Ichor slowly dribbled from its underside in a slimy trail.

"When I cut out Stalvos the White's heart at the end of my own world's destruction, he gave me this. A mature seed of power." Myuna's soul still spoke all languages simultaneously, but her voice was garbled by the flaring gills along her neck.

The Void played out the scene as she narrated it. A different pair stood next to us. A male creature rendered in white, offering this same heart to a living Myuna, who was covered in fish scales that glimmered teal and green. Her battle armor was covered in greasy white blood, and her alien spear dripped with it.

"*I accept,*" her apparition said, swallowing the heart in one bite.

In a blink, the memory was gone. Myuna's soul said, "It

is yours. *You* are the goddess now, the one to own all the power in the universe. The souls you need are already within you. Consume them and rise."

Some evil power in the heart called to me, whispering to do it. To swallow it and ascend, to become the next reaper of worlds. I could still return to Earth and finish what she'd started.

The many souls within me clamored, screaming, their terror filling my every pore. I jolted and shook my head sharply, my stomach turning with disgust.

"Power...so delicious. It is the way of things," she whispered, leaning forward with anticipation when I lifted the heart.

I stared at it, astonished that I'd been tempted for a moment. How insane, to willingly become a soul-eating monster for power.

"Myuna," I stated. I met her bulging fish eyes to watch her reaction when I filled my palm with light, pure and searing, and coated the seed in a white-hot bath of magic. It crumpled to dust, drifting into fine particles the Void absorbed. "The answer is *no*. Go to hell, where you belong!"

The white apparition's mouth dropped open, despair clearly etched over her alien features. She released the opening strains of a scream of denial before the Void ripped her apart with tendrils of gray magic, dragging her back toward her corpse for a feast that would only leave her voice and memories behind to haunt its depths forever.

I breathed out with relief to see her dead for good, then looked down at myself and wondered, *What now?* Because I was full of unknown magic and half again as tall as I usually was. The internal glow hid my nakedness at least, as it did for the souls now climbing out of Myuna's husk and standing in a clump whispering and looking around.

I walked over to my friends and mates, feeling like I was lumbering with my change in stature.

"That. Was. Amazing!" Wren declared loudly, clapping with each word. "I got it all on film, don't you worry. The whole supernatural world is going to know about this!"

A smile split my lips out of sheer disbelief that she'd been filming the fight. "There's no internet in the Void, Wren. There's no way you streamed any of it," Ben corrected.

She fixed him with an impatient look. "I *recorded* it. Now we have video evidence that Myuna is, like, majorly dead, so we can get out of godforsaken Cerris City."

"Good thinking," I said, wincing at the boom of my own voice. "Um, I need to be de-goddessed now."

Pretty much everyone turned to Phaeron. He'd released his shadowborn form and was talking quietly with a Moihan tribe male until he felt our attention on him. "How exactly did this happen?" he asked, gesturing up at my face.

"Well, you see...I think Braza's energy gave the souls left within—"

Phaeron's eyes dilated, and he whipped his head around. "Where's Braza?" he demanded.

"The last I saw her, she—oh shit." I turned toward Myuna's corpse. "She was grabbing the other half of her soul from you and diving back inside Myuna."

In a blink, he was next to the corpse, pulling open the rip in her belly and sticking his head in to look inside. He released a muffled howl and fished in her stomach, removing something and turning to show me when I loomed behind him. It was the dragon scale...cracked into two uneven pieces. The runes on it flickered with the last vestiges of energy.

"There's almost nothing left," he said, looking at me with new realization. "All of the energy she gathered as a powercore went to awakening the souls of Myuna's victims."

A bolt of dread thrilled through me. This couldn't be. She was an ancient powercore, the venerated protector of Moongrove Library. And the other half of her soul was tethered to me...a shiny little thread still connecting us to my awareness. Yet I had no idea where she was.

"I-I'll just give some of the magic back to her. T-that's possible, right?" I stammered, reaching for the broken scale.

He jerked away from me, his breath growing shallow. We were both panicking, feeding into a feedback loop that was no good for either of us.

Geo inserted his steadiness between us, both physically and emotionally. That loop of negative emotion broke upon his stone form, even as he laid an obsidian palm on Phaeron's shoulder and my arm. "Braza is a being of shadow, and right now, you are glowing like the sun," he rumbled. "Undo this magic, and perhaps she will show herself."

"Well said," Phaeron sighed, scrubbing at his face. "All right, Cress. Try again to tell me how you became like this."

I did, leaving no detail out, not even flinching away from the fact that it was his deceased mate that kicked off the whole change that had led us all to freedom.

"Make me anew in your light," he repeated slowly. "No..." He switched to Soiluirian, which I didn't understand without Braza's presence. "Clearly, you must release all these souls that have bound their last vestiges to you. But we are still in the Void. What will become of them afterward?"

The spirit he'd been talking to stepped forward again, asking Phaeron a question. They spoke for a minute while I shifted with nerves. "My father claims to sense the way forward to the next life," he eventually translated.

My jaw dropped. He was being really casual about having his father right there. But they were both standing rigidly, avoiding eye contact. It had to be a matter of pride at this point. "So, once I release these souls, they will be able to go too?" I asked.

Phaeron wore a troubled frown as he considered. "In theory. It would be for the best to release them and have them try, at least, my bright mate. It is not right for you to hold on to them for much longer."

I completely agreed. So, I took part of his knowledge of Soiluirian along the mating circle and repeated the phrase he guessed would do the trick. "I have made you anew in my light, and now I release you from your vow."

The pressure within my body released like a deflating balloon. It was a near-immediate flood of souls, countless spirits fleeing the confines of our temporary pact. Many winked out of existence immediately, especially the older ones that'd been consumed before the fall of Soiluire.

Phaeron confirmed with his father that they'd gone on to the next life rather than been consumed by the Void. "He claims it has little power over them. Less than over us...but that may be because the Void has Myuna to feast upon for the moment. You may notice that it's gone suspiciously quiet," he said.

I hadn't noticed it'd shut up, but that was probably because I was feeling like a limp spaghetti noodle as I quickly lost the power of numbers that'd made me a "goddess." My inner glow winked out, and I slumped into his arms. Phaeron glanced down at my bare skin with brows rising, having accidentally cupped my belly. His cool shadows enveloped my modesty.

Actually, everything felt super cold all of a sudden, except for his body heat. I snuggled into him for more of it, and he snuck a gentle nip on my ear. "Glad to have you human-sized again," he murmured.

"I thought being taller than you was the best part of all of this," I sighed.

He whispered in my ear, "I'd get on my knees for you in a heartbeat." Phaeron was nuzzling into my hair when the last two souls emerged from me...Ravai and Keshora. It was only my stiffening that had him look up.

I still had that basic grasp of his language that I'd borrowed, so I understood Keshora saying, "So it is true."

And Ravai bulldozing straight past the awkwardness with a cry of, "Father!"

He gently nudged me aside and caught her when she flung herself into his arms. They spun and touched their foreheads. "My Ravita. How blessed I am to see you again," he said tenderly.

I met Geo's eye, tilting my head in suggestion. They deserved some privacy.

Keshora intercepted me before I took more than a couple steps. "Wait. Braza spoke highly of you...Cress. She's not with you?"

"I'm going to go looking for her," I said, hitching my thumb in the direction I felt our fraying tether pointing. With a nod, she fell into step with Geo and me.

It wasn't a long walk, but I kept shooting glances over my shoulder, knowing from some hazy secondhand memory that it was a death sentence to stray too far from others in the Void. Keshora kept me occupied with questions, fitting in some pieces she'd missed by dying before the Age of Decay.

She keened with pain when I told her how Braza had died and of the desperate decision made to sustain her by making her a powercore. "She sacrificed herself for us. No wonder I felt her the moment I woke... It was a fraction of her magic that revived me," she said.

My eyes filled with tears as we closed in on where Braza was and spotted her lying there. What had once been a hearty connection bolstered by her nearly endless pool of energy was nearly nothing because the half of Braza I'd carried was *literally* half of her now.

The Hungering Darkness had bisected her messily, cutting her soul from hip diagonally to her opposite shoulder. She had one wing and one arm like this. Her soul was still black and purple shadows, the jagged wound less ghastly with the details obscured. *"You came for me,"* she whispered in my mind.

"Oh my god, Braza," I said in English, sinking to my knees beside her. "I'm so sorry. I had no idea you were sacrificing *everything*."

"Would you have stopped me if I told you?"

"Yes! At least, I would've told you to save some for yourself. Anything but this." I took her hand in both of mine. Hot tears trickled down my frozen cheeks. "Let's get you back to Phaeron. He has the other half of your soul...maybe there's a chance..."

"Allow me," Geo offered, bending slowly and offering his steady arms for the task. I clued a distressed Keshora in on what we were doing, and she helped me lift Braza into his hold. He carried her while I tried to calm her mother with reassurances I wasn't sure were true.

It seemed pretty certain that Braza was fading. Her

black shadows were looking more like gray vapor, and the purple was sparsely intertwined with it.

Sensing my distress, Phaeron met us halfway with Ravai and the broken scale. Ben tagged along as well, rushing to hold me to share body warmth. After rubbing my arms, he shrugged off his shirt for me to wear. He was nearly too hot to the touch... I must've been more chilled than I realized.

"The scale is in two pieces. Could it hold both halves of her?" I asked desperately.

Phaeron tapped the larger piece of scale. Out flowed the bottom half of her, in the same drained state. Worse, actually, with her legs and tail flickering in and out of sight. "If Lucas were here..." he muttered. "She just needs some energy to stabilize her."

"Can anything be done for her?" Keshora fretted.

"It is my time. But I cannot feel the next life..." Braza whispered. She watched souls winking out of sight around us.

Phaeron answered Keshora with, "She gave away too much. All of these souls moving on around us do so with her energy. She'd need at least a spark returned. But that will deny a soul the power to move on to the next life."

Ravai gasped, exchanging a glance with her mother. "It has to be me."

"Ravita, no," Phaeron said immediately. "After everything you've been through, you deserve paradise."

"Mother, he told me he has a plan to return her to life. To living, breathing life. I could do this for her. She sacrificed so much for everyone else..." She looked past him to her, clasping her hands together.

"What's happening?" Ben whispered.

I explained the argument in English as Phaeron grew more dismayed. Keshora was nodding, moved by Ravai's plea. "There's no way for you to go to the next life if you do this," he put in.

"I'll do it," Keshora said firmly.

"There's no way for them to move on to the next life," I echoed.

The air stirred beside me in a way I was intimately familiar with by this point. My birth mother took form, and Ben gasped. I guess in the Void, all spirits were visible, as he'd never seen her before this moment. "Is the problem that they don't have someone to show them the way?" Eris asked, uncharacteristically solemn.

"It's a matter of energy, Mother," I said.

"Well, I have plenty of that." She smiled over at me, distinctly bittersweet. "It is time I moved on, dear one. I could think of no better way to go than in helping others...if they will let me." Keshora was eyeing Eris with suspicion.

Phaeron and I spoke at the same time. He invited her over to try, while I blurted, "Are you sure?"

In reply, Eris hugged me. I stepped away from Ben, letting my birth mother hold me as an adult for the first and only time. More tears leaked out of the corners of my eyes.

Eris said, "You are the core of a mating circle. I watched you defeat a goddess. Yes, I would say I fulfilled my purpose here...to help you."

"Thank you for everything, Mom," I murmured. When I let her go, she gave me one last look and nod before heading over to the ghostly dimensional family. At Phaeron's direction, she held Keshora and Ravai's hands, while they each grasped a hand attached to one of Braza's halves. They were both donating their spark back to Braza.

With a glance my way, Phaeron said, "I beseech my goddess for a miracle." He wove shadows and soul magic, feeding energy from Eris to the two dimensionals. They glowed with a new infusion of power before a portion of it passed into Braza.

Her shadows darkened considerably, but I continued to hold my breath, not feeling my connection to her grow any stronger. Phaeron blew out a tense breath and held out the two pieces of the dragon scale. Braza's bottom half went into the larger shard without trouble. He chanted a new spell and held the smaller shard toward her head.

With a wrench I felt down to my own soul, he cut the connection between us permanently, and Braza's top half turned into curls of shadows that absorbed into the smaller shard. The mark along my back burned and tingled, making an unpleasant crawling sensation.

He tilted both shards to inspect the steadily glowing runes on them. Satisfied, he lashed them together with a tendril of shadow. "It is fortunate the scale broke. I believe she will be okay," he said. His eyes shone with a mix of grief and relief as he drew in first Keshora for a hug goodbye, then Ravai. My understanding of their language disappeared, tugged away by him for a few private words to them both.

Eventually, the two spirits turned to Eris and took her hands again. Together, they faded to nothing, heading off to the next life together.

I hiccupped a sob. It hurt a lot worse than expected to say goodbye, and Phaeron echoed that feeling. Even though he'd come to peace with their deaths long ago, it was hard to have them back for such a short visit.

"Maybe you could see them again on Samhain," I suggested quietly.

With a sigh, he adjusted his swords and sat. "Perhaps." He began unlacing his boots and passed them to me.

Though they were far too big, they enveloped my icy-soled feet in much-needed warmth.

We watched the last straggling souls wink out of existence and the Void break down what was left of Myuna's corpse. Soon, it was just us, the living, and Áine came over, scuffing her hoof. "I know this was intense and all…but shouldn't we be heading back?" she asked.

Phaeron quirked his lips. "You all may as well be sitting for this news." He waited, and everyone but Geo had a seat around him. "I don't know the way back."

"What?" Roe spluttered.

"I sense my mate like a second heartbeat and led you straight to her due to that alone. But wayfinding in the Void is impossible to all but the Vess," he explained, putting his palms up in apology. "If we try to go back without assistance, we will only become hopelessly lost."

Ben scowled. "What the fuck, Big P?"

"If Auric knows what's good for him, he'll rescue us!" Phaeron shouted up at the Void's sky. "He owes us for sending Cress here in the first place."

I looked at him in astonishment. "You came after me without any guarantee you'd return?"

"To clarify, Ben, Geo, and I did." He slanted a look in my three friends' direction.

"No." Ben held up a finger. "To clarify his clarification, I did *not* know that was what I was signing up for."

Geo cracked a smile in his stone form. "I would do it again," he rumbled.

I propped my chin on my fist, shivering head to toe. "I love you all so much," I said. Ben snagged me to pull into his lap to share more body heat.

Wren rolled her eyes, warming her fingers by rubbing

her hands together. "*Please* stop there before you start kissing."

Áine and Roe exchanged a glance. "I'd do it again too. That fight was fucking awesome, and it was even cooler that you all saved so many souls," the faun said, with Roe nodding emphatically in agreement.

Some of the good cheer faded from Phaeron's face. He ran his thumb over the cracked dragon scale he still held before slipping it into his pocket. "We may as well make something of our time while we wait." He laid out on his back. The lengths of his sheathed swords sank into the Void's ground like it wasn't there.

He spoke sternly at our surroundings. "All right, Void. We've delivered you a feast today. How about you provide a boon in return for Myuna? As you will have my most dire enemy's memories and voice forever... this is the last time I shall visit you with any semblance of willingness."

Moments passed in silence before Roe asked, "What are you doing?"

"Shh." He pointed upward. "Look."

I exchanged a glance with Ben, who shrugged, and settled onto his back. I lay on top of him, observing the swirling mist far above us. It patterned the sky with tones of blue, gray, and black, rolling like a muted aurora.

Those colors became a backdrop when the Void started showing us pieces of our possible futures; whole and coherent scenes, though they were split between all of us evenly. It was a rare moment of kindness for the darkness between worlds. I began to smile, seeing happiness in each, no matter whose future it was.

"Remember, it could be ages before any of this comes true, if it ever does," Phaeron murmured. But his eyes glimmered like topazes from the last vision the Void shared, and the slow leak of grief from his side of the mating circle turned on its head so intensely that my heart felt full.

The Void showed us an apple tree covered in autumn leaves. If I wasn't looking closely, I'd have missed the trio of kids sitting on its lowest boughs.

My breath caught as I noted a few details. The girl, who was maybe nine, sat with her back to the trunk. She ate an apple slowly while thumbing through a book. Her little lopsided smile as she giggled over something she read was so familiar that I nudged Ben, and he pressed a kiss to my crown.

Meanwhile, the two boys shared the bottom branch. Geo's son was the second eldest and could've been all of seven years old, but he was a little protector already with his arm around his brother. He'd plucked a pair of apples from the next branch up and shared one. *"Here you go, Tezzy."* The dimensional boy was too young to have gotten onto the tree on his own and had his tail wrapped around the branch underneath them nervously.

It ended there, to an aggrieved sound from Geo and a softer sigh from Phaeron. "Ages? I hope it's soon," the gargoyle said. At some point, he'd shifted back to human form, and though he was frustrated at the brief vision, he wore an optimistic smile with his gaze fixed on the sky.

Me, too, I thought.

Auric showed up soon after, just as I was starting to shiver even in Ben's hold. "So *I* owe *you* hmm?" he grumbled. He and Phaeron snipped at each other in Soiluirian before the Vess opened a new rip in reality that radiated much-needed heat.

43

CRESS

It took us a week to convince the governing supernatural councils and covens of the world that Myuna was, in fact, dead and that Wren's video wasn't heavily doctored footage. But eventually, we were released from Cerris City and allowed to go back to normal life.

Whatever "normal" was.

A day after our return to New Salem, I was in a familiar office in the center of a semicircle of five chairs facing the cupid woman behind the sandy wood desk. The other chairs were filled by my men and my sister. Dr. Aurina was as flawless as ever, resplendent in a green dress that offset the candy pink of her flowing hair and the gleam of her rose gold wings.

"Rowena Ashbough sent me to represent A Little Wicked Coven in her place. She's in the Crystal Court right now, recovering with her family," I said as soon as small talk faded.

It was a bit of a white lie. Yes, Roe was in the Crystal Court, but she was preparing for her visit to the much more cutthroat Autumn Court with Áine and Ambrose. She'd texted to tell me that the changeling was more than a little disgruntled. His undersea stay as Willow had included one test of magic he'd had to fib his way out of and two assassination attempts.

The real Willow was happily ensconced in my dorm room as my unofficial roommate, though she'd soon have the room to herself. We planned to hide her comings and goings for now, until the attention on her identity as maybe-royalty faded.

For now, it was spring break, a real slap in the face after losing track of time for so long in an otherworldly situation.

"Of course. From what I hear, you're quite the celebrity," Aurina simpered. She opened a folder on her desk and shuffled paper. "But you are also a scholarship student who's missed over two months of coursework."

"Surely vanquishing an ancient eldritch goddess qualifies for an exception," I replied.

When Aurina laughed, it sounded like the tinkling of bells, high and sweet. "Oh, it does! It is so exceptional, in fact, that I don't know what to do with you and your friends except reenroll you all for a summer semester. You will still have access to your dorm room and campus services if you need to speak with anyone about your ordeal."

Through our mating circle, Phaeron made me aware of Aurina's emotional magic slowly filtering into my mind. She was projecting sympathy and kindness, but now that I was aware of it, she simply seemed tired and a little bored. As important as this meeting was for us, it was just another Tuesday for the University President.

"Thank you," I said, grateful for her generosity anyway.

Aurina nodded, picking up a pen. "Are any of your coven

mates interested in changing their major? Now would be a good time to make it official."

It was Ben who spoke up. "Yeah, I want to go into Criminal Justice."

"A bold choice, Mr. Cross," she replied, scribbling something down.

He flinched at hearing his old alias from his Garroway days. "And an opportunity to update my file would be great, too," he added.

She hummed in agreement and continued writing as I listed the other change. I was going into Occult Studies with Wren, the two of us minoring in our witcheries now. It'd be fun. My former nemesis promised to give Ben and me access to all the notes and lectures from her celestial witch classes so we could continue practicing on the sly.

"There's one more thing I was hoping you could do for my coven. This is my sister, Carly."

I rested a hand on her ghostly white arm and gave her a little squeeze. Carly turned her head with uncanny slowness to look at me. It'd taken five bottles of magical hair dye, but the bleached color of her hair was transformed into a shiny teal with only a few white highlights showing. We'd fit her with contacts to make her eyes appear blue, but she forgot to blink them still. Under the guise of scratching my cheek, I tapped the side of my lips.

Mechanically, she smiled. Ah, god, we needed to work on this. On the bad days, it seemed like she'd forgotten how to be a person.

"You may know that one of my coven mates died during the slaughter used to summon Myuna to Earth. His name was Heath Storm," I continued, turning back to Aurina with one last pat of Carly's arm. "We would like to keep his spot open to honor his death. We didn't get the opportunity to do that for Lanie Graygazer, so you would understand that it would mean a lot to us."

Aurina's pen halted for a moment. "Of course. Unfortunately, your coven leader will still receive applications for that spot until it's filled. And given your fame, the application pile will only grow."

I lifted a shoulder. Roe could handle it. "Carly will be coming to NSU in the fall. We plan on holding the spot for her."

There was a whole intricate plan for her, in fact, including forging high school graduation information for her and Lucas so they could both live on campus starting next school year. She was always a person around Lucas, who was still trying to mend the damage done to her soul despite not having the best understanding of his own magic.

Unlike everyone else twisted by Myuna's control, Carly was still an unnatural, her soul and body stained by death and corruption. Though Lucas and Phaeron had saved her from a fate worse than death by pulling the seed of entropy from her soul and destroying it, she had a long, hard road of recovery ahead.

"I don't see any problem with that." Aurina spared Carly a smile before glancing away in discomfort. Though she wouldn't know why, she'd find my sister unsettling.

I met Phaeron's eye and nodded, turning the floor over to him. "About the matter of my employment," he said. He hadn't wanted to talk to her, finding Aurina's presence barely tolerable. If I weren't happily mated to him, I'd have bristled by the way his voice had her beautiful feathers rustling.

"You are welcome in Moongrove Library in your old position, of course. If there is any professor turnover at the end of the semester, you'd have no trouble getting promoted, Prince Sudair." Her pink brows jumped with a purr of his title, which she used as a surname since she didn't know better.

"Darkmore," he corrected.

"Pardon?"

He raised his left hand. On his ring finger glittered a black band with a stripe of shimmery gray crystal. "Prince Phaeron Darkmore et Sudair. Did we fail to inform you of our mating circle?" He smirked, enjoying the way her mouth popped open as the rest of us flashed our rings, gifts courtesy of the Crystal Court.

Geo's was the heaviest, a platinum band inset with a shiny crystal that matched the multicolored glimmer of his quartz. It was made to flex for his shifts into gargoyle form. Ben wore a gold ring, his crystal yellow with veins of red and orange. And mine was a traditional style for the core of a mating circle, a single gold band with a triangle-cut diamond and three smaller crystals set along each edge, their colors matching what my men wore.

"Well...wow...congratulations," Aurina said grudgingly.

He nodded. If she understood dimensional culture, she'd have realized he was mated earlier into the conversation. He'd gotten his hair cut and accepted adornment, gratefully acknowledging that he was at peace after an immortal lifetime of war. I mourned the loss of his longer hair but loved running my hands over the silky black feathers that framed his horns and sharp ears.

As for his makeup, I'd dusted his eyelids and cheekbones with shimmery black, an understated modern style that wouldn't get him second glances. Though I was still learning the markings that should decorate his horns, I'd convinced him to let me paint them in yellow edged with gold. They popped against his usual monochromatic outfits.

"Many thanks. So...my position. I would like it back once we return." This, he said with the same level of reluctance as she'd displayed. He'd give it five years, long enough to get Carly through college and comb through the library's resources for any mention of gargoyle creation. Though we had the help of Geo and now Madigan and her men, who called Braza a silent hero for what she'd done, there was much we didn't know about the process. Especially since Braza was a split soul housed in a questionable vessel.

It'd put Phaeron at ease to put both halves together on the shelf of a stasis room in Moongrove Library, where she would sleep without pain until we figured out what to do to bring her back properly.

Geo put in, "We will all start our lives again after our honeymoon." He still had the tickets in hand, fanning them with an excited half smile.

I don't think I imagined the jealousy that flashed in the cupid demigoddess's eyes as she read the name of the supernatural-friendly cruise company. They were another incredible gift that'd arrived today and hadn't left Geo's grip since. Generously paid for by the Ashbough, Evenstar, and Graygazer families...our honeymoon. Two blissful months, just the four of us, with no expectations other than to have fun and solidify our mating circle properly.

Everything else was taken care of for now. I'd be placing Carly's hand in Lucas's after this meeting was finished. They'd live in the Crystal Court for now, under the watchful eye of Madigan and Mom, who'd officially become an Ashbough Protective Services medic, complete with an apartment in the peaceful court. She was within walking distance of her maybe-boyfriend, if she would ever admit whether she actually liked the fae male who followed her like a forlorn puppy.

Pushing to my feet, I waved to Aurina and held my arms out to help Carly to her feet. "If you'll excuse us," I said with a brilliant smile. "We do have a plane to catch."

"Wishing you all the happiness in marital bliss," Aurina replied. She watched us leave and jotted one last note down on a new file marked with Carly's name.

We passed by a moderately full waiting room, pausing as Lucas glanced up from his phone and scrambled to join us. He looked like any ordinary kid now, dressed in a hoody with his hair shaved on the sides and permed on top. "How'd it go?" he asked Carly, taking her hand.

She blinked slowly before lighting up. "Good, I think. I'm joining Cress's coven in the fall. Hey, do you want to get something to eat? I'm *starving*..." We descended the stairs ahead of them, in a hurry where they were not.

"Now kiss," Ben murmured. He made no secret of how he thought they looked good together.

Phaeron rolled his eyes, slipping on a pair of sunglasses that'd been pinned to his collar. "Give them a few years to mature, Little B."

Geo echoed the gesture. "Not everyone needs to be shipped," he said in agreement.

"On the contrary, G Man." Ben held up a finger. "It is the law that two people who help one another heal should get together."

The gargoyle attempted to stare at him stonily, but he was also fighting a smile at the new nickname he'd finally approved of. We'd vetoed Hard G, Gigantic G, and It's Just Geo until Ben had finally come up with something the big man liked.

"You're going to be a terrible policeman if you keep making up laws," he rumbled.

As they continued their back and forth, Phaeron offered his arm, and I took it. The sunglasses were doing a world of good for his eyesight, but I already missed his otherworldly smolder. "Let us be off to experience this...plane," he said, still highly suspicious of modern air travel.

"We're flying first class. You might have some knee room," I said, lifting to my tiptoes to kiss him. The moment we were finished, I turned to see Ben and Geo lined up for their kisses. My heart swelled for all three of them and the uninterrupted time we were about to have.

I kissed them too, then we walked out into the sunlight to go enjoy our new life together.

I HOPE you have enjoyed Cress and her men's story! Thank you for reading.

CONSIDER JOINING MY FACEBOOK GROUP: Ella Hendricks Library Nest! Stay up to date with planned releases, chat about favorite books, and enjoy the occasional giveaway!

PLEASE REMEMBER TO REVIEW! Reviews help other readers find stories they may love. Consider leaving a review for Bright Soul on Amazon and other websites.

ABOUT THE AUTHOR

Ella Hendricks is an author of romances with dark roots and steamy twists. She loves getting lost in fantasy worlds, especially if the monsters are naughty and the lady saves the day in the end. When Ella is not writing about swoon-worthy men, she's off collecting video game achievements. She holds a master's degree in journalism and lives in Texas with her family.

Find out more about her books at: www.ellahen-dricks.com